RISE AND REVERENCE

The Valmenessian Chronicles
Book Two

Rebecca Camm

Find me at: www.rebeccacamm.com
Instagram: @readingwritingdaydreaming
TikTok: @readingwritingdaydream
Facebook: @readingwritingdaydreaming

Printed in Australia.

Hardback ISBN: 978-0-6453455-5-1

Special thanks and acknowledgements to:
Editor; Chloe Hodge – chloehodge.com
Proof-reader & Editor; Emily Morrison – emilymorrisoneditorial.com
Cover Design; Story Wrappers – storywrappers.com
Formatter; Rebecca Camm – rebeccacamm.com

This book is written in British English

The Valmenessian Chronicles

Alta: A Valmenessian Novella

Liars and Light

Rise and Reverence

Content Notes

Rise and Reverence is an adult fantasy novel. It contains cursing, sexual references, violence, assault, and other adult themes. A full list can be found on my website, www.rebeccacamm.com or by scanning the QR code below.

For Liam

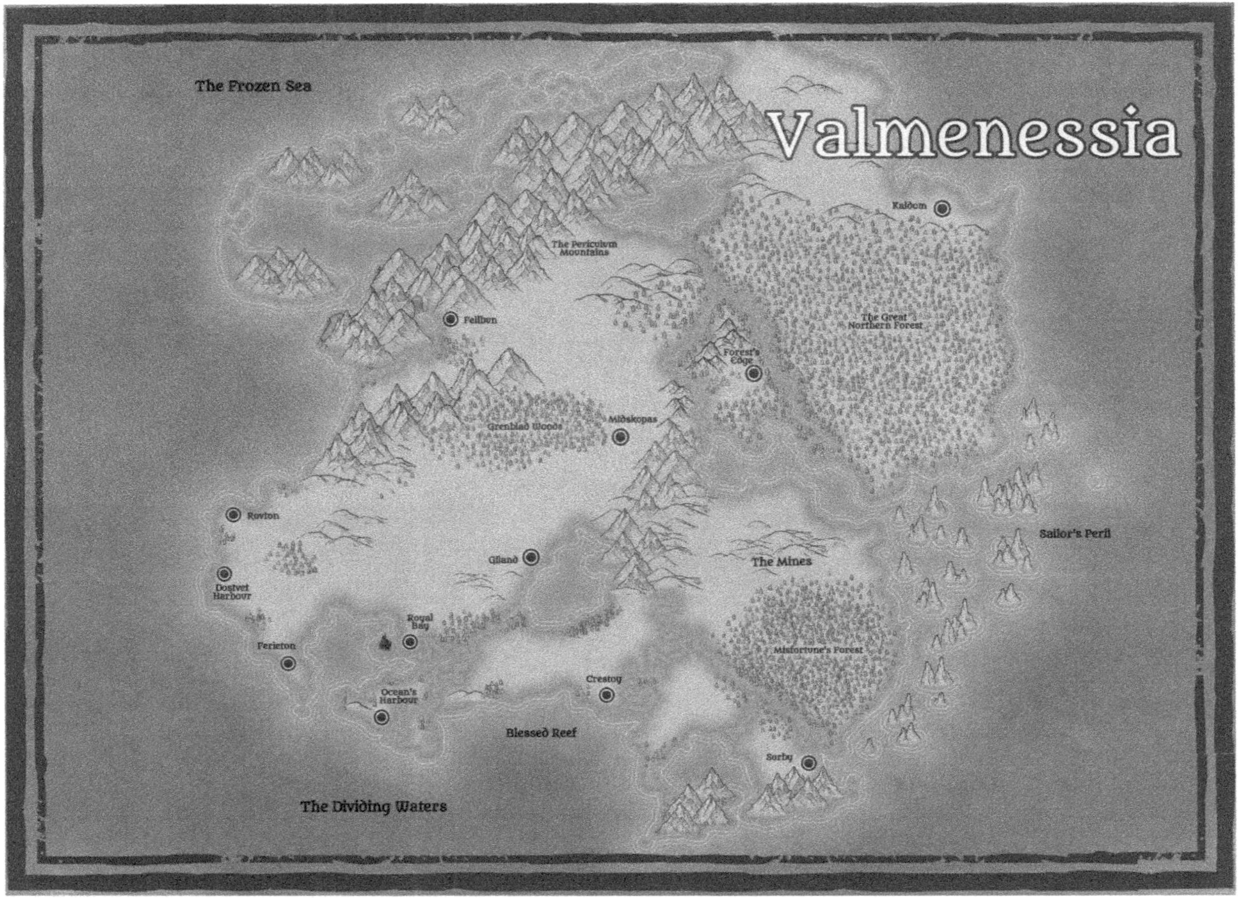

Valmenessia

Sailor's Peril

Raldon

The Great
Northland Forest

The Mines

Forest's
Edge

Surfay

Mishkrygna

The Everburnt
Mountains

Chwang

Fellien

Blessed Reef

Gilund

Royal
Bay

The Frozen Sea

Rorton

Ocean's
Harbour

Dogent
Harbour

Feranton

The Dividing Waters

PROLOGUE

August
8 Years Ago

A faint crack in the stone ceiling ran the length of the room. Even though there were no windows, nor was the usual bright ball of flame conjured by Nora floating in the space, August was able to make out the black line that snaked above him from the soft flickering light of the sconce near the door. He lay on his bed, head resting on his folded arms, and stared into the dark while listening to Nora's breathing on the other side of the room in their underground Alta quarters.

Tomorrow was his birthday, and he would be thirteen years old. He'd been looking forward to this birthday for as long as he could remember as it was the day he'd officially become an Alta. He'd receive his tattoos, be bound to King Dominic, and finally be sent on missions. August had trained hard his entire life—especially over the last few weeks—and he was excited to put his skills into practice.

At least… he had been excited.

Today, August and Nora learned more about recent history in their lessons with Rana. Troubling thoughts had him feeling like something was gnawing on his insides—an uncertainty was trying to eat him alive. Part of him feared voicing it aloud, but the other part was desperate to know, to be reassured that he had a chance unlike the others of his race.

There was only one person he trusted in the whole world to utter his thoughts to and she was fast asleep. August chewed the inside of his cheek. Tomorrow, everything would change, and if he didn't ask Nora now, he might never get the answers to the questions making it impossible for him to sleep.

"Nora," he whispered into the darkness.

She didn't reply. Her breathing was a steady rhythm as she slept and he briefly second-guessed his decision to wake her. Rolling onto his side, August sought her silhouette in the shadows. Nora was only a year younger than him yet she barely took up much of her bed. She looked like little more than a small lump under the blankets. What Nora lacked in size though she made up in personality and her attitude often got her in trouble.

She'd probably kill him for waking her, but he needed to know...

With a steady breath, August steeled his resolve. "Nora."

She grumbled in her sleep, rolling onto her back and throwing an arm over her face, but she didn't wake. Undeterred, August reached for the book on his bedside table—a tale of an adventure in an ancient forest—and threw it across the room. It landed on Nora's chest with a loud thump, and she cried out, jolting upright. A gust of wind shoved August back, and the single sconce extinguished, plunging them into darkness.

"What the fuck!" Nora shouted as bright light and heat filled the room. She was sitting on her bed, one hand rubbing her chest whilst a burning ball of flames crackled and hissed aloft in her other. Her dark gaze scanned the room for possible threats. "Who's there?"

"It was just me," August said calmly, rolling back onto his side to face Nora, drawing her attention.

"Shit! You scared me!"

"Sorry." August stifled a chuckle, leaning on his elbow. Nora would have received a beating for swearing like that. Rana kept saying it was no language for a twelve-year-old, but Nora wasn't one to be deterred by punishment. "I tried calling your name—"

Her shoulders relaxed and Nora flicked her wrist, extinguishing her orb of flame and relighting the candle by the door with the same movement. August's eyes quickly readjusted to the change in light, but not fast enough to catch Nora's swift action.

The book she threw back hit him in the head. "I'm sure you tried hard."

August bit his tongue on a snarky reply, rubbing his forehead where a bruise would undoubtedly surface. Arguing with her was a waste of time. He wanted her genuine opinion, so he'd better not piss her off any more than she was already.

"Can I ask you something?"

"It better be important," she groaned, flopping back onto her bed and throwing an arm over her eyes, "or I'll start plotting my revenge for waking me up."

August fiddled with the edge of his blanket, ignoring her threat. He wouldn't have taken it seriously even if he didn't have something more important consuming his thoughts. Nora would never truly hurt him. "You know how Rana taught us about when King Dominic got rid of all the Mors Alvs?"

"All but one," Nora replied, and he swore he could hear her smile if that were even possible.

"Yeah, all but one," he said with a sigh, tugging at a loose thread. Finally, it came free and he twirled it around his finger. "Anyway, he made the law because Mors Alvs are dangerous and kill people. They can't even help it; it's in their nature. Like how General Natsky had killed Queen Helen. He was supposed to protect her, but even he couldn't control the dangerous part of him."

"Did you wake me up for a history lesson?" she grumbled, then let out a long sigh. "You know you have your ceremony tomorrow. I don't think King Dominic will be happy if you fall asleep during it."

"I know," he said, rolling onto his back and staring up at the crack in the ceiling once more.

His heart raced in his chest, and he hesitated. Would Nora agree with the thoughts that haunted him? He couldn't lose her; she was all he had. He twisted the thread tightly around his finger until it throbbed and cut into his skin.

"August is that all you woke me up for?" she asked irritably, though he thought he'd heard the tiniest hint of concern in her voice. Maybe he imagined it though, hoping to hear something that may not have been there. "Because if it is, I'm going to think of something awful to pay you back."

He snapped the thread, blood rushing back into his finger.

"If Mors Alvs are so bad, why hasn't the king killed me?"

The silence was thick, interrupted only by their breathing as August *waited. He felt as though he were standing at the very edge of a cliff, his fate not yet decided. Would he fall into the sea, or would he be pulled back to safety?*

His bed dipped, and August looked to see Nora by his side. He hadn't heard her move, and yet here she sat on the edge of his bed in her nightgown, her long brown hair hanging loose down her back.

"I don't know why he saved you," she admitted softly, her brow scrunching. "But I do know that you're not dangerous. Just look at the other Alta. They're all assholes, and the king keeps them alive, so the Mors Alvs must have been worse for him to make those laws."

August swallowed hard. "What if I turn evil?"

"No one can see into the future. Plus, I know you." Nora shrugged, then tapped her finger on her chin. "You know the other day when Rana had us look at that dead body to learn all the different parts?"

"Yeah?" August grimaced, unsure where Nora was going with her story.

"Well, the other Alta are like the bones and nails—all the hard and scratchy parts," she said. "You're the—"

"Heart?" he asked with a smile.

"No, you idiot." Nora laughed. "You're the guts. All soft and squishy."

"Thanks... I think." August sighed, his doubts crashing back in. "How could all the other Mors Alvs have been bad then?"

She shrugged, a frown on her face. "Who knows? They must have done something wrong. The king protects the people."

"I guess," he said. An uneasiness lingered inside, but he refused to give fuel to the fire. If he dwelled on it, it would only lead to more questions and uncertainty.

Nora lifted his blanket and slipped into his bed, pressing close to his side and wrapping an arm around him. August welcomed her embrace, her closeness helping to ease his troubled mind.

"You're a good person," she whispered. "The best one I know. Maybe the king sees that too."

"Maybe," he replied softly, staring above him.

Nora yawned, snuggling close. "I'll still love you, even if that changes. Even if you stop being all mushy, like guts." She poked him in the ribs. "You'll always be my best friend."

Tracing the crack in the ceiling with his eyes, August listened as Nora's breathing deepened. Maybe one day, he would turn evil like the other Mors Alvs, and there was nothing he could do about it. He would try his hardest not to be like them, but if he couldn't stop it—if that was just how his race was— then at least he'd have Nora. And as long as they were together, everything would be okay.

August closed his eyes, pressed his forehead to the wooden door, and tried to contain the emotions threatening to undo him. Guilt wrapped tightly around him, pulling him in every direction. He was only one man, and though the decision to leave had been hard to make, he had made it, nonetheless.

Nora would forgive him eventually. He hoped.

Unlike Evelyn, Nora was only a danger to herself, but she wasn't *in danger* so there was less urgency in her need for him. Not that his friend would ever admit to needing him. Nora was beyond stubborn when she set her mind to something, and right now, she was determined to hate him. He'd seen the betrayal in her eyes, contradicting the unaffected mask she was so desperate to portray to the world.

They had known each other nearly all their lives, and after freeing her from King Dominic's shackles, August had expected her to detach herself from him once she'd been free to feel and make her own choices, knowing that she would have wanted to punish him for what he'd done. He had planned to stay by her side and show her they would always be family—that he would always be there for her and that what he'd done was because he loved her, but now, things had spiralled out of his control.

He just hoped Nora would remember their bond once she'd processed everything that had happened. It tore his heart in two to leave his best friend, but Evelyn's life was at stake. He could only pray their friendship was strong enough and Nora would forgive him in the end.

Taking a steadying breath, August straightened, collected his pack from the floor, and strode away from Nora's room. He moved through the Forest's Edge Manor, keeping his head down as he passed others walking through the hallways of the ruling family's home. He didn't want to be noticed, but he also didn't need to crowd his thoughts further with reminders of Evelyn. She was already consuming his mind.

Despite the fact Jasmine had ordered him to stay put, nothing would stop him from going after Evelyn. He'd promised to protect her, and he'd failed. Zaim had taken her from right under his nose. The wily Alta was one of the worst people August had ever known. Zaim had spent many years torturing him and Nora as children, leaving scars both on their flesh and their minds. He was about ten years older than August, but instead of those years providing Zaim with maturity and a scrap of empathy, they had twisted him into a monstrous creature.

The guilt August felt for letting Evelyn down and his fear of what Zaim may have done to her was a storm of energy that drove him forward. Each step August took towards the stables behind the Manor was purposeful, his focus as clear as the ice that would soon freeze the northern lakes.

Boots crunching on the path, August tugged his cloak tighter, bracing himself against the cool Frost Season chill. August had donned his charcoal cloak, the shadow of the hood hiding not only his dark eyes that would give away his race but his pointed ears, chin-length, dirty blond hair, and his pale skin. He was used to being covered up; being able to walk around freely without his cloak was strange to consider outside of Alta quarters or in the company of the few people he trusted.

A light dusting of snow had fallen the previous night, coating the grounds in white. As he neared the stables, the sounds of life came from within, and August pushed open the heavy doors to find a young boy mucking out the stalls whilst another groomed a horse nearby. Neither looked up from their task, which August couldn't help but think was a good thing. Jasmine and the others may have been okay with him being a Mors Alv, but that didn't mean everyone else in Forest's Edge would be.

Unfortunately for him, hiding behind a cloak wasn't the antidote to people's fear, even if it solved one problem. Being tall with broad shoulders tended to draw the eye. He was stuck between a rock and a hard place regarding his options, but at least the one he'd settled on had fewer consequences. Fear of Mors Alvs was something that had been ingrained in society for the last two decades. August was unsure he wouldn't be inclined to fear or judge someone of his race.

King Dominic's prejudices had twisted even his mind against himself.

As August scanned the stalls with his dark eyes, his gaze snagged on a sturdy-looking horse with a rich brown coat. The steed was a good size for the distance and speed to which August was planning to travel. He made to step forward but was hauled back outside and shoved against the stable wall.

"What the fuck?" August growled, tearing Felix's hands from his cloak and shoving the man away.

"Going somewhere without me?" Felix asked, patting down his thick coat, he looked up at August with a wry smile.

Felix always had a way of appearing more refined than August knew he was. His clothes were of a fine make, his black hair cropped neatly, and there wasn't a scar or blemish on his brown skin. If it weren't for the glimmer in his dark brown eyes, there would be no obvious tell of the man beneath the cloak at all. August couldn't believe he'd spent all those weeks searching in vain for Felix with Nora on the king's order, only to have the man reveal himself in Forest's Edge.

"I know what Jasmine said, but I need to go after Evelyn," August replied, turning away from Felix. "She's in danger, and I promised to protect her."

Felix placed a gloved hand on August's shoulder, stopping him. "And how do you suppose you'll achieve that little goal of yours, hmm?"

"I'll figure it out on the way."

"The king and Alta know who you are, not to mention as soon as someone sees your face, you'll have sentries and Royal Guild members after you, too. You don't have Nora to help you."

"I'll take my chances," August said, attempting to shrug Felix off, but the man's grip held strong. "Take your hand off me."

"Not until you realise what a big mistake this is," Felix argued, refusing to let August turn away. "Now that you are no longer bound to the king, you have full access to your magic. You are stronger without the tattoos binding you and need to learn how to control it, or you'll be a danger to anyone with magic. What good will you be to Evelyn if you steal her health and magic just from being by her side? You admitted that you unknowingly took magic from Evelyn and Nora. Look what it did to your best friend—how easily the Faction subdued her because of something you cannot control."

"I have a few weeks' travels to learn how to control it," August grumbled. "If I travel fast, I'll be able to reach Evelyn and the others before they enter Royal Bay. Besides, any excess magic I have will be directed at Zaim. Not going after Evelyn is more dangerous."

"Zaim and King Dominic won't kill her yet. They wouldn't have gone through all this trouble to end her life immediately. The king will have a plan up his sleeve to use her against Jasmine and everyone else in opposition to him."

"Like staging her execution in Royal Bay to set an example?"

"Possibly," Felix said, earning a pained groan from August. Felix placed a reassuring hand on August's shoulder. "But I highly doubt it. He's up to something."

"I don't like those odds."

"Evelyn is alive and will remain so for the foreseeable future," Felix said firmly, though August still had doubts despite the other man's sense of assuredness. "Come with me to the Periculum Mountains to meet with the Mors Alvs. Learn how to master your magic. Not only will it benefit Evelyn and Nora, but you'll also be an asset to the entire country."

August rubbed his stubbled jaw. "How do you even know Mors Alvs are there anyway? King Dominic would surely have had them all killed if there was a community living in the frozen mountains."

"King Dominic doesn't know of their existence."

"And you do?" August scoffed. "I call bullshit."

"You can call whatever you like," Felix replied. "That's the truth."

"Whatever." August stepped towards the stable door. "I'm not wasting time hunting for ghosts. I'm going after Evelyn. I promised to protect her, and I will. You're not going to get me to break my vow."

"I'm not trying to make you break your promise to her. I'm trying to help you keep it if you'd just listen to me. Is your skull so thick that you can't see reason?"

"Fuck you," August growled, turning and swinging a fist in Felix's direction, rage rising in him rapidly. The man dodged the blow, stepping back with a smirk. "Just because you think you're some kind of leader or god or some shit doesn't mean everyone else does."

"True," Felix said with a chuckle, side-stepping another of August's swings before spreading his arms wide. "Let's make a deal, seeing as you're so eager to hit me. How about if you can beat me without using a weapon or magic, then you can go after Evelyn? If you can't then you have to go with me. Deal?"

"Fine," August grunted, then lunged.

The two men wrestled, their fists flying as they brawled. Felix managed to strike a hard blow to August's ribs, earning a grunt from the Mors Alv. August tried to elbow Felix in return but missed, his frustration growing as all his punches either missed or were deflected. Anger coursed through him as he'd never known, and the next thing he knew, he'd launched himself at Felix, dragging the man to the ground and letting his magic flow. His breathing steadied as he absorbed Felix's magic, and reality returned with a vengeance.

He released his hands as though burned, his bright blue-and-black eyes wide at not only his actions but the amount of health that swarmed beneath Felix's skin.

Felix lay beneath August, his breath billowing like a cloud of smoke as he panted. "You lose." He grinned up at August despite just having his magic fed on. "You weren't supposed to use your magic."

"Fuck," August swore, sliding off Felix and slumping to the ground beside the man. "You did that on purpose."

"Yes, I did, and now that I have sufficiently proven my point, wait here while I collect my things. We can leave for the mountains within the hour."

August grumbled, accepting defeat, and ignored Felix as the man left. He remained to lie on the cold path, letting his cloak dampen until the chill seeped through the fabric. He didn't care that he was cold; if anything, he embraced the punishment for his lack of control. Felix was right. He was no use to anyone if he couldn't control his magic. With a deep sigh, he accepted his fate. He would go to the Periculum Mountains.

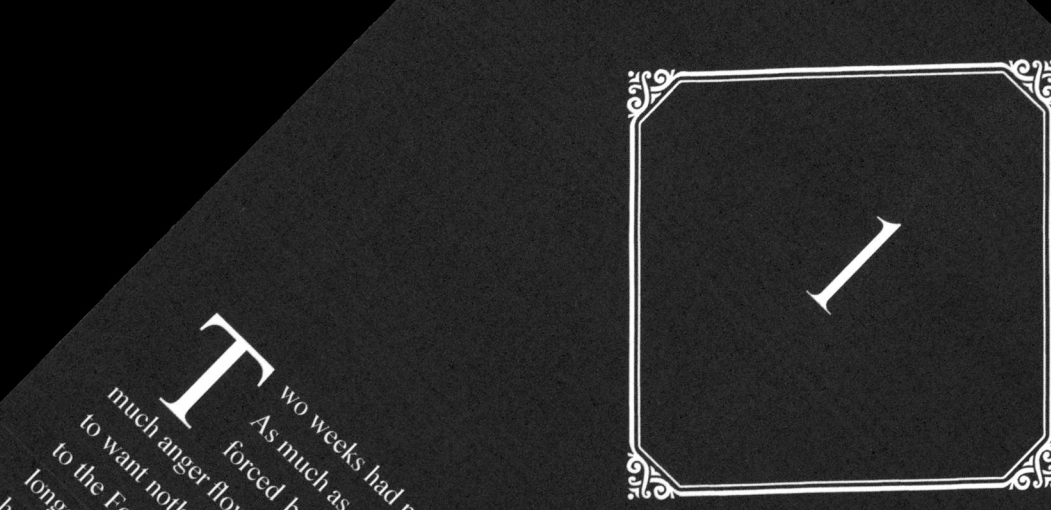

1

Two weeks had

As much as

forced b

much anger flo

to want noth

to the F

long

The truth was, she hated herself for not asking him to stay.

And therein lay Nora's new emotional state, because upon realising she couldn't blame August for the conflicting feelings that had arisen since losing the tattoos, she only had herself to hold accountable. There was no one else to blame for all the things she'd said and done, the horrors she'd inflicted or hadn't lifted a finger to stop.

Nora chewed her lip and picked at her fingers. They bled as she tore away skin and nails; no doubt scars would be left. Not that she didn't already have those. The most prominent being the line on her cheek and a few scratches that crept into her hairline on her forehead. Nora stared out the window and wondered whether this was how she would feel for the rest of her life. A pathetic shell of whom she used to be.

"What are you thinking about?" Florence asked from where she lounged on Nora's bed. She fiddled with the buttons of her violet shirt, tapping them with her fingers as she stared at the ceiling.

The Faction member and partner to Will—who had also been Nora's old boss at the florist shop—turned up right after August had left, and the redhead was currently holding the bed hostage. Florence was a high-ranking Forest's Edge Faction member, so Nora found her frequent visits surprising. Surely Florence had more important things to do with her time than babysitting her? Florence oversaw meetings with newcomers seeking refuge within the Faction, as well as her duties as one of Gemma's advisors. The Faction leader had a select few she kept close—Florence being one of them—which was one reason why Nora's infiltration had angered Gemma so greatly. Nora wondered if Florence still held those roles, considering she was always busy visiting her.

"Nothing," Nora sighed deeply, tugging her knees to her chest and tilting her head so that it rested on the back of the armchair. "You know, you don't have to be here."

"I want to be here," Florence replied, rolling onto her front and propping her chin onto her pale hand, her red braid falling over one shoulder. Her socked feet kicked lazily at the air as she continued to speak. "Also, Jasmine asked me to pop in now and then. She thinks your allegiances are still debatable."

"And you?"

Florence grinned broadly, accentuating her freckled cheeks. "She knows I'm loyal to her, but I also trust you."

Nora rolled her upturned brown eyes. Despite telling Florence she didn't have to be there; she was glad for the company. No one else visited, so she often found herself torn between wanting to be alone and not wanting to be in her head. She hadn't been put in a cell, if anything they'd given her more luxury than she'd ever been granted before in her life. The bed was large and as soft as a cloud, the blankets finely made, and the other furnishings were all crafted by skilled workmanship. Even the meals she'd been given were exceptional; she was sure she was being served the same as the ruling family that resided in the Manor.

She tugged at her shirt sleeves to reveal her pale wrists and the pearlescent shackles that glimmered in the light. They hadn't removed the shackles preventing her from using her Elementum magic, but they had cut the chain linking them, turning them instead into oversized bracelets. Tacky and uncomfortable bracelets.

"Because I can't use my magic?" Nora asked with a sigh.

"Nope," Florence replied. "Now that you aren't under the king's command, I think you'll do the right thing."

"How would you know? I may understand a lot about you and the Faction, but you hardly know me."

Florence shrugged. "Call it a feeling. Once you stop moping, you'll see I'm right."

"I'm not moping."

"I've been visiting multiple times a day for the last two weeks, and you have spent the entire time moping."

"I have not."

"Yeah, you have. No point denying it."

"What's the other alternative?" Nora asked. "Join Gemma or Jasmine? Fight against the king?"

"Both are good options," Florence said, winking at Nora. "But you should only do what you believe is right."

"How would I know if they don't share their plans with me?"

"They have a pretty good reason not to share anything."

"Fine," Nora said, grimacing. "I guess I'll have to get used to being treated like I'm the Morken risen from the land for following King Dominic," she added, referring to the story Daphne had told those children the night Nora went with her to the Anima celebration in the forest.

She missed Daphne.

The woman ran a sanctuary in Forest's Edge for those needing shelter from dangerous people or situations, taking them in without judgment and providing somewhere safe to stay and a community if they sought it. Nora felt terrible for betraying Daphne's trust; she'd taken advantage of the woman's kind heart. It was just another thing Nora felt shit about.

"You're not an evil being with sharp claws and fangs that spreads darkness all over the world," Florence said, her blue eyes running over Nora. "At least, I don't think you are. Show me your hands and teeth."

"Ha, ha, very funny."

Nora groaned at the woman's teasing as Florence flashed her teeth, goading Nora to do the same.

"Look, King Dominic is evil in a nice outfit, and he forced your loyalty through those shackles," Florence said when Nora didn't play along. She pushed off the bed and effortlessly stepped her feet into her boots then bent to tie the laces. "No one thinks you're the Morken, far from it. That's why I keep visiting you, why Jasmine is keeping you here. We all know you won't run back to the king because you can see his actions are wrong."

"I don't see anything," Nora mumbled, looking back at the icy garden beyond the window.

"Keep telling yourself those lies," Florence said, glancing up at Nora through strands of her hair. "But you know the truth. It's why you're so miserable."

"If you say so," Nora replied, though she knew Florence's words to be true. "So, what makes following Gemma or Jasmine's orders without question any different from me following the king's? Other than you believing one is bad and one is good."

"Choice."

Florence came to stand before Nora, looking her dead in the eyes. "Gemma and Jasmine want equality among the races and to fix the mess the king has made. I share that vision, so yes, I choose to follow them without knowing everything, but I trust them to do the right thing. They tell me what I need to know, sometimes more. Ultimately, I don't need to know everything to choose to follow them. It's my judgement."

"You all put so much emphasis on choice," Nora said. "It's not all it's cracked up to be."

"Decisions can be hard," Florence agreed, nodding. "But it's what makes life exciting. You can't tell me you'd rather be the pawn in a game than a player?"

"We're all pawns," Nora said with a sigh. It didn't matter whether the king was pulling the strings or if it were Jasmine or Gemma; there would always be someone in control of her life. "We're all doing the bidding of those in power, and I'm fucking sick of it."

"Maybe," Florence shook her head. "In the end, when I'm taking my last breath, I'll at least know that everything I've done was because I believed it was right. Can you say the same?"

Nora frowned. She couldn't, and it was eating her up inside—that and the fact that August had left her. Oh, and dare she forget a certain unrequited emotion she had for someone else that was making her feel worse? Nora had never felt so many unpleasant emotions in her life, and it was hard not to feel sorry for herself. It was pathetic, but she didn't deny it … at least not to herself.

"Come on," Florence said. She pulled on her black coat, straightening it, and the gold buttons flashed in the light. "It's been weeks since you've been cooped up in here. Let's go do something fun."

"I'm fine here," Nora replied, waving her off dismissively.

Florence took Nora's hand and attempted to pull her to her feet. "Yeah, but I'm not."

"Then go," she said, narrowing her eyes at Florence and snatching her hand back. "I'm not—"

A knock at the door had Nora's mouth snapping shut, and she looked at the entrance to see Jasmine stride in. The woman looked immaculate, her flowing black hair pinned neatly at the sides of her head and her thick forest-green gown swaying with each of her purposeful steps. There was no outward sign of sorrow for her late father, nor fear for her kidnapped sister. Instead, the Lady of Forest's Edge looked calm and confident in her newfound position, just as she had been in her previous occupation as the city's best pastry chef. Thanks to her conjuring abilities, Jasmine's baking was renowned in the city.

Nora didn't stand in greeting. Judging by the disgruntled looks of Jasmine's personal guards, it was certainly rude, but she just didn't have it in her to rise.

"Lady Royd," Florence said, bowing her head. It was strange to hear her refer to her friend so formally.

"Good morning, Florence. Good morning, Nora," Jasmine said, coming to sit on the edge of the bed. She turned to her guards. "You can leave us, thank you." She then looked at Florence. "You too, please."

Florence and the guards nodded at their lady's request, the door closing with a soft click as they left the two women alone in silence. Nora must have looked utterly pathetic, but she had no idea, nor desire, to bring back the woman she was.

"If you could look into the future and see yourself, where would you be?" Jasmine asked, her rich brown eyes studying Nora intently. "What would you be doing?"

"Laying on a warm beach and slowly spending a small fortune that I somehow inherited from a long-lost relative," Nora replied sarcastically.

Jasmine gave a half smile as though placating Nora. "What does the rest of the world look like?"

"I don't know or care," Nora grumbled.

"That's a lie," Jasmine said instantly. "Where would your friends be? Would they be with you?"

"I'm not sure if you have noticed," Nora said, spreading her arms wide, "but I don't have any friends, so my future self is much like I am now. Alone."

"Just with a little more coin and sunshine?"

"Exactly."

"Do Florence and Will know you don't consider them friends?" Jasmine asked. "What about August or Evelyn? Sage?"

"Florence and Will liked the person I pretended to be," Nora told her. "I'm not sure your sister is a very good judge of character. Sage most definitely doesn't want to be my friend and August…"

"He doesn't count because he is your family?"

Nora shook her head. "He doesn't count because… because…" Her throat constricted, and she fisted her hands at her sides. "He just doesn't count. Besides, it's not like anyone visits me, so I think you're off base about the whole friend thing anyway. Florence only turns up because you make her."

"Maybe, like you, they just needed time to come to terms with what happened? You aren't the only one who had their life turned upside down." Jasmine pursed her lips, giving Nora a pointed look. "How long are you going to feel sorry for yourself?"

"Excuse me?" Nora asked incredulously, eyes wide.

"I knew you'd be upset before I came in here. It would be a huge shock to your system to suddenly feel the consequences of all you have done in the name of King Dominic," Jasmine said. "I let you be these last few weeks thinking you were a fighter, but judging by your current state, I was wrong. You've given up. Decided you're all alone and no one cares for you."

"I am all alone."

"Is that why all the people I mentioned tried to help free you from King Dominic's slavery? Is that why you are currently in my home, being taken care of and allowed a fresh start?"

"I—"

"Is it because you are all alone?" Jasmine raised a brow. "I have to say, this is strange behaviour from people who apparently care so little about you."

Nora shut her mouth. She had nothing to say about what Jasmine had just disclosed. The lady of Forest's Edge had a point, even if it was something Nora struggled to see on her own. Was it her current state that wouldn't allow her to see it? Or was simply her pride preventing her from admitting that she had others she could rely upon?

"Get up," Jasmine announced, rising from the bed and smoothing her skirt with a delicate brown hand. "We're going for a walk. The fresh air will do you good. At least that's what Evelyn always tells me when I'm in a mood."

"She's still missing?"

Jasmine nodded. "I will bring her home, but I can't let my concern for Evelyn stop me from caring for the people in this city and those seeking help. King Dominic has denounced my rule as Lady of Forest's Edge. He will come for me like he did my aunt and cousin, just like he was planning to murder my father. It is only a matter of time."

"He's such a dick," Nora said, dragging herself from the bed and taking the cloak Jasmine held out for her. She shoved her arms through the sleeves, the pearlescent shackles making the process difficult.

Jasmine chuckled. "He is, and I never want to be anything like him. Your restraints will come off once I can trust you won't do anything stupid."

"I'm not sure I can ever promise that."

Nora dropped to her knees to search under the bed for her boots. Dragging them out, she stuffed her feet into them and tied the laces, then followed Jasmine from the room and into the frosty garden. A dusting of snow had fallen, speckling the greenery with tiny diamonds that glistened in the sun's glow. Florence and Jasmine's guards trailed behind them at a distance, providing them with some semblance of privacy.

"I have a proposition for you," Jasmine said, breaking the silence.

"Mmm? What do you want from me?"

"I'd like you to make a choice," said Jasmine, stopping on the path as she turned to face Nora.

"What are my options?"

"That's up to you. I have a few suggestions, but it's your life. What you do with it is your decision."

Nora quirked a brow. "Why do I feel like that isn't entirely true?"

Jasmine smiled but pushed on, ignoring Nora's statement. "If it were up to me, you'd help us take King Dominic down. However, I believe you aren't partial to that path, so I would also suggest staying here and lying low so he cannot use you as a weapon against the people here."

"In other words, be an accomplice or a prisoner."

"*Ally* or *guest*. You'd be exceptionally valuable to our cause if you chose the former. You could make a difference, Nora."

"And if I choose something different?"

"You'll find that there is a delay in enacting anything other than the two choices I'm offering," Jasmine said. "You are not the only person I am trying to protect in this city."

Nora held up her shackled wrists. "Not much of a choice, then, is it?"

2

The roof caved in amber gemmy her, and crouching low, from the hea flames. eyed, *drenched from perspiration and water magic after trying to use the latter as a glistening shield, only to have it boil against her skin. Nora could still hear the calls from inside—hysterical cries that twisted amongst the roar of the inferno.*

She needed to find her family.

Sobs escaped her as she circled the farmhouse, her body trembling with each step. She couldn't leave them in the fire. Nora tried to control the flames with her fire magic, but they were too unruly to listen to her command, and when she attempted blowing the fire out with her wind magic they only became fiercer, as though angry with her interference. Finally, as she neared the back of her home, tears streaming down her cheeks, she called on her water magic, begging for it to come to her aid.

It didn't come. Not a single drop.

Panic crept up her spine to wrap sharp claws around her heart. The world grew blurry before her eyes. Even though her chest heaved with all its might, she couldn't breathe. What little air she could get in scratched against her burnt throat. She ran from her home to the field bordering one side. She knew it wasn't safe there, that the fire could spread to the field, but not being able to see if anyone made it out terrified her more. There, she stood and watched, fear coiling in her belly.

All was lost.

...Until she was swept away, her tiny body shielded in a calming, safe embrace. The image of her burning family home dissolved, her smouldering flesh no longer smarted, and her broken heart mended back together. Maybe everything would be okay.

Nora woke wrapped in warm blankets. Sunlight trickled in through the gaps in the curtains. The memory of the pain from that night, not only of her injuries that she'd been lucky to have healed entirely by a Lys Alv but of her loss that had never had a chance to heal. She wriggled back, pressing herself into the furs, only to realise she hadn't been given a fur blanket. Her eyes snapped open and she spun, twisting in her sheets, to find a familiar grey leopard with black spots sleeping beside her.

"Who the fuck are you?" she said in alarm, shoving the snow leopard.

It barely moved an inch. She knew it wasn't a wild animal, remembering the creature had arrived with Felix when the ex-Alta had revealed his presence. She shoved them more vigorously. "I know you're an Anima, so just shift and tell me who you are!"

They cracked a cloudy grey eye open, raking their gaze over her before yawning and flashing sharp teeth.

"Well?" Nora demanded, gripping the sheets in her fists. If they didn't answer her soon, she would wring their neck with the fabric. "This is not a slumber party. I don't share beds."

The leopard shifted to reveal a lean man with dark hair, wearing a crumbled olive-green coat and brown slacks. He stretched out and propped his head on his pale hand. "Now, that's not entirely true. You share with August."

"That's different," she huffed. "Not that it's any of your business."

"Why?" he asked casually. "Because you're together? Are you two like one of those fairy-tale love stories where you start as childhood friends who date other people, only to find each other again years later and try to make up for lost time?"

Nora scrunched her nose. "Don't be gross."

August was her friend—her family—or at least he used to be. There was, nor would there ever be, anything romantic between them. The idea made Nora feel unclean.

"So that's a no, then?"

"Definitely."

"Oh, you are together?"

"No! It's a definite no." She groaned, kicking him, though the thick blankets between them made it little more than a nudge. "And don't try to twist my words or think that by asking ridiculous questions, you could make me forget that you were sleeping in my bed."

He winked. "I don't think I could say anything to make you forget that I slept with you."

"We didn't have sex."

"I never said we did. Get your mind out of the gutter, buttercup."

Nora shoved at his chest, throwing him off the bed. He landed with a heavy thud accompanied by what could only be described as a growl.

"No pet names! And stop trying to distract me! Instead, tell me who the fuck you are," Nora demanded, then quickly added. "And don't sleep in my bed."

"So many rules," the man replied, rising to his feet and rubbing his shoulder. "I'm Ashe."

"*Why* are you here?"

"You were having a nightmare."

She scoffed. "No, I wasn't. I would have woken up."

"Well, you did, and thanks to yours truly, you calmed down and slept through the night."

Nora's brows rose, and she turned to look at the clock. "I slept the whole night?"

"Mm-hm." He nodded, looking smug. "You're welcome."

"What did you do?" she demanded, looking at him suspiciously. "How did you get in here?"

Ashe raised his hands. "Just slept, as I said. It turns out all you needed was a little contact, and I like a good snuggle when I sleep, so it was a win-win."

"Well, you can go now," she snapped, wrapping herself in the blankets and preparing to return to her self-pitying from the previous day.

"No can do," he replied with a playful grin. "I promised August I'd watch you."

"You know August?"

"Sure do."

"How? Wait, never mind. That's not important. August is not entitled to make any decisions for me," she stated through gritted teeth. "You can leave, and if I find you in my bed again, you won't be walking out of it."

He winked. "Kinky."

Nora slipped an arm out from under her blankets, grabbed the nearest heavy thing she could find, and threw it at him, hitting him square in the chest.

"Fuck." He rubbed his chest as the wooden box fell to the floor. "No need to get violent."

"Don't force yourself on me, and I won't need to defend myself," she snapped. "It's creepy to come in here and sleep in my bed without my knowledge."

"You're making me sound like a pervert."

"Don't act like one and you wouldn't have a problem."

Ashe narrowed his gaze, his mood instantly shifting. "Jasmine asked me to watch you, seeing as you're a murderer."

Nora jolted, his words hitting her like an arrow to the chest, drawing in the dark clouds that had only just started to recede. She would never be rid of the stain of her past.

"Go get dressed," he told her, his playfulness gone. He dropped into the armchair and spread his legs out wide before him.

"Why?" Nora asked, scrunching her brow.

"You're moving."

Nora groaned, pulling her blanket over her head. If they were to hold her prisoner, why couldn't they leave her in peace? The dark clouds hanging over her soul wanted to storm, and she was pretty content to lie in bed and be drenched by guilt.

Ashe pulled the covers back and said, "get dressed and pack your stuff."

"I don't have anything beyond the second set of clothes."

"Good," he barked, grabbing her wrist and pulling her to her feet. "It should take you no time at all then."

"Don't fucking touch me," she said, snatching back her arm.

Florence appeared at the threshold, a disapproving look on her face. "I'll take it from here."

"Lady Royd told me to watch her."

"Looks like you're doing more than that."

"Fine," he grumbled, snatching his cloak from the wall. "I've got shit to do anyway."

Nora smirked at his departing back, then slowly dragged herself from the bed, heading into the bathing room to clean up. She dressed in slacks, a navy shirt and a thick woollen sweater that fell almost to her knees with sleeves that covered her hands. Then, throwing on a cloak and stuffing her feet into leather boots, she strode back into the room and left the manor with Florence.

Passing through the Manor Grounds, Nora cast an appreciative eye over the statues of the five Gods and Goddesses of Valmenessia that guarded the temples. They were sprinkled with snow, the pools beneath them frozen solid. Like the statues, the Healing Centre was also iced like a sweet cake, the canopy of the giant tree at its centre speckled with white. There was one thing Nora could say with absolute certainty: this city was beautiful.

As they ventured into the more populated district, the streets filled out with people going about their business, and, despite the cold, there was a sense of urgency about the place that wasn't there a few weeks before.

"Did something happen?" Nora asked as she walked beside Florence. She angled her head towards a woman who swiftly strode by with her arms full of bundles. "Why do they look like they're gathering supplies for Frost Season?"

"Maybe that's exactly what they're doing," Florence replied with a coy smile.

"There are enough Elementum here to aid in growing food and maintaining temperatures. So I doubt people would be fretting about dwindling supplies."

"You're an observant, violent little one," Florence noted, turning a corner.

"Jasmine mentioned something about King Dominic denouncing her rule."

Florence nodded. "He sent a decree to all the cities and towns; that's why she is closing the city."

"Really?"

"Yes. Fortifications are being built just beyond the southern perimeter, so the citizens are preparing for its completion. Some supplies will be harder to get because we have less access to trading once the city is closed off, but Lord Royd had contingency plans for situations like this, so the city is somewhat prepared."

"Lord Royd planned for Forest's Edge to stand against King Dominic?"

Florence grinned. "He expected the king's greed to grow and the inevitability of him removing people's rights. It's not like it's a wild prediction. You'd have been blind not to see it coming."

Nora frowned. She *hadn't* seen it coming. She hadn't seen anything wrong with what the king had been doing. Now that she was unbound to him, had her feelings changed? Nora would have liked to think that they hadn't, but she was no longer unperturbed by what was happening in Valmenessia, nor was she blissfully unaware of the effects of her actions. It was like she'd been bundled in a knitted blanket—able to see through the gaps in the yarn, yet her view was still obscured to some degree. It was hard to wrap her head around the fact that so much of her life had been hidden from her by the shackle tattoos the king had bound to her wrists.

"How does Ashe know August?" Nora asked, blowing a loose strand of hair from her face and dodging someone rushing past. "I remember him arriving with Felix. Did Felix introduce the two of them?"

"All I know is that Felix had him follow you and August."

"So he went from stalking me to climbing into my bed," Nora grumbled, thinking of her journey with August from Royal Bay to Forest's Edge. She'd spotted Ashe in his leopard form multiple times, only to dismiss it as nothing. Just another facet she'd been truly blind to.

"Ashe has difficulties with boundaries," Florence said. "Not that I'm condoning his behaviour. We've tried to tell him, but he refuses to listen. Luckily, he won't be bothering you where you're staying from now on."

"And where's that?"

"You'll see," Florence said. "I will say this much about Ashe; he's a stickler for following orders. It's how he interprets them that's the problem."

Florence led her to a row of houses, knocking on one of the doors. Unlike Daphne and Sage's homes—which were nestled amongst the trees or suspended in the branches—these houses were smaller and squashed against each other. Moss grew on the rooftops and vines tangled up the walls.

"Welcome to our humble home," Will declared, grinning broadly as he opened the door for Nora and Florence. His mop of black hair tumbled over his pale forehead, and he swiped it away, revealing his green eyes.

"I'm moving in with you guys?" Nora stepped through the threshold, glancing around the small living space. The furniture was minimal and well-worn, with the odd personal belonging scattered around the space. Though it was hardly sparse, plants were dotted here and there, filling the corners and shelves with lush green leaves. "This is it?"

"That's an interesting remark coming from someone who doesn't have a home," Will said as he sat on a small sofa by the fireplace. "Spending two weeks at the Forest Edge Manor has spoiled you."

"Oh yes, my imprisonment and the forced removal of my tattoos complemented the expensive furniture and fancy food perfectly."

"And here we were under the impression you'd lost that wonderful sense of wit." He chuckled, crossing his legs and leaning back in his seat. "From what Florence said, you were a moping mess."

"I—"

"A shadow of your former self."

"She—"

"Like the routine of getting ready for work in the morning."

"What?"

"Dull and somewhat depressing."

"I thought you liked your job?" Florence asked, dropping onto the sofa beside him.

Will looked at her in adoration and smiled. "I do, but sometimes even I dread the monotony of the day-to-day."

"Maybe you could hire someone to help out?"

"I tried that," he smirked, his emerald eyes flicking to Nora. "Look how well that turned out last time."

"I'm glad you still remember I'm here," Nora quipped.

Florence laughed and proceeded to point around the space seeing as Nora had never been there before. "Kitchen, living, and bathroom are through that door." She pointed to the back of the room and then to a set of stairs beside it. "There are two bedrooms upstairs."

"I get my own room?" Nora asked, running her finger over the back of one of the dining chairs. Their home had a warmth to it, the furnishings clearly lived in, not broken but well loved.

"We like you, Nora," Will said. "But not enough to share a room with you. I bet you're the type to kick in your sleep."

"Your room is the one on the left," Florence said. "You should have everything you need. All your belongings from Daphne's are here, and I managed to get you a few extra clothing items too."

"Thanks," Nora replied, stuffing her hands into her pockets, her eyes not quite meeting Florence's green ones.

"Do you want to have a look?" Florence asked.

She nodded.

"I'll show you, come on." Florence jumped to her feet, placing a quick kiss on Will's cheek. "You need to go to work. You'll be late."

"Lucky the boss likes me," Will replied.

"Terrible." Nora shook her head, amusement quirking her lips. "Truly terrible."

Florence laughed, striding over to the stairs. "I like his jokes."

"That's because you love me," Will said with a grin.

"True."

Nora faked gagging as she followed Florence. "Show me the room before I vomit."

"I'll see you both later," Will called. "I *love* you, Florence."

Nora opened her mouth to reply, but the words never passed her lips. Instead, Florence swung her arm around Nora's shoulders, urging her up the stairs. "If you start your sassy talk, we could be here for hours."

"What's that supposed to mean?" She eyed Florence with narrowed eyes.

"Nothing," Florence said with a mischievous grin. "Do you want to see your room or what?"

3

Evelyn

The sun slowly bled into the sky, with orange and pink hues illuminating Royal Bay in the distance. Evelyn's horse slowed in the tall grass, picking its way through the undergrowth. Zaim had been cautious, taking care to avoid well-travelled roads, opting for the cover and relative quiet of lesser-known paths. The Alta was always on the move, never letting Evelyn out of his sight. She'd tried to find a way out of her predicament, but Zaim kept Poppy close, the unconscious and vulnerable body of her best friend more effective than any chain.

Evelyn glanced at her friend, who sat strapped to Zaim's back. Her head drooped to one side and her body wobbled with each of the horse's movements. The rope holding Poppy to her captor was the only thing keeping her upright. Zaim had been drugging Poppy regularly, enforcing Evelyn to heal her friend of starvation and dehydration with Lys Alv magic. It was a smart move—not only did it keep Poppy unconscious, but Evelyn was constantly drained due to using her magic so often.

If the long days of riding, magic use, minimal sleep and little food weren't enough to exhaust Evelyn, thoughts of her father were the icing on the cake. Not a day went by in the weeks of travel that Evelyn did not think of him and his sudden passing. He'd unknowingly sacrificed himself via his conjuring skills to remove Nora's tattoos and free her from the king's hold. Even if he'd been aware of the outcome, Evelyn knew he would have done it anyway. She found it hard to comprehend that he was gone. It was a concept too far from possible in her thoughts. Yet, she refused to mourn. To let herself crumble. Evelyn was determined to remain strong despite her predicament.

That she was forced to abandon her mother and Jasmine without a word—especially with her father's death still so raw in their hearts—saddened her terribly. They should have mourned together, but what choice had she been given? Zaim had vowed to kill Poppy if Evelyn didn't accompany him without protest, and she couldn't stand to watch her loved ones be hurt, even if that meant she might hurt others in the process. She knew her family worried for her, but they would understand once she'd explained Zaim had forced her hand… *if* she ever found her way back to them.

Zaim halted his horse as they reached an outcropping of trees where a wooden cabin sat not too far in the distance. Evelyn wondered whether she could alert the residents, but doing that meant leaving Poppy alone with Zaim, and that was *not* an option.

"Dismount," Zaim ordered, untying himself from Poppy before getting off his horse. Poppy fell forward, her golden hair tumbling around her.

"You don't have to be rude," Evelyn reprimanded Zaim, dropping from her horse and hurrying over to her friend. "And be careful. She'll fall."

Zaim folded his arms over his chest, the fabric of his dark coat straining over his arms and shoulders. He narrowed his eyes like a predator eyeing its prey. "Someone's forgotten her place. Do you need a reminder of who I am?"

Evelyn held his stare. Oh, she knew exactly who he was. An Alta—one of King Dominic's lethal soldiers—and a trained killer. He'd murdered her aunt and cousin, lured Poppy with kisses and false words, and then plotted to kill her father. Zaim may not have been the reason for his death, but Evelyn knew Zaim would not have hesitated to end her father's life himself. She would never forget the crimes he'd committed against her loved ones, and she would never forgive. He would one day suffer for them. She didn't know what she would do yet, but she would make Zaim and King Dominic pay.

"I'll take that as a yes," Zaim said, drawing Evelyn from her thoughts of revenge and striding over to her. He shoved her out of the way and her ass hit the ground hard, earning a gasp. "Here's your reminder."

He grabbed Poppy's hair and dragged her from the horse. Poppy almost looked as though she were kneeling, but her body was limp in his hand, and Evelyn winced at seeing her friend being held up by her hair. Then, quick as a wink, Zaim drew a knife and pressed it to Poppy's pale throat. A scream ripped from Evelyn, and Zaim stilled the blade, laughing like it was some innocent joke. Evelyn made to dive forward, but Zaim released Poppy and caught Evelyn before she could reach her friend, pulling her away and jostling her roughly.

"You promised she wouldn't be hurt if I cooperated," Evelyn said, twisting in his grasp. She elbowed him in the ribs and stamped down on his foot, yet Zaim appeared frustratingly immune to her attacks.

"Then cooperate," he grunted in annoyance, absorbing the blows from her elbows.

"I will!" Evelyn screamed, thrashing in Zaim's arms. "Just don't hurt her!"

"Not so cocky now." Zaim sneered, his breath hot against her cheek as he pressed his lips to her pointed ear. "Step out of line again and I'll kill her."

He released her, and she fell to her knees with a sob, his leather boot connecting with her side and shoving her back. Evelyn rose, trying to remember Jasmine's lessons as she lashed out, but he moved too quickly, his grasp too strong, and she soon found her wrists bound.

"You'll pay for all you've done," Evelyn shouted as she was lifted and draped over Zaim's horse. The cabin in the distance showed no signs of life, despite her cries. Either there were no occupants, they couldn't hear her screams or, worst of all, they didn't care.

Zaim chuckled, though there was no humour in his voice. "I doubt that. You've proved to be a terrible adversary already."

Evelyn struggled on the horse, but there was no use. She was stuck.

"The three of us are about to get real cosy."

Laughing at his own joke, he gripped the hair at the back of her head, holding her firm as he stuffed his hand into his pocket. He produced a vial of the concoction he'd been using to drug Poppy and shoved it between her lips. Evelyn refused to open her mouth, but that didn't deter him. Zaim smashed the vial against her teeth, and she cried out at the impact, the pain shooting up her face. The broken glass cut her lips, tears streaming down her face as he held his hand over her mouth, forcing the liquid inside.

"Drink up," he said, grinning wickedly at her.

The tiny shards of glass tore inside her mouth, and she was forced to swallow the liquid along with her blood. If she were any race other than a Lys Alv, she'd die from the internal bleeding. Instead, her magic would heal the internal wounds from the glass for days, and that's if she was lucky enough for it to pass through her system without getting caught anywhere. Evelyn's vision blurred and the last thing she saw before darkness took her was his horrible grin.

Smack!

Evelyn's cheek stung, her lashes fluttering as she woke to Zaim's evil eyes glaring down at her. She ran her tongue along the inside of her mouth, surprised to find it healed. He must have cleaned out her mouth, though she doubted he would have been thorough enough to stop any glass from being swallowed.

"Time to walk," he said, grabbing her by her still-bound wrists and tugging her to her feet from where she was slumped on a cool stone floor.

"Where are we?" she croaked as he roughly dragged her along. Poppy hung limply over his shoulder, and he carried her with the ease of a baker carrying a sack of flour.

Zaim ignored her question as he dragged her down a corridor and up a staircase. Evelyn stumbled after him, trying to keep her footing in the low light. Her golden eyes slowly adjusted, but that didn't stop her from tripping on the steps and needing to brace herself against the wall.

"Where are we?" Evelyn spluttered again. Were they underground? Evelyn shuddered at the thought. Her captor just marched upwards.

At the top of the stairs, Zaim halted, watching her with a sneer as she clambered up behind him. When she reached him, he continued through a narrow corridor before opening a thick wooden door. Evelyn was immediately accosted by the bright sunshine flooding the garden.

Outside, the scent of salt enveloped her senses, followed by a strange *whoosh*. "What's that sound?"

"What?" he grunted, unperturbed by the sudden change in the environment.

"That whooshing sound?" she explained, blinking a few times. Her vision finally cleared, and a courtyard lined with blossoming flowers appeared around her. The flowers surrounded an immaculate lawn, trimmed to near-perfect precision and were bordered by polished tiles. An elaborately sculpted water feature depicting Elementum children using their magic stood in the centre of the space.

He laughed—the sound wretched to Evelyn's ears—and she watched his shoulders shake as he continued. Evelyn narrowed her hooded eyes at his back, wishing, not for the first time in the last few days, that she had Elementum gifts or could turn into a tiger or an equally strong Anima shift so that she could do some actual damage to him.

"You have got to be one of the most naïve, sheltered people I've ever met. Second only to your silly little friend," he replied, his tone akin to speaking down to a child. "That sound is the waves crashing against the island."

"We're on the castle island?" she asked, halting and causing Zaim to stop in front of her.

He'd knocked her out, and she'd missed how they'd got there. Questions flooded her mind, the most prominent being why they had been underground. Zaim pulled out his knife and cut the ropes binding her wrists before turning away once more, clearly expecting she would keep following.

All her questions were quickly replaced with awe at where she was now walking. The farthest she'd ever travelled from her home in Forest's Edge was to that tiny village with her mentor, Margot, for her final examinations as a Healer. The idea of being in Royal Bay, not to mention on the island that housed the castle, was beyond anything she'd ever imagined. Evelyn had read many geography and history books filled with stories of the Elementum who'd held back the sea so the island could be created. It was hard not to be a little excited about the prospect of seeing the place in person. It didn't take away her anger at being forced to leave her family and friends, of course, but it was a pleasant distraction. And Evelyn sure loved distractions.

Evelyn spun as she walked to fully appreciate her surroundings, only to find herself face-to-face with a sentry dressed in silver armour that sparkled in the sunlight. He appeared unbothered, his face remaining neutral as he stood stiffly with his arms at his sides.

"Sorry," Evelyn said hastily, stepping back and running a hand down her dress. She must have looked dishevelled compared to the two sentries before her, but *someone* hadn't offered her a chance to wash, let alone change since she'd left her home. Her skin felt as though it was caked in dirt, and her black hair was a knotted mess.

"Seems your father didn't bother to teach you any etiquette," came a deep voice, chilling Evelyn to her bones.

The sentries stepped to the side, revealing King Dominic in all his glory. The man stood tall, his broad shoulders back and chest puffed out as though his sense of self-importance was desperate to burst from his ribcage. His hazel eyes took Evelyn in, and she did her best not to quake beneath his gaze. She could only imagine what he saw when he looked at her.

"My—"

"It is customary to bow before your king," King Dominic hissed, cutting her off as one of the sentries stepped forward and shoved her to her knees with a firm grip on her shoulder. "You will do well to remember that you are beneath me. Do not speak unless I require an answer."

Evelyn remained silent, her knees smarting from colliding with the ground. She'd known the king was horrible, but a small part of her had hoped the stories had been exaggerated to some degree.

"Now," the king continued. "Where are the other three?"

Evelyn scrunched her brow, unsure of how to answer the king, but then Zaim spoke. King Dominic's question was obviously for the Alta. She remained on her knees with the sentry's hand still firmly on her shoulder. She clasped her hands before her to stop them from shaking and focused on her breathing.

"My king," Zaim began, and Evelyn could see slight movement to her side as he bowed. "August and Nora are still in Forest's Edge. They had yet to find Felix last I spoke with them."

"They better find him soon," the king growled. "Or so help me..."

"There may be a problem with that, my king," Zaim replied, a slight tremor in his voice betraying the man's fear. The way Zaim usually behaved, she would not have believed him to be afraid of anyone if she hadn't heard it herself.

"What?" King Dominic ground out.

Zaim audibly swallowed, and Evelyn lifted her head to see the man shifting on his feet. He licked his lips, his eyes flitting to the sentries in their silver uniforms before returning to the king. "They have betrayed you."

"That's impossible," the king hissed.

"I saw it myself," Zaim replied, his pale hands rubbing over his covered wrists.

"You mean to tell me you witnessed with your eyes, proof that two of my soldiers are no longer loyal to me? Two people that are privy to important information, and you let them live?"

"Ahh... I was tasked with bringing you the key to the north and dealing with the lord," Zaim stuttered. "Ending Nora and August would have been detrimental to fulfilling the tasks you set before me."

"Don't you dare attempt to make excuses for your failings!" the king roared, fire igniting in his pale palms. "It is your duty to eliminate threats! Two elite soldiers are now in the hands of a treacherous ruler because you failed to kill them whilst they were in your grasp. Now there are three Alta no longer in my service!"

The burst of heat flared, warming Evelyn's face as she watched King Dominic's features twist with rage.

"No one leaves the Alta!" the king seethed as he began pacing.

Evelyn quickly looked at the silver sentries' blank faces despite the king's mention of the Alta. Did they know about the secret soldiers the king tied to him through magic? Zaim must have been wondering the same because when she looked back at him, he too, was eyeing the sentries, his brows scrunched in confusion.

"Now I have three deserters roaming the country," the king continued as he walked back and forth. He extinguished the flames in his hands before running his fingers roughly through his dark hair. He halted abruptly, glaring at Zaim. "Send for Rana to meet me in her office in five minutes. I will have to send others to fix this mess. I will not let three traitors ruin my plans. Go! You will receive your punishment when I am done."

Zaim dropped Poppy to the ground with a thud that had Evelyn cringing, then quickly bowed before running across the lawn and disappearing through an archway.

Evelyn clasped her hands before her to stop them from shaking and focused on her breathing as she waited for the king's wrath. To her surprise, he didn't spare her a second glance before storming off in the opposite direction, a silver sentry following close behind.

"Follow me," the remaining sentry said as he removed his hand from her shoulder. He picked up Poppy, cradling her in his arms, then turned and marched away. Everything about him appeared uniform—from his neatly combed black hair to his precise strides.

Evelyn quietly followed the sentry through the courtyard into a grand hallway lined with giant portraits and busts of past rulers. Her jaw dropped as she gazed at the grandeur of the place. Light filtered through tall windows, casting a glow on the polished tiles and the finery on display. They ascended a grand staircase, reaching a set of double doors that revealed a magnificent room.

Poppy had once said the manor in Forest's Edge was fancy, but her home was a rickety shack compared to King Dominic's castle. Tears threatened to fall, but Evelyn blinked them away. She would not be seen as weak. She may bow to the king and keep her mouth shut, but she would bend no further.

Without a word, the door shut behind Evelyn, the lock clicking with finality. Poppy lay on the sofa, and Evelyn dashed to her side, kneeling beside her and summoning light from her hands which she placed over her friend's chest. Her Lys Alv magic coursed through Poppy, seeking injuries in need of healing.

Her magic could not clear the drugs in Poppy's system, but it could heal Poppy's malnutrition and dehydration since Evelyn was last able to tend to those needs.

Once satisfied that Poppy was well, Evelyn let the magnitude of her predicament wash over her. Then, with a heavy sigh, she dropped to sit with her back to Poppy.

Her friend's hand hung over the sofa's edge, and Evelyn held it tightly, staring into the fire crackling in the hearth. She'd never felt so powerless in her life. Nothing nailed that sentiment home more than being locked in a strange room in a dangerous castle with no idea of what came next.

4

Nora

Nora bit into her toast, resting her cheek lazily on her hand as she chewed. She was sitting at the small table in Will and Florence's home, contemplating her next move. Will was set to leave for Florence's flower shop any minute and, according to him, Florence had left hours before; at least, that's what he had told Nora when she'd woken up. Anticipation danced in her stomach, disturbing the breakfast she was forcing down. Just a little longer and she'd be alone. Then she'd make her escape. The pearlescent shackles were still firm around her wrists, but that would be tomorrow Nora's problem. Today she needed to leave the city.

Jasmine had given her two choices, but Nora wasn't ready to give up freedom or anything. Freedom was her main priority now, not being tied to that third option. She just needed to wait for the right moment.

"What's going on in that head of yours?" Will asked, leaning against the kitchen bench and taking a sip of his tea. His inquisitive gaze glanced down at her now empty plate, avoiding Will.

"Nothing," Nora replied, stuffing the rest of her

"I think I'm going to enjoy this little ritual of what comes out of your mouth is sarcasm up to see a grin tugging at his lips. "Right now, I'm guessing a lie because we both know there is never anything *not* going on in your head."

"You're not just a pretty face, then." she teased.

"Sarcasm." He winked as the front door opened and Florence stepped inside. "Tell me a truth, so I can hear all three before I'm on my way."

"Good morning," Florence sang, striding into the living area.

Nora's shoulders slumped. "Will said you had already left for the day."

"I did," Florence replied with a mock salute, "but I'm back now, reporting for babysitting duty."

"For the love of all that is holy," Nora groaned. "I do *not* need a babysitter."

Will paused putting on his cloak and cast Nora a knowing look. "I asked for a truth, not two lies."

Nora shot him daggers with her eyes. If only she had her magic. She would have washed that look right off his face with a good jet of water. As if understanding her would-be intention, he laughed, dragging the rest of his cloak on before wrapping a brown scarf around his neck.

"I'll see you two later," Will said, kissing Florence on the cheek before striding to the door. His hand stilled on the knob, and he turned to look at Nora sternly. "Be good."

"I can't make any promises!" Nora called after him as he stepped onto the street.

"There's my truth!" He laughed, shutting the door and leaving her alone with Florence.

Nora couldn't help the smile spreading across her face. Despite being under the king's command when she had worked for Will, she'd enjoyed the florist's company. If only her life had been different, maybe she and Will would have been friends.

"Go get ready," Florence said, rummaging through the cupboards. "We have a few jobs to do today."

"Are you sure I can't stay here?"

Nora had contemplated using brute force to free herself, but every time she did, it brought back memories of her attempted escape from the Manor after her tattoos had been removed. She still felt horrible for what she'd done to those guards—they had only been doing their job and she'd hurt them. And then there was Aeolus. The second in command of the Forest's Edge Faction would most likely be sent after her and, without her magic to ward off the frost chill, he'd catch and punish her. The thought of how he might use his water magic sent chills down her spine. As part of her Alta training, Nora had been taught to endure torture, but without the tattoos controlling her emotions, she couldn't keep the fear at bay anymore.

Florence laughed at Nora's request like it was some big joke. Begrudgingly, Nora went upstairs to retrieve her jacket and a scarf before returning to find Florence waiting by the door. With a tight-lipped smile, she held eye contact with the woman and pasted a sarcastic look on her face as she shoved her feet into her boots. As promised, Nora had received new clothes—all much better made than anything she'd owned before—not that she'd ever had personal belongings. The king had provided the bare necessities, but they'd never truly been hers. The few items she'd come to acquire, like books and trinkets, all technically belonged to King Dominic. Nora dropped her gaze to study her boots. *Her* boots. Nora couldn't help the smile that tugged at the side of her lips.

"They are nice," Florence commented. Nora glanced up to see Florence was looking at her boots, too. "Not as nice as mine, but you can't all be as stylish as me."

Nora quirked a brow. "You are not what I would call stylish."

"Pshh, that's exactly what someone without style would say," she replied, turning towards the door. "Come on, we have things to do."

Nora followed Florence outside, rolling her eyes and stuffing her hands into her jacket pockets.

"At least when I leave, I'll have some nice stuff to take with me," Nora said as they walked.

Florence reached for Nora's arm, giving it a gentle squeeze. "I want you to stay," She said with a small smile.

"Why?"

"Because we are friends."

"We are?"

"Yes," Florence laughed. "Will and I consider you a friend. I hope you consider us yours too."

Nora found her insides warming from the woman's declaration. Jasmine had said as much, but hearing it from Florence made it hard to deny. She let herself be steered through the bustling streets as the citizens of Forest's Edge went about their business. There were a few light clouds this morning but beams of sunlight still managed to weave through bare tree branches. Only the evergreens remained green, their needles still providing colour despite the cold weather. They passed by the markets, and the smells of baked goods and roasting meats filled the air before they passed the busy thoroughfare and headed southeast.

The tree coverage grew wilder, and Nora spotted a tall stone wall spanning around the city border that hadn't been there the first time she'd arrived in Forest's Edge. A large wooden gate was closed, blocking access in and out. When Nora had first arrived, the city had no barrier stopping people from entering, only outposts high in the trees with one or two guards on watch. Now, multiple Faction members and green-coated guards monitored the wall from the outposts, their faces stern, whilst others went about their duties on the ground. Nora had always found it strange that Forest's Edge had a city guard instead of sentries like every other city. Before King Dominic, every city had a guard and only the royal family had sentries, but his reign changed all that. He dictated that all cities have his specially trained sentries, claiming it would ensure superior and unbiased security for all. Even though some were reluctant, citing tradition as a reason to refuse, eventually all but one city fell into line. Nora was surprised the king hadn't come after the Royd family decades ago.

A group strode passed Nora, and she noted that even though the Forest's Edge guards still wore their green coats, distinguishing them as the city's protectors, they all had a fabric band around their upper arms. Nora noted the faction's symbol, five interconnecting squares all on their points, stitched into the band.

"Lou," Florence said, greeting a man wearing a thick travelling cloak and well-worn leather boots. She extended her hand to him and Lou smiled broadly, shaking Florence's palm exaggeratedly. "Where's Mya?"

"Behind you," Mya said, popping out from behind Florence and causing her to jump. "I see your senses are still awful."

"My senses are in top condition," Florence replied with a shrug. "Maybe it's not whether my skills are lacking, but that your skills are excellent."

"Always the diplomat," Mya said, adjusting her woollen hat. "No wonder Gemma has you as the first port of call for newcomers."

Florence smiled. "How are things in the south?"

"Getting worse each day," Lou replied. "Messenger Anima have been spreading the word of Lord Royd's passing, not to mention that the new Lady Royd is outwardly opposing the king. Already King Dominic has demonstrated he isn't impressed. He passed another ridiculous law. Have you heard?"

Florence shook her head. "We've had no updates for a week."

"In addition to registering and being told where we can and cannot live, Anima must now declare all assets and are subject to inspections without warning. He's disguising it as crime prevention. Not only are we 'aggressive' and 'wild', but we're also alleged thieves now." Lou said with a scowl pointing in the direction of Royal Bay, which lay far to the south and out of sight.

"As you can imagine, more and more people are fleeing north," Mya added. "We're on our way to Carl to update him on numbers. I don't think he has the space for all the Anima flooding this way."

"I'm sure Jasmine will help," Florence said. "She has already made it clear that Forest's Edge will shelter anyone seeking refuge in the city."

Mya nodded and said, "We know she is an ally, but many Anima are finding it hard to trust anyone but our own. As you know."

Lou frowned. "People are afraid."

"They have every right to be," Mya said. "The further south we travelled, the more Anima were reported missing or sent to the mines. And it's not just the king. The Makers' Murders are worse down there. We did our best to help, but the Faction numbers are smaller in the south and most of the southern wolf pack is gone. Only those actively sabotaging the king or aiding others to flee have remained, but even their numbers have dwindled. I know Lady Royd, Gemma, and Carl are doing what they can, but I fear there will be no helping anyone below Midskopas soon."

"Who's Carl?" Nora asked.

"He's the leader of the Northern Wolf Pack," Florence replied. "He recently acquired the Southern Wolf Pack and many Anima from other shifts, too. He's basically the leader of a hidden city."

Nora didn't know much about the wolf packs—only what Rana had taught her during Alta training and from intel she had gathered on jobs. The wolf packs weren't deemed a real threat to the Kingdom, more of an unsophisticated nuisance. But now that Nora could think freely about everything she'd seen, she was starting to deeper examine those beliefs more and had many questions about where they originated.

"Any news from Fellbun?" Lou asked.

"Lord Halivor should have received Jasmine's letter by now, and we have no reason to believe he will not side with us," said Florence. "The Halivor and Royd families have always worked together and shared similar beliefs throughout the years. A message has also been sent to Lord Ulmer in Kaldom. We await his reply. He isn't likely to send aid, but we expect he will side with Forest's Edge from a political standpoint. His people have strong ties to the Anima, as we do here. I expect his only assistance beyond written support will be to take in those wishing to relocate. He may be an Anima, but he won't risk his city."

Mya and Lou glanced at each other with brows pulled together.

If an Anima lord wouldn't come to the aid of his own race, what were the chances the other lords and ladies of the other races would do so, Nora wondered.

"Incoming hostiles!" a guard cried, and suddenly everyone was gathering weapons and racing towards the wall.

"See that building over there?" Florence asked Nora, pointing to a small cabin nestled between two large trees. "Go inside and wait for me."

"Not going to make me defend the city?"

"Your work ethic isn't great at the moment," Florence replied as a boom echoed through the air and water sprayed over the wall. "Go!"

Florence shifted and ran to help, and Nora was suddenly unguarded. Dropping her hands, she flexed her fingers and quickly scanned her surroundings. She could disappear and be long gone before the sun had made its descent beyond the horizon.

Nora bit her lip. She could easily leave Forest's Edge and all its inhabitants behind, but where would she go? King Dominic wouldn't take her back, even if she had information he could use. He'd deem her a liability. She could follow August to the Periculum Mountains…

Nora shook her head. No. She was done with him.

Realisation dawned on her. She had nowhere to go. And if she was honest, making excuses to stay was so easy even after everything. Nora strode to the cabin and opened the door, her gaze snagging on a familiar figure sitting at a table in the corner. Nora could blame her inability to leave on having nowhere to go. Not when the real reason was a few steps away.

Sage was devastatingly beautiful, dressed in a navy coat with charcoal tights and chocolate brown leather boots. Her tight curls were tied into two pigtails with ribbons that matched her coat, and her gold-rimmed glasses were doing their usual trick of attempting to slide off her dark nose. Nora's heart raced in her chest, worsening when Sage looked up and her brown eyes connected with Nora's. It was a miracle from the Goddess Thyra herself that Nora could breathe at that moment.

"Hey," Sage said softly, a hesitant smile gracing her face.

"Hi," Nora replied awkwardly, her tone not as strong or confident as she would have liked. She closed the door and stepped closer to the table. "Hiding from the fight, too?"

"Not initially," Sage said, flinching as another boom sounded.

"Don't worry, it's probably just the King's Guild. They're more of an annoyance than anything."

"You're certain?"

Nora nodded. "If I can take on the Guild with little help, I'd say the guards and Faction will be fine. It's good practice for them for what's to come anyway."

Sage scrunched her nose. "Last I remembered, you almost died both times you tried to fight the Guild."

"Maybe, but I'm still here and they're deep in the ground being eaten by bugs, so who's the real winner?" Nora said. "Why are you here?"

"Meeting someone, though I hadn't expected to see you."

"Still mad at me?"

"No," Sage replied, exhaling deeply as she spoke. "At least, I'm trying not to be. I know you were under the king's control, so your shitty behaviour wasn't your fault, but it's hard to marry my head with my heart."

"And what does your heart tell you?"

"To be mad at you for lying to me. To be angry at you for manipulating me and using me."

Nora winced, avoiding Sage's eyes. "Quite the predicament you have yourself in then." It was hard for her to look at Sage when the other woman was so visibly hurt by what Nora had done. Instead, she fixed her gaze on a corner of the room and forced her emotions away. She tried to emulate the stoic version of herself when the king's tattoos spared her emotional distraction from interfering with what needed to be done. But it was so much harder now.

"Look at me," Sage said. She appeared at Nora's side, placing a hand on Nora's upper arm and turning Nora to face her. "Don't shut me out."

"I don't remember ever letting you in."

Sage's brows drew in. "You're pushing me away again, and you need to stop. I know I haven't seen you since... since it all happened, but I've been trying to work up the courage to come. I want to give you another chance because I think I was able to glimpse enough of you beyond the king's control to see that you are an amazing person."

"Irritating, antagonistic, sarcastic, self-centred, and stubborn, I think are the terms you once used," Nora added, ignoring how Sage's words were affecting her. They were exactly what she wanted to hear, but at the same time made her feel like a rabbit running from a predator. She felt the urge to do exactly that. Maybe she'd have a better chance of survival on her own.

As if noticing Nora's instinct to flee, Sage gripped Nora's arm tighter. "Apparently, I like all those personality traits," Sage smiled, making Nora's heart skip a beat. "I think we could be something. But that's up to you. I won't force you to do anything you don't want to. Just think about it," she said, releasing Nora and backing away. "You're free. Your life is yours. So, you might as well start living it."

"With you?"

"I don't know yet. Maybe we could try first as friends?"

Nora found herself liking the sound of that. Any small crumb Sage offered felt like a gift.

"I thought you two were already friends?" Ashe asked striding into the cabin. The last place Nora had seen the guy was when she'd kicked him out of her bed, and Florence had then added salt to his wound by making him leave the room too. He placed an arm over Sage's shoulders, tugging her to his side and forcing her to stand still. "Sorry about having to run off."

Nora clenched her fists, her heart rate rising. The warmth that Sage ignited inside her cooled at the sight of the man. Sage had been there to visit Ashe.

"We are friends, just like you and I are *only* friends," Sage replied, slipping out from under his arm. The movement calmed Nora instantly. "I was only making sure Nora knew that our relationship hasn't changed despite everything that has happened."

"I do," Nora nodded.

"Good," Sage smiled, then turned to Ashe. "I better be getting back. If it's safe now?"

"All safe," Ashe replied. "I'll walk you. Like old times."

"Something like that," Sage said flatly. Her face brightened as she looked at Nora. "I hope I'll see you soon."

"You will," Nora replied with one last smile. Sage turned away from them both and strode out the door.

Her plans to leave were definitely on hold now—the idea of spending more time with Sage was too good to give up. So, with a sigh and a shake of the head, she flopped into one of the chairs to wait for Florence.

"Sage is a good person," Ashe said, coming to stand in front of her and folding his arms over his chest. "If you truly cared about her, you would leave her alone."

"You seem to be confused." Nora leaned back in her seat. "It appears you think I give a shit about your opinion."

"I'm not asking you to care about what I say," he replied. "I'm asking you to consider what's best for Sage."

"How about you stay out of my business?" Nora said. She aimed for a bored tone, despite the emotions whirling inside her. "I already told you I don't want you around—that August asking you to watch me is unnecessary—so why don't you do us both a favour and fuck off?"

"Stay away from Sage, and I will."

"Are you threatening me?" Nora stood, closing the distance between them and jabbing a finger at his chest.

"Only offering friendly advice," he replied with a smirk. Ashe made to leave, pushing past Florence as she tried to enter the cabin at the same time he exited.

Florence's eyes flicked between Nora's and Ashe's backs. Her hair was still in a tight braid and, to Nora's relief, there were no injuries on her pale, freckled skin. Between the conversation with Sage and Florence being unhurt, Nora felt her mood was a bit brighter than it had been in a long time. She wouldn't let Ashe dim that feeling.

"Judging by your appearance and how long I was left without you watching me," Nora began, sitting down with a smirk, "I'm going to assume there was only one threat."

"Close," Florence replied. She sat opposite Nora, propping her boots on one of the other vacant chairs. "There were about ten King's Guild members."

"Ten? —so I guessed the right number of brains then," Nora said and tapped her chin in mock thought. "Or am I being too generous?"

"Definitely generous."

"Removing the tattoos has put a dent in my hard exterior. Next, I'll be offering to braid your hair."

"I wouldn't say no," Florence said with a laugh. "I see you and Ashe still aren't getting along."

"He's an asshole."

"He is," Florence agreed. "Be careful."

"I'm not going to let him get away with being a jerk," Nora said, sitting back and stretching out her legs. "I can handle him."

"I'm sure you can."

5

Evelyn

Evelyn lay on the sofa looking up at the ceiling and spotting her reflection in the gems attached to the intricately designed golden chandelier. The suite she had been allocated was the definition of luxury, with multiple rooms decorated exquisitely. She was in the lavish sitting area where two sofas were placed in the centre of the room, accompanied by small, handcrafted wooden side tables and a large, grey fur rug. She glanced at her breakfast plates where they were stacked on the coffee table, the half-empty pot of tea beside them now cold.

"I just can't believe Zaim kidnapped us," Poppy declared for the thousandth time since they'd arrived yesterday. The temperature in the room rose each time the Elementum expressed her feelings. "There has to be a reason."

"He's an Alta," Evelyn replied. "The king commands, and he follows. There's your reason."

Poppy frowned. "I don't think I could ever trust him again."

"I'm glad," she said. "Now we just need to work out what the king wants with us."

Her anxiety rose with each passing minute of waiting to find out why King Dominic was holding them hostage.

"To make your sister bend to his will? Although that only tells us why *you're* here," Poppy said, tapping her pink lips with a finger. "What's *my* value? It would have been easier for Zaim to just take you without worrying about an extra prisoner."

"Any powerful relatives?" Evelyn asked, raising an eyebrow at her friend. "Or do you know any secrets?"

"Nope." Poppy laughed. "And next to your healing skills as a strong Lys Alv, I'm worthless."

Evelyn frowned. "You're not worthless."

"I didn't mean it in a sad way," Poppy said, flicking her golden hair. "I have enough self-worth to know that I am priceless."

Other than the silver-armoured sentries who had delivered their meals, they had been left alone. Their time had comprised of Poppy angrily marching back and forth, spitting hate for Zaim after she'd awoken, and Evelyn contemplating their predicament.

After succumbing to the realisation that they were stuck, the two women explored the rooms, and then Evelyn excused herself. She'd stoked the coals to generate steam and filled the bath with hot water and perfumed oils, sitting in it until the water had gone cold and her fingers had been a map of hills and valleys. She'd longed to be in the company of her mother and sister—to mourn her father with those she loved—but once she'd risen from the bath, she had been more determined not to lapse into despair. She didn't want to feel the loss of her father, nor the anxiety of being kidnapped. Evelyn refused to break when she needed to keep her wits about her. She was in a lion's den, after all.

A soft succession of melodic knocks on the door had Poppy stilling, and Evelyn quickly jumped up to see that a woman dressed in black-and-white clothing and carrying a bundle of fabric had let herself in. She had dark brown hair tied into a bun and a pink flush to her high cheekbones.

"Miss Evelyn," the woman said, halting before her and bowing her head. "I am Louise, your handmaid. I am here to make sure all your needs are met."

"What we *need* is some answers!" Poppy shouted, storming over and forcing herself between Evelyn and Louise. She pointed a finger, glaring up at the handmaid.

Louise took a step back and frowned, her brown eyes moving between Poppy and Evelyn. "I'm sorry, I—"

"It's not her fault," Evelyn said quickly, placing a hand on Poppy's shoulder. "I'm sure she has very little say in what is happening, being a servant, and so I'd assume has even fewer answers."

Evelyn didn't want to be mad at the staff when it was King Dominic's fault for her predicament, though she wasn't about to let her guard down so easily. She couldn't trust a single person in Royal Bay aside from Poppy.

"I know this is not ideal," Louise said, offering Evelyn a small smile. "But I will do my best to make you comfortable."

Poppy threw her hands in the air and dropped onto the sofa with a huff. "What about me?"

"Someone is coming to take you to your own rooms," Louise replied, then looked to Evelyn. "Right now, you need to get ready."

"For what?" Evelyn asked, tucking a strand of hair behind her pointed ear. She glanced at Poppy, who merely shrugged, clearly giving up on taking her anger out on the handmaid. "Louise, what am I being prepared for?"

"King Dominic has requested your presence," the maid replied, ushering Evelyn through the room. "I wasn't told any more than that."

They passed the set of double doors leading to the extravagant, oversized four-poster bed. It had been luxurious to sleep in. Evelyn had never slept better in her life and, considering she'd slept beside Poppy—who had wriggled constantly in her sleep—as well as the traumatic events of the past few weeks, it had been a massive achievement.

"Do you know what he wants?" Evelyn asked, stepping into the walk-in closet. The average home in Forest's edge could easily fit multiple times inside the wardrobe, let alone the rest of the suite. Evelyn had never felt more out of place in her life, and she was part of the Forest Edge's ruling family. She thought she knew what luxury was until now.

"Everything," Louise whispered, then giggled as though it were a joke, not a weighted statement. "Let's not waste any more time."

She hung the fabric she'd been carrying on a hook, then unravelled the outer layer to reveal a gown that shone like gems in the sunlight. Louise fluttered around Evelyn, removing the simple dress she wore and forcing Evelyn into the new one, while Poppy stood at the door, watching the whole display with creased brows. The powder-blue fabric was soft against Evelyn's skin, the colour complementing her golden-brown complexion. Behind Evelyn, Louise pulled on ribbons, tightening the bodice until Evelyn let out a gasp.

"You look beautiful!" Louise exclaimed after securing the dress to Evelyn's figure. "Come, sit, and I'll do your makeup."

Louise gripped Evelyn's arm, dragging her over to a chair, and the woman set to work using an array of brushes to apply powders and creams to Evelyn's face. She watched in the mirror as Louise hummed while she worked, her personality oozing positivity that was so contagious, Evelyn felt herself almost forgetting her reality. She had to fight to keep the walls she'd put up in place.

Evelyn wouldn't treat Louise poorly because of the king. The handmaid was only trying to do her job and being nice to her didn't mean Evelyn had accepted her fate.

Louise ran a comb through Evelyn's black hair, sighing wistfully. "Your long hair is so lovely and glossy. I wish I had hair as nice as yours. Unfortunately, I have this brittle frizz that can only be tamed with a bun and a dozen or more pins."

"I'm sure yours is beautiful in its own way," Evelyn replied, picking up a gem-encrusted pin and twirling it between her fingers.

"You're just being nice," Louise said, playfully tapping Evelyn's shoulder. "I am plain. The current fashion certainly favours your natural beauty."

"The fashion is biased," Evelyn said, pricking her finger with the pin. A tiny bead of blood appeared on the pad; it was all that could escape before her magic healed the tiny wound. "Sometimes, I think they only invented it to make us conform and loathe ourselves." She turned to Louise, looking the woman in the eyes. "You are one of a kind, and all rare things are beautiful and should be cherished."

"Such pretty words." Louise smiled broadly, stepping back and waving her over. "Go have a peek in the mirror before leaving."

Evelyn did as told and was surprised by the reflection staring back at her. The dress's bodice sat snugly against her curves thanks to Louise's handiwork, accentuating her breasts and hips. Her hair hung loosely with diamond pins threaded through the strands, making it look as though she'd been walking in the snow. Louise waved her hands, fluffing the flowing skirt around Evelyn's feet with her wind magic.

"Is it a bit much?" Evelyn asked hesitantly as Louise crouched before her and held out a satin slipper. Poppy shook her head, her reflection visible in the mirror from where she stood behind Evelyn.

"Not for a lady of your station," Louise replied, helping Evelyn into her shoes. "King Dominic will be very pleased."

Evelyn's gut twisted. That was the last thing she cared about.

Besides being a pawn to force Jasmine's hand, she had no idea why the king wanted her. Not a single word had been uttered, and even Zaim had been cagey during their travel. All she could do was pray to the Goddess Nyssa that whatever it was, it wouldn't be painful, though she had little hope there. Judging by her first encounter with the king, she would be forced to give him whatever he wanted, and she wouldn't be happy about it.

Poppy pulled Evelyn into a hug. "Stay safe."

"You too," Evelyn replied, squeezing her friend tightly.

The skirt of her dress billowed around her as she left the suite and was escorted to meet with King Dominic. A silver sentry walked a few steps ahead of her, his footfalls like a steady beat of a drum that, along with his clinking armour, echoed throughout the grand hallways. As they strode towards their destination, they passed finely dressed people whom Evelyn could only assume were members of the court. They unsubtly whispered degrading comments about her appearance and mean-spirited speculation as to who she was and why one of the king's sentries was guarding her.

Evelyn tried to ignore them, but it was difficult to block out the way they looked down on her. She knew their words shouldn't affect her—after all, she didn't know them nor want to be there in the first place—but it was difficult not to take their comments to heart. Unfortunately, cruel words had a way of piercing even the toughest of armour at times.

As they stepped out onto the castle grounds, Evelyn was surprised to see three carriages lined up before the entrance. Her shoes crunched on the gravel as she was led to the end carriage and helped inside.

Where were they taking her?

Evelyn leaned forward to spy on the front carriages but before she could get a good look, she was abruptly forced to sit back. A man stepped into the carriage, sitting opposite her before patting down his black trousers and opening a book. Evelyn's brow scrunched as she took him in. He had styled black hair, a strong pale jaw, and an air of confidence about him. His posture was relaxed, his broad shoulders filling out his immaculate uniform. Who was this man? There was something oddly familiar about him that reminded her of some*one*, but she couldn't quite put her finger on it.

"Hello," he said, his piercing blue eyes lifting from his book.

"Hi," she replied, feeling awkward. What was it about him that was so familiar?

"I'm Kylan."

The prince? So *that* was why he looked familiar. She'd never seen him in person but had heard enough stories. Evelyn's golden gaze dropped to the prince's outstretched hand.

"You must excuse me, but I don't know who you are," he said.

"Oh!" Evelyn sat up straighter, taking his hand and shaking. "I'm Evelyn Royd."

"From Forest's Edge? Your sister is causing some problems for my father."

"I would argue that your father is causing problems for everyone."

Prince Kylan fixed his gaze back on his novel. "You might want to keep that opinion to yourself."

"Yes, of course," she replied quickly, sitting back in her seat, her cheeks warming as a footman shut the carriage door and it began moving.

They travelled in silence. Evelyn didn't attempt to engage in conversation again, not wanting to get herself in trouble. She shouldn't have said what she did so blatantly to one of the king's sons. Royal Bay was not like Forest's Edge—other than Poppy, she had no allies here and her mouth could get her in trouble.

Instead of letting her mind spiral with worry, she admired the view beyond the window. The castle grounds were enormous, the gardens filled with colourful plants lining the road that led them over a bridge and back onto the mainland where the city of Royal Bay was located. Evelyn marvelled at the yellow-cream buildings with reddish-brown roof tiles that lined the cobbled path causing their carriage to rock as they made their way to their destination. Citizens dressed in fewer layers than those in Forest's Edge at this time of year moved about freely. To Evelyn, Frost Season meant thick coats, scarves, and woollen hats, but in Royal Bay, there were none to be seen. The weather wasn't the unforgiving hot and humid of Scorch Season, but more that of Bloom or Harvest Seasons. Cool, but not cold.

The people appeared happy enough, but there was something Evelyn couldn't put her finger on that had her feeling uneasy. What was it about this city that made her stomach churn? The buildings were well-maintained, and the people were smiling and well-dressed. Evelyn tapped her pursed lips. She felt eyes on her, but when she glanced at the prince, he appeared invested in his book, unbothered by her or the city they travelled through.

As they continued, the streets became busier and grey-uniformed sentries appeared beside the carriage, forming a barrier against the public. Unlike the silver-armoured sentries, those in grey were part of the king's forces established in each city to show his power and reach. Everyone was heading in the same direction as the carriage, which had her craning her neck to see where they were going. Unfortunately, the window didn't open for her to get a better look, so she was left to imagine what awaited. The thoughts she conjured ranged from a public execution to some sort of twisted ritual. By the time the carriage pulled to a stop, her heart hammered in her chest and her palms were slick with sweat.

The carriage door opened, and she quickly wiped her hands on her dress before following Prince Kylan outside. They made their way along a guarded path towards a wooden stage, where she was quickly ushered up to stand before the gathered crowd. From the stage, Evelyn could see hundreds of people had squeezed themselves into the city square. She spotted King's Guild members, identifying them by their bare chests that proudly showed off their tattoos. The king's symbol, a three-pointed crown with a flame, droplet, and swirl hovering over its tips was marked on their skin like a brand. Everyone in Valmenessia knew of the Guild and their blind devotion to the king. They saw him more as a God than anything.

Turning her gaze from them, she saw that many who had gathered were cheering whilst others stared adoringly at King Dominic. He stood front and centre, waving at his people as a woman with long, flowing copper hair spoke in his ear. Her blue eyes spotted Evelyn, and the woman held her gaze as she continued whispering to the king. Evelyn wondered whether the king had remarried or if she was an advisor of sorts. The woman looked too regal to be anything less, and Evelyn couldn't help but think there was something off about her.

The woman smiled at Evelyn, though it felt more like a threat than a warm gesture. Then, with a quick peck on the king's cheek, she stepped away. The woman's long, golden lace dress danced around her feet as she halted beside a man Evelyn guessed was Prince Xander. Like his brother, idle gossip made him easy to place. He was slightly shorter than his younger brother, with unruly, dark curly hair, yet his eyes and smile seemed genuinely delighted as he waved at the people gathered. Prince Kylan stood between him and Evelyn, his book no longer in his hands and a tight smile on his lips.

"Welcome!" King Dominic boomed, drawing not only Evelyn's but that of everyone gathered. "My people, I come before you with a promise and a gift!"

The people cheered, shouting their love for their king, some Elementum even sparking fireballs into the air that exploded like shooting stars. Evelyn's eyes dragged over them, widening in surprise. As far as she could tell, there were no Anima present. Unless they remained in their human forms, the crowd consisted of humans, Elementum, and Lys Alvs, the latter in small numbers. The native birds perched on rooftops gave her a spark of hope that some Anima may have been present, but she knew better.

"First, my promise!" the king shouted, gesturing as a group dressed in sleek, black uniforms appeared and stood in formation. Evelyn spotted Zaim amongst them and glared. "We are moving into a new phase in history. I will no longer be lenient on disturbers of the peace, who threaten the lives of my citizens. The Alta is your newly formed specialised security. They will weed out those who seek to harm all that we have built and the prosperous lives we live. *Feeling* safe and *being* safe are two different things. I want both for my people and, with the Alta, no longer will the Anima and the Makers' Murders be a threat to you!"

The crowd erupted, crying out their approval for the man who had, unbeknownst to them, just revealed how he had been manipulating and controlling them for decades. The Alta weren't new, despite being kept a secret, but King Dominic had twisted a tale that painted them as peacekeepers rather than what they truly were: the king's assassins, torturers, puppets, and, as she'd recently learned, enslaved people.

King Dominic waved his hands, quieting the crowd as he smiled broadly at them. "And now for your gift!"

A rumble started in the crowd as feet stamped in time like a collection of drums. The sound was deafening and, as the king turned, gesturing for her to come forward, Evelyn's heart rate joined the quickening beat. Finally, Evelyn forced her feet to move and stepped to King Dominic's side.

The king waved his hands again, silencing the crowd. "This is Lady Evelyn Royd of Forest's Edge, the true heir to the northern city. You may have heard her sister claims this title, but she is a traitor who presumes to rule."

Evelyn's body tensed and a roaring sounded in her pointed ears as the boos and shouts of displeasure rumbled through those gathered.

"I blame myself," he declared, placing a hand on his chest and frowning. "The northerners believe I have forgotten them, but I will prove that they, too, will prosper in this world we are building! I will depose the traitor in their midst!" He waved his hand towards the youngest prince. "And to prove my goodwill, I will give them my son to show that I care for the north! And so, my people, I gift you a wedding! My son, Prince Kylan of Valmenessia, is to wed the Lady of Forest's Edge!"

The crowd cheered, and Evelyn froze. The king's announcement replayed over and over in her head. When she finally regained herself, she looked at the prince. His face remained a blank mask, impossible to read unlike hers. There was no way to hide her wide eyes or the way her shoulders shook with each breath.

Judging by the sound of the crowd, no one noticed or cared whether Evelyn was happy or not. Their king had promised to provide them protection, stability, and a cause for celebration. If she was the price, they were glad to pay it.

6

August

The city of Fellbun was at the base of the Periculum Mountains' most southern point, built on either side of a river. Stone buildings were scattered in a disorderly fashion, each painted in a bright colour, stark against the snowy surroundings. From what he'd heard about the Lord of Fellbun, August had expected a man of the people. What he didn't expect was the lord's reaction to August's race, or lack thereof, to be exact.

"Welcome, welcome! I'm so happy you are here," Lord Havilor said, beaming from where he stood in the hall of his home. He was tall and thin, dressed in a fur-lined ensemble with golden buttons that matched his eyes.

August had removed his hood before entering the mansion that overlooked the city, as per Felix's instructions, and, thankfully, the lord and his servants didn't bat an eye. They didn't seem the least bit surprised to see a Mors Alv in Valmenessia.

"Thank you for hosting us in your home," Felix replied, hugging the lord as though they were old friends. "We'll be out of your hair in a day or so, I promise."

"Nonsense," Lord Havilor snorted. "Stay as long as you like."

Felix grinned and waving August over said, "this is August."

"Pleased to meet you," Lord Havilor said, taking August's outstretched hand in both of his. "You must be starving. Let's have a bite, and you can fill me in on news from the other cities."

It felt strange to interact with anyone besides Nora, Evelyn, and Felix, who had no issue with him being a Mors Alv. Those three were unbothered by his presence or touch. He couldn't say the same about his allies in Forest's Edge.

Those in Forest's Edge who became aware of his race had acted in a way that indicated they were uncomfortable with the revelation. Their lingering looks and body language were telling enough without anyone saying it outright. It was like it had been ingrained in their subconscious to distrust his kind. As much as they didn't want to believe what the king had said about Mors Alvs, it had still slipped between the cracks.

As for the Alta and King Dominic, they had never bothered hiding their disdain for his race in all his time with them, and August never expected that to change.

August followed the two friends chatting happily ahead of him through the lord's home. Despite its size, it was minimalistic. Glass walls overlooked the city and a waterfall nearby. When they reached the dining room, he saw a table set with what August could only describe as a feast. The scents of roast meat and freshly baked bread filled the air, causing August's stomach to growl.

"So, tell me," Lord Havilor began, sitting at the round table. Tiny orbs of flame floated above them, adding to the sunlight illuminating the space. "What news do you bring?"

August and Felix also took a seat each at the large table and waited for Lord Havilor to serve his plate before they made any selection from the various dishes.

"Unfortunately, Lord Royd has passed unexpectedly, and his daughter, Jasmine, now rules over the city," Felix said, serving himself some vegetables. "It was the king's doing, albeit indirectly, so she plans to make a stand against him."

Lord Havilor frowned. "I am sorry to hear about Lord Royd. He was a good man."

Felix nodded.

"The king has used one of the Alta to kidnap Evelyn, too," August added gruffly. He thought of Evelyn every day, still torn over his decision to head for the mountains rather than rescue her. Each morning, he prayed to the Goddess

Jord that he had made the right choice.

"Lord Royd's other daughter?" Havilor asked. This left August surprised once more as he had expected the lord to seek clarification on what an Alta was. The man clearly knew more than August had assumed.

"Yes," Felix said. "We don't know what he wants with her, but I'm sure we'll soon find out."

"And Jasmine will oppose the king," Lord Havilor mused, pursing his lips. "Fellbun will stand with our kin in Forest's Edge."

"You will?" August asked, impressed with how quickly the lord offered his allegiance.

"Of course," the lord replied. "The king is a bigoted old man with an ego rivalling the Gods and Goddesses themselves."

Felix barked a laugh, earning a wry grin from Lord Havilor.

The lord moved on to another concern, "and the rest of the country?"

"Anima are fleeing," Felix said, taking a sip of water to clear his throat. "More ridiculous laws, which I'm sure you're aware of."

The lord nodded, "I am, though I am not enforcing them. The king believes our city at the foot of the frozen mountains is beneath even his Royal Sentries. Not that I would want them interfering here." He wiggled his brows. "Makes it easier for me to keep secrets without his spies."

"Secrets?" August asked, stilling the fork that was almost in his mouth.

"Do you think your kin would have remained hidden this long without a little help?"

Felix smiled. "Lord Havilor's great, great, great, gr—"

"There are a lot of those," Lord Havilor winked.

"—Grandfather," Felix continued, "was charged with ruling the city of Fellbun. It was hoped the role would rein in the rebellious spirit of his kin, but it turns out that trait continues to pass down through each generation. The distance from Royal Bay has only made them bolder."

August frowned in Felix's direction, "how do you know so much about it?"

Felix shrugged, "I like history."

"He's also so confident in his delivery, he could be lying for all we know. We just can't help believing him," Lord Havilor teased. "Now, what other news do you have for me?"

The two men continued their conversation, ranging from politics to conversations between old friends. August was coming to understand that Felix was well-connected, but he did not understand how that could be. The man was about August's age and had been raised as an Alta, too. When had Felix had the time to meet all these people, let alone charm them into friendship?

Maybe he was too exhausted from travelling to be thinking clearly. The journey had been taxing, but the true nature of his fatigue had been his constant hold on his magic. He didn't want to use it on anyone, subconsciously or not. The only positive this afforded was it made him too tired to be angry. Ever since his magic had dissolved the tattoos binding him to King Dominic, he'd found his temper eager to snap and show its teeth. He hated this newfound part of him.

Once they'd finished eating, servants showed August and Felix to their suite, a sitting area with a shared bathing room and two separate bedrooms. He'd cleaned himself up, then chose the room on the right for himself. Settling onto the bed, he rested his back against the headboard, took out his sketch pad, and began drawing.

The next morning August vigorously shook his upturned pack, eyes scanning the contents as they thudded to the floor. Clothing, maps, a dagger and a book landed at his feet, but his sketchpad was nowhere in sight.

Running a hand threw his hair, he twisted around, taking in every inch of the room he'd been allocated. There was only a bed, armchair and side table, so it wasn't like there were many places for his sketch pad to be. It wasn't a dark room either; the far wall was a wall of glass that let in copious amounts of sunlight. Like the rest of Lord Havilor's home, the view over the city was a feature that was always on display. You'd think his sketch pad would be easy to find with this light and minimal spots to search.

Apparently not. Where the fuck was the thing?

He dropped to his knees with a huff to look beneath the bed again. Nope. It was the same as the last time he'd looked about two minutes ago: nothing but a few dust balls in the far corner.

He rose to his feet with a deep grumble, frustration curling through his veins. His sketch pad was one of the only possessions he gave a shit about. It held not only drawings but memories and ideas, a visual diary of sorts. Unlike the other things in his pack, it was irreplaceable.

"Fuck," he grumbled. Closing his eyes, he clenched his fists and tried to think where it could be.

Maybe someone else had come into his room and moved it. A knock sounded at the door and his eyes snapped open, nostrils flaring at the servant who entered.

"Where did you put it?"

The servant backed up; their eyes wide as they placed a hand on their chest. "I'm sorry, I don't know what you're talking about."

"My sketch pad," August said, his tone clipped. "It's gone."

"Would you like me to help you look for it?"

"Obviously," he snapped. He stormed around the room, roughly moving the curtains that fell on either side of the window in his search.

"Is this it?" the servant asked nervously.

August spun, finding the man standing by the bed, a pillow in his hand. The sketch pad sat on the mattress as though he'd stuffed it beneath the pillow before falling asleep, which he must have.

August dragged a hand over his face. He was losing his mind. Taking a few deep breaths, he tried to regain control of himself, but it was no use.

"Breakfast is in the sitting room when you're ready," said the servant, a slight waver in their voice as they retreated towards the door.

"I'm sorry," he said through gritted teeth. "Thank you."

The servant nodded, then shut the door, leaving August alone. His words had sounded insincere even to his ears. Striding over to the sketch pad, he picked it up and flicked through the pages. There were plenty of blank pages, but he didn't feel like drawing anymore. The moment had passed. Throwing the pad onto the bed, he stomped from his room.

His actions since waking had been utterly pathetic, and August was mortified with himself.

A breakfast spread had been set up in the room that separated his and Felix's. The smell of bacon, eggs and roasted vegetables filled the room. Felix was finishing up his meal when he entered, but August didn't feel like eating. His stomach was too twisted in knots to even contemplate food. So instead, he stood before the window and hoped the view would calm him.

Beyond the glass, the vast waterfall fell to the river below, cutting the northwestern city of Fellbun in two. It appeared to glow a bright red—a trick of the afternoon light that turned the cascading water into liquid flames.

"There was another attack south of Fellbun," Felix said. "A group of people were found strung up on the side of the road, the King's Guild emblem painted on a sign before them."

August's anger fed on Felix's word. His feelings over this crime weren't unwarranted, but the need to track down and murder Guild members in torturous ways was excessive.

He was feeling less rational with each passing day.

Seething, August tried to squash the anger within him. His hands tightened into fists causing his knuckles to turn white. Was this rage inside him merely an aspect of his nature as a Mors Alv? He'd always been told as much. He'd just never wanted to believe it.

"Talk," Felix said, coming to stand at August's side.

The man hadn't looked at August. He was staring out the sitting room's floor-to-ceiling window at Thyra's Firefall, yet he'd somehow sensed August's mood change.

August huffed, but no words left his lips. He didn't want Felix to psychoanalyse him; he was doing that enough on his own. He didn't reply, letting the irrational anger stew in his stomach, hating that he had no way of stopping it. It was like the water that rushed from the waterfall—unruly and fiery, despite the snow-capped mountains around it.

Felix didn't push him to divulge his thoughts, and they both continued staring at the natural wonder, waiting for Lord Havilor to arrive.

"Fine," Felix said after a time. "Continue to clench your jaw and grind your teeth to dust. Don't talk about what's bothering you and let it fester. That's always the best way to deal with things."

"I assume that's sarcasm," Lord Havilor said.

August turned to see the Lys Alv lord stride through the suite towards them. It was modestly decorated with scenic artwork, warm-toned fabrics, and furs draped over the comfortable sofas—a contrast to the harsh terrain north of the city.

"You'd be correct," Felix said, facing the lord and placing his hands behind his back. He glanced sideways at August, then cocked a grin. "I think August has missed it though and taken my words to heart."

August rolled his dark eyes. Felix was getting on his nerves, and the more time he spent with the man, the more irritated he became.

"Ahh," Lord Havilor said, patting August on the shoulder as he came to stand beside him. "Still eager to head north?"

"Plans haven't changed," Felix replied, leaning against the glass and casually folding his arms over his chest. "Any advice about the trip?"

"Move as fast as you can," Lord Havilor replied. "My people and I do not venture as deep into the mountains as you're planning, but we hear things. The mountains are louder than usual."

August frowned. "What's that supposed to mean?"

"To reach your kin is not as simple as it once was, but not impossible."

Felix grinned, "sounds like my kind of odds."

"I've sent word to Lady Royd of our continued allegiance," the lord said. "Nevertheless, Fellbun and this Faction will stand by her side against King Dominic."

"It's an easy thing to promise when you run both the city and the Faction," Felix said, chuckling.

Lord Havilor smiled, "I'm sure Jasmine will soon be in a position to offer the same."

"You think Gemma will let go of the Faction reigns?" August asked. "She didn't seem like the type to forgo power to me."

"Not likely," Felix replied, "but given the right incentive, I'm sure she could be persuaded to move to another job. It makes sense for Jasmine to run everything—having two leaders in one city never works. The people need one authority to look to. They'll create a divide if they're not careful, and that's something we can't risk, not with the king breathing down our backs. His people are united, as we must be too."

"What about the north as a whole?" August asked, turning to face Lord Havilor. "Would you cede power over your city and your people to merge with the other cities under one ruler?"

"I would do whatever was needed to keep my people safe. If that meant bowing to another leader, one that I knew would protect them against the king? Yes, my ego is not so great that I would sacrifice my people for my pride. That doesn't mean that I wouldn't offer my services, but my seat will not be as the leader of the northern cities. My role is here, with the people of Fellbun. My duty is to them."

"You never know what the future holds," Felix said. "We shouldn't worry about it now. We need a unified front, and we have it, so let's not let it fall."

A sentry in blue came rushing through the door, halting before the lord and hastily bowing, his brow beaded with sweat. "There's been another one, my lord. Another Makers' Murder."

"We haven't had an attack in weeks. I thought we'd apprehended the people involved in this city?"

August tucked that knowledge away. He wasn't aware that the Makers' Murders were rarer here than in other cities, with incidents occurring multiple times a month, if not several times a week. What was it about Fellbun that was keeping the murderers away? Or had been, at least. It seemed they had returned to this city.

The sentry shook his head. "The latest report matches the murder a few weeks ago."

"I wonder what has drawn them back," the lord said softly, frowning at Thyra's Firefall as the red reflected in his eyes. "Call a meeting."

With a nod, the sentry ran from the room to carry out his orders.

"It seems I have a pressing issue to deal with," Lord Havilor said. "I hope to see you both when you return, whenever that shall be. Stay safe."

The lord patted August's shoulder, then turned, striding towards the door and leaving August and Felix alone once more.

"Ready?" Felix asked.

"No," August replied. "Though I doubt that matters to you."

"What you want does matter, August. I'm not so horrible that I've completely disregarded it. However, I think that going is what you need. So maybe I'm putting what you need above what you want in the hopes that you will see that doing this was the right move to make in time."

"That little speech was quite convoluted. Felix, God of raiding people's inner thoughts and determining what they need before they know." August sighed heavily, giving in to the inevitable. "Which way to the Mors Alvs? Didn't you say something about a temple?"

Felix laughed, playfully knocking his shoulder into August's. "This way, Mr Sarcasm."

7

Evelyn

As she stared at the drop below, Evelyn contemplated whether jumping to escape was worth the risk of dying. Waves crashed against the castle island, hitting the rocks with a vengeance. Her magic would heal her if she didn't die from the fall, but that was only if she didn't lose it in the waters. Those with magic couldn't leave Valmenessia without sacrificing it in the process. Beyond the seas surrounding the country, there was no magic and no races besides humans. Evelyn found it hard to imagine a world without magic. No. Definitely *not* worth the risk.

She pushed off the balcony railing and walked back to her rooms. Even if she was brave enough to risk it, she had Poppy to think about. Evelyn couldn't leave her friend behind.

After shutting the glass doors that caged her in and sealing off the wind from the balcony, Evelyn crawled onto her ridiculously big bed. She sat crossed-legged, drawing the soft blankets overhead as though she were a child hiding from a monster at night and not an adult trying to escape the real demons of the world. Monsters that had declared her Lady of Forest's Edge, denounced Jasmine and gifted the Royal Bay citizens a wedding all at once.

Marrying Prince Kylan—King Dominic's youngest son—was something Evelyn couldn't accept. She'd spent the morning compiling a list of reasons why beyond the fact she simply didn't want to.

First and foremost, the king wanted her to wed his son. King Dominic never did anything without cause and she didn't want to be a part of furthering his agenda or to be used as a piece in his horrible game.

Secondly, she didn't love Prince Kylan. She didn't know him beyond the gossip and their time alone the previous day. He hadn't been unpleasant, but they hadn't really conversed, which wasn't helpful when trying to decipher his personality. On the carriage ride back to the castle, he'd communicated less, not uttering a single word about what his father had announced. Instead, he focused on pointing out various architecture of note when he wasn't immersed in his book.

Even if Prince Kylan turned out to be a good person, it didn't change anything.

Evelyn was with August. *She hoped.* At the very least, she'd thought they were about to be an item before she'd been blackmailed into leaving. They'd just begun opening up to each other, and now the distance had her second-guessing his intentions and reading into their whole relationship.

Sighing heavily, Evelyn drew the blankets from her head, wrapping them around her slumped shoulders. She wondered whether August was in Forest's Edge helping Jasmine and the others stand against the king or if he was searching for her. It felt selfish to want the latter, but Evelyn couldn't help herself. She wished for August to swoop in and rescue her like a knight in a fairy tale.

The door to her quarters opened, and Louise rushed inside, swinging the door shut behind her.

"Prince Kylan has requested you join him for lunch," the maid said as she approached the bed, with a frown at Evelyn's hair.

Dread pooled in Evelyn's stomach at the prospect of what other plans the royal family had for her. "He has?"

Louise nodded, extending a calloused hand towards Evelyn. "We need to make you a little more presentable first."

"What if I don't want to go?" Evelyn asked, narrowing her eyes at the woman's hand.

"In this castle, you must do as they wish," the handmaid said, "at least for now."

Evelyn tilted her head at Louise's words, though she didn't get a chance to ask the handmaid to elaborate. Evelyn's blanket was pulled from her shoulders in one swift movement, and she squeaked at the sudden chill. From what she'd seen of Louise, the handmaid wasn't what Evelyn had expected of a castle servant. The maid could be rather careless with her words and behaviour.

"You don't want to be late," Louise said as she strode away.

"Do you know where the lunch will be? Or who will be there?" Evelyn called to where the woman had disappeared into the closet.

"All I know is that you will be escorted to his study."

Evelyn chewed her lip. What were the chances she'd be subjected to more life-changing declarations?

"Lady Royd! I have other things to do today!"

Deciding there was no point in arguing with the handmaid, Evelyn shuffled out of bed and let Louise prepare her. Evelyn thought of what her parents had taught her and tried to keep an open mind. She didn't know Prince Kylan. Who was she to assume he was like his father?

Once dressed, Evelyn was escorted from her rooms, reminding herself not to worry about what lunch would bring.

Be open-minded. Don't rush to any conclusions. She told herself as she walked.

The sentry with her was one of three assigned to her in some rotation. As they walked, Evelyn listened to the patter of rain against the large windows. Grey clouds darkened the midday sky and the air smelled salty from the sea. They made their way downstairs and through a passage bordering a garden on one side. The sentry halted at a set of double doors, and Evelyn looked out at the garden beyond as she waited. It was a glossy green thanks to the rain that continued to pour, and she couldn't help but be reminded of her home.

She missed Forest's Edge and the people in it with all her heart.

"Look who it is," a woman said to her companion as they passed, raising her button nose in the air. "The most ungrateful person in all Valmenessia."

The man beside her nodded, adjusting his finely made coat as his blue eyes ran up and down Evelyn. "It would be a dream come true to marry into the royal family."

"There's no pleasing some people," the woman replied as she walked, her silk skirts flowing around her. Neither one lowered their voices as though they wanted Evelyn to hear precisely what was on their minds. It seemed because she wasn't jumping around with joy through the streets, she was an awful person.

Why should she be happy about something she was being forced into?

"I'd heard stories of what the northerners were like," the man said as Evelyn's cheeks heated. "I didn't want to believe them. You know me, I try to give everyone the benefit of the doubt, but you can't deny the proof so clearly before our eyes."

"It's almost sad how backward they are up there. It's a shame they have such difficulty rising to our standard."

"Mmm, it's a pity," the man said, glancing back, his bushy blond brows furrowed as he gave Evelyn one last look before the duo disappeared around a corner.

"We'll need to fix that," a voice said, and Evelyn turned to see Prince Kylan standing in the doorway, frowning at the direction they had gone. He towered over Evelyn, his broad shoulders outfitted in a pressed maroon coat that was open at the front to reveal a dark shirt beneath matching his black hair. He was handsome in every sense of the word.

"Thank you for joining me." The prince raised a hand and beckoned to Evelyn before turning and striding into the room.

Evelyn followed him inside. The sentry shut the door behind her and remained out in the hallway. Inside, the room was modest compared to the rest of the castle. The walls were plain, lined with shelving that housed books stacked in neat piles, and a desk sat in a nook with parchment, inks, and quill pens placed in an orderly manner atop it.

"I'm not sure they'll change their minds about me."

"They will," the prince said, sitting at a round table set for two in the centre of the room. He gestured for her to follow suit. "Once you are taught the correct etiquette."

"Excuse me?" Evelyn sputtered, stopping suddenly. She placed her hands on the back of the chair he offered her and narrowed her golden eyes at him.

"That came out badly," he replied with a shake of his head. "I only meant they will help you understand how to act around here."

"Are you saying I don't know how to hold myself?" Evelyn asked, steeling her spine and ignoring the grumbling of her stomach thanks to the food set out before them.

"No, but I am saying you don't know what is expected of you here."

"I was raised by the best tutors in Forest's Edge. I am part of the ruling family."

"I know," Prince Kylan sighed, running a hand over his face. "I do not wish to offend you. I have merely organised lessons to make your life easier. Please sit."

Evelyn frowned.

Open-minded, Evelyn.

She sighed, sitting down as he served himself from a tray filled with cheese, dried meats, pickled vegetables, and savoury tarts. Fresh bread rolls, a plate of cut fruit, and a pitcher of water were also laid out on the table.

"The lessons will help you act like the future royal you are intended to be."

"Don't imply that my upbringing is subpar simply because I don't meet your standards."

"Those are your words, not mine," he said, filling her plate after she made no move to do so herself. "I want us to get along and thought helping you to fit in and know what is expected would help. You are the one who determined I thought you were lesser."

"You want to be friends?"

"Yes," Prince Kylan said with a nod. "I would like us to get along."

"You have an odd way of showing it."

"I'm not usually this bad at explaining myself," he sighed again, cutting into a tart. "Our marriage doesn't have to be a chore."

"We can't get married. I have a boyfriend."

Prince Kylan stopped cutting and focused his attention on her. She felt her skin warm under his gaze and did her best not to squirm in her seat.

"Is he here?"

She shook her head.

"Will he come for you?"

"I don't know," she replied, pausing to chew her lip as she thought. August had promised to keep her safe. Surely, he wouldn't leave her here. And then there was Jasmine. "I think he will, and my sister will not let this marriage happen when she finds out."

"Then let's work on playing our parts for now," he said with a smile. "Your lessons begin tomorrow and will occur every morning. Learning our ways will help bring the gossips to our side."

"So, we are pretending?"

"About our engagement? Yes, but I would like to get along as well. I was sincere about that."

"I'd like that too," she replied.

"Good," He said and held up his glass of water. "To pretending to be happily betrothed."

Evelyn smiled, raising her glass. "To our fake engagement."

Their glasses clinked, and Evelyn felt the beginnings of a plan forming in her mind. Despite agreeing to the friendly alliance, she was still suspicious of any ulterior motives Prince Kylan may have. There was no way she'd let her guard down entirely in this place, so if Prince Kylan was leading her into a trap, she would not walk into it unaware. She would play the part King Dominic wanted of her if only to learn the inner workings of Royal Bay and end his reign.

As far as tutors were concerned, Tina was nothing like Margot, Evelyn's healer mentor, back in Forest's Edge. Margot hadn't been the softest person in the world, but after meeting Tina, she longed for her old mentor. Tina was a wiry older woman with grey hair cut short to a chin that always lifted to the sky.

"As you walk, I want you to pay close attention to each step you take," the woman instructed Evelyn from where she stood by the window. She was dressed in a soft blush gown with no embellishments bar the neckline, where pearls were sewn into the fabric. "Remember to keep your back straight and look ahead, not at your feet."

Evelyn bit back her reply as she stepped from one side of the room to the other, doing exactly as she was told.

"Don't do that with your mouth," the woman scolded. "Princesses do not make faces. She must remain pleasing to the eye."

What a load of crap! Evelyn had been locked in her rooms with the woman for the entire morning, forced to practise how to sit and stand on different occasions because, according to Tina, there were specific ways for every event. It didn't sound like much, but when she was made to repeat the movements, the hours had stretched on and Evelyn's temper was fraying.

"Head up, head up!" Tina ordered. "I used to teach the princes how to walk correctly and they were never so difficult."

Evelyn stumbled at that, thinking of the two men being ordered around by the woman.

"Straighten up!" Tina snapped. "Those boys could barely read when they were learning what you are now, yet they mastered my teaching perfectly. *You* are not so inclined, which is a pity, but I never shy from a challenge. I will have you walking like a princess in no time."

The way Tina was acting, it was as though she believed Evelyn had run wild. Evelyn had been taught how to behave when she was younger. When her aunt ruled Forest's Edge, the woman insisted on Evelyn and Jasmine learning the basics for when ruling families would visit from other cities. In comparison, Evelyn felt these measures were extreme.

Under Tina's scrutinising gaze, Evelyn continued to walk back and forth until the woman deemed her competent. When Tina asked her to stop, her shoulders sagged in relief, but instead, she was ushered to the large mirror in her dressing room.

"Hold your posture. We have one last lesson for the day. Watch my face as I speak," Tina said, staring at her reflection as she pointed to her mouth. "Notice how the movements of my lips are refined. I don't gape like a fish."

"Neither do I," Evelyn mumbled under her breath.

"You could have fooled me," the woman replied with a shake of her head. "Now, I want you to copy my words and pay close attention to your mouth."

As Tina began speaking, Evelyn straightened her back and looked at her reflection.

"Thank you, your majesty."

Repeating the words, Evelyn was careful not to move her lips too much. Naturally, Tina was unimpressed.

"Don't mumble," the instructor said, slapping Evelyn's wrist. "Enunciate, but remain demure."

Evelyn fought the roll her eyes were desperate to do and tried again.

"A little better. Now say, 'It is a fine day for a stroll through the city.'"

"It's a fine day—"

"No, no, no! Why are you smiling like a jester on the word 'day'? Say it without opening your mouth so wide."

A sigh escaped her, but Evelyn repeated 'day' with the best solemn expression she could muster. Tina must have found it acceptable as she moved on, having Evelyn parrot more sentences, which Evelyn thought were beyond ridiculous.

By the time the etiquette tutor left for the day, Evelyn was sure she'd just been subjected to some sort of torture. Flopping onto her sofa, she cursed Prince Kylan for his supposed good intentions and dreaded the following day when she would have to do it all again.

8

Nora

Florence opened the familiar door of number four Emerald Lane, gesturing for Nora to enter before her. Nora grimaced. The last time she'd been there, Aeolus had interrogated her and her only friend had betrayed her. Not exactly nice memories. She raised her chin and strode down the passage towards the back room, stopping abruptly at the sight of Aeolus, her expression slipping.

So much for trying to appear unaffected.

The Faction's second in charge stood in the open space, the tables around her were scattered with papers and equipment, and a banner was draped over a sofa, the faction's symbol stitched to the green fabric. A fire burned in the hearth behind Aeolus, warming the room and providing a backdrop to his imposing figure. He was wearing leather armour that showed off his muscular build, the weapons strapped to his person combined with his towering height giving him a daunting aura.

It wasn't that Nora was afraid of him—he wasn't like Zaim or Hyde from the Alta who had spent years tormenting her—but Aeolus still gave her pause. He had tortured her to uncover King Dominic's secrets. As trained as Nora was to withstand pain, without the king's bond to control her and suppress her emotions, she couldn't help when her body flinched of its own accord.

"I see you haven't attempted to run again," Aeolus said, his hazel eyes narrowed, as though disappointed that she'd stayed. She didn't think he would have wanted her to return to the king. Perhaps he was just disappointed that he couldn't chase her down himself.

"Obviously not," Nora snapped, staring him down. Despite her newfound feelings, she still refused to be intimidated.

"Hey, Aeolus," Florence said, sitting on a stool at one of the nearby tables. "I see you got up on the wrong side of the bed this morning. Maybe push it against the wall, so that's not an option." Aeolus's lips thinned as he turned his disdain on Florence. He straightened his back, standing as rigidly as the spikey caramel-brown hair on his head. Florence held up her hands, smiling mischievously. "Just a suggestion. Take it or leave it."

Nora smirked, enjoying Aeolus's discomfort but refraining from commenting. Riling him served little purpose when she was eager to learn why she had been asked to come to the Faction headquarters. Florence hadn't elaborated when she'd told Nora of their plans that morning, only that Gemma had requested her presence. Nora would have liked to feign indifference, but curiosity got the better of her. As if summoned by Nora's thoughts, the door to the back room opened and Gemma appeared on the threshold. Her long white-blonde hair hung over an open navy coat, revealing a charcoal vest and tights. She was mid-conversation and as she stepped out Ashe appeared behind her.

The Faction leader's eyes landed on Nora, and her calculating expression had Nora feeling all kinds of unnerved. The last time she'd seen Gemma, the woman had been pissed at Nora for not only spying but getting close to the high-ranking members of the Faction. A woman like her did not forget such a blow to her ego.

"Ah, you're here," Gemma said, placing her pale hands on her hips. Ashe said nothing as he glared at Nora. "I'll get straight to the point. Florence has informed me that you have taken Jasmine's offer and decided to help, so I have a job for you."

"What?" Nora asked, brows furrowed. Her eyes darted to Florence, who was grinning broadly. Nora hadn't accepted any sort of offer. That sneaky little... "I—"

"Don't worry, Nora," Florence said, cutting her off. "I know you were worried about the tasks you would be given, but Gemma has arranged something I think you'll like."

"Enjoyment wasn't among the criteria," Gemma said, drawing Nora's attention back to the Faction's leader. "Based on your skills, I think this job will be the most beneficial for us."

"What is it?" Nora asked, folding her arms over her chest.

"You are to meet with Aeolus each morning to train Faction members in combat," Gemma stated. "You will teach them physical combat and help the Elementum hone their magic, too."

"Are you telling me your Faction dedicated to standing against the king is completely untrained to fight him and his soldiers?" Nora asked, quirking a brow.

"Of course not," Aeolus huffed, turning to Gemma. "This is unnecessary. We don't need her involvement. Our people are defending our borders just fine."

"Against the King's Guild, but we need to prepare for trained fighters. To attack as well as defend. I'm not too proud to know when we need help," Gemma told her second, her golden monolid eyes narrowing on the man. "Nora has the skills. We'd be stupid not to utilise them."

Aeolus didn't back down. His posture stiffened as if on guard as he said, "and if she tries to sabotage us?"

"Then we'll deal with it," Gemma said. "It's a risk I'm willing to take, considering there will always be someone with her, so unless you're telling me you're not up to the task, my decision is final. Jasmine is forming an army to defend us against the king's forces whilst also dealing with the ongoing Makers' Murders and, now that we know the rumours of the Alta are true, we must prepare counteractive measures. If we stand any chance of defending the north, then we need to be smart. Nora's knowledge of combat is one way to do that."

"I was trained for fourteen years to be an Alta," Nora said. "There's no way any of your people will reach the same standard in what, a couple of months. If you're lucky?"

"You joined the Alta when you were six?" Florence asked, her brows disappearing into her red hair as Nora glanced around to see everyone staring at her.

"I—ah," Nora began, shuffling her feet. "It's not important."

"She was sold," Ashe announced as if he were telling them all what was for dinner.

"You were sold?" Florence asked, eyes wide. "Your parents sold you to the king when you were six?!"

Nora shot Ashe a glare, to which his lips twitched subtly. She had no idea how he knew about her childhood, but she suspected August or Felix had most likely told him. Why they hadn't told the others as well was beyond her, but it didn't matter now anyway.

"It wasn't them," Nora sputtered, feeling her cheeks redden. Stupid fucking emotions! "Look, it doesn't matter. Can't change it, so let's just move the fuck on, shall we?"

Gemma nodded, though her golden eyes now looked at Nora with something suspiciously close to pity. "You'll start training Faction members tomorrow morning."

"Perfect," Nora said with an unconvincing smile. "Can't wait."

Nora's shoulders drooped as she glanced around the library. The shelves were filled with rows upon rows of books on every topic imaginable, not that Nora had checked the accuracy of what she'd been told. Once the meeting at Faction headquarters had finished, Florence dropped Nora off at the library to meet with Sage. She hadn't lingered, eager to complete whatever tasks Gemma had assigned her. Of course, she'd still told Sage not to let Nora out of her sight. Nora didn't care. After Ashe announced her admission to the Alta, she wanted time to clear her head and be away from those that had been there. Ashe had spilled her secrets, and she was sick to fucking death of people disregarding what she wanted. She was supposed to be free of the king controlling her life, but she felt as though she'd merely found herself under another master.

"Are you okay?" Sage asked, her brows furrowing when she looked at Nora with obvious concern.

"Yeah," Nora said, sighing. "Just a lot going on."

"Anything you want to talk about?"

Nora shook her head.

"How about I provide a distraction, then?" Sage suggested.

Nora raised her brows, her lips tugging up at one side.

"Not that kind. We're trying to be friends, remember?" Sage laughed, smacking Nora on the arm. "I want to show you something."

Nora followed the woman towards the offices at the back of the library. She had never been in this area, but she'd seen Sage disappear and appear from the hallway entrance many times before.

"Oh, there you are," Phillip said, coming out of the third door on the left. He shoved his hands behind his back, his beady blue eyes darting between Nora and Sage.

"Were you looking for me?" Sage asked her boss.

"Yes," he replied more firmly. "I need a sample of a Malachite crystal."

"I can grab it for you now."

"No," he said with a shake of his head, the few strands still attached bounced around with the movement. "I don't have time now. I'm much too busy to wait around for you. Bring it to my office before you leave today."

"Will do," Sage said as he stormed away, his coat flicking around his calves.

"What. A. Dick," Nora commented.

"Yeah," Sage replied with a sigh. "It's better to tolerate him than try to be too friendly."

Sage pushed open the door Phillip had come out of and waved for Nora to enter first. The room was more extensive than Nora had thought it'd be. Shelves lined the walls, filled with books, parchment, and boxes brimming with various objects. In the centre of the room was a large desk with metal stools tucked underneath, and on top, a heap of papers and quills were scattered messily on the wood.

"I see organisation is your strength," Nora commented, dragging a stool out and sitting atop the cool metal. Her gaze ran over the papers before her. "So, what's all this stuff?"

"It's an organised sort of chaos," Sage said. "They're all things I have collected as part of my research." She picked up a wooden box with a familiar pattern on the top, a collection of light pink crystals nestled inside. "You brought this box to me from Will, remember? They're rose quartz. Will has contacts that send me things."

"Of course he does," Nora replied with a small smile. "That man knows everyone."

"And he has style, hence the pretty boxes." Sage laughed, moving around to the opposite side of the desk. She picked up a piece of paper and passed it to

Nora. "I wanted to show you this."

Nora examined the instructions on the parchment and asked, "it's a potion?"

"Not quite," Sage replied, coming to stand beside Nora and placing a silver pendant on the desk. A vibrant pink gem, much brighter than the rose quarts had been, shimmered brightly in the centre. "The gem's made of a powder. A dust of sorts."

"What does it do?" Nora asked, picking up the pendant. She held it in her palm and felt it heat against her skin as the surface of the pink gem swirled, revealing the dust within.

"It absorbs magic," Sage said, taking the pendant from Nora and placing it back on the table. "You may wear those," she indicated to the shackles around Nora's wrists, "but I can't guarantee they will stop it from taking the magic inside you. Just because you can't use it doesn't mean it's not there."

Nora frowned. "Is it permanent?"

"As far as we can tell, it is," Sage replied. "Once the dust takes your magic, it's gone, but we are working on various methods to reverse the process or at least utilise the magic within the dust in other ways. We want to be able to create weapons, nullify them, or—"

"Remove magical tattoos that bind someone to another?"

"Exactly," Sage said. "The possibilities of the dust's uses could be endless, and not just in capturing magic. If we can work out how to utilise it, who knows what we could do? Maybe even heal people of ailments for which Lys Alvs can't use their magic."

"But you'd be taking it from someone?"

Sage shook her head and said, "not necessarily. The aim would be to take it from something manmade, and if that doesn't work, then to receive small donations from multiple people."

Nodding, Nora glanced down at her wrists. "If you could take my magic and make me human like you, would you?"

Soft fingers gripped her chin and lifted her face. Nora looked into Sage's brown eyes and felt that gaze strip her bare.

"Your magic is part of you," Sage said. "I never want to change who you are."

"I've used my magic to kill a lot of people," Nora said, tugging her chin from Sage's grip. "For no reason other than them being in the way. I've tortured people."

"It wasn't your choice. You did those things because you were bound to an evil king, forced to do his bidding. Those things are not on you."

"Not everything is his fault! I used people, was cold and brutal because I could be," Nora shouted, though her voice held no real strength. "I used you because I wanted to, not because he commanded me to."

Sage nodded. "You know how I haven't seen you since that meeting at the Manor? I spent that time deciding what I wanted to do about this whole situation between the two of us. I know full well what you did, and I decided to forgive you."

Nora slapped a hand against her chest. "*I* don't forgive *me*!"

Sage stepped towards Nora, her hands reaching out, but Nora moved away, slipping off her stool and wrapping her arms around herself. "Don't."

"Why? You've finally opened up, why are you pushing me away? You don't have to do this alone. I want to help you. I want to be your friend."

"I'm not a problem you can study," Nora said, earning a frown from Sage. "Something that you can fix."

"I never said you were," Sage replied, putting her hands on her hips. "I see no point in you going through this alone, but if that's what you want then fine. Be insufferable and let your pride get in the way." She huffed. "Your stubbornness is so infuriating, you know that?"

"I think it's best if I go," Nora said and turned towards the door. "Maybe this whole friendship thing is a bad idea."

"No. Nope," Sage said. Nora turned to see her shaking her head. "You don't get to decide what's best for me when you don't even know what's best for yourself. You don't want to be here right now? Okay, I'll take you to Will and let him watch your miserable ass, but just so you know, I'm not going anywhere. You're stuck with me." She marched to the door, opened it and turned back to Nora. "You're not the only one who gets to be stubborn around here."

9

Evelyn

Evelyn chewed her lip, contemplating her next move. It had almost been a week since she'd been confined to her room with only Poppy, Louise and Tina for any kind of outside human interaction—not that the maid stayed long or the etiquette lessons were a delight. Instead of succumbing to boredom or feeling sorry for themselves, Poppy and Evelyn had spent their time plotting. There were no signs of a rescue attempt, so they would save themselves… but not before doing something valuable for the Faction.

What that entailed, however, still evaded them. Everything they'd schemed so far varied in extremes from learning the king's secrets to stabbing him with a knife, though Evelyn was smart enough to know they would hardly be privy to the king's plans, nor would they have the chance to murder the man. Not to mention they lacked the skills to succeed in the latter. Poppy may have been an Elementum, but ultimately, they were healers, not killers. No matter how much they hated the king, Evelyn very much doubted they'd be able to end his life.

It didn't mean she would sit around and wait to be married off to Prince Kylan, though. She would play the part of his betrothed only to keep them safe, even though her heart belonged to another.

"I can't *actually* marry the prince," Evelyn groaned, wrapping her arms around herself.

"But he's so attractive," Poppy said as she propped herself up on a fluffy blanket in front of the fire. "I'd marry him."

Prince Kylan *was*, by all means, an attractive man. He was tall with a strong jaw, styled black hair and sky-blue eyes behind unfairly long eyelashes. She could certainly see why gossips as far and wide as Forest's Edge had giggled and daydreamed of spending time alone with him.

"Then you marry him!" she exclaimed. "And you're forgetting August."

"To be fair, I never had a chance to meet him."

"You haven't met the prince either."

"No, but I've seen him," Poppy replied wistfully, looking far off into the distance. Then she shook her head, returning to reality. "Also, take it from someone who was betrayed by who they thought was the love of their life. You think you know someone, but then they turn out to be completely different. If only I could speak with Zaim—"

A knock at the door caused them to fall silent. Evelyn assumed it was only Louise bringing dinner, but she could never be complacent in this place. It would be no good for their conversation to be overheard by the wrong ears.

Just as Evelyn had guessed, Louise opened the door and stepped inside, though she wasn't carrying a dinner tray. Tilting her head to the side, Evelyn forgot her manners, her curiosity getting the better of her.

"No dinner?"

"Good evening, Lady Royd and Miss Poppy," Louise replied cheerily, using Evelyn's formal title—according to the king, at least. "You have been summoned for dinner with the royal family this evening." She waved her hand at Evelyn, gesturing for her to join her in the closet. "We need to move quickly. Miss Poppy will have dinner in her room."

"Great," Poppy mumbled, rolling to face the fire.

"No."

Louise halted abruptly. "Sorry, Lady Royd, but you must."

"I don't want to." Evelyn shook her head. "I'm sick of being at the king's mercy."

"Lady—"

"That's not me! Jasmine is the lady of Forest's Edge, not me. I'm a Healer, that's all."

"Eve," Poppy began, wetting her lips, her eyes darting to Louise. "Maybe you should go."

Louise nodded. "I don't mean for this to come out as a threat, but there will be consequences."

Evelyn scrunched her nose, hating that she was forced to do the royal family's bidding.

"Fine." Evelyn's anger fizzled and her shoulders slumped. By not going and angering the king, she could put her loved ones at further risk. "I'll go."

"Maybe you'll hear something interesting?" Poppy suggested.

"You're right," Evelyn replied. She should think of these orders as a means of gathering information.

"His time will come," Louise muttered, though Evelyn was pretty sure the woman wasn't speaking to her or Poppy.

Evelyn frowned at her friend, then quickly changed her attire and sat for Louise to adjust her long black hair and apply light makeup. There was no point in fighting what the king commanded; she wouldn't survive long if she chose to defy him outwardly. Not to mention she was intimidated by him. Evelyn wished it wasn't so, but King Dominic scared her.

Evelyn was soon following the silver sentry who'd been guarding her door downstairs. In the limited time they'd spent together, he'd barely spoken more than a few words a day, speaking only to provide directions.

As they arrived at the dining hall, Evelyn was taken aback by the size. The room was deep, with high ceilings and a wide wooden table that ran the length of it, set with expensive-looking dinnerware. There was no one there yet, so she took her time, taking in the details of the room. Painted depictions of rulers and nobility lined the walls in golden frames, staring down at those who dined. She recalled some of the faces—old kings and queens, priestesses, knights, and faces she'd seen in history books—but there were others she'd never laid eyes on before. She wondered what they might have done to earn a place on the royal walls.

"Everyone sit," King Dominic ordered, earning a jump from Evelyn. She spun to see the king striding into the room towards his chair at the head of the table, the rest of his family filing in behind him.

Evelyn nodded stiffly, her eyes catching Prince Kylan's. He angled his head towards the seat next to him, and she quickly straightened her skirt and moved to sit down.

"Thank you," she said, offering a servant a warm smile as he placed a napkin on her lap. The man inclined his head, then moved away, and she looked around the table at the royal family.

Opposite Evelyn sat a petite woman with black hair braided into a single plait and shimmering gold dust on her eyelids and dark high cheekbones. The woman gave a little laugh, a soft and girlish sound, as King Dominic's eldest son, Prince Xander, placed a plump pale hand over hers. Everything about her was immaculate, as though she had been groomed to marry the man beside her, which was likely true. But, unlike the princess, Prince Xander was less refined. His dark hair was unruly as it fell to his shoulders. Tufts of hair were scattered along his jawline, and his nose was bright red and bulbous. Prince Xander and Harley—princess upon marriage and now the future queen of Valmenessia— had been married four years prior, after a well-known political match arranged before their conceptions.

A muffled huff to Evelyn's right drew her gaze from the doting pair to the man sitting beside her, and she couldn't help but quirk her brow at Prince Kylan.

"You are to visit the eastern cities," King Dominic stated as wind magic lowered fragrant roast meats and vegetables in the middle of the table, and servants began serving.

The king leaned back, allowing his servants to pile his plate with large slices of meat and little of anything else. At the head of the table, King Dominic's presence commanded the entire room's attention. Besides his broad shoulders, the man wasn't an overly large figure, but his authority drew the eye and demanded submission. Evelyn looked to the king, curious to see whom he was speaking to, but the man was eating, his gaze firmly on the meal before him.

"When am I leaving?" Prince Xander asked, looking at his father.

"Tonight," the king replied.

"Will Harley be joining me?"

"No." The king shook his head, then looked up and pointed his fork in Evelyn's direction. "Your wife is to remain here and rectify the mess the late lord of Forest's Edge has created with her." He flicked his fork for emphasis, gravy and meat splattering the pristine white tablecloth as his lip hitched into a sneer. "The north has not only strayed in their morals, but they've failed to produce a lady of the elite class."

"She is being tutored in etiquette by Tina," Prince Kylan said.

The king huffed, pointing his finger at Evelyn. "It is not enough to fix this."

Her cheeks heated, her heart beating at a rapid pace as she listened to the king bad-mouth her father and herself. No words left her lips, nor did she reveal any emotion except for her golden eyes widening.

"I'm happy to help, my king," Princess Harley said politely. "I will assist Lady Royd in finding her place."

"It was embarrassing enough to announce the engagement with her in this state." His hazel eyes remained on Evelyn, his square jaw twitching as he took her in.

Evelyn gripped her cutlery tightly, her knuckles paling around the silverware. She opened her mouth to retort but was cut off by the prince beside her.

"Do you have time to listen to my proposal?" Prince Kylan asked, earning a glare from Evelyn. Not only had she been insulted by the king, but her betrothed had decided to speak over her. She thought they were trying to be friends.

"Can you not see that I am eating?" King Dominic replied without looking at his son.

"Yes, but I tried to make an appointment."

"Then wait for your appointment."

"They wouldn't give me one," Prince Kylan said, gritting his teeth.

"And you thought to impose on my dinner time instead?" The king shot his son a scathing look, his hazel eyes like daggers. "You appear to have an elevated sense of importance. You may be a prince, but you are my second son. You will do well to remember your place."

Prince Kylan nodded; his narrowed blue eyes directed at his meal—the only sign of his displeasure. Evelyn felt a pang of sympathy for the prince.

"The plans to extend the tutor rooms at the city library have been finalised," Prince Xander said, changing the conversation. "Harley has been working hard to ensure everything is running smoothly."

"The women at tea are excited to access the classes currently occupied by mostly men," Princess Harley said. "It will be wonderful for the women of this country to be able to extend their education. Think of all our advancements and how we will progress even faster with more educated citizens."

"At this rate, we will be able to build classrooms in the other cities, too,"

Prince Xander added between mouthfuls of his roast meat. "I know Lord Gudrid is eager to implement Harley's plans in Giland."

Princess Harley beamed at her husband at the mention of her father, saying "and we have solved the issue of funding, too."

"And?" the king said, though it was more of a demand for more information than a show of any real interest.

"The royal family can't possibly fund the construction as there is so much to do in this country, so we have decided to allow citizens to make donations. Of course, priority placements for classes will be given to those who donate, as well as their families."

"Not everyone wants to further their education," Prince Xander said. "So, it makes sense to prioritise those who value exploits of the mind."

"I agree," the king huffed. "Some would rather keep to their base instincts."

The married couple nodded in agreement, but Evelyn felt unable to eat another bite. How could they not see that they were simply creating an education system to which only the wealthy had access? Despite her feelings, Evelyn kept her mouth shut. What would be the point of making a scene? Instead, she moved her food around her plate and waited for the king to dismiss her for the night. She hated being locked up in the room she'd been given, but now all she wished for was to return to her quarters and be left alone.

"You two have done well," King Dominic said as he sliced his vegetables. "As rulers, you must remember that you know what is best and follow your instincts. Your job is to do what is right for the people, even if they cannot see it for themselves."

Without waiting for a reply, King Dominic rose from his seat and threw his napkin on the table, striding away without a word or gesture of goodbye. Once the king was out of the room, Evelyn stood, eager to leave. Of course, Tina would scold her if the woman discovered her bad manners, but Evelyn simply didn't care.

"I'll meet you in the morning," Harley said, a soft hand catching Evelyn's elbow. She'd almost made it to the door and had thought she was free but hadn't noticed the princess follow. "We will start with the basics, and then you can attend tea with me."

"She has lessons with Tina in the morning," Prince Kylan said as he also approached the door.

Princess Harley pouted. "Can't she skip it for the day?"

"You heard my father."

"I did," Princess Harley replied. "And he asked me for help." Prince Kylan's cheeks tinged pink as he nodded stiffly. "Excellent," Princess Harley grinned. "We will have so much fun together."

"Yes, Your Highness," Evelyn lied through her teeth. She highly doubted she would have any fun with the future queen. Maybe she could backtrack and get out of it. She'd still be stuck with Tina, but wasn't there a saying… 'better the demon you know?' "I'm sorry, but my Poppy, I mean, my friend—"

"Can join us. It will be wonderful." Harley clapped her hands. "Now call me Harley. I have such high hopes for you and me. I've always wanted a sister."

"You have a sister, darling," Prince Xander drawled, placing a hand on his wife's back and ushering her out the door. He gave Evelyn a quick nod as he passed, his locks covering his face with the movement.

"I'd rather not think of that brat in Giland, my love," Harley said, her voice trailing off as they disappeared down the hallway.

Tingles spread along Evelyn's exposed skin, and she glanced beside her to see Prince Kylan standing all too close on that side. The tall man loomed over her, his blue eyes watching her curiously. She was taken aback to see the expression on the prince's face, and they both stared at one another. Then, like a snap of the fingers, the moment passed, and Prince Kylan frowned.

"Be careful with Harley," he said in a low voice. "The smiles and laughter are all for show."

"Duly noted," Evelyn replied as they strode from the room together.

"Everyone here has an ulterior motive."

"Even you?" she asked, halting at the intersection of the hallway.

He smiled. "Even me. Good night, Lady Royd."

Evelyn watched him go before she turned and followed her guard back to her room. The entire time, she wondered what each of the royals was after and how she would survive them.

Evelyn grumbled, dragging her nightgown over her head, the silk soft against her skin. Ever since she'd arrived back in her room, the night's events had replayed over and over in her head. The most prominent being the king discussing her as though she weren't in the room. She hated how he'd spoken of her—as though growing up in Forest's Edge was beneath him. Hearing of his prejudiced ways was one thing, but having them directed towards her was something Evelyn could do without. And then there were the plans Prince Xander and Harley were discussing as though they were providing a gift to all citizens, rather than the upper class. It was great that women were given more opportunities to learn, but when it didn't apply to *all* women, it didn't feel so progressive.

Louise appeared, ushering Evelyn towards the seat before the mirror and retrieving a brush from one of the many drawers.

"You don't have to do that," Evelyn said as the woman began to brush her long hair.

"It's all part of the job," Louise replied simply. "Plus, you seem a little stressed, and this always relaxes me."

"It does feel nice," Evelyn admitted, her shoulders slumping.

"You miss home."

"Yeah."

The brush stilled, and Louise dipped her head next to Evelyn's pointed ear. "I imagine the people here are not helping the situation."

"Err…"

"The world has become a dangerous place, full of evil," Louise said, straightening. "We shouldn't be living in such a divided world. The hate for each other is sickening."

"It's hard to come together when…" Evelyn swallowed hard. Was Louise setting her up? "Never mind."

"When the king wants to tear us apart?"

Louise stepped away, bustling around Evelyn's quarters. She wasn't sure if she'd heard the woman correctly. Was Louise against the king? Or was she testing Evelyn's loyalty in the hopes of selling her out? Hesitantly, Evelyn rose, following Louise from the dressing room.

"It's okay," Louise said, fluffing the pillows on the bed. "We are on the same side."

Evelyn's golden eyes widened. "Are you…" She licked her lips, unsure what to say. "Are you—"

"Hoping to change the world?" Louise asked.

"Yeah."

Louise winked, a glint in her eyes, then clapped her hands. "All right, I've wasted enough of your time. It's getting late and you should get some rest. You'll be no good to anyone if you are sleep deprived."

"Thank you," Evelyn said, climbing into bed.

"Good night, Lady Royd," Louise said, pausing at the door, her hand on the handle. "I'll be back in the morning."

Evelyn was left feeling tired and confused. Was Louise part of the Faction? Did Evelyn have an ally in the city? The idea of having someone other than Poppy to talk to and possibly plan with was a thrilling prospect. She'd been worried that she wouldn't be able to make an impact, but with help, maybe she could do something worthwhile.

Laying back on her pillows, Evelyn couldn't help the smile that graced her features. Dinner had left her frustrated and angry, but after speaking with Louise, she felt hopeful. Finally, she could make her time in Royal Bay count.

10

Evelyn

Sitting at the dining table, Evelyn pointed at each utensil as Tina called its name. She felt like she was ten years old again sitting in the dining room of the Manor in Forest's Edge. When she was younger, it was at her aunt's request that Evelyn and Jasmine learn etiquette. Her father and mother cared little either way if their children learnt dinner etiquette, but at that time, there had never been the thought her aunt would die and leave her father in charge. Back then, her father was a Healer and her mother an artist. All they were concerned with then was being happy.

"Soup spoon," the royal etiquette teacher said. She glided back and forth on the other side of the table, her hands clasped behind a perfectly straight back. The woman's lilac skirts barely swayed with her steps and the fabric was inexplicably crinkle-free and in impeccable condition, just like everything else about the woman.

Evelyn pointed to where the silver spoon rested on the table. Nothing was like it was supposed to be. Now, her father was dead with her mother confined to her bed in mourning the last Evelyn had seen of her, and Jasmine was running Forest's Edge, while Evelyn was trapped in Royal Bay—identifying cutlery.

"Sal-," Tina began but was cut off by the doors opening. She pursed her lips, her gaze narrowing at the armoured man who entered.

A sentry strode in their steps heavy thuds on the floor. "The Lady Royd has been summoned," they said.

Evelyn sat up straighter at the prospect of being able to leave. Surely whatever Princess Harley or Prince Kylan wanted couldn't be as dull as the lesson she was currently enduring.

"Who, may I ask, has she been summoned by?" Tina said with a tight-lipped smile.

The sentry stood taller, puffing out his armoured chest and replied, "his Majesty, King Dominic."

"Of course," Tina said. She quickly turned towards Evelyn and gestured with her hand towards the door. "You mustn't keep the king waiting."

Evelyn's stomach dropped. How could she have been so presumptuous to think the princess or prince had called for her? Slowly, she followed the sentry from the room and as her anxiety grew with each step she fidgeted with the sleeves of her cream-coloured dress, where the lace was already fraying in some areas thanks to her nerves.

The castle hallways were quiet with the sun shining through each of the windows, yet Evelyn felt no warmth from its rays. Her mind worked overtime, compiling reasons why King Dominic could want her. Each thought was more worrisome than the next. Had she done something to make him angry? She tried to think about her actions since arriving in Royal Bay that may have pissed him off but was coming up short. She'd barely been let out of her room beyond lessons and having dinner with the royal family.

After walking for what felt like an eternity, they stood on the castle's second floor before a set of guarded doors. Sentries moved quickly to open them, their armour clanking as they revealed a darkened space within. Unlike the brightness of the hallways, no sconces nor candles were lit, and black curtains were drawn over the windows inside, blocking out the sun.

Light pressure on her back had her reluctantly moving into the room, her slippered feet shuffling against the wooden floorboards. Evelyn glanced around as she hesitantly stepped inside, finding the room bare. She wondered why the king had brought her there of all places. It wasn't a place for receiving guests like the drawing room, yet it wasn't hidden beneath the ground or behind some secret door like she might've expected if he were hoping to commit some horrible act against her. Fear gripped her; whatever was going to happen, she knew for certain she wouldn't like it.

"Shut the doors," came a booming voice and Evelyn spun to see the king striding into the room, adjusting the cuffs of his maroon coat as he walked. He appeared completely unbothered by the location, which sent a chill down her spine.

King Dominic had a presence that bordered on suffocating. As soon as he entered a room, he commanded attention without a word, and when he did speak, people rushed to comply. He was a tall man, with broad shoulders and calculating eyes that could make others quiver.

The sentries moved swiftly at his command to close the large doors and Evelyn was quickly plunged into darkness. Her breath came quickly as she stood frozen on the spot.

They were alone.

She had no idea where he was, and without her sight, nightmares surfaced in her mind. Monsters in stories she'd been told as a child, unwelcomed touches and looks from strangers, and memories of the night she'd been attacked and almost murdered filled her with fear.

A ball of fire crackled to life before her, lighting the king in a sinister glow, and Evelyn gasped at his nearness.

"I am a fair king," he said, stepping closer. "So, I'm going to give you one chance to do the right thing."

Despite the heat of the flames, Evelyn shivered. He couldn't be further from the truth and this lie only made her situation feel worse. A pretence of benevolence when she had no choice in the matter. She didn't know what he wanted yet he would interrogate her anyway. She would fail whatever chance he gave her; he was far from fair.

King Dominic looked down on her. "What is your sister planning?"

She didn't know her sister's plans, but she could make an educated guess. Not that she would tell the king anything of value. She was afraid. The king's presence and the echo of her memories haunted her, though her love for her family and friends was stronger than her fear. There was nothing he could do to make her tell him anything. At least, she hoped that was the case.

Evelyn shook her head, her lip trembling. "I don't know. I was forced to come here before she became the lady of the city."

"Your father then?"

"I don't have anything to do with running the city. I'm a Healer."

"And a liar too."

The king slapped her hard, causing her to stumble backwards, almost falling over her skirts. Tears streamed from her eyes, and she cupped her stinging cheek.

"I never like to hit a woman," the king said, running a thumb over the palm of his hand. He straightened his shoulders. "But if you are going to lie, you give me no choice."

Evelyn wiped her eye, then dropped her hand to her side and steeled her spine.

"Now, let's try that again," he said. He cracked his neck before looking her deep in the eyes. "Your father. What actions was he taking against me? I know he was friendly with that little rebellion group."

"I had nothing to do with the politics in Forest's Edge."

He stepped forward and slapped her again, this time with more force that had her falling to her knees. The skin beneath her eye stung from being split open and blood mixed with tears down her face.

King Dominic kicked her in the gut, and she gasped, clutching her stomach. "You must think I'm an ignorant fool."

Evelyn shook her head. "No, I'm telling you the truth, I swear."

"Is this how that slum of a city teaches you to respect your king?"

He kicked her again, his boot connecting with her ribs repeatedly. She could feel her Lys Alv magic rising in her to repair the injuries he was causing. She prayed to the Goddess Nyssa for the courage to keep any knowledge she had from him. She was trying to be strong but could feel her resolve breaking along with her ribs. Black spots danced before her eyes, and she didn't know whether she feared passing out or welcomed it.

"August," the king demanded once he'd gone still. Sweat beaded on his forehead and something flickered in his eyes at the Mors Alv's name. "Where is he?"

"Forest's Edge," she panted. "That was the last place I'd seen him."

"What has he told you? What do you know of him?"

A sob escaped her. "Only that he is a Mors Alv and was an Alta."

Flames sparked in his palm, and Evelyn flinched away. Would he burn her now? Turn her to ash? Her magic wouldn't help her then. King Dominic narrowed his gaze at her, and she could feel him weighing her words.

Evelyn prayed again to her Goddess to make him believe her—convince him that she knew nothing and to stop hurting her. She feared she would speak truths if he kept up the torture.

"What does your sister want with him?"

"Nothing," she replied, her voice coming out strained. She was shaking where she lay crumpled on the floor. Her Lys Alv magic was healing her as best it could, but it was becoming increasingly harder for her to stay conscious. "She is only giving him refuge."

"You mean to tell me she doesn't want to use his heritage against me?" The king glared at her.

Evelyn's voice trembled, her fear of being punished unable to be hidden. "I don't know."

She braced herself for his attack, but it never came. King Dominic paced before her, a frown creasing the sides of his mouth. Evelyn watched, her blurry vision clearing and her anxiety rising with each step he took. Even as her magic healed her, she knew it was only a matter of time before he inflicted more pain. She could tell by the set of his tense shoulders and the ferocity of the ball of flame in his hand that he was not done with her.

"It appears your only use is to be tied to my son and produce heirs," he stated, straightening his back and staring down at her once more. "That is if you can birth Elementum children."

"Women have more value than just having children," Evelyn replied breathily, shocking herself with the words that spilled from her lips.

"You are either dense or your pathetic family taught you nothing." King Dominic's eyes glowed orange before he kicked her once more, his boot making contact with her chest. "Without children, I don't see you surviving very long."

She fell backwards, wheezing as she clutched her chest. The pain burned through her as the king extinguished his ball of flame and strode through the darkness away from her.

Evelyn held in fresh tears as the doors were pulled open and bright light flooded the room. She held in her sob when she was left to lie on the wooden floor for what she was sure were hours. And she did not cry when a sentry finally decided to escort her back to her room.

It wasn't until she was alone, beneath her blankets, that she let herself weep tears of not only hurt but anger too. She knew giving in to her emotions wouldn't do her any good and so she pushed her feelings away. She wasn't going to let herself crumble here. She'd known King Dominic was evil, but being at his mercy like that had only made her more afraid and yet more determined to end his reign.

If only she had something she could use against him.

She wiped her tears away and went over all that had happened to see if there was anything she could use against King Dominic. There had been nothing in the room, nothing to indicate his plans, or what he knew or didn't know—so that was no help—and he'd asked the sort of questions she'd expected about her sister and father. Evelyn frowned. He'd asked about August too, but it made sense for the king to be interested in one of his Alta.

Except he hadn't asked about Nora. Not a single question. And he'd seemed almost desperate to know about August's involvement with her sister.

Evelyn stared into nothing, her mind whirling.

Why did the king care so much about August?

11

August

Here," Nora said, placing a small box in front of August, a giant grin on her face. They lay on their bellies beside the trunk of a tree deep within the castle gardens where no one could see or hear them. *"Open it."*

It was late afternoon on Frost Solstice, and they'd just finished training, enjoying a break before heading on a mission later that night. August and Nora were going to a ball to assassinate a traitor to King Dominic and, despite the mission objective, they were excited to go. It was their first ball, and at sixteen and fifteen years old, the prospect of dressing up and staying out late at a party was exciting.

"Did you steal it?" August asked with a wry grin.

Nora shook her head and said, *"nope, Rana helped me."*

The leader of the Alta wasn't allowed to give them gifts for Frost Solstice, but that didn't stop her from 'helping' them find gifts for each other.

August picked up the box and rolled it deftly between his fingers.

"Don't break them," Nora exclaimed, snatching at the box, but he was too quick, extending his hand out of her reach.

"There's more than one thing in here? And they're breakable?"

She rolled her eyes. *"Just open the box, you idiot."*

August lifted the lid and looked inside to find coloured sticks in shades of red, yellow, and white.

"To add a little colour to your pictures," she said with a broad smile.

"These are expensive," he said in a low voice, looking in awe at his new drawing materials. Only the wealthy could afford anything beyond charcoal or cheap inks.

"No shit," Nora scoffed, then wriggled her brows. "So, what did you get me?"

August sighed, "It's not as good." He rose to his feet and went to collect the basket with a check fabric draped over it from the other side of the tree.

"I'll be the judge of that." She grinned, sitting up and extending her hands towards him. He passed her the basket, and she lifted the fabric, her brown eyes widening and her mouth popping open almost comedically. "You got me a cake?"

"I told you, it—"

"A whole cake?"

"Sorry."

"This is the best gift ever," she laughed, tearing into the side of the cake and stuffing it into her mouth. She moaned loudly, tossing her head back with her eyes rolling in exaggerated pleasure.

"The cook wasn't happy about the jam."

"It's the only way to make a sponge cake," Nora replied, licking the cream and jam from her fingers. "So, what are you going to draw?"

August shrugged, sitting opposite her and resting his back on the tree trunk. "I'm open to ideas."

"Ooh, how about something for Frost Solstice? Like a snowy scene?"

"It doesn't snow in Royal Bay."

"I know, and it is fucking disappointing," Nora groaned, breaking off another bit of cake. Of course, she didn't offer him any, but he didn't expect her to. It was her present, after all.

"You don't like the cold," he said, laughing. They'd been friends for nine years and each Frost Season, Nora was very vocal about her hatred for cold weather. "You were complaining about it just this morning."

"That's because no one likes freezing winds from the sea," she replied, her mouth full of cake. "Maybe I'd like snow."

As August found himself knee-deep in the freezing whiteness, he imagined Nora sitting in Forest's Edge, complaining about the weather. Her attitude towards snow would have changed the instant she experienced it. The terrain of the mountains was horrendous, and his bones chattered along with his teeth. It had been a week and a half since they left Fellbun, and he was starting to wonder whether it was such a good idea to have trusted Felix. He knew he should have stuck with his instincts because right now, freezing atop the peak was a high probability, and he wasn't even that good at math.

"I think I'm going to die before we reach the Mors Alvs," August said through gritted teeth.

"You are so soft sometimes!" Felix laughed. "It's just a little snow. You Royal Bay people are so fragile. It's not even that cold."

"There are icicles on the end of my hair," August grumbled, eyeing the crystals that had formed at the tips of his dirty blond hair. He probably should have cut it before they left Fellbun; any longer, and he'd be able to tie it up.

Felix waved him off. "Come on, grumpy, if you slow down you will freeze, and your miserable prophecy will come true, which I won't be taking any blame for. We're almost there anyway, and then your training can begin."

As much as he was pissed at Felix because of his current predicament, August was eager to have something to do beyond trudging through snow. He wanted to not only exercise his body but keep his mind busy too. Unfortunately, all this walking was giving him too much time to brood.

A rumble echoed through the mountains, and snow slid from the taller peaks in a rush. August dropped to his knees, bracing himself as it flowed past his left, splattering him with slurry.

"What the fuck was that?" August shouted as the mountain stilled beneath his feet.

"Don't you remember what Lord Havilor said? The mountains are known for causing a commotion, and he said they were more active than usual."

"Is it safe walking up here with the risk of snow slides? We'll get thrown straight off the mountain and return to Fellbun as frozen icicles floating through Thyra's Firefall."

"The snow sliding is not our biggest concern," Felix said grimly.

"What do you mean by that?"

Felix pointed over August's shoulder, his lips tugging down at the sides. "They are."

Turning on the spot, August looked behind him. At first, he thought Felix was pointing out mounds of snow that had collected from the tremors, but then the snow moved, and two sets of large, black eyes looked in his direction.

"What are they?" August breathed as he backed up.

The mountain shook beneath August's feet as the giant white bear-like creatures roared. Their jaws stretched, appearing to almost dislocate, as their mouths opened wide to reveal long, sharp fangs made of clear ice.

"Guardians of the mountains," Felix replied, grabbing August's cloak and tugging him out of the path of a snow slide.

The creature swung for him, its fur made of tiny icicles and its claws smaller versions of the teeth in its obscenely large jaw. He jumped out of the way of the enormous icy fist and crouched behind a boulder.

"How come I've never heard of them?" August shouted.

"Maybe because you don't read much," Felix yelled, lunging out of the way of a swipe from the other creature.

"I read," August shot back, drawing his sword and swinging it, slicing at the claws. The creature howled, sky-blue blood dripping from the wound on its paw, though not enough to dissuade the beast from continuing its tirade.

"Not the old history books, it seems," Felix replied, though August had lost sight of the man. "There are a lot of things this world has forgotten. Out of sight, out of mind and all that."

"How could these things possibly be out of sight?"

"*You* didn't notice them until now," Felix said.

A howl ripped through the other ice bear from whatever strike Felix had made, causing it to stumble in August's direction, much to his dismay. He was already fighting in limited space against the other one. Felix ran to the edge of the mountain and leapt forward, shifting into his eagle form and disappeared into the cloudy sky.

Both bears now had their attention on August. They towered over him, their fangs gnashing as they lunged, and he was forced to dodge their blows. If he could get behind them, he might be able to use his magic without getting caught in their teeth or claws. They were huge, and it would take more than a fleeting touch to incapacitate them.

"I need to get behind!" August shouted, spotting Felix's eagle form as he swooped towards the creatures, aiming for their dark eyes with his sharp beak.

"Give me a second!" Felix shouted back, surprising August so much that his face was nearly clawed.

"How the fuck are you talking?!" August shouted, swiping his sword against the bear's limb closest to him. The creature roared, kicking its leg and hitting August in the chest. He flew backwards, landing in the snow with an *oof*. His ribs ached from the impact.

"I'll explain once we've dealt with the Guardians!" Felix called back, followed by the whistling sounds of his bird call. "And while I'm at it, I'll also explain this!"

Felix took off into the cloudy sky and suddenly, his form grew, his wings spreading wider as his form morphed into a giant eagle. If it weren't for the bears making their way towards him, August would have stared in awe at the Anima. Felix turned in the sky and descended upon the bears, aiming for their faces. August shook his head, clearing his thoughts and remembered the task at hand. He looked for an opening and took his chance when the bears were too occupied by Felix's harassment. August ran through the thick snow and launched himself onto the back of one of the bears. His hands gripped tightly on the creature's icicle fur as he released his magic. The bear stumbled, a groan escaping its lips as August continued to pull on its health, drawing it into himself. His magic flared, his essence growing, and he revelled in the high of what he was taking on. It was like igniting a spark within him, the fire burning, ravaging as it grew with each drip of health he took as the bear fell beneath him.

"Don't kill it!" Felix shouted from above.

Remembering himself after being distracted from such a high, August swiftly jumped, launching himself onto the second bear before summoning his magic once more and stealing its health. The first bear fell to the ground with a large thump, the mountain reverberating around them. Snow slid from higher up the mountain, accompanied by large rocks that tumbled and skipped, crashing against each other. August braced himself against the bear, using it for protection as he continued to drain its vitality.

Overhead, Felix wove between the debris before once again shouting to August not to kill the bear. August groaned, finding it harder to release himself.

For the second time, his power demanded that he take all the creature had to give. It went against every instinct to release it, and he found himself warring with the part of him that desired to take it all. Felix swooped down, diving into August's side quite literally knocking sense into him. It did the trick, and August released the bear, then quickly slipped from its back as it fell to the ground beside its companion.

August crouched beside the bears as more snow slid, and rocks fell from higher up using their unconscious forms to protect himself. Finally, when the mountain calmed, he stood, and Felix landed before him, shifting back into his human form.

"Thanks," August said. "If you hadn't—"

"Once you are trained, you won't need help. You'll be able to stop on your own," Felix replied. "Don't beat yourself up over it."

"I wasn't going to," he said with a shrug. Though Felix—judging by the smile on his face—didn't buy August's attempt at nonchalance. "So, are you going to explain how the fuck you were able to talk while in your animal form? I've never heard of anima being able to do that. Or how one minute you were your usual eagle, and then suddenly you were giant?"

"I'll explain, but I doubt you'll believe me," Felix said, brushing snow from his cloak.

"Try me," August replied. He folded his arms over his chest.

"Felix is not my birth name. My real name is Aren."

"As in, you were named after the Anima god?"

"As in, I *am* the Anima god."

At first, August stood in stunned silence, unsure what to make of Felix's calm revelation. Then his sanity got the better of him.

"Fine, don't tell me the truth, but you can at least say why. If you could turn into a giant eagle, why the fuck are we climbing this freezing mountain? Couldn't you have just flown us?"

Felix's lips tugged up at one side. "I'm not flying you anywhere when you can't control your magic. I'm not keen on falling from the sky to my death."

"A little harsh," August replied with a smirk.

"But true," Felix grinned, waving a hand for August to follow, "we need to keep moving. We don't want these guys to wake up and rouse any friends."

"There's more of them?"

"As with all things in this world," Felix said. "Better to assume there is a threat than being lulled into a false sense of security."

"What a bright outlook on life," August replied sarcastically, rolling his eyes as he followed Felix through the snow.

"Better than to think everything is doom and gloom like you've been doing for the last few weeks."

"I haven't been doom and gloom."

"No," Felix said with a laugh. "You've been a shining ball of positivity."

"It's okay for me to feel like crap sometimes," August replied. "My girlfriend has been kidnapped, my best friend won't talk to me, and I'm stuck with you while my magic refuses to be controlled."

"It could be worse."

"Yeah?" August asked with a huff.

Felix stopped, spinning around to face August. He slapped the man on the arm and smiled. "You could be dead."

"Silver lining." August quirked a brow.

"Exactly." Felix winked before continuing on his way.

August shook his head and chuckled. His life was becoming a collection of tragedies, and he was starting to see why Felix had such an upbeat attitude. It was one of those if you don't laugh, you cry things. Or, in August's case, go on an angry rampage and steal everyone's magic and health.

12

Nora

Assisting Aeolus in training the Faction members of Forest's Edge was something Nora quickly found she did not have an ounce of patience for. Some people were capable of teaching others, but Nora, on the other hand, felt herself becoming more pissed off with each passing minute. It was a combination of two things; the bad attitudes from those that didn't like her teaching them and the basic lack of skill. It wasn't that they weren't trying. On the contrary, most were putting in a lot of effort, possibly because of the impending threat looming over their heads. So, rather than direct her annoyance at them for not doing the drills right, she targeted it at their old teacher. As far as Nora was concerned, Aeolus had taught them nothing.

She strode between her trainees as they moved through drills with wooden swords in hand, attempting to disarm one another using the techniques Nora had shown them. A woman thrust her blade at her opponent, who deflected, sending the wooden weapon flying to the ground.

"You need to pay more attention to your opponent's movements," Nora said, picking up the sword and handing it back to the woman. "People always have tells. Look at how he moves his feet and whether he protects a part of his body when you fake an attack. Watch carefully and then take advantage of his weakness."

"Aren't we supposed to fight with honour?" the man asked as he and the woman began circling each other.

"Trust me, there is no honour when you're fighting for your life," Nora replied. "If we had years to train, then you might stand a chance with skill alone, but we don't have that luxury, so I'm teaching you how to win. You can let your pride get in the way, but it won't shield you from magic or a sharp blade."

He grunted a curse under his breath, an irate look in his brown eyes. Nora moved on before he could argue. She moved among the trainees, adjusting stances and offering advice before returning to where Omari stood watching on the sidelines.

"What has he been doing with these people?" Nora said in a low voice for only Omari to hear as she stood beside him. She continued monitoring her trainees as they spoke, her eyes never leaving them as each pairing moved through the steps.

"They look pretty good to me," Omari replied. He'd come on behalf of Jasmine to see how she was going with her new job. It made sense that the Lady of Forest's Edge would want to know about her progress, and she didn't mind that Omari was the one to check up on her. He had always come across as level-headed, and she would never forget how he'd questioned Aeolus's brutality towards her when she'd been a prisoner. He was a good match for the leader of the city.

Not to mention the people of Forest's Edge adored him. Who wouldn't look up to a tall, broad man who looked like he could take on multiple men in battle, but who also had a relaxed and welcoming manner? He projected strength. And strength was exactly what Forest's Edge needed right now.

Nora rolled her eyes. "Pretty good is just a nice way of saying they are adequate. Adequate is not going to help them against the king's soldiers."

"I'm sure they'll be able to defend themselves."

"Defence is not the problem; they need to be able to attack, not be on the back foot. If there is no offence, they won't be of use to anyone."

"That's a bit rough," Omari said with a frown.

"It's the truth," she replied. Nora sighed. She watched the trainees move through the dance of hand-to-hand combat as though they were toddlers still learning to walk.

"It's only been a week," Omari said, bumping her shoulder playfully.

"I'm sure they will be up to your standards in no time."

Nora groaned. "You weren't here the whole time."

"How about you think of this in another light?" Omari said.

Nora raised a brow at him. "I'm listening."

"Training these people is showing that you're trustworthy. Whether they are good isn't the question. It's all about the effort you put in. So, keep it up and you'll have those"—he inclined his head towards the pearlescent shackles on her wrists—"taken off in no time."

"I guess," Nora replied, biting into her bottom lip. *Omari had a point.* "You might be right."

Omari grinned broadly, his dimples showing on his cheeks. "Why do you sound so pained when you say that?"

"Because of that look," Nora said, pointing at his face and scrunching her nose.

"What's so wrong with making people smile?"

Nora groaned again and strode towards the group of trainees, leaving Omari's question unanswered. It's not that she didn't want to make people smile. Seeing the expression on some people's faces brought her joy, but there was something else that she couldn't quite put a finger on that made her feel uncomfortable.

"Okay, we're done for the day," Nora declared as she reached the group. She ignored the heated looks from a few as she put her hands on her hips. It didn't matter whether they liked her, she was there to do a job, and they were there to learn. "Meet back here tomorrow morning."

The group disbanded with heavy puffs, one grumbling under his breath at her lack of approval, but she wasn't going to offer any praise when they weren't as good as they should have been. Nora hoped that by meeting in the morning rather than in the afternoon, as it was now, she would see more effort and improvement from her group. As much as she liked the idea of using them to gain trust and get her magic back, her pride would suffer if her group was not the best anyone in Forest's Edge had ever seen. She was determined to excel in her training, and these people had been assigned to her, so they would damn well be just as driven and skilled.

"Hey," Ashe said, coming to stand beside her. "Let's go get a drink."

"Not going to happen," she said without a hint of consideration. "Where'd Omari go?"

"He had stuff to do, and I told him I'd take you home."

"What? Why?" Nora asked, her brows scrunched in confusion as she looked for the other man. "Where did he go?"

"He's long gone, and *you* need to relax. You're so wound up." He stepped behind her, gripping her shoulders and squeezing. "We need to loosen you up a bit."

Nora shoved him away. "Don't touch me."

"Chill," he said, raising his palms. "All I'm asking is you come for a drink. Is that really so hard for you?"

"Yes," Nora said and folded her arms over her chest tapping her foot. She eyed Ashe suspiciously. "You want something."

Ashe nodded. "Obviously."

"Spill."

"We started on the wrong foot," he said. "Let's begin again. Sage is my friend too—we should at least try to get along for her sake."

Nora frowned. *Sage.* He was playing that card then. She couldn't think of anything worse than spending time with Ashe. He was beyond irritating and frankly, she had no reason to agree to his suggestion. At least, she'd had no reason until he'd brought up Sage. If the two of them were friends, it would most likely make Sage happy if he and Nora could at least hold some form of conversation or pretend to be friends. Old Nora wanted to tell him to fuck off, but new Nora was trying to do the right thing, and everything about Sage screamed right. Nora pursed her lips. For Sage, she'd do anything.

"Fine," Nora replied.

Ashe grinned broadly, then swiftly grasped her wrist and dragged her away from the training area, which had been set up on the Manor Grounds alongside the guard's outpost. She pulled out of his grip but allowed him to lead her back into the main city.

"Where are you taking me?" Nora asked as they turned a corner. "Is this some ploy to lead me down a darkened alley to slit my throat?"

Ashe chuckled darkly. "It would make things easier, but no, I'm not planning on murdering you."

"You actually want to have a drink and make nice?"

"Is that so hard to believe?"

"Hmm," Nora murmured, pursing her lips. "To be honest, a little."

Ashe chuckled, picking up his pace, and she matched his speed, happy to move quickly. There was an iciness to the air and now that the afternoon sun was setting she was eager to get indoors. Missing her fire magic more than ever with the cold looming, she tugged her cloak tighter around herself. They hurried on and only stopped once they reached his intended destination. Ashe led her up a set of stairs that wound around a large tree trunk to a door on the second storey of the building that stood beside the tree.

"Why can't we enter from the ground floor?" Nora asked as Ashe opened the door.

"Different owners," he replied. "Downstairs is an office building."

Nora stepped inside the warm space, finding it relatively quiet. There were a few tables though more standing room, a long wooden counter to the right, and a large red curtain partially covering the entire back wall.

"What is this place?" Nora asked, glancing around at the almost empty space. Usually, the lack of people said a lot about the quality of the establishment.

"Haven't you visited any places in the east?" Ashe said, nudging Nora towards a table near the fire.

"You must be a shitty stalker if you don't know the answer to that," Nora said with a smirk.

"I wasn't following you every waking minute," Ashe said, rolling his eyes. "You might have snuck off to do something fun. You seem like the type."

Nora narrowed her eyes, folding her arms over her chest. "What's that supposed to mean?"

"Correct me if I'm wrong, though I highly doubt I am, your personality doesn't scream 'sit at home and be in bed before nightfall'," Ashe explained. "I wouldn't call you a wild child because you were very diligent where the king was involved, but you have the potential for trouble."

Nora couldn't help the smile that tugged at her lips. Maybe Ashe wasn't so bad, not that she wanted to befriend him. He'd been nothing but a jerk since she'd met him, not to mention the whole stalking thing.

"Which," Ashe continued, "is why your sullen mood is, quite frankly, depressing by association."

Her smile dropped. And here she was feeling like she'd been more herself lately. The guilt had been ebbing as she was coming to terms with all she'd done under the king's control, though she always felt it rise stronger than ever at night. Nora tried blaming King Dominic for her actions, but she couldn't give him all the credit. He'd asked her to kill and torture people, but there were many she'd killed or hurt because they were purely an inconvenience. They were in her way, and she needed them not to be. She had killed purely because she couldn't be bothered with the fallout. It was those actions that kept her up at night, alongside memories of a burning farmhouse. Overall, though, Nora had begun feeling more like her old confident and sarcastic self each day, but after hearing Ashe's words, maybe she hadn't come as far as she'd thought.

"I saw you walking in," a man said as he approached their table, snapping Nora from her thoughts. With a wave of his hand, he lowered two mugs of ale onto the table. "Sticking around for the show tonight?"

"Thanks, Paul, this is Nora," Ashe said, shaking the man's hand. "Who's the big act?"

"The Three Macs. Gonna stick around for them?"

"Yeah, we'll stay," Ashe replied with a nod. "We're taking the night off to enjoy ourselves and find common ground, aren't we?"

Nora rolled her eyes. "Apparently."

"The Three Macs are very good," Paul added. "There are a couple of acts before them. I'll leave you both to it. I have some setting up to do before this place starts to fill up."

"Thank you for the drinks," Nora said before the man could leave.

"Anything for Ashe and his friends." The man smiled, then turned and went back to work.

"That was very polite of you," Ashe said, taking a drink of his ale.

"I have manners."

"So I see."

"Whatever," Nora said, leaning back in her seat. "So, this place is for performers?"

"Musicians," Ashe said. "Only the best play at Paul's."

"How do you two know each other?"

"He was friends with my father," Ashe replied, shrugging. He pulled out a deck of cards and placed them on the table. "Wanna play a game?"

Nora raised a brow. "What kind of game?"

"You'll see, but first, we need different liquor." He winked. Then he pushed back his chair and rose from his seat. "Don't go anywhere. I can still see you from the bar."

"I won't move a single muscle," she replied, folding her arms over her chest.

As she waited, the red curtains parted and a young man stepped onto the stage and began strumming his instrument. He wasn't bad, though she could see why he'd been scheduled to play whilst the crowd was yet to grow. More people trickled in, some now watching the man perform on stage whilst others conversed with their companions. Despite all the shit going on in the world, it was nice to take a break from it, and these people around her must have felt something similar. At least, Nora assumed the other patrons felt the same. She longed to spend time with her friends and just enjoy life.

"He's really good," Nora said as Ashe returned to their table, a bottle of amber liquid in one hand and two small glasses in another. He poured a measure into both glasses. "You took your time."

Ashe handed Nora her drink, clinking his glass against hers and then downing his in one go. "I was talking to Paul. Now for our game."

Nora watched curiously, drinking the liquid he had poured her as he split the deck and handed half to her. She lifted the top card only to have him slap her hand.

"No peeking," he chastised playfully.

"What is this game?" she asked, placing her empty glass on the table. Ashe refilled both glasses before answering.

"It's simple. You guess what the card is. If you get it wrong, you drink. If you get it right, you don't."

Nora smirked. "This is going to get messy."

Ashe laughed as he picked up the top card of his deck and motioned for Nora to do the same. "That's the point. Five Flames."

"Jord's Throne," she guessed. They flipped their cards over to find they were both wrong. With a sigh, Nora emptied her glass. "Why are we doing this?"

"To relax around each other and become friends, thanks to a shared memory," he said, refilling their glasses. "Aren's Arrows."

"Three Droplets."

Again, they were both wrong. Nora and Ashe continued playing as more customers filtered in, ordering drinks at the bar and mingling in tight groups. Now that the venue was filling, the room was alive with chatter and music, anticipation filling the air.

"I'm looking forward to hearing the Three Macs," Nora told him, raising her voice over the people crowding around them. "I used to like seeing the bands play in Royal Bay."

Ashe quirked a brow as he finished his latest drink. Neither of them had gotten a single card correct yet, and Nora was pretty sure she would be vomiting before the sun rose in the morning. "Are you making small talk? Conversing like a normal person? Are we friends now?" Ashe said.

"Do you need to analyse everything I say and do?" Nora snapped, tapping the top card on her deck. "I'll just sit here and shut up unless I'm guessing the stupid card then, shall I?"

"Wait." Ashe frowned at his empty glass. "I'll stop," he said and ran a hand through his dark hair before leaning forward. "So, the king used to let you out to see bands?"

Nora shook her head. "Nah, I only got to see them when a job took me there. Like most things."

"That's a little sad."

"I've seen and done a lot of things I'd never have been able to without the king."

"Yes, you're very lucky to have been given the opportunity and means to murder so many people."

Nora huffed, leaning away. "I wasn't trying to make it seem like my life has been fucking sunshine and daisies."

"Sorry," Ashe said, grabbing her hand and halting her movement. "I don't mean to—"

"To what?" Nora asked, snatching her hand back. "Bring up all the bad shit in my life? Do you think I don't know what I've done? Do you think I've just forgotten all that's happened? I don't need you to remind me. Have you ever thought the reason for my moping could be because I didn't get a chance to try to be like everyone else? To be happy?"

"Fair point," Ashe replied, scratching his chin. "You're right."

She nodded stiffly. "Nyssa's Healing Hands." She picked up the card and flipped it over to find a drawing of the Lys Alv Goddess staring up at her, the Alv's hands glowing brightly.

"I don't think anyone has ever guessed a card right before," he said, eyebrows raised.

The performer on the stage bowed and left to a round of applause that only grew louder as a trio stepped up. Cheers added to the sound, and soon an upbeat rhythm joined in.

"Make your guess."

"Eight Droplets."

Nora watched as he turned his card over and found Two Flames. "Drink up!" she shouted over the growing noise of the musicians and the crowd who were singing and clapping along.

Ashe laughed, downing his drink and smacking his lips. "So, you and Sage."

"We're friends."

"Really?" he asked, raising his right brow. "I thought you two…"

"Sage suggested we try to be friends," Nora amended, the alcohol making her more open to divulging her thoughts.

"She did, did she? That's good."

"What's good about that?"

"Well, if you're still planning on leaving, at least you won't hurt her," he explained. "You still want to leave, don't you?"

Her heart skipped a beat. She'd initially wanted to leave, but now? Her plans had changed.

"Look, all I'm saying is if you don't want to be here," he continued, oblivious to her reluctance, "it'd be shit to make her think there's something more going on."

"Who says I don't want to be here?"

Ashe scoffed. "I can see you don't want to, and I get it. There's not much here for you. You're more of a big city in the sunshine kind of person."

"The sun shines during Scorch Season."

"Yeah, but not like you'd be used to." He raised his hands before him. "I'm just trying to be a good friend to Sage. I care about her and don't want her to get hurt. She deserves to be with someone who puts her first and plans on sticking around."

Nora frowned, her head aching from the drinks and Ashe's words. She wasn't sure where she fit anymore if she was, to be honest with herself. However, the idea of leaving her new friends and Sage didn't sit right with her. Her heart ached at the thought of not being around Sage. The real question though, was if she could put Sage first.

"Keep playing?"

"Yeah." Nora nodded, sitting up straighter. Now was not the time to question her current predicament. "Let's see if you can get any of the cards right."

Ashe laughed, reaching for the bottle to fill up their glasses, only to have his head slammed forward into the table. Nora jumped back, her heart pounding in her chest as she spun, searching but coming up short. Whoever had attacked him must have done so with wind magic, meaning she was searching for an Elementum. Ashe groaned, lifting his head, and Nora sucked in a breath at the blood spilling from his broken nose.

"Fuck! We need to get you to a Healer," Nora said, coming around the table to scan the room. Everyone was either emersed in the performance onstage or pretending to be. Whoever had attacked Ashe was smart. "You're lucky you didn't smash your face into a bottle."

Another gust of wind propelled their way, and Nora crashed into the table beside Ashe, sending its contents toppling to the floor and cracking the wooden table.

"Fucking drunks," someone grumbled nearby as the ever-growing crowd shifted around them.

Nora winced, her hip and elbows smarting from the impact. Ashe pressed a hand to his face, trying to stem the blood flow from his nose as he stood. He pointed to the exit with the other. She kept close as they pressed through the crowd and made their way down the spiralling stairs outside.

At the bottom of the tree, Nora froze. The street was deathly still, nothing but the hum of the music above to be heard. Nora scanned the darkness as she crept forward, only to knock her foot on something in the way. She looked down at a body and, when she bent to feel for a pulse, she found only cold blood. The night's chill and the dead body instantly sobered her as she was left wondering how many more bodies could be found in the shadows.

"Take these fucking things off!" Nora hissed in a low tone, rising and shoving her wrists at Ashe. "If someone is attacking us, which I'm pretty sure they are, I need my magic."

Ashe shook his head, his words coming out nasally. "I can't. Only Jasmine has the key."

"Fucking fantastic!" She threw her hands in the air at the same time a gust of wind propelled her through the street.

Nora braced herself for the impact, hitting the icy ground hard. She scrambled to her feet despite her tailbone hurting and glared at the familiar faces that stood just beyond Ashe. They must have been sent by the King to bring her back to Royal Bay. Their sinister smiles were visible in the moonlight, igniting a fire in her stomach. She wasn't afraid of these assholes. Even without her magic, she refused to let any member of the Alta have that power over her.

"Leave or die," Hyde said to Ashe. "This doesn't concern you." The older Alta stepped forward with a hand rubbing his scarred chin as his predatory gaze snapped to Nora.

To Nora's surprise, Ashe shifted into his leopard form and took off, racing down the street without a backward glance. She hadn't picked him for a coward, but it's not like he owed her anything either. Why should he fight for her? Her gut clenched at yet another person letting her down. He'd said he wanted to be friends. He'd *lied*. She stupidly forgot the cardinal rule: everyone was out for themselves. She turned her attention back to the three Alta dressed in black who were now striding towards her. Each one had tormented her growing up in one way or another.

"How lucky am I that you came to visit?" Nora drawled, slowly rising to her feet. They may have scared her as a child, but she'd promised herself many years ago that she wouldn't be afraid of them ever again. "I didn't realise we were so close, yet here you are. It's very sweet."

"Removing the tattoos didn't rid you of the smart mouth," Jolene said on Hyde's left. Her hair was up in a tight bun, lifting her face and making her features appear as sharp as the blades Nora knew were hidden beneath her cloak.

"Apparently not," Nora said, keeping an eye on Owen, who was now making his way around her, prowling like the lion he could shift into. "Which is lucky because it would have been such a shame if it was lost to the world."

"A tragedy," Owen said behind her.

A chill ran up her spine at his nearness, despite her determination to put on a brave face. She was surrounded and had no access to her magic or even a weapon as they drew closer. She was in deep fucking shit.

"King Dominic is very displeased with you," Hyde said as Jolene stalked nearer, closing the distance between the two women. "No one is allowed to leave the Alta and for that, you will be punished. But first, where are August and Felix?"

She shrugged. "No idea."

Jolene moved quickly, slapping Nora across the face, splitting her lip. "Don't lie. It will only delay the inevitable. We know August is never far. You two are as thick as thieves."

Nora spat blood. "Then why bother with your idiotic questions? If we are as close as you say, then I wouldn't tell you anyway." She tapped her temple. "Think, Jolene, I know you've always found it hard, but you need to keep working on it if—"

Her cheek stung from Jolene's second slap if it could even be called that. Her palm may have been open, but it had the force of a punch. Spitting out more blood, Nora righted herself and glared at Jolene.

Nora tutted, "JoJo, if only you put the same amount of effort into academics as you did in combat."

Jolene made to hit her again, but Nora stepped back, knocking into Owen and avoiding the strike.

"Nyssa have mercy," Jolene hissed, her golden eyes shining brightly. "You're such a mouthy fucking bitch."

Nora smirked, but it quickly died as Owen's arms wrapped around her. She struggled to be free by elbowing him in the ribs. But he held her firm, absorbing the blows and lifting her higher so that her legs swung in the air. Nora flung her head back, making contact, which earned a sickening crunch from Owen's face.

"Fuck," Owen grunted.

His grip tightened, and Nora cried out in frustration, only to have Hyde step forward to grip her neck firmly in his large hand.

"Last chance," Hyde said, bringing his face close to hers. "Where are Felix and August?"

13

Nora

"Fuck you!" Nora spat at Hyde's face. Blood and saliva peppered his cheeks and the man growled, looking like a demon in the night.

"Do you know why King Dominic sent Jolene with us?" he asked in a low tone that sent shivers up her spine. Of course, Nora knew why the Lys Alv was here. "We will get the answers we want, even if she has to keep bringing you back for days… *Weeks.*"

Hyde released her throat and Owen dropped her to the ground. Nora couldn't help the tremors shuddering through her. The night was dark, the music still audible from the venue down the street. The Three Macs must have been putting on one amazing performance for none of the patrons to notice Nora and her attackers outside.

The Alta may have had the advantage, but Nora wouldn't go down so easily. She lowered her head and rose to her feet.

"Oh, look, she's given up already," Jolene exclaimed. "Ready to play nicely?"

"Yes," Nora replied, then lunged, throwing a fist at Hyde.

Her fist collided with his face and she made to strike again when Owen's hand wrapped around her ponytail and tugged hard. She didn't let it bother her as she spun, using the advantage of Owen having only one free hand to launch herself at him. Nora grasped his face with her fingers, digging her thumbs into his eyes as hard as she could.

Owen screamed and they fell to the ground hard with her on top of him, though it was short-lived. Nora was quickly dragged from Owen by the back of her coat, who kicked her in the chest and cracked a rib as she was pulled off him. Nora thrashed despite the pain but was quickly subdued and flipped onto her stomach with her face shoved into the ground. Something held her down, her ribs screaming as they were squashed into the dirt. It felt different to a boot—spread over her entire body. Hyde had to be using his wind magic rather than risk getting too close to her again.

"Fucking heal me, Jolene!" Owen was shouting, though he was getting nowhere with his fellow Alta. Jolene was yelling back about it not being her problem, the two arguing whilst Hyde came closer and knelt before Nora.

She swallowed, her eyes searching wildly for a weapon and finding nothing. This was it. She was going to die. Nora had been told there was supposed to be a moment of clarity before death. Laying on the ground with Hyde pinning her down, what she wanted became clear. She wanted to stay in Forest's Edge with her friends, see August again, and do something meaningful with her life. If only she'd realised it all sooner.

"Silly little girl," he said, reaching out to tuck a strand of her hair behind her ear. "You—"

Hyde never finished his threat. The pressure of his wind magic released her the instant an arrow pierced through his head and stuck out his eye. He fell to the ground, and Nora's mouth dropped to see shadowy figures standing down the street.

"On your knees!" Gemma shouted, Nora instantly recognising the voice. The Faction leader strode forward, her shoulders pushed back and chin high, Faction members flanking her on either side.

"This is none of your business!" Jolene shouted back. "Leave or face the wrath of the king!"

"Fuck the king!" Gemma declared, tapping Aeolus on the arm.

Aeolus grinned, launching a water jet over Nora's head and knocking Jolene and Owen off their feet. Drenched, Owen swiftly jumped up and shifted, roaring and running towards Nora despite his wounded eyes. She rolled out of his path as another jet of water flew overhead. Jolene's cackled laugh echoed down the street as Owen came for Nora again, but he stumbled before he reached her with an arrow piercing his shoulder.

He veered sharply, charging for the archer. They went down with a high-pitched scream that was cut short. Owen snarled, looking back in Nora's direction with bloody teeth and unfocused eyes, relying on his other senses after Nora half-blinded him. Owen prowled forward but was knocked away by a grey snow leopard. Another snarl tore through the air and the two fought. The leopard snapped at the lion's neck and was quickly joined by a falcon in the fight, which swooped at Owen as he fought Ashe.

"I want them both alive!" Gemma called as more water flew.

Jolene was still laughing loudly as Faction members tried to seize her. Magic and weapons cracked in the night, but she refused to give in, taking on multiple members. She was stronger and more skilled, managing to kill and injure a few, but the sheer number was taking its toll.

Ashe continued fighting Owen with the falcon, but once Aeolus stepped in, it was all over for the Alta. The lion roared as Aeolus threw a jet of water, hurtling him into a tree trunk. Owen was knocked out cold, flopping to the ground at the base of the tree like a sleeping kitty.

Maniacal laughter turned into shrieks as Jolene was overpowered, and soon both Alta were restrained and hauled away.

Gemma strode over to where Nora lay panting on the ground, a hand over her broken rib. "Are you okay?"

"You came to help me," she whispered, staring at the woman's outstretched hand. "Why?"

"You're with us," Gemma said, a fire burning in her golden eyes. "We protect our own."

"But you lost people."

Gemma frowned. "Their sacrifice wasn't in vain. One dead Alta and two prisoners who I'm sure will give us vital information with the right incentive."

Nora took Gemma's hand. She hissed in pain as she moved until Gemma's healing magic flooded through her aching body like a warm caress. Standing, she pressed a hand to her lip, finding it no longer split.

"I've only lessened the pain and healed the minor injuries," Gemma said, her lip splitting and then healing closed. "It should help you get to the Manor where you can heal fully. Presuming you aren't in any more danger."

"Thanks," Nora said, noting how her rib was the only sore spot on her body. It hurt, but it was manageable. "You know, I would have been fine if I didn't have these."

Nora rolled up her sleeves, revealing the pearlescent shackles she wore that resembled chunky bracelets. They were so simple in design yet held the power to suppress her magic completely. The loss of access to a vital part of her made Nora feel ill.

"Perhaps we should do something about them," Gemma said, surprising Nora. "Come, I think it's time we visited Lady Royd."

Gemma left to speak with Aeolus in hushed tones, though it was obvious they weren't pleased about the Alta being able to infiltrate the city so easily. Soon a horse and wagon rolled up, and Owen and Jolene were loaded onto it along with Hyde's body. Horse-drawn wagons and carriages were not overly common in Forest's Edge. It didn't take long to walk through the city, and the uneven streets made cart travel uncomfortable. In Royal Bay, the wealthy would take carriages everywhere. The city was more extensive than Forest's Edge, but even if it were smaller, Nora doubted the elite class would walk anywhere regardless.

"Go with them," Gemma said, her voice carrying. "Drop the injured off at the Healing Centre."

Aeolus nodded, climbing onto the front of the wagon and sitting beside one of the Faction members. A few others hopped into the back with the Alta, and then the horse took off, pulling them towards their destination. Gemma, Nora, and Ashe left soon after, making their way on foot to the Manor to meet with Jasmine. The streets were dark, the air icy cold as they walked. Nora kept a hand to her broken rib, the area smarting with each step, and wondered if it would snow. It didn't take long for them to reach the Royd family home, and whilst they sat in a room waiting for Jasmine, Gemma used her Lys Alv magic to finish healing Nora's rib. Even though she'd been partially healed earlier, it was still surprising to Nora that the Faction leader bothered to heal her at all, especially as Nora had infiltrated the Faction on behalf of the king. Gemma had been far from impressed and had no reason to heal her. She could have made someone else do it, or let Nora's wounds heal naturally which would take weeks. But then, maybe she realised Nora was more useful if she could train the Faction without any hindering injuries.

Gemma moved on to heal Ashe and Nora settled into her end of the sofa to contemplate the direction her life was taking as the fire warmed her. King Dominic didn't want her back. He wanted her *dead*. She would never have gone back to him anyway, and it was clear her place was no longer in Royal Bay, but could it be here? Ashe didn't seem to think so, but she didn't care. Almost dying had made her realise what was in her heart and running away was no longer an option.

The doors to the sitting room opened, and in strode Jasmine and Omari, followed by a guard. The pair embodied what a ruling family should be, not only in how they presented themselves but in their manner. Jasmine, as always, was a picture of grace and calm, whilst Omari was reliable and comforting at her side. King Dominic had never made Nora feel at ease, always leaving her with the constant need to prove herself, do better, and be worthy of him even looking her way. To think she'd once craved his attention and love when he didn't deserve her loyalty or respect.

Jasmine and Omari did though. Nora could see that now. They hadn't expected such things as the king nor forced her through magic or fear to get it. That was true power.

Ashe made to stand, only to receive a slap on the shoulder from Gemma, who was still healing his broken nose.

"Don't move," she hissed nasally. "I'm almost done."

"How did they get in?" Jasmine asked, coming to sit in the armchair beside Nora. Omari took up a spot beside the fire but stayed close to Jasmine.

"I don't know yet," Gemma replied, sitting back on the coffee table and wiping the blood from her nose with a handkerchief. The swelling from the break was already going down. "Aeolus has taken the two surviving Alta to the cells and will question them. We will find out soon."

"Not unless you can take their tattoos," Nora said. She sat up straight as they looked at her. "They can't betray King Dominic, even if they wanted to. Remember what it was like when I had them? Not to mention they are trained to endure torture. Even if you can remove their tattoos, you still might not find out for weeks."

Jasmine sighed. "She's right, but we must try." She turned to the guard. "Fetch Phillip and Sage. They can test their new research on the two Alta."

The guard nodded, leaving swiftly.

"Are you okay?" Jasmine asked Nora. "Three-on-one with no magic is tough odds."

"Yeah, I'm fine," Nora replied. "I mean, it was looking like I was a goner there for a bit, but it worked out."

"Almost dying seems to be a bit of a pattern of yours," Omari commented, his lips tugging up one side.

Nora smirked. "Better than going through with it completely."

Omari laughed, and even Gemma let out a small chuckle.

"I've heard your training sessions are going well," Jasmine said with a grin. "And that you're a disciplined teacher. It's worth it for the results."

"Is that what Omari told you?" Nora smiled, looking at the man by the fire.

"I used the words hard-ass instead of disciplined," he replied with a laugh.

"Have you thought any more about my offer?" Jasmine asked.

"Actually, I have," Nora said, sitting up in her chair. "I want to—"

"Just tell them, Nora," Ashe interrupted with a huff.

"That's what I'm trying to do," she replied, confused at what he was getting at.

Ashe shook his head. "No, tell them how the Alta got into Forest's Edge. Before you spin lies, tell them what you did, or I will."

"Maybe you should because I have no idea what you're talking about," she hissed. "I was going to say that I want to help more."

"I'm talking about the deal you made," Ashe said, shaking his head. "I saw you sneaking out of Will and Florence's place the other night. I followed you." He turned to face Jasmine. "She met up with the Alta and offered to help them in return for passage back to King Dominic and affirming her loyalty to the king."

"What the fuck are you talking about?" Nora snapped, pushing her shoulders back. "That never happened. Not to mention your story makes no sense at all. Why would they have tried to kill me tonight if I was helping them?"

Ashe shrugged. "Who knows? You Alta aren't exactly respectable citizens. The deal must have gone sour, but it doesn't change what you did. Do yourself a favour and stop lying about it."

"I'm not lying! You are!"

"What reason do I have to make it up?" Ashe shot back. "I am loyal to the Faction and Forest's Edge. Always have been."

"Shit!" Gemma growled, jumping up and glaring at the Lady of Forest's Edge. "I knew she would betray us again!" She pointed a long finger at Jasmine. "This is what I was trying to warn you about. You are too trusting and naive!"

"Hey!" Omari shouted, coming to stand between Gemma and Jasmine. "Back the fuck off and remember whom you're speaking to!"

"Omari," Jasmine said calmly, "can you find Florence and Will?" When the man didn't move she stood and placed a hand on his upper arm. "Please."

With a huff, Omari stormed out of the room.

"I didn't do what he's saying," Nora said, meeting Jasmine's gaze. "I swear, Ashe is lying."

"Why would I lie?" Ashe scoffed.

"I don't fucking know, but you are!" Nora clenched her fists. "How would I even know to meet them? I'm watched nearly every minute of the day!"

"Don't pretend you're not smart enough to find a way," Ashe replied. He narrowed his grey eyes at her.

"Are you kidding? Do you hear yourself?" Nora asked, eyes wide. "I have no access to magic, coin, or anything besides what has been given to me. I can't even take a piss without someone on the other side of the door, yet you're accusing me of colluding with people who basically tortured me my whole life until I was strong enough to fight back?"

Her chest heaved in rapid succession and she could feel the tears welling in her eyes. Fuck Ashe. Fuck her emotions. And fuck everyone who decided it was their right to mess with her life.

"Fuck you!" Nora said, standing. "I'm done with this shit. Lock me up, throw away the key for all I care. I'm done. To think I wanted to be a part of all this, to stay here willingly."

"Nora, sit down," Jasmine said, her voice like a calm light in the dark. Yet roaring anger surged through Nora's veins. "Let's get to the bottom of this."

"Wonderful," Gemma replied, dropping into her seat and rolling her eyes. "Give her a chance to fill your head with more lies."

"It would be irrational to decide her fate without hearing all the evidence," Jasmine said, swallowing hard. "My father always listened before casting judgement, and I plan on doing the same. If you don't like it, perhaps your position in this city may not be the right fit for you."

"Are you threatening me?"

Nora stared into the distance, ignoring the two women as they argued. The unfairness of the situation writhed like one of the fire snakes she used to summon, taking up residence in her stomach. Only, this one wasn't slithering around but coiling itself painfully tight around her insides. Why was it that as soon as she started to feel a little normal, something shit had to come along and ruin it? She wished other people would stay out of her life and stop trying to manipulate everything she did.

"I'm warning you, not threatening," Jasmine stated. "This is my city."

"Understood, my lady," Gemma said, looking to the fire burning in the hearth, her spine rigid as she folded her arms over her chest.

"Now, Ashe," Jasmine began, turning towards the man. "Why were you monitoring Nora? Had Gemma or Aeolus asked you to?"

Ashe shook his head. "August had asked me to watch her. He had a feeling she would betray us."

Gemma threw her hands in the air. "Even her closest friend thought she was a risk in need of monitoring."

Nora felt like she'd been doused with a jet of water, extinguishing the fire burning in her. Had that been the reason August asked Ashe to watch her? Had he believed she wasn't capable of change? Of doing the right thing?

Dropping her gaze, Nora looked at her hands. "Looks like no one trusts me."

"We trust you."

Nora lifted her chin to see Florence and Will standing in the doorway with Omari.

"We trust you, Nora," Florence repeated, striding into the room.

Her words were Nora's unravelling. Tears fell, as unstoppable as the rain, releasing all she'd felt over the last few weeks. The guilt, betrayal, and anger poured from her, but what surprised her were the feelings of sadness and loss. Her life had been taken from her—twisted into someone else's creation. She'd lost herself the day her family had died all those years ago and had no idea how to find the person she was supposed to be.

Warmth enveloped her, and she looked up to find Florence's arms wrapped tightly around her and Will sitting where Jasmine had been. Everyone else had left, though she hadn't heard a single footstep. Nora brushed her cheeks, feeling embarrassed about her meltdown.

She sniffed. "Sorry."

"Don't be," Will replied with a warm smile. "It's nice to see a side to you that isn't sass and sarcasm."

"Will," Florence groaned, loosening her hold on Nora. "Don't listen to him. Well, do, but read between the lines. Sometimes he's a lot like you and you need to work out the feelings behind the words rather than the words themselves."

"I didn't do what Ashe is accusing me of," Nora said.

"We know," Will replied. "Omari told us about his accusation. We'll vouch for you."

"Why would he do that?" Nora asked. "I know he doesn't like me much, but he was the one who'd asked me to go for drinks. He said he wanted us to get along."

"Hmm." Florence cupped her elbow with one hand, tapping her lips with the other. "Ashe can be unpredictable."

"All smoke and mirrors," Will added, wiggling his brows and waving his hands like a human magician. "But I didn't think he had anything against you. Nothing that would warrant accusing you of something like this, at least."

"He wants to get rid of me," Nora said. "He told me he wanted to be friends for Sage's sake. It looks like it was just a way to get me to go with him."

"Or…" Florence said, cocking her head at her partner in silent conversation. "Do you think…?"

"Possibly," Will said. "I wouldn't put it past him to be petty."

Nora had no idea what they were insinuating. "What?" she asked, looking between them.

Florence sighed. "Ashe and Sage used to be a thing, but it was short and they ended things on amicable terms."

"You think he did this because Sage and I are... friends?"

"Sure," Will laughed, shaking his head. "Just friends."

"I think it's the most plausible reason why he's trying to make you look bad," Florence said. "Sucks for him that it failed."

Nora chewed her lip. "Do you think he sold me out to Hyde, Jolene, and Owen too?"

"Who?" Will asked.

"The Alta who attacked me."

"Now that's an interesting question," Will replied. "If he did, then he's just put himself in a very bad position with Jasmine and Gemma."

"Speaking of those two, Gemma said Jasmine trusted too easily and was naive," Nora said, thinking back to the Faction leader's outburst. "I thought they were getting along."

"They are, sort of," Florence said. "I think Gemma wants to be in charge, but Jasmine is the rightful lady of Forest's Edge. Her father was training her, and yes, Gemma has experience in leadership, but Jasmine has other qualities that make her a great leader for everyone, not just soldiers."

"They will sort it out. They have a common enemy, which always helps remind them to work together," Will said as he rose from his seat. "In the meantime, we should go home. Let them worry about how to run a city and rebellion."

"I'm allowed to go home?" Nora asked.

Florence smiled broadly, nodding her head a little too eagerly. "You just said home."

"I mean if that's…" Nora's cheeks heated as she stumbled over the words. "I can—"

"It's your home," Will said warmly.

Nora nodded stiffly, looking away as she rubbed the back of her neck. "So, I can go?"

"Yes, Jasmine said she'll speak to Ashe tonight and as long as we watch you, she will meet with you tomorrow to hear your side." Florence turned to Will, a mischievous glint in her eyes. "We should steal some cake before we leave."

Will laughed. "My God, I love you."

"I don't know why you're invoking Frode. He's not going to sneak into the kitchens for you." Florence grinned, darting out of the room but quickly sticking her head back through the doorway. "Oh, and I'm so happy you've chosen to stay! I'll meet you both out front!"

Nora laughed and realised her chest felt the lightest it had been in a long time. Who would have thought admitting to herself what she truly wanted, along with a good cry, could do that?

14

Evelyn

Evelyn had been expecting a room filled with precious porcelain, delicate cakes, and dainty women with gentle temperaments. What she found after an hour of sitting on soft cushions with the upper-class women of Royal Bay was contradictory to all she had believed. To a degree, at least.

So far, the women she'd interacted with believed in the elitism of the Elementum race above all others, which didn't surprise her, but that was not where all their interests lay. Despite having this core moral in contrast to her own, Evelyn found it challenging to dislike these people entirely. The villain was supposed to be horrible, and in the case of King Dominic, he lived up to that image. However, these women didn't fit that mould, and Evelyn wasn't sure what to make of it.

Sunlight streamed through the large drawing-room windows overlooking the sea below. Bright bouquets in shades of pink and red were placed around the room, and a calming melody filled the space, the music drifting from a harpist who sat in the corner. Trays of miniature cakes and savoury tarts were displayed on a table in front of the windows, along with pots of freshly brewed tea kept warm by the Elementum servers.

Evelyn sat beside Harley, the queen in waiting, and drifted between the conversation nearest to her and the one Poppy was having just a few steps away. Her best friend's blonde hair glowed in the sunlight as she spoke with a rather animated woman about the latest fashion where they stood by the small cakes. Evelyn had rarely used her Lys Alv hearing in Forest's Edge, but she was finding it exceptionally useful in Royal Bay.

"I love the fabric," Poppy said as the woman opposite her gripped her skirt and twirled on the spot. "You're so lucky to have such a huge supply to choose from. We barely get anything good in Forest's Edge."

"Really?" the woman asked with pity in her brown eyes. "You'll have to join me next time the tailor visits. We can help each other choose our next gowns for upcoming events. There is always something happening in Royal Bay."

"I'd love that!" Poppy squealed.

Her friend seemed to be enjoying herself and Evelyn couldn't help but feel Poppy was more at home amongst the women here than she was. Unlike her friend, Evelyn wasn't sure she'd ever feel truly comfortable in these circles.

"Xander told his father all about my women's education plans," Harley said, drawing Evelyn's attention to the group she was sitting with. "The king was very pleased."

"That's wonderful, Your Highness," the woman seated next to the princess said with a broad smile. Her lips were a bright shade of red that matched the hem of her dress. The gown looked like a sunset of sorts, with the fabric dyed yellow at the top, slowly becoming orange, then red at the very bottom. "Your contributions only strengthen his reign and the livelihoods of all women."

Harley beamed at the praise.

"Speaking of the achievements of women, the efficacy of the new potion is promising," the lady across from Evelyn said as she stirred her tea. Her hair was pulled back into a bun, showing off large diamond earrings. "We require further trials, of course, but the outlook is promising."

"Perhaps I can host a luncheon to generate additional funds for your work?" asked another in an olive-green gown and white fur shawl. She wiggled her fingers, and a tart hovered over to her, thanks to her wind magic. "I may not be positioned for your style of work, but I do know how to throw a party, do I not?"

The women laughed, though Evelyn only offered a hesitant smile, not wanting to appear rude for not understanding the inside joke.

"No one would question that, Hilda," a woman with thick, curly black hair replied. "What was the outcome of the last one?"

Hilda smiled and said, "we raised enough to fund a new orphanage."

"You are too good to the people of this city. The old one should never have been destroyed in the first place. It only proves the king's need to enforce his laws," commented another as she pressed her lips into a thin line and nodded.

"An Anima lost control and rampaged through the last one," Harley whispered to Evelyn as the women continued their conversation. "Shifted into a bear and destroyed all the buildings in the area."

"Why?" Evelyn asked, tilting her head closer to the princess.

"Oh, you know, he was upset because he'd lost his business and threw a tantrum," she replied. "Ridiculous, I know. It's not Hilda's fault he was deemed unfit to run the business. Childish behaviour if you ask me. We are only trying to do what's best for this country and its people, and the Anima continue to fight any real progress we make." Harley shook her head. "They simply will not see reason. Hilda is so good to have raised the funds to repair the damaged buildings. It wasn't her responsibility, but the Anima would never pay for it. She has once again shown herself as an integral member of the community."

"Why did the man lose his business?"

"I don't know the details, but it wouldn't be without cause."

Evelyn frowned. How could these intelligent and eloquent women be so blinded by the injustices around them? She was finding the tea gathering mentally exhausting.

"Evelyn," the woman with curly black hair said. "How are you finding Royal Bay? I'm sure it is a wonderful change to Forest's Edge."

"It's different," Evelyn replied, picking up a miniature cake from the small plate on her lap and stuffing it into her mouth. She had nothing nice to say, so she spoke as little as possible.

"I can imagine," said another woman. "We have so many advancements in Royal Bay."

"She will flourish," Harley said, reaching over and clasping Evelyn's hand in her own. "I look forward to her wedding to Prince Kylan, and then we will be not only friends but sisters, too."

Evelyn swallowed. She already had a sister and was desperate to return to her. The people she'd left in Forest's Edge were constantly on her mind and made her heart ache. It was hard not to worry about them when she saw how determined and horrible King Dominic was in person. Surely these women didn't see him properly—didn't know how evil the king truly was. How could they agree with his worldview if they did?

Evelyn glanced at Harley's hand on hers.

Harley saw King Dominic often, yet she still believed in him. It was hard to marry the two sides to these women: the dynamic, intelligent, strong, caring side and the one with no regard for the rights of races besides Elementum. It was easy to forgive disagreements on cake flavours or who won a card game, but a person's fundamental rights were non-negotiable. Evelyn found their ignorance on this too hard to overlook.

"I've had a lovely time today," Harley said, rising to her feet and dragging Evelyn with her. The plate on Evelyn's lap tipped but was caught by the wind magic of a server who swiftly prevented it from falling. "I look forward to next week. Come, Evelyn."

Evelyn's smile was strained as she nodded at the group, her eyes catching on Poppy who didn't seem to notice their imminent departure. Rather than interrupt, she let herself be led from the drawing room, feeling glad the tea was over. Her shoulders slumped from the exhausting contradictions she'd endured for the last hour, but there was one small silver lining. She'd had ample time to practice Tina's teachings, so perhaps the woman would go easier on her now that she'd put it to use.

"How did you find your first tea?" Harley asked, almost gliding along beside Evelyn in her rose-pink and gold-trimmed gown. They made their way towards the left wing of the castle; an area Evelyn had never been permitted to go to.

"Different," Evelyn replied, studying the artwork lining the walls and wondering what was behind each closed door.

Harley raised a brow. "Are you going to be evasive with me, too? I was hoping we could be friends."

"I—" Evelyn began, then chewed her lip. If she were being honest, she and Harley would never be friends. But what could she say without getting herself into trouble whilst also being truthful at the same time? "It was interesting. I learned a lot about the women of Royal Bay."

"A little better." The future queen grinned. "I can work with that, but I hope you eventually open up to me. We, women, need allies in this world."

Evelyn nodded. "Of course."

"I'm glad to hear it," Harley said, flicking her long braid over a shoulder. "Now, I have other meetings to attend. I'll see you at dinner."

Harley strode away and Evelyn looked around realising she was alone for the first time. No silver sentry was haunting her steps and no nobility or servants anywhere. Did she have time to make a run for it? She chewed her lip. No, she wouldn't leave Poppy behind, especially after what Evelyn had endured at the king's hand only a few days prior. She wouldn't risk anything happening to her friend too.

Voices echoed from the far end of the hallway and Evelyn feared it was a sentry come to dictate her back to her room. She quickly opened the nearest door and slipped in, closing it softly behind her. Resting her forehead on the wood, she took a few breaths and listened as the voices passed. She contemplated her next move. If she could reach Poppy without being seen, maybe an escape was possible. Except her friend was most likely still at tea, which meant she'd be surrounded.

Shit. She was no good at this sort of thing. Evelyn sighed deeply. Perhaps if she took a few breaths and calmed herself a plan would come to her.

Evelyn turned around and faced an extensive library. The room's ceiling was over two stories high and lined with shelves filled with books. Tall ladders leant against the shelves, and a cluster of leather chairs gathered in the centre of the room. Light streamed in from the large windows adorned with thick burgundy curtains on either side, the sun's rays making the floors and other polished wooden surfaces shine.

"Wow," Evelyn breathed, the sight distracting her from her escape. She approached the shelves, tentatively running her fingers over the spines. It would take years for someone to read one shelf, let alone the entire room's collection.

"Look what we have here," came a voice from behind, and she spun to see an unfamiliar man.

"I was only looking," Evelyn said, backing up until her back pressed against the shelves.

"Do you have permission to be in here?" the man asked, crossing his arms over his chest as he widened his stance.

"I didn't know I was coming here," she admitted, raising her chin despite her mind warning her to cower. "I found it by mistake."

"Who are you?"

"Lady Evelyn Royd," Prince Kylan said, strolling out from between some shelves. The prince was taller than the man, broader and more handsome, though she didn't want to admit the last part even to herself. He winked at Evelyn, and she felt her heart skip a beat.

"So this is your future wife," the man said, rubbing his chin as he looked her up and down. "She's a Lys Alv. I knew you'd been given a lower-class woman to marry, but your father has to be making some sort of joke at your expense with her race. Unless you've pissed him off. Have you?"

Evelyn's cheeks heated. "Excuse me?"

He ignored her, his laughter reverberating through the library, though it was short-lived. A gust of wind blew him across the room, pinning him against the shelves beside Evelyn. She dodged out of the way, avoiding the books tumbling down as he flailed, unable to release himself from the prince's hold.

"Enough," Prince Kylan commanded, his voice deep. His display of magic without moving a single muscle spoke volumes of his strength and training. Yet, despite using his magic, his eyes never strayed from Evelyn's. "You won't speak to or about Lady Royd that way again. Do you understand, Blaine?"

"Yes," the man panted, still struggling against the prince's magic.

"You will be lord of Ocean's Harbour one day," Prince Kylan continued, placing his hands behind his back. "You won't gain any allies speaking of fellow lords and ladies like that."

Prince Kylan released him, and Blaine fell to the library floor where he panted hard with a hand pressed to his chest. Evelyn looked between the two men.

"You should go to your room," Prince Kylan told her, his soft voice like a caress against her skin. "I'm sorry he spoke to you like that."

"It's not your fault," she replied, narrowing her gaze at Blaine. "His bad behaviour belongs to him alone."

Prince Kylan's lips quirked to one side.

"Thank you for—" she waved her hand at Blaine awkwardly, her cheeks flushing as she dropped the prince's gaze "—this."

"You're welcome," the prince replied, his eyes lit with amusement.

With a jerky nod, she practically fled the room. Evelyn ran down the hallway, not paying attention to where she was going; she just wanted to get away. Turning a corner she pulled to a stop, her eyes going wide at the sight before her. Two sentries stood guard over a sheet-covered body.

Blood-splattered silk slippers peaked out the bottom of the sheet, and crimson blooms stained the white fabric over the chest and abdomen. Evelyn's stomach lurched as a ringing sounded in her ears. The hallway disappeared, visions of the night she was attacked replacing the scene before her. Yellowing teeth, a blade and fingers dipping into the blood of her neck to be used as ink. Unlike when the king had questioned her in the darkened room, this time, when the memories of her attack flooded her mind she was shaken to her core.

A hand gripped her tightly, jolting her from her waking nightmare. She trembled as the sentry dragged her away. She let herself be dragged along, focusing instead on steadying her breathing.

Push the feelings away, she told herself. She could not let herself break here.

When she finally felt calmer, she looked around to find herself back near the library. There was a flurry of activity. More silver sentries were standing around, barking orders as servants were being ushered into one of the many rooms. The servants didn't protest and followed orders with their heads lowered.

"She's the prince's betrothed," a sentry said to the one who gripped her arm painfully. "Put her in the drawing room with the other women."

"Wait!" Evelyn gasped, trying to tug out of the sentry's hold. "You're hurting me!"

"Do as you're told," the man holding her growled. "I don't have time for your tantrum."

"Let her go."

The sentry froze, releasing her as though he'd been stung. Evelyn sighed with relief, her magic healing the bruising from his grip. She looked to see who had helped her, only to find Prince Kylan standing before them.

"My apologies," the sentry said, bowing to the prince. "We are under orders to gather all guests and servants until they can be questioned."

"Does she look like a servant or guest to you?" Prince Kylan asked, one dark brow raised. He stepped closer to Evelyn's side, his fingers brushing hers.

The sentry frowned, shaking his head. "No, my prince."

"Someone has been killed," Evelyn said, looking up at the prince.

Prince Kylan raised a brow, looking to the sentry. "Is that true?"

The sentry nodded.

"I must speak with my father," Prince Kylan stated. He gave her wrist a gentle squeeze and then stepped away. "Take my betrothed to her room and stand guard until someone comes to relieve you."

"Yes, my prince," the sentry replied, bowing his head. He turned, gesturing for Evelyn to follow.

"Thank you," Evelyn said with a polite smile. She tried not to think about how his touch had both reassured her and sent her stomach fluttering at the same time. "That's the second time you've helped me in less than a few minutes."

Prince Kylan stuffed his hands into his pockets and grinned. "What are friends for?"

With a stern glance at the sentry, he strode away and Evelyn was left to follow the guard in the opposite direction.

Opening the door to her room, Evelyn found Louise moving about dusting and cleaning as she hummed along.

"Did you hear what happened?" Evelyn asked, striding towards the handmaid. "Everyone is being ushered around and no one will tell me anything."

"I was questioned about an hour ago with some of the other maids," Louise replied, placing a trinket she'd been polishing back onto the table. "Your etiquette tutor was murdered. They're saying it's one of the Makers' Murders."

"Tina was killed? In the castle? How is that possible?" Evelyn asked, her golden eyes wide. She hadn't been Tina's biggest fan, but the woman hadn't deserved to die. And in the castle, too. How did the killer get in past all the sentries?

"There is always a way if you're determined enough."

"The poor woman." Evelyn frowned, wrapping her arms around herself. "Have they any idea who did it?"

Louise shook her head. "I don't think so. I'm not sure if they will find the culprit now."

Evelyn felt her entire body shudder at the prospect of an assassin freely stalking through the castle. The handmaid must have noticed her fear as Evelyn was tugged towards the sofa. Louise placed a hand on Evelyn's back as they sat, and Evelyn's thoughts once again went straight to the night she's been attacked. She'd been walking home from work when a man had tackled her to the ground to slit her throat. If it hadn't been for Gemma Evelyn would likely be dead. The Faction leader had fought the man and combined her Lys Alv magic with Evelyn's so they could work together to heal Evelyn's wound. The memories still gave her nightmares and knowing that a killer could get into the castle made Evelyn feel like those nightmares were coming to life. If they could kill Tina, what would stop them from coming for her next?

"It will be okay," Louise said, her hand rubbing up and down Evelyn's back. "She is with the Goddess Jord now. You are safe."

Louise was only trying to be comforting, but until the killer was found and the murders stopped, Evelyn wasn't sure she'd feel safe. Though right now, she needed to get a hold of her emotions. Locking her fear behind a wall in her mind, she tried to focus on the facts.

The most prominent being: King Dominic's castle was not impregnable by those who wished to harm his people.

15

Evelyn

E velyn stared at the jewellery in Princess Harley's quarters and couldn't help but think about how just one item could pay to feed a large family for years. Crowns, necklaces, earrings, bracelets, broaches—all resting on the table before her.

"I think I quite like this one to wear with your wedding dress," Princess Harley said, pointing out a gold diamond necklace. "It's simple and timeless."

"Is that simple?" Evelyn asked, looking at the draped design that would cover her entire chest and blind anyone if the sunlight were to catch it.

"Yes." Harley laughed. "It will pair well with whichever tiara we choose. It will be a long day, and you won't want to be weighed down by too many jewels. Not to mention your dress."

"My dress? Wait." Evelyn raised her hand. "Did you say tiara?"

"What did you think they were here for?" Harley smiled, drifting to the array of crowns. "These aren't for me."

"I have to wear one?"

Harley nodded. "For the wedding, yes, then only on special events."

"It's a shame," came a voice from behind, and Evelyn turned to see Lady Elizabeth walking towards them, her hips swinging with each step. The movement was accentuated by the light fabric of her gown. She stepped up to the table, choosing the most ostentatious of crowns and placing it upon her red head. "They demand attention and respect."

"King Dominic doesn't wear one," Harley replied curtly. "And he is well loved and respected by the people."

"Perhaps." Lady Elizabeth smiled, though it held no hint of warmth. She strode towards the mirror, looking at her reflection as she moved her head left and right. "Though they look so good on."

"Was there something you needed?" Harley asked, her tone clipped. "Why are you here?"

Evelyn was surprised by Harley's attitude towards the king's advisor. She'd never seen the two women interact, but she'd assumed the nobility and royals got along. Judging by this exchange, her assumption was incorrect. The future queen clearly disliked Lady Elizabeth and wasn't shy about letting it show.

"I only came to see how you were both faring. It can be such taxing work choosing jewels and drinking tea," Lady Elizabeth replied, lifting the crown from her head and striding back to them. "When I heard you had these out of the vault, I couldn't resist coming to try one on."

She placed the crown down, her fingers running along the others before choosing a simple tiara and trying it on.

"Prince Kylan and Lady Royd's wedding plans are secret," Harley snapped, using her wind magic to lift the tiara from Lady Elizabeth's head and floated it back down to the table. "I'd ask that you leave."

"Harley—"

"*Princess* Harley," the future queen corrected. "Only my closest friends are permitted to use my first name."

Lady Elizabeth's bright blue eyes burned like the centre of a hot flame. The two women stared each other down. The room became heated with not only tension but their Elementum magic. Evelyn watched the silent battle warring before her curiously.

"I'll be leaving then," Lady Elizabeth announced with barely a bow of her head. "Princess Harley."

She looked at Evelyn, a twinkle in her eye, before departing from the room. The instant she was gone the temperature dropped and Harley let out a frustrated sigh.

"She is awful," Harley said, gesturing towards the two armchairs perched before the fire. "An entitled bitch. I have no idea what the king sees in her."

Evelyn ran a hand along the back of the armchair, the fabric soft against her fingers as she walked around it. Most of the people she'd met in Royal Bay were entitled, so it was strange for Harley to single Lady Elizabeth out. There was more to the story there.

"Before you suggest that her qualifications or values make her a worthy advisor, let me tell you that I had some of my associates investigate her. It turns out she has no noble breeding and no experience that warrants serving the king beyond warming his sheets."

"They're having an affair?"

"It's hardly an affair when neither are married, though she did arrive in Royal Bay when Queen Helen was alive, so who knows what happened back then." Harley sat back, her fingers picking at the seam on the arm of the chair. "She doesn't deserve to be here and will ruin everything."

"What do you mean?" Evelyn asked, tilting her head to one side. "You think she has a personal agenda?"

"Doesn't everyone?" Harley replied. "The problem is that she so obviously wants to be queen. She flirts with Xander too, you know. King Dominic isn't the only royal she is trying to sink her claws into."

Evelyn raised her brows, intrigued that Harley felt threatened by Lady Elizabeth. "Prince Xander is in love with you. There's no way he'd fall for such an obvious scheme."

Harley smiled. "I know he is. I just don't trust her."

Was Harley worried about her marriage or her standing in the royal family? One thing was for sure, Lady Elizabeth was a sore spot for the princess, and Evelyn tucked that information away.

"Is there anything you can do?"

"Unfortunately, no," Harley replied with a shake of her head. "King Dominic would never listen to me. You've seen what he's like with Kylan— his reply would be worse if I of all people tried to tell him anything."

"What about Prince Xander? He listens to you, right? Maybe ask him to speak with the king about your concerns," Evelyn suggested. "He could phrase it as though you both are worried."

Harley sighed and said, "I've tried. He won't fall for Lady Elizabeth's flirting, but he doesn't believe she is a threat." She turned to face Evelyn. "You can see what I'm talking about, though, can't you? Please tell me it's not just me imagining things."

Evelyn took the opportunity to stoke the flames and said, "I saw how she challenged you. She didn't outwardly say it, but her behaviour spoke volumes. If that's how she is all the time, then you're not imagining it."

"Do you think I should do something more to get rid of her?"

Evelyn nodded. "She can't be allowed to manipulate the king."

"You're right. I must protect my family," Harley replied, flopping back in her seat. The movement and her current sitting position were the most unqueen-like thing Evelyn had ever seen.

Evelyn tried not to feel bad for influencing the princess this way. She reminded herself that Harley was the future queen who agreed with King Dominic's prejudices and actions. Still, she was a young woman who had feelings and dreams. A woman who had interests beyond ruling a kingdom and was concerned with protecting her family, just like everyone else.

The world was never simple. Good and evil were not descriptors easily placed on people because people weren't absolutes. Everyone had varying degrees of both. Good and evil were all about perspective.

The night breeze caressed the exposed skin of Evelyn's arms as she stepped out of the carriage. She took Prince Kylan's hand, and the moment their fingers touched, sparks danced beneath her skin.

Evelyn shook her head. Prince Kylan was her pretend betrothed, and she was still in love with August. Those were the facts, and she needed to remember them. Taking a deep breath, she focused her attention ahead as Prince Kylan escorted her to the mansion towering before them.

Hilda, one of the women from tea, had decided to throw a party instead of hosting a luncheon to raise funds for her friend's research into healing potions and tonics. Harley had said the reason for the event was to bring some joy to their lives after the Makers' Murder. Evelyn felt they were only looking for an excuse. Thinking of Tina had a wave of sadness flow over her, stifling any of the feelings Prince Kylan may have elicited in her. Her tutor's killer was yet to be found... a fact Evelyn didn't like to think about.

Music filled the air as they drew closer and they were greeted by two servants dressed entirely in black at the open front door. Light spilled out from the luminous hall within and Evelyn stared up at the garlands of white lilies hanging from the ceiling as they entered a busy ballroom.

Everyone was dressed in their finery. The women wore gowns of sparkling jewels and vibrant colours while the men were fitted in immaculately pressed coats adorned with medals. Musicians played an upbeat tune that those in the centre danced to. Poppy twirled amongst them, her movements quick as she laughed and spun. Evelyn had seen less and less of her friend in the last few days. Poppy had been given more freedoms than Evelyn since the tea luncheon and her friend seemed happy meeting the people of Royal Bay. Poppy was assimilating without difficulty which worried Evelyn. Royal Bay was stealing her friend and she felt helpless.

"Welcome, welcome," Hilda greeted as she approached them, a short man Evelyn assumed was the woman's husband followed close behind. Her brown hair was in a plaited arrangement like some sort of tower atop her head and she was once again dressed in olive green. Hilda's skirts were so large no one could stand within a foot of her. The woman did her best to bow though needed her husband to help her rise. "We are so happy you could join us this evening."

"Your cause is worthy of support," Prince Kylan replied, inclining his head.

"You are kind, my prince," the husband said, bowing at the hip. Unlike his wife, his simple grey attire was demure and his caramel hair was neatly combed to one side. "I must offer our congratulations on your engagement. May the Gods and Goddesses bless you with prosperity and happiness."

"Thank you, Mr Thomas," Prince Kylan said with a smile as the other man gestured for the prince and Evelyn to join the rest of the party.

Eyes followed them as they joined the guests and Evelyn tried her best not to feel affected by the attention. The rest of the royal family were yet to arrive, so Prince Kylan and Evelyn were in the spotlight.

"Don't let them intimidate you," Prince Kylan said under his breath, drawing her closer to him so that their sides pressed. "Appearance is everything to these people."

"You don't seem to think highly of them," she replied, trying not to think about how close they were and how his pine-scented cologne reminded her of home. "I have met some of the women here. They have passions beyond high society."

"I never said they were two-dimensional. Everyone here has proven ruthless enough to have risen to their station or hold on to their birthright."

"Perhaps some have been forced into this life like me," Evelyn quipped as they did a walk around the room. Why she was defending these people she had no idea. They didn't deserve it. "What they show you isn't necessarily the truth."

"Precisely. You see what they want," he said, turning her to face him. His bright blue eyes captured hers. "You should remember that," he smiled. "Dance with me."

The prince took her hand and lead her onto the dance floor. She could still feel the eyes of everyone in the room on them, but now she kept her head high. Prince Kylan spun her in one quick movement then tugged her close. Their bodies pressed together and he placed a hand on her hip igniting a fire beneath her skin.

"Did you finish that book you were reading the day we first met—in the carriage?" Evelyn asked in an attempt not to fixate on where his hand was resting.

He nodded. "I did. I'm currently reading a story about a man who shifts into an owl and is sent on a quest to fight a monster in the sky and free a princess."

"I'm not sure your father would be happy with you reading about Anima."

"Then you'll have to keep my secret," he said with a wink.

"Maybe I'll store it away and use it against you," she replied. His grip tightened on her hip, making her hyper-aware of all the places they touched as they moved through the steps.

Prince Kylan grinned, saying "you're mischievous."

"I have never heard anyone describe me that way," she said, laughing.

"Well, when I write a novel about you, I will have to make sure to include it," he replied, spinning her on the spot. "Once it is written down it is part of history."

"You write novels?"

"I try," he said, pulling her close once more. "I'm still learning, hence all the reading. I find the best way to learn to write is to find what I like to read. Our library is quite extensive and I have read some interesting stories, though I think I'm starting to narrow down my preferences."

Evelyn smiled broadly, imagining the stories that lined the shelves. Her mind instantly when to August and him reading about a fuzzy peach in the Forest's Edge library. Guilt instantly deflated her mood. She unlocked her gaze with the prince and when the song ended they left the dance floor silently to move through the guests once more.

"Prince Kylan," came a voice, and she looked to see the man from the library striding towards them. "Lady Royd," he added.

"Blaine," the prince replied, a tight smile gracing his lips.

"I was wondering when you would get here," Blaine said, looking between the prince and Evelyn. "I have some businessmen I'd like you to introduce me to."

"I'm occupied with Lady Royd right now."

"She is more than welcome to join us," Blaine replied.

"No, no," Evelyn said quickly. She needed some space from the prince. "You go with Blaine. I think I see Poppy over there and I'd hate for you to miss an exciting conversation."

Prince Kylan gave her a pleading look. "I think we should stay together."

"I need to do my rounds," Evelyn insisted with a small smile. "It'd be rude to ignore those I know and stick by your side all night. Wouldn't give a very good impression, would it?"

"She's right," Blaine said smugly.

Prince Kylan didn't look convinced, but Evelyn *had* seen Poppy on the dance floor and wanted a moment to speak with her friend alone about her sudden guilt at dancing with the prince.

"I'll find you later," Prince Kylan relented and stepped away. "I won't be long."

With one last look over his shoulder, he disappeared amongst the crowd. Searching for Poppy amongst the other dancers, Evelyn made her way in the direction she'd last seen her friend. Only to find Poppy seated at a table surrounded by nobles looking at her with broad smiles and bright eyes. If Evelyn hadn't known better, she would have thought Poppy had been born to this life. She was making many new friends and appeared happier than ever. Evelyn chewed her lip, unsure how to feel about it.

"I wouldn't do that," a man said, standing beside her. "I don't believe biting your lip with a sad face is in the etiquette handbook."

"Don't tease her."

Evelyn turned to see a woman she recognised from tea playfully slap a man on the arm. She had been the one speaking with Poppy about fashion the other day, but Evelyn couldn't remember the woman's name. "She has enough to deal with."

"Excuse me?" Evelyn asked, her cheeks flushing.

"Sorry," the woman replied, bowing her head. "My brother has a terrible sense of humour."

"Gotta keep the spirits up if we must attend all these things," he replied, grinning as dimples appeared on his stubbled cheeks.

"Indeed," the woman said, her brown eyes glimmering.

"I thought you enjoyed dressing up?" Evelyn asked, then remembered that she had never spoken to the woman, only overheard the conversation between her and Poppy. "I mean, Poppy said that you liked it. Didn't you invite her over to have a dress made for this party?"

"I do like the fashion," the woman said, looking to where Poppy sat. "The company, however... Your friend is not what I expected."

"What do you mean?"

"She thought Poppy would be a little different," the brother said, stuffing his hands into his trouser pockets. "She fits in nicely here."

"And you thought she wouldn't?" Evelyn asked, quirking a brow.

The woman shrugged, her hand gripping her brother's arm. "We should keep moving."

"It was nice to meet you, Lady Royd," the man said, bowing his head as his sister did the same. "You are not alone here."

What did he mean by that? Evelyn opened her mouth to reply, but the siblings strolled away before she could ask for clarification. Prince Kylan had said the people here showed only what they wanted. Had the woman been acting the part at the tea party, or were she and her brother playing some sort of game with Evelyn's mind?

Evelyn's gaze darted around the room and she suddenly felt too warm. She moved through the crowd towards the doors in need of air. Everything about this place felt so intense. She was constantly on her guard, wondering what people's motives were. Stepping out into the hallway, Evelyn placed a hand on her chest and let herself breathe.

She wouldn't let this place break her.

Soft voices sounded down the hall and Evelyn walked towards them.

"I'm taking her to a healer," a voice said as someone else whimpered.

"No one leaves," another said firmly. "You have a job to do. She can have her hand sewn closed when the party is over."

"It's not a simple cut!" the first barked back. The door flung open, and a woman spilled out. Her arm was around another figure who was clutching her hand to her chest.

"There are servants' passageways!" a man scolded from the doorway. "You two will lose your jobs traipsing about in the main hallway."

"Let me help you," Evelyn said, approaching the two women. She kept pace beside them, the injured woman's eyes widening at the sight of her.

"No, my lady," said her companion with a shake of her head as she tried to scurry down the hall. "You must go back to the party."

"I will once she is healed," Evelyn replied, reaching for the woman's hand and forcing them to stop. "It will take no time at all."

The woman in pain bit her lip with tears falling down her face. Her hand was deeply sliced and Evelyn took no time to summon her light.

It felt good to use her magic, and she directed it into the injured hand, mending the tear in the woman's flesh as her own hand split. She bit down on a cry of pain, instead focusing on sewing the woman's hand closed with her magic. It was a simple wound and would only take a few more moments to heal.

"What do you think you are doing?!" bellowed a familiar voice. She turned her head, her body instinctively flinching at the king striding toward her.

A crowd spilled from the ballroom, eager to witness King Dominic's wrath, and the women stepped away, bowing their heads. She hadn't finished healing the woman's wound and her own, but at least now they were only superficial.

"I asked you a question," the king barked, halting his stride a foot from where Evelyn stood. His face was red and his hazel eyes were alight with anger.

"I was healing her," Evelyn replied, her voice soft and with a tremor running through it. Her body was angled away from him as though ready for his blow.

"It is not your job to tend to wounds like some common Healer," he growled in a low voice. He grabbed her arm, his grip bruising as he drew her closer to him. "You are not a Healer. You are the Lady of Forest's Edge and a future royal."

"I think the people would be happy that their leaders care for their wellbeing," Prince Kylan said in a low voice that couldn't be overheard by the crowd. He came to Evelyn's side. His breathing was quick as though he had run to Evelyn's aid.

"It is not acceptable behaviour."

"She won't do it again," the prince replied with a shake of his head. "Please, Father."

King Dominic huffed, releasing Evelyn's arm. He straightened his coat and cracked his neck before taking a deep breath and turning away. He strode towards the party as though he ruled the entire world, and in some ways, he did. If people with magic could never leave Valmenessia without losing it, then the country *was* their world.

"I'll have someone bring about our carriage," Prince Kylan said as Evelyn clutched her hand. A faint red line was all that remained from the wound her magic had created. "I think it's best if we go home."

Evelyn agreed with him, though in her mind, there was only one place she called home and it was certainly not in Royal Bay.

16

Nora

Accorﬂ to Florence, Ashe admitted spotting Hyde, Jolene, and Owen trying to enter Forest's Edge when he was patrolling along the wall and, rather than raise the alarm, he'd decided to make a deal with them. At first he'd tried to maintain his original story of Nora's betrayal, but after Jasmine had spoken to Nora, the Lady of Forest's Edge had interviewed Ashe again. Apparently, he'd been quick to divulge what he'd done after holes had appeared in his story, in the hope of earning Gemma and Jasmine's forgiveness. Nora hadn't seen the man for days and was quite happy for him to stay out of her life.

"I still can't believe Ashe did that," Sage said, her breath clouding before her. "I mean, I can believe he would. But it's such a shitty thing to do. Now Gemma and Jasmine will question whether he is trustworthy at all."

The Manor Ground's training area was filled with the sounds of weapons and the occasional growl from an Anima in their shift. It was a chill wasn't so bad when Nora was moving, demonstrating between her trainees to offer advice—if they accepted it.

The grey clouds blocked any warmth from reaching them on its hill wasn't so bad when Nora was moving, demonstrating with Nora train her group of Faction members and hang out, which Nora wasn't complaining about. They stood close enough that their gloved hands brushed each time they moved, but neither made to permanently close the gap.

"Florence thinks he's jealous," Nora said, focusing her attention on a duo sparring before her instead of the other woman. She suddenly found herself *very* interested in their technique.

Sage made her feel vulnerable and Nora was still unsure why the woman was giving her another chance. A part of her kept expecting Sage to turn around and declare their 'friendship' over. Ashe's actions were making Nora second-guess herself.

"Oh really?" Sage asked in a sing-song voice. "And what does she think he's jealous about?"

Nora shrugged, though there was a fluttering in her stomach. "Oh, this and that."

"Sage!" Phillip called, shuffling into the training area. Nora's brows rose at the sight of the man. She'd never seen him step foot out of the library and had started to think he never left the building. A woollen hat was pulled over his balding head with a long scarf wrapped around his neck that dangled in the dirt behind him.

"I was told you would be here." He glanced at Nora, his upper lip twitching. "And you..."

"Hey, Phillip, so lovely to see you again," Nora replied sweetly. She'd met Sage's boss a few times, but their interactions had not been positive. Phillip outwardly disliked Nora, and she enjoyed being particularly antagonistic whenever he was around. "Is there something you need? A combat lesson? Toothbrush? New personality perhaps?"

"You shouldn't be here," he hissed, turning to Sage and tugging his cloak tighter around his thin frame. "You have work to do."

"Lady Royd put me on her watch for the morning," Sage replied, and Nora smiled at how easily the woman lied. "Nothing I can do about it, I'm afraid."

"How are you expected to watch her," he said, sticking his pointed nose up at Nora, "when you have so much to do? You need to document our progress with the prisoners."

"Is your dusty pendant thing working at removing the tattoos?" Nora asked Sage, perking up at the idea of Jolene and Owen's tattoos being wiped off their skin.

"Dusty pendant thing?" Sage chuckled.

Nora grinned, shrugging. She didn't know what it was called. Around them, wooden swords clashed, and the sound of grunts and shuffling of feet filled the air.

"So far, the pendant is working," Sage continued with a smile, her eyes brightening behind her gold-rimmed glasses. Nora loved how Sage's passion for her work was so evident on her face. "We are taking it slow, seeing as it's mostly theoretical. We have only been able to do minor tests, but it's looking promising."

"She doesn't need to know everything," Phillip snapped, thrusting a sheet of paper at Sage. "I want samples of everything on this list brought to my office before you leave this evening."

"Can do," Sage said. She didn't chastise Phillip for his behaviour; she just took his attitude in her stride. Nora wasn't sure if she was impressed or annoyed by that. Part of her wanted Sage to tell Phillip to go jump off a cliff, but the other part was awed by Sage's ability not to let her boss bother her. Sage had never shown such restraint with Nora. "Is there anything else?"

"That's all. Don't forget anything," Phillip said before spinning on his heel and storming away.

"How can you be so calm when he's such an asshole?" Nora asked as she watched the man go. "You've never been that way with me."

"You, Nora, have a way of getting under my skin," Sage replied, pursing her lips. "You're hard to ignore."

Nora's cheeks flushed. "I presume you mean in a good way. I doubt I'd be alive right now if you thought otherwise."

"You think I could take on Nora, the highly trained assassin, soldier, spy, and smart mouth?"

"Probably, considering I wouldn't fight back." Nora shrugged a shoulder. "Why not?"

"There's no way I'd hurt you. I know I have in the past, but..."

"You didn't have full control then," Sage offered, running a hand down Nora's arm. "Things are different now."

Nora nodded, then looked deep into Sage's brown eyes. "I would stand against anyone who tried to lay a single finger on you now."

"I had a feeling," Sage said, leaning in and capturing Nora's lips with her own.

The kiss was soft and tentative at first, but Nora allowed herself to feel and truly want for the first time. And what she wanted was Sage. Gripping the back of Sage's neck, Nora drew the other woman closer, sparking a fire in their kiss that had Nora blazing. Sage's hands came to Nora's hips, pulling them flush against each other, moulding them into one. Everything about Sage felt right. From how she made Nora feel emotions she'd never felt before to how perfect her body felt pressed against her own.

"I thought we were trying to be friends?" Nora said breathily, drawing back slightly.

"Like that was ever going to work," Sage chuckled, pressing her lips to Nora's once more and smothering the smile there.

Nora savoured the moment. She felt so lucky to have been given a second chance, not only with the woman she held but with life. She would not let anything ruin her future. Nora was determined to be happy with Sage and make right all she'd done in King Dominic's name.

"Hate to interrupt—" Florence coughed and Nora reluctantly released Sage's lips and stepped back, feeling instantly colder without Sage in her arms "—but you have an audience."

Nora's trainees quickly turned their heads away and refocused on their fights. *Shit.* Nora got so caught up in Sage it was easy to forget the world around them.

"Also, I have something to show you both," Florence declared, handing a box to Sage.

Nora recognised the packaging from her time working at Will's flower shop. "Plants?"

"Nope," Florence said, carefully lifting the lid whilst Sage held the box.

"Looks like plants to me," Nora said, angling her head to see what was inside. "You better not be making Sage hold Thornapple?"

"I'm not." Florence glanced sideways at Nora and smirked. "I can't believe you remember what was written on my other order."

Sage grinned, peering over the lid. "She *was* spying on us. She wouldn't be very good if she didn't pay attention."

Nora smiled brightly at Sage, loving the woman's confidence in her abilities. Sage's praise was a hundred times better than any she'd ever received from the king. He could have told her the sun shined out of her ass and it wouldn't compare in the slightest to a compliment from Sage.

"What was in the last box?" Nora asked, watching Florence gently sift through the leafy contents. "Was it actually Thornapple?"

Florence shook her head. "No, but it's handy to label the boxes with Nightshade varieties to keep people from being nosey." She pulled out a velvet bag and Sage put the box on the ground. "It was those lovely bracelets around your wrists. Gemma had been interested in them and they turned up at a rather convenient time."

"Is this the handheld cannon?" Sage asked as Florence drew a metal contraption from the bag.

"That sounds extremely dangerous," Nora commented. "A good way to blow your hand off."

"It's safe," Florence replied, handing the weapon to Sage who took it reluctantly, holding it like she would a spider. "The blacksmith conjurer has been refining the design for years. It's called a gun."

"It has magic?" Nora asked, taking a closer look at it. The weapon comprised a long tube that was attached to a handle, with some sort of lever.

"No, it uses explosive powder to propel a small iron ball," Florence replied, taking the gun back and demonstrating how to hold it. "You load the ball in this chamber, aim, and squeeze this trigger." She directed the gun towards the trees in the distance. "Then shoot at your opponent."

"Looks barbaric," Nora said with a frown.

"It isn't any different to swords or your Elementum magic. The king has the upper hand with all his devoted Elementum. This will level the odds," Florence replied. "And I have an idea that will hopefully give us an advantage."

"What's more advantageous than shooting holes into people?" Sage asked.

"How about instead of iron balls, we harnessed your research to create projectiles that we can shoot? Then when they are lodged in our opponents—"

"They are both injured and losing their magic," Nora said, paling as she finished Florence's sentence. "Injuries can be healed. What you're suggesting is permanent loss of magic."

Florence's face was grim as she packed the gun away. "Yes. they'll be weaker in both aspects."

"Hey!" a man shouted and Nora turned her attention to the training group. "Are you teaching us or what? I told Aeolus you weren't fit for the job."

"Maybe if you could do the drills successfully, I wouldn't get bored watching you fuck up," Nora called back, placing her hands on her hips.

"You're a fucking traitor bitch with zero skill," he snarled. "Your drills are shit. I heard about the fights you got in with the King's Guild. Everyone is talking about your exploits. You would be dead if it weren't for someone saving your ass. You can't fight so why the fuck are you pretending to teach us?"

Nora narrowed her gaze then strode over to the weapons rack and drew a steel sword.

"Steel against wood?" he scoffed, holding up his wooden sword. "What was it you said when we first started? Something about cheating to win?"

"This is for you actually," she said, throwing the sword in the dirt at his feet. "Pick it up."

The man's face reddened, but he threw his wooden sword away, retrieving the steel one and readying his stance. Nora removed her coat, handing it to Sage, and stepped into the circle the man had been practising in. As she looked into his eyes, she realised she had never tried to learn his name—or any of her trainees' names. She thought for a moment, trying to recall whether she had ever heard it, but nothing came. A bird called as it flew overhead, drawing her attention back to the present. The training area was silent as all eyes watched Nora and her opponent.

"You can have the first move," she said casually as she pushed up the sleeves of her shirt and left her pearlescent shackles on display for all.

The man didn't argue. He ran for her with his sword raised and a feral snarl ripping from his throat as he swung the weapon towards her. Nora didn't bat an eye, dodging the blow by moving swiftly to her left and following up with a fist to his shoulder. The man stumbled but managed to save himself from falling on his face. He turned, charging at Nora once more. She dodged by rolling over his back and landing on the other side of him. As he turned his head she punched him square in the face and felt his nose crack beneath her fist.

Blood spilled down his face, and he growled, "Fucking bitch!"

He summoned an onslaught of fireballs, throwing them at her in quick succession. Nora moved with speed, weaving between them without a single burn as his attack pursued her around the circle. Then she jolted to a stop and ran for him. The man hadn't been ready for her course change and was barely able to lift a hand to cover his face before she was on him, throwing her fists into his chest and cracking a rib.

Crying out, he made to knock her away, but she jumped back to avoid his arm. Seething, he narrowed his gaze on her. She smiled sweetly, unable to stop herself from winding him up further. It was just too fucking fun.

He came at her again and she ducked beneath the swipe of his blade, knocking out his feet in the same movement. He landed flat on his ass, and she quickly stomped hard on his hand, earning another cry and forcing him to release the sword, which she picked up and pointed beneath his chin.

Nora was barely out of breath as she looked down at the man. He gasped for air, nursing a broken nose and several broken fingers—judging by the odd angles they were currently in. She smirked down at him. "Maybe this demonstration will improve your skill, seeing as nothing else has helped so far."

The man bared his teeth, but he wasn't given a chance to reply. Florence's voice rang out over the training area. "Anyone else want to question *why* Nora is the one training you?"

Nora looked over those gathered. No one spoke. She couldn't tell what their silence meant. Dropping the sword beside the man, she strode back towards Sage and Florence.

"That was impressive," Florence said as Nora approached and Sage nodded beside her. The girl's heated gaze roamed over Nora in a way that made her feel warm and tingly all over.

Florence said, "I've seen you fight before, but let me tell you, I'm glad you're my friend."

Nora chuckled. "Why, because I won't hurt you?"

"Yeah, and you will also defend me from my enemies," Florence replied with a grin. "Come on, we are late for our little meeting."

"How am I late if my job isn't even finished yet? Training isn't over. Sounds like you're late to me."

"That's how friendship works, Nora, we're in this together," Florence replied. "We're late *together.*"

Sage laughed and Nora couldn't help joining her.

"Training isn't over," Nora repeated.

"They can miss you for five minutes," Florence said, waving Aeolus over from the far side of the training area. "Aeolus can watch them. Show them a few moves."

"He'll ruin all my progress." Nora pouted. "I thought you guys wanted an effective army."

Florence scoffed. "You're so up yourself sometimes."

"Sometimes?" Sage laughed and Nora stuck her tongue out at the woman.

"Sage, you should come for dinner tonight," Florence said with a wink. "Then you two can pick up from where I so rudely interrupted earlier."

"Florence," Sage groaned at her friend.

"What?"

Sage huffed but looked sidelong at Nora with a coy smile on her face. "I'll be there."

Nora grinned and placed a quick kiss on her cheek. "I'll see you later then."

Florence and Nora left Sage and strode across the compacted dirt together.

"You're cute when you're happy," the redhead commented, nudging Nora in the side.

Nora stuck out her tongue. "Whatever."

"You both are," Florence said, scrunching her brow at Nora. "I like seeing my friends happy. I don't know why you're looking at me like that's a crime."

"It's not, it's just…" Nora threw her hands in the air and laughed. "Thyra have mercy!"

She was still getting used to what her life had become—how she'd gone from being a member of the Alta to an emotional mess, and now to navigating friends and whatever was going on with Sage. She'd never considered being able to choose her future and was looking forward to the prospect of what it may hold.

"This way," Florence said, placing a hand on Nora's arm and pointing to the row of buildings that ran beside the training area.

They strode through a hall leading to an office that had been set up for Jasmine's higher-ranking guards.

"I thought we were late for some meeting," Nora said as Florence opened the door and gestured for her to enter. A chill ran through Nora, and she hesitated, fearing what awaited her inside. Her mind flashed back to the Faction headquarters when Aeolus had thrown her against the wall with water magic and tortured her for information. She'd just won a fight without a weapon or magic and yet, stepping through the threshold was nearly enough to bring her to her knees.

"No one is going to hurt you here," came Lady Royd's voice as the woman stepped into view. "Though after seeing you out there, I think you'd be able to hold your own if it were the case."

Nora's hands felt clammy, her heart racing in her chest. "Have I done something?"

Jasmine shook her head with a smile on her face. "No, I wanted to surprise you but I'm not sure that was the best idea."

"Surprise me?" Nora scrunched her brow.

"Yes, though I have some news I think you should hear first," Jasmine said, a frown tugging her lips down. "King Dominic has declared Evelyn the true Lady of Forest's Edge and has betrothed her to Prince Kylan."

"What?" Nora asked, her eyebrows drawing upwards. "He's going to marry her off to that pompous ass?"

"You've met him?"

"No, not exactly, but I lived in Royal Bay my entire life," Nora replied. "He's what you'd expect of a royal. All self-importance, though he's not cruel. She'll spend her days rolling her eyes at his nonsense until they roll right out of her head."

Florence chuckled beside her. "What a picture you paint with your words."

"You don't think he will hurt her?"

"He's not the type," Nora said.

Jasmine released a heavy sigh. "Of course, I want to get her back before she is forced to marry him, but if I can't—"

"She'll be okay," Nora replied. "She may be pushed to murder him to save her sanity, but that's not exactly a bad outcome, is it?"

"Maybe not. I'm relieved to hear you don't think he'll hurt her though," Jasmine laughed. "Okay, now for the surprise. I'm to remove your shackles. I think it's about time and, to be frank, I feel a little too like the king making you wear them."

Nora couldn't believe her ears. Her magic would be free. *She* would be free.

"What are you waiting for?" Florence asked, bouncing on her feet like a child on their birthday.

"Oh." Nora smiled, shoving up her sleeves and extending her arms. "Thank you."

"You're welcome," Jasmine replied, taking a key from her pocket and pushing it into the first lock.

There was a clicking sound—one Nora would never forget—and the first pearlescent shackle fell to the floor with a clang. The second followed and Nora breathed in deeply. Her magic was still dormant, the effects of the binds needing time to wear off, but that didn't matter to her. For the first time in her life, she was truly free.

17

Evelyn

T here you are!" Poppy exclaimed, hurrying into Evelyn's dressing
room. "I need to talk to you."

"Is everything okay?" Evelyn asked from where she sat before
the mirror as Louise finished pinning her hair. The handmaid had spent the last
hour getting Evelyn ready. "Did something happen?"

"Yes!" Her smile was broad, her sapphire eyes brighter than they had been
in weeks. "He came to see me!"

"Who did?"

"Zaim! He explained everything and it all makes sense now. I feel terrible
for thinking the worst of him."

Evelyn scrunched her brow, dread pooling in her stomach. "What do you
mean? He attacked you and kidnapped us!"

"No," Poppy replied, shaking her head and making her blonde hair sway.
"He had to follow orders and this was the only way we could be together. I
knew there had to be a reason behind his actions. He loves me and I still love
him. We are fated, Evelyn."

"Poppy—"

"Trust me. He did all that for love. He had to make it believable otherwise
the king would never have let us both come here."

Evelyn stared at her best friend, stunned by what she'd just heard. Surely Poppy was mistaken or Evelyn was simply misunderstanding. There was no way Poppy could be declaring her love for the man who'd abused her. "Is this a joke? Because to be honest, it's not funny."

"Evelyn," Poppy sighed and sat on the edge of the dresser, taking Evelyn's hands in her own. "I know you're hesitant to believe what I'm saying but trust me. He apologised for how he had to behave to deceive the king. He is controlled by those awful tattoos and the king's commands. It's not his fault that he has to be so cruel sometimes. But I looked into his eyes and could see how torn up he was about the whole thing. He wants to apologise to you too and explain himself. If you let him, I'm sure you will understand."

Evelyn gaped at her friend. Was she having a nightmare? She pulled her hands from Poppy's grasp and pinched herself on the arm.

"This is real," Poppy said, folding her arms over her chest. "I want you to be happy for me. My life is all coming together. I have the man of my dreams and live in a freaking castle among the most amazing people! Except for the king, of course, but everyone else is wonderful!"

"Is this really what you want?" Evelyn asked, unable to hide the anger lacing her words.

"Yes! The women here think I can really be someone. That I have the potential to make an impact," she replied excitedly. "I love it here."

"Pop—Ouch!" Evelyn hissed as Louise stuck a pin into her head.

"Oops, sorry, I slipped," the woman said, though she gave Evelyn a stern look that Poppy couldn't see. Not that her best friend was paying attention. She'd turned to look in the mirror and used her finger to blot at the makeup around her eyes.

"Look, I get that you aren't over the moon for me right now and it's okay," Poppy said. Her reflection offered Evelyn a small smile. "But I hope you come around to the idea of forgiving him. I'd love for you to give him a chance."

She turned and looked at Evelyn as though she was a child in need of reassurance. "I'll see you at the ball, okay?"

"Not like I can be anywhere else," Evelyn grumbled, offering a tight-lipped smile. "I'll see you there."

Now that Poppy had grown so close to the other women, and with Zaim re-emerging in her friend's life, Evelyn wasn't sure she could entirely trust her.

She felt terrible about it, but she was no longer confident that Poppy would keep her secrets. Not knowing where that left their friendship made Evelyn's heart hurt. They had always been there for each other, and she didn't want to lose her best friend to Royal Bay. Especially not to Zaim. He had a terrible hold over Poppy and now Royal Bay was curling its claws around her friend too. Evelyn felt powerless to stop it.

"Be careful with that one," Louise said, stepping back and running her gaze over Evelyn's hair and face. "She is easily misled."

Evelyn chewed her lip, looking at her reflection. Louise had done a wonderful job. Evelyn's black hair hung in loose curls around her shoulders, the upper half pinned back in a style she associated with her sister, Jasmine. Her makeup was simple. The light blue dusting her eyes made her golden irises glow brightly.

"I didn't expect her to be sucked in by all this," Evelyn said, waving her hands around her as she stood. She dropped them, gently running her fingers over her beaded bodice and feeling the intricate design sewn there.

"It's hard for her to see a place she perceives as welcoming in a negative light," Louise said, fluffing Evelyn's dress with her wind magic. "Don't be too hard on her."

Evelyn said. "I'm trying not to be. I just wish we'd never been brought here."

"Even if you were still home, she wouldn't remain the same person. People grow and change over time, and so do friendships."

"I wish they wouldn't."

Louise offered Evelyn a warm smile, then busied herself tidying the rooms and leaving Evelyn to wait to be escorted to the party. Ever since the Makers' Murder, Louise had been spending more time in Evelyn's company. As far as Evelyn knew, the murderer was still at large. Sleep had been difficult, the night's silence letting her mind wander in the dark and bringing her back to when she'd been attacked. She hoped she wouldn't be targeted again, but with her poor luck, anything was possible.

A knock sounded, drawing Evelyn from her disturbing thoughts. She opened the door and her eyes went wide as she found Prince Kylan there instead of the sentry. The man was exceptionally handsome in his immaculate suit with his dark hair styled.

"I wasn't expecting you," she said, her stomach flipping as she looked up into his bright blue eyes.

"It's our engagement party," he replied, stuffing his hands into the pockets of his red coat and grinning. The action was so casual, making him appear even more confident than he already was. "It would be odd for us not to turn up together."

Evelyn tucked her hair behind a pointed ear. "I guess."

He offered her his arm and, at first, she found herself staring at it. Something had changed between herself and Prince Kylan. They had agreed to be allies—friends of sorts—but there was more there now. He was always smiling at her, and he'd defended her, not only against Blaine but his father too. She was starting to see him in a different light and she wasn't sure what to make of it.

Louise cleared her throat from somewhere in the room and Evelyn quickly looped her arm through his. Her handmaid was working hard to protect Evelyn from herself tonight.

"You look beautiful," Prince Kylan said, a sparkle in his blue eyes.

Her heart beat harder in her chest and her cheeks warmed. "Thank you," she said.

His flirting had two effects on her: One was making her feel all warm and fuzzy inside, and the other ignited guilt for August. She tried not to act upon the feelings Prince Kylan elicited in her, but she couldn't deny they were there.

They walked downstairs in silence and Evelyn focused on the art hanging on the walls, the tiled floor, even the colour that was painted along the trim, *anything* to not look at or speak to him.

On the ground floor, they stepped through a side entrance to the ballroom, avoiding the guests still arriving and mingling in the main hallway. Inside the ballroom, vines with red and gold painted roses climbed the walls and draped over a small stage where a group of musicians played soft music. Tiny balls of fire floated near the ceiling and a towering ice sculpture depicting the image of the king sitting on his throne stood before the open windows, the night sky providing an epic backdrop. A light breeze caressed Evelyn's cheek, and she watched as golden stars drifted on by, carried by the wind that was no doubt summoned by an Elementum. The stars drifted towards a buffet big enough to feed the entire city. At least ten tiers of cakes, tarts and pastries in every flavour lined the table, alongside roast meats and vegetables cooked in more combinations than Evelyn thought possible. Even she had to admit the aromas were tempting.

Royal Bay's elite knew how to throw a party—if one enjoyed extravagant food and decorations, a guest list with egos bigger than the sun, and a dash of bigoted conversation that is. The ostentatious decorations only made Evelyn more annoyed at the whole spectacle that was her engagement party, which only fuelled the anger that was still simmering in her gut since Poppy's announcement. Evelyn abruptly released the prince's arm. Though she remained by his side as they moved amongst those gathered. She didn't speak unless spoken to, choosing to endure the event rather than participate. She hated the situation, hated being away from her home and, most of all, she hated King Dominic and all those who followed him.

"It is lovely to see you both again," said a woman moving towards them. "Everyone is so excited about your nuptials."

Evelyn smiled, keeping her mouth shut and letting Prince Kylan do the talking. He must have sensed her mood because when more people approached, he conversed enough for them both. The action only made him more endearing and she didn't want that. Or so she kept telling herself. Her anger rose as she added herself to the list of those she hated at that moment.

Instead of stewing, Evelyn focused on finding worthwhile pieces of information that she could use against King Dominic. Evelyn had always thought her hearing didn't live up to the Lys Alv expectation but living amongst only Elementum these past weeks had proven her wrong. That or the surrounding people weren't trying very hard to hide their comments from anyone but the prince.

"—to think she thought it was acceptable to stoop so low as to heal a servant with her magic," a man said as Evelyn and Prince Kylan walked past. "Such behaviour is not befitting a future princess."

"I feel sorry for him," another man commented. "Not only does he have to bed her, but his children might not be Elementum."

There may have been a shift in her and Prince Kylan's relationship, but she wasn't going to cross *that* line. Evelyn frowned. She couldn't help but wonder why she hadn't heard from August. Part of her was glad because it meant he wasn't putting himself in danger, but it stung that he hadn't come for her. There had been no word from anyone she loved. It was hard not to let it get to her.

"What can we expect when the sister is single-handedly destroying the north?" a woman said to the small group around her.

Evelyn kept her head high, feigning ignorance at their words as they moved through the crowd. They were greeted with smiles to their faces and ridiculed behind their backs. She was finding the room too hot and her palms began sweating by her sides.

"How are you finding Royal Bay so far?" the man opposite Evelyn asked, drawing her back to the conversation. He stood in a dark suit with his wife's hand resting on his arm and showing off the many jewels on her wrist and pale fingers.

"I'm not sure whether it is exactly as I expected or completely unlike what I'd hoped," she replied with a strained smile.

"She hasn't had a chance to see much of the city," Prince Kylan said politely when the man frowned. "She's been occupied with wedding planning."

"Oh, wonderful," the woman exclaimed, smiling broadly. "It must be a dream come true to plan such an event, with every wish at your fingertips."

"Some things wealth and power can't buy," Evelyn said softly.

"True, but they come close." The man laughed and the woman and Prince Kylan joined him. "You'll have your hands full with this one."

"I hope so," Prince Kylan said as the couple walked away.

Evelyn pursed her lips as she gazed at the ballroom where the guests mingled and danced. They were all revelling in the luxuries of the night despite what was happening in the world. It wasn't that she didn't want anyone to enjoy life, but these people had the power to change what was happening. Instead, they chose to ignore it or simply held the false belief that King Dominic was doing the right thing. This engagement party was just another way for him to assert his power and twisted worldview.

"You should at least try to pretend to be happy," Prince Kylan said, placing a hand on her upper arm. "Even a fake smile draws less attention than a frown."

"I'm finding it hard to pretend tonight," Evelyn said softly, glancing up at him.

"I noticed," he replied with a wry smile. "I was only offering advice because we are friends now."

"And because my behaving like a puppet benefits you," she snapped. "We're friends because you want something from me."

"It benefits us both, and—"

"I'm such a fool to think there is hope for people like you," she said, cutting him off and focusing back on the guests. "It is hard to comprehend that you all think your father's laws are just. Trying to understand that and thinking you all could change your view if I could just make you see…" She shook her head. "I am a fool."

Evelyn jolted as Prince Kylan placed a hand on her back, steering her around the guests who were all happily mingling. The music bounced off the walls, but Evelyn couldn't focus on her surroundings, her mind fixated on his hand. Her feet carried her towards the doors opening onto the gardens and the night beyond.

"Where are we going?" she asked finally, the cool air soothing her flushed skin.

He didn't answer, smiling at the guests as they passed through the gardens before finding a secluded area by perfectly sculpted hedges. Evelyn glanced around, but there was no one in sight. The moon shone brightly casting the green leaves around them in a pale glow.

"You have us all figured out," Prince Kylan said, his voice low.

Evelyn narrowed her eyes at his admission, but she held her ground, refusing to back down. "I have been here weeks and given everyone I meet an opportunity to show their true selves."

"And you have concluded they are all devotees to my father and care for no one but themselves?"

"Of course not," Evelyn replied. "There are some who haven't fallen for his manipulations."

"But I'm not one of those people?" He shook his head. "I thought we were friends, but I see you've obviously taken your time to scrutinise not only them but me as well and have now passed your judgement."

"I'm not—"

"Not what?" He stepped closer. "Judging everyone in that room? Judging me?"

"You say that like I'm at fault for having an opinion on the horrible things you support."

"You think you're better than me. You think because I don't outright reject my father's discrimination that I share his views. You think because I don't behave as you would like that I don't care. I'd hoped you could see there was more to me," he spat, turning away from her. "Why do you think I'm here?

Do you honestly think I want to be? With my father imposing his twisted will upon the people?"

"Then do something about it!" she shouted, storming after him as he made to walk away.

"I am!" Prince Kylan threw his hands in the air. "I tolerate him because one day my brother will be king and I will be his advisor. We can undo everything my father has done."

"And in the meantime?" Evelyn asked, blocking his path. She wouldn't let him hide from her. "What about the people being killed or displaced? Are they supposed to thank you for living in this palace, biding your time until you can convince a new king to do the right thing?"

"The alternative is leaving and having no power at all."

"Can't you see that leaving and speaking out against him *is* powerful? Doing so would show the people they are not alone. That even the king's son can see he is wrong."

Prince Kylan's shoulders dropped. "They won't care and my father would just brand me a traitor. I'd be assassinated and what for? I'd be even more useless."

"You'll never know if you don't try." Evelyn's chest heaved as she pleaded with the man before her.

"I am trying," he said, tugging his collar as though it were chaffing him. "But there are better ways to go about things. If you haven't noticed, your way isn't exactly working. you are being used as a puppet. A prisoner dressed in fine clothing."

"I am doing my best with what I have!"

"So am I!"

Evelyn stared at the prince's blazing eyes. How could he treat her like she's the one worthy of criticism or judgement for her family's resistance when he's being complacent to his father's tyranny?

"Your silence says otherwise," she told him, raising her chin and squaring her shoulders. She would not back down from him. "You stand by his side and say nothing."

He stepped closer, forcing her to tilt her head to maintain eye contact. They were so close their chests almost touched, but she wouldn't let his proximity unnerve her. "Last time I checked, you do the same."

"I have no power here."

"What makes you think *I* have any?" he asked in a low voice that sent tingles running all over her skin. His blue eyes dropped briefly to her lips, and she licked them before thinking better of it.

The prince stepped back abruptly and Evelyn instinctively wrapped an arm around herself, suddenly cold. Had she gone too far with her accusations?

"Prince Kylan—"

"Don't. We have to go back," he said, turning on his heel. "We've been out here alone for too long."

"Fine," Evelyn replied as she strode past him, schooling her features. Her lilac dress flowed behind her as the cool breeze grasped at the finer lace.

They did not speak and she didn't look his way until they were back in the ballroom. It was only his arm brushing against hers that made her acknowledge his presence.

"There you are!" Harley exclaimed, appearing before them. Xander was still visiting the eastern cities, so the princess was left without an escort, not that she needed him to work the room. The future queen was confident amongst these people, and they loved her for it. "The king will address everyone any moment."

"And then I can leave," Evelyn mumbled under her breath.

"Have you seen Blaine?" Harley asked Prince Kylan, oblivious to Evelyn's comment. "I think he's taken a liking to Poppy."

Evelyn searched the crowd, spotting the pair dancing. Poppy had a broad smile on her face as Blaine spun her, her orange dress fanning out around her.

"He's wasting his time," Evelyn said before she could think better of it. She was sure Zaim was worse than Blaine, but the idea of her best friend being with either of them made her stomach churn.

"Have you been holding out on us?" Harley asked, leaning closer to Evelyn. "Spill. I want all the details."

"There's nothing really to say," Evelyn began, regretting opening her mouth in the first place. "I mean, it's not my place."

"Okay, now I'm really interested!"

"Look, Father is about to speak," Prince Kylan said, taking Evelyn's arm and steering her away.

"We can talk tomorrow," Harley called after them before turning to join in the conversation around her.

"You could thank me," Prince Kylan said as they moved.

"I don't need you to rescue me," Evelyn replied flatly, dropping his arm.

He stepped in front of her, making her stop. "Thyra forbid that I do something nice for you."

"Only because you want something from me. Your words, not mine," she said, hands on her hips. "And like Poppy, I am with someone, so you can get the idea of us being happily married out of your head. I don't plan on being here when it's time to say our vows."

Prince Kylan rolled his eyes. "They must love you dearly. Where are they? Are they here, waiting in the shadows to rescue you?"

"You're an asshole, you know that?" she hissed.

"Why is it that you are so reserved with everyone else?" he asked, tilting his head to one side. "You let them say and do whatever they like around you, yet I get no such luxury."

"Because—because…" she stuttered, wishing she could be anywhere else than at this stupid party with him. "I don't like you and I'm not interested in pretending. This alliance was a mistake."

"Fine," he said, nodding stiffly. "No more pretending."

She watched as he wove through the guests with her lips pressed tight into a grimace. Her shoulders slumped and she slowly shook her head. She wished they hadn't argued and along with the disappointment in how the night had gone, she was also left wondering what he meant by those three words.

18

August

The wind howled as it danced through the pass, weaving between the towering mountains. Harsh stone bordered either side as August and Felix continued up the narrow path. The snow trickled around them despite the eager wind trying to sweep it away. August was sick of being cold and the uncertainty of how much longer they had to travel. They'd spent the previous night in a deep cave, huddled close around a small fire and sharing rations. He was hungry and tired and beyond ready to arrive at The Temple of the Faithful. Unfortunately, August knew very little of the place, and what he did know wasn't promising. Last he'd read, the temple had been destroyed around the time the kingdoms were passed from the Gods to mortal rulers. The fact that he was yet to glimpse any hint of civilisation up here was not helping his mood.

He was beginning to regret the decision to trust Felix. With each passing day, he felt certain Felix was leading him on a never-ending quest that would end in August freezing to death, buried in snow. Not to mention the whole god thing. If he'd known Felix was deluded enough to think himself a god, he definitely wouldn't have agreed to come.

August swore. His fists clenched in his gloves as his magic responded to his temper. He'd fucked up. Not only was he wasting time that could have been spent rescuing Evelyn, or supporting Nora with her new life, he was probably going to die. The anger swirled within him like a dark storm on the horizon and he contemplated using his magic on Felix. He would gain enough strength to make it back to Fellbun and then to Royal Bay as he'd initially intended. The thought was tempting; it would be so simple to do and no one would ever know.

August stopped abruptly and shut his eyes, tugging his scarf from his face and taking deep breaths that clouded in front of him. He needed to remain calm and avoid letting his anger cloud his judgment. So, he continued his breathing exercise, letting the emotion leave with each exhale. Tempting or not, he was not a murderer.

If the journey had given him anything, it was the patience and space to calm himself. It took longer each time, but he refused to let that deter him from attempting to rein it in. August didn't want to be the monster everyone thought his race was.

"Everything okay?" Felix asked, glancing over his shoulder. "Do you need a break?"

August shook his head, deciding to ask the question that had been bothering him for a while.

"Is there any truth to the qualities King Dominic accuses Mors Alvs of?" He didn't look at Felix when he posed the question.

"I have a feeling you aren't referring to the *magical* traits of Mors Alvs," Felix replied from ahead, sounding closer as he slowed. "Do you mean character traits?"

"Yeah."

"Well, you all have dark eyes and pointed ears—"

"I know that." August sighed. He hadn't wanted to broach the subject with Felix but bottling up his thoughts was getting harder. His control over his anger—and hence his magic—was slipping and he needed to know before he did something he regretted. "I mean personality traits. He describes us as dangerous killers with no empathy and an insatiable greed for magic."

Felix laughed and stopped walking. The wind whistled past them as though joining in on whatever joke Felix thought was funny.

"Why the fuck are you laughing?" August asked, his brows raised.

"It's just ridiculous, that's all," Felix said with a light sigh and shake of his head. "To believe that every person of one race has the same personality.

Do you know what it would mean for that to be true? Not only would they have to have the same disposition, but they would also need the same life experiences and upbringing. Even then, nothing is guaranteed."

August frowned. Felix's words made sense, but he couldn't help the niggling feeling in his mind. The evidence of the changes in him.

"I'm not going to tell you that you don't fit the description King Dominic declared of your race," Felix said, placing a hand on August's shoulder. "Anything is possible, but you have a choice. You can be that person, or you can be someone else. Granted, you will experience hardships that may push you towards that, but ultimately, it's up to you whom you want to be. If you are content in your life, that's all that matters. One man's villain is another's hero. Remember that."

Felix squeezed August's shoulder and turned away, continuing until there was a gap in the narrow passage. Then, turning right, he began descending large stone steps that seemed to appear from nowhere.

"You're playing up the god thing a bit there with the poetic advice," August said as he followed, looking down the path beneath his feet. "This little bit of magic we are following is also nicely timed."

"If it makes you feel better, that so-called poetic advice was given to me a very long time ago," Felix said over his shoulder. "From a Mors Alv, actually."

"Let me guess, the Goddess Jord?"

"Yes, actually, smart ass." Felix paused, the path ending beyond where he stood. "It was Jord."

Felix removed a glove and lifted his hand against an invisible barrier, splaying his fingers and shutting his eyes. The air around him rippled and a stone building appeared out of thin air. Grey stone walls stood against the expanse of snowy white and August's eyes trailed over the arched windows to where three towers spiralled overhead, disappearing into the cloudy sky.

"I present the Temple of the Faithful."

"This is a palace," August said, staring in awe.

His dark eyes flicked from feature to feature, taking in the ornate masonry that decorated the walls, the colourful glass windows, and the ornate large stone doors that Felix now stood before. The doors swung open soundlessly and Felix swaggered inside as though it wasn't unusual for a building to just appear out of nowhere. August hesitated before following, the tempting

169

warmth inviting him in. He stepped forward and his gaze instantly fell to the mosaic-tiled floor. The colours were a stark contrast to the dull tones he'd been used to while travelling.

"What brings you to my doorstep, Aren?"

August's eyes snapped up to see a tall woman striding towards them, her navy-blue gown flowing behind her. Black hair hung loose to her waist with a sharp fringe falling over her pale forehead, almost reaching her obsidian eyes. Bright emerald-coloured rings stood out against the darkness on slender fingers.

"Can't I visit you anymore, Jord?" Felix replied, extending a hand. She took it, her long fingers resting in his grasp. "Are you still holding a grudge?"

Not only was Felix under the belief that he was a god, but that this woman was too. She was playing her part well, her appearance identical to what August would have expected the Mors Alv Goddess to look like. These two must be deranged playing the roles of Gods and Goddesses he thought.

"You did nothing to help my people," Jord replied, turning her back and walking down the hallway. Felix took it as a signal to follow, so August did the same. "It has barely been two decades. What is half a lifetime to them is a blink for you and me. For me, it is still too fresh to call it holding a grudge."

As they delved farther into the temple, August was amazed at the architecture that should, by all accounts, be a crumbling mess. Somehow, it was in near-perfect condition. The murals on the walls were brightly painted and the coloured tiles beneath his feet looked barely worn, as though very few boots had trodden on them.

"That's not true and you know it," Felix argued. "I helped your people by aiding you. If it weren't for me, you'd be dead or still trapped."

"Perhaps," Jord said, shrugging a shoulder as they passed under an archway and into a large hall.

She was trapped? August didn't get a chance to ask how or why.

Sofas and tables were arranged beside fires burning in hearths on every wall, occupied by clusters of people. All of whom looked up as Jord entered the room. August had been expecting Mors Alvs, but he'd never expected to see this many. Judging by the sounds coming from adjacent hallways, there were even more than what he saw. A smile spread across his face. For so long, he'd thought he was all alone. He couldn't wait to tell Nora about this place.

Felix wasn't fazed by the staring onlookers, continuing his conversation with Jord as though it was a regular occurrence. If he was telling the truth about the god thing, he'd be used to the attention. The Mors Alvs returned to their conversations, though some continued watching the three as they strode by.

"I also have the Anima to think of," Felix told Jord as they left through a narrow archway.

"Yes. How's that going?" she asked, glancing back at him with quirked lips. "Last I heard, you're destined for the same fate."

"Not if we can stop him."

"There is no 'we'."

"Even after I came to your aid?"

Jord halted at a dark-stained wooden door, pushing it open and gesturing for Felix and August to go inside. The door opened to an office—the walls on either side were lined with shelves filled with trinkets and books. A desk backed onto a floor-to-ceiling stained glass window that filled the room with a rainbow of light. Jord sat in the chair at the desk and looked very much like the Goddess whose name she claimed.

"If you find yourself in the same predicament I was in, then I will repay the favour, but the Anima are not my problem," she told Felix, leaning forward and clasping her hands on the desk.

Felix flopped into one of the opposite seats, kicking his legs up so his feet rested on the desk. "Are you planning on hiding here forever, then?"

Jord narrowed her gaze at his boots. "There are many threats beyond these walls other than the king."

"The Makers' Murders?"

"Among others," she replied. "They are non-discriminate in their kills and hold fanatical views about the Makers."

"They are delusional," Felix said. "I spoke to one in Forest's Edge. The man believed enough sacrifices would trigger the purification of the world."

"There is no magic that can do that."

"What about the Morken?" August asked. "Didn't it wipe out parts of the world?"

Felix smirked. "That story has been exaggerated over the years."

"Nevertheless, multiple murders cannot create a magical wave to rid the world of evil," Jord said. "Terrible acts do not bring anything good and those that believe they do are just as bad as the evil they are trying to eliminate."

"Couldn't have said it better myself," Felix replied.

"But I doubt you've come all this way to discuss the murders with me," Jord said, looking pointedly in August's direction. "What do you want, Aren?"

"Where are my manners?" Felix waved a hand in August's direction. "I have brought someone in need of your assistance. He is having difficulty controlling his magic. Will you help him?"

"I would never turn away one of my own."

"I didn't think so," Felix replied. "And he isn't just anyone. He was one of the king's Alta."

"Ahh, you were bound to him by magic," Jord said, turning her attention to August. Her dark eyes raked over him and August stiffened, feeling the weight of her assessment. "One of the king's little pets."

"I'm not anyone's pet," August growled.

"You are the Mors Alv that was kept as a little trophy. A relic of his supposed victory against us," Jord said.

August clenched his teeth. "I am none of those things."

"Good. Mors Alvs are no one's to control or keep as a sick prize." Jord's smile was razor-thin and frosty as the breeze beyond the stone walls. "The binding magic is old. A conjuring I had believed long forgotten until the Alta's appearance."

"*She* never forgot," Felix added with a grimace.

"Now, that is a woman who knows how to hold a grudge," Jord said, earning a chuckle from Felix.

"Who?" August asked, looking between them.

"Thyra," Jord replied. "But we can discuss her later. For now, we need to remedy what the binding has done to you. Holding you captive to the king's will limits your magic by inhibiting your emotions. You can't be compliant to his will if you can truly feel for yourselves."

"So, this anger inside me... that's all me?" August asked. He leaned against the nearest shelf disheartened. "I'm constantly trying to hold back the irrational, violent side that makes me want to use my magic on everyone in sight. I'm becoming exactly how the king has painted our race."

Jord shook her head. "Those traits are not unique to us. Your magic, like everyone else's, feeds off your emotions. It is likely that because you have never learnt to master the intensity of your unsuppressed emotions that it is more difficult for you now to control both emotions and magic. There may be years' worth of pent-up emotion you need to come to terms with… rage you never knew existed inside you. You said yourself that it feels irrational, so I presume this is the case. The question is, what caused your anger and how do we work through it now so it doesn't destroy you?"

"What caused it?"

"You weren't born angry, so what would you be most angry about?" Jord asked. "The lies you were told? Your murdered parents? Enslavement to an evil king?"

"To name a few," August replied with a heavy sigh, his thoughts going to his best friend. He looked to Felix. "Does that mean anyone who once had the tattoos would feel the same? Would Nora be like me?"

"To a degree," Felix said. "There is no way to know what Nora feels. She may have different traumas to deal with. When we left, her magic was still bound, so it's likely she isn't affected like you and perhaps never will be. Nora is a different person. Her personality may react to the removal of the tattoos in ways that yours doesn't. We're all individuals, after all."

"I—"

"She has support in Forest's Edge, so before you feel guilty and say you shouldn't have left her, remember what I said. You *must* help yourself before you can help others."

"He's right," Jord said. "Here, we can help train your magic and heal your mind."

"Why are you so willing to help me?"

"Because I am your Goddess," she replied, a sparkle in her dark eyes. "The Mors Alvs are my people, my children. I failed to protect them once. I won't fail again."

Whether she was the Goddess Jord or not, the woman obviously felt responsible for the Mors Alvs and she seemed knowledgeable. August needed her help, so he wasn't going to argue.

"What's your name?" Jord smiled warmly this time. "Aren rudely neglected to introduce us properly."

"August."

"August who?"

"I—"

"Natsky," Felix said. "His name is August Natsky."

"Ahh," Jord replied, leaning back in her chair like one who found the missing piece in a puzzle. "The son of the General and Queen Helen."

19

Helen

21 Years Ago

Queen Helen caressed her stomach as she stared out at the glistening waves that crashed against the cliffside. It had taken decades to construct the island that housed the castle. Elementum had worked in shifts to hold back the water while other teams built the land up and reinforced it. It was not only an admirable feat of magic and skill but the strength of the Valmenessian people. The castle sat upon the island with one side overlooking the drop below whilst on the other, it opened onto an expansive garden, barracks and the Makers' Temple. The only way to enter the island was by a single bridge that stretched to the mainland city of Royal Bay. Reaching the island without permission by sea or sky was a sure way to an early meeting with the Goddess Jord in the afterlife, thanks to the sentries monitoring the area.

The window beside Helen was ajar which let in the salty sea breeze that blew loose strands of her curly brown hair around her face. Like every day over the last few months, she questioned the wisdom in acting on her affections for General Natsky. It's not that she didn't love the man—she loved him with her whole heart—but their secret affair was at risk of being discovered and it wasn't only hers and General Natsky's necks on the line. Helen glanced down at her stomach where a precious life was growing inside her.

She had been selfish and now as the birth drew closer her worries were all-consuming. If the child was not born an Elementum the king would know he was not the father. The whole world would know.

What a mess they had found themselves in.

The king's ambition was something she had originally found herself drawn to in the early days of their courtship. Their marriage had been a political match, but she had been just as keen to be his bride as their parents had been... until she'd seen his ugly side. His beliefs and quick temper had been kept hidden behind smiles and kind words. He'd never laid a hand on her in anger, but his words were sharper and more brutal than any physical blow he could have ever made.

Helen might have loved him, but when she'd seen King Dominic cut down their sons with his sharp words, that had been the end. The way he spoke to the boys made her Elementum fire burn in her veins. She wanted to leave, take the children and flee to a distant city where they could be safe. Perhaps they could leave Valmenessia and their magic behind altogether. But such things were just a dream. The king would never let them leave. As much as they were his family, they were his prisoners too. So, she employed more nursemaids to keep the boys occupied and away from their father as much as possible. Helen had later found her solace in the arms of a kind man with a gentle heart.

"My Queen," said one of her handmaids, inclining her head to the door as General Natsky strode into the sitting room. He halted before her, maintaining a few paces between them as was appropriate for show, then placed his hands behind his back and bowed his head.

Helen did her best to hide the reaction ignited within her whenever she was in his presence. Yet she could still feel the blush creeping up her neck—an effect she could not control. She prayed to the Goddess Thyra that none of her handmaids would notice the flush or the way her blue eyes lingered taking in the man before her. General Natsky had long, muscular legs and a broad chest that showed off the efforts of all the physical training he undertook daily. As the leader of the Royal Sentries and advisor to King Dominic, he was an example to all who served below him. And what a prime example he was. When General Natsky lifted his blond head, she was presented with a chiselled jawline, a strong nose, and dark eyes with honey irises that made her feel bare when he looked at her.

"My Queen," he said, an eyebrow quirked and his lips tugging to one side as he tried to contain his amusement.

"G-General Natsky," she replied, stumbling over her words slightly. She glanced down, cleared her throat, and then straightened her back before looking back at the man with a firm grasp on her heart. "What brings you here?"

Helen rarely referred to King Dominic as her husband, the words no longer felt right on her tongue. Not when the man she wished was her husband stood before her.

"I was hoping to speak to you," he said, eyeing the handmaids. "In private if possible."

"Is everything all right?" Helen asked, immediately thinking of her children. The general never approached her during the day and certainly never with witnesses around. "Has something happened?"

"Everything is fine. No need to worry," General Natsky replied calmly, as though noticing her rising panic. This time his smile was unhindered, brightening his handsome face.

Helen returned his smile. The general made her feel warm and safe, something Dominic hadn't done since they had exchanged vows. He had changed utterly once she'd officially become his.

"We can speak on the balcony," she said, pushing herself up from her seat. Her lower back smarted with the movement and she rubbed it as she crossed the room.

The general's hands twitched, but he made no move to touch her. The handmaidens were watching and the consequences would be great. At least on the balcony, they would not hear what was said. The salty wind blew Helen's skirts around her as she leaned against the railing and looked down at the waves below. The waves crashed against the cliffside as if angry the castle island had been erected in its territory.

"Helen," General Natsky said, no longer using proper titles now they were alone. They may not have been able to be overheard, but their movements were still visible to those indoors and so kept their distance. "We are running out of time."

She sighed, knowing he would press the issue, and looked up into his dark eyes. "We can't leave."

"We can," he assured her. "It's not safe here."

"It's not safe anywhere. He would find us."

"He doesn't have eyes everywhere."

"Maybe not," Helen agreed, rubbing a hand up and down her arm as she hugged herself. "But at least this way, we have a chance."

"A chance for what? For our love to remain in the shadows? For Xander, Kylan, and our unborn child to spend their lives enduring Dominic's abuse?" General Natsky said, clenching his jaw. "And that's if our child is born an Elementum. If they're like me, their fate is sealed."

"He'll kill us if we leave."

"If we stay and he finds out, he will kill us anyway."

"Leaving is not as easy as you make it out to be," she huffed.

"It's not as hard as you think either."

They held each other's gaze and all Helen could think of was how unfair life was. All she wanted was to be happy with the man she loved and for her three children to be safe.

"You Majesty," her handmaid said, appearing at the door to the balcony and breaking the tense silence. "King Dominic is on his way."

Helen nodded, not sparing General Natsky a glance. She was only a few steps in when the door swung open, and her husband appeared.

"Ahh, you're both here," Dominic boomed as he entered the room like a gust of wind. "I want to discuss the plans for my wife whilst we are in Giland."

The king dropped into an armchair, draping his arms over the armrests and spreading his legs as he leaned back. He dominated the space. Even the way he'd said 'my wife' was just another way in which he asserted ownership. Helen felt no affection from those words—they were purely a statement of property.

"I'm sure the sentries General Natsky has organised to guard me are well-trained for the job," Helen said, moving to the seat by the window. She did her best to mask her emotions, wiping her face clean of any hint of the prior conversation.

"If only I could be as blissfully ignorant as you," Dominic replied, leaning forward in his seat. His hazel eyes were on Helen for the briefest of moments before he focused his attention on the general. "Lady Elizabeth will be joining us on our journey. You will have to re-evaluate your plans to ensure adequate protection."

"Yes, my king." General Natsky bowed his head. "It will be done."

"Why is she going with you?" Helen asked. The woman had arrived at the castle a few months prior and had already wormed her way into the king's good graces. If he wanted to bed Lady Elizabeth, that was one thing, but Dominic had grown even more brutal since the woman's arrival. The coincidence had not been lost on Helen.

"Because I wish for her company, that's why," he spat. "It is none of your concern. You are lucky I tell you anything at all. Jealousy doesn't suit you."

"That is not the reason I asked," she replied. "I am concerned that woman has too much sway over you."

The king stormed towards her. An aggressive gust of wind moved with him that knocked a vase from a table and shattered, scattering flowers across the floor. He towered over her, his nostrils flaring as he gripped her upper arms painfully.

"Do not speak to me like I am a fucking fool," he said, his voice low and menacing. "No one can control my mind."

Helen pursed her lips, already feeling the bruises forming.

"You are my wife, not my counsel and will give your opinion only when I ask for it. Do you understand?"

She nodded and he released her, turning his attention to General Natsky. "Make the arrangements."

The king stormed from the room and the door slammed behind him. Helen wished their lives weren't so full of politics and secrets. King Dominic knew she was unhappy. Unfortunately, her husband was too proud and selfish to free anyone captured in his web.

"Is there anything else you needed?" Helen asked suddenly feeling tired and looked up at the general. He stared at the door with his fists clenched at his sides.

"I have said all I needed to, my queen," he replied, looking back at her and sighing heavily. "I'd better go."

"Of course," she said, her smile not reaching her eyes.

With a look of regret, General Natsky left the room and Helen was left wondering if she was making the right choice.

The sky was dark beyond the windows though Helen had no idea of the time or any recollection of its passing. It was what she had come to expect from her labours. The pain was so intense, her mind would sometimes leave the room and she would drift somewhere else entirely. Now, she was faced with reality. The midwife had given her a potion to ease the pain and a Lys Alv Healer had been brought in to restore her energy. It was almost time to meet her child.

When her first two children were born, Helen felt nothing but relief and joy at the sight of her boys. With her third child, she was filled with fear. She'd laboured for most of the day, her rooms closed off but for a trusted few. She would take no chances. With one last push, the queen cried out and her call was answered by a high-pitched scream. The baby was here. The time had come to see where their futures lay.

General Natsky had come to meet with her the night before, begging once again for them to run, to take the children and leave. It had taken all her strength to deny him. Dominic would search for them; he would never give up, especially if she took Xander and Kylan and she would never leave them behind. There would be no peace. Their only option was to stay and pray the child was born an Elementum.

She lay back on the bed panting heavily. Sweat beaded on her forehead and the fear inside grew as her baby was placed on her chest. She ran her fingers gently over her baby's pointed ears and stared into his dark eyes. *What had she done?*

Tears fell down her cheeks as she looked at her son, terrified for her precious baby boy. There would be no passing him off as one of the king's own. The evidence of her affair, with General Natsky, was plain as day. She loved her new child and would do whatever she could to protect him, even if it was the hardest thing she would ever do.

"Take him," she said, tearing her eyes from the baby to look at the midwife. "Please, I beg you. He must be hidden."

The midwife's eyes widened, and she stepped back only for Helen to reach out and grasp the woman's wrist.

"Please," Helen begged, her grip tightening. "I'll pay you. Whatever you want I'll give it to you. Please, the king will kill us all if he sees him."

Blanching, the midwife nodded and Helen released her so she could take the baby carefully into her arms. Around them, the handmaids were silent, the terror of facing the king's wrath falling over them all. If the baby's nature was not kept a secret, they would all perish.

"The king must never know. Tell him the baby did not survive."

"I will make arrangements," the midwife said. "He will be safe."

"Thank you." Helen sobbed. She would have to tell General Natsky the baby did not survive as well in case he tried to seek him out. All ties needed to be cut.

Helen felt her heart break in two as a sob broke free. Leaving was still not possible, but hopefully, her new child would have a chance at a happy life and her eldest sons would not be punished for her actions. The midwife stepped away and her place was immediately filled with a handmaid who held the queen's hand tightly. She wanted to reach for her child, to change her mind and never be parted from him again, but it would mean his death. King Dominic would not stand for her to bear a child that wasn't his.

The midwife paused at the foot of the bed, with the baby bundled in her arms. "What is his name, Your Majesty?"

Helen looked at her child once more. She may not be able to be in his life, to give him the love she felt so deeply, but the least she could do was give him a name.

"August," Helen replied through her tears. "His name is August."

20

Nora

There were two sources of light in the darkness: the moon and a roaring fire that put the moon's light to shame. Nora stood in a field filled with seedlings brushing her ankles watching the little girl a few steps ahead. She didn't move to comfort the girl. The scene before her was all too familiar, freezing her to the spot.

The little girl shivered in a thin, soaked nightgown that clung to her burned skin. Strands of her long brown hair escaped the braid that ran down her back. The two of them stared beyond the field to where the fire greedily licked up the walls and devoured the farmhouse that was once home. What Nora was seeing was too real, bringing back the anguish of the night she'd lost everything.

Taking a deep breath, she strode to the girl's side and the child's little fingers wrapping around Nora's as she looked up at her. Nora stared into the eyes of her younger self, noting the cracks in her heart that had already begun to form and would grow deeper.

The girl looked away. Silent. Not a single tear trickled down her sooty cheek as she lost everything she'd ever known. By some luck, she had escaped the flames and smoke, but there was still no sign of her mother and brother. Nora squeezed the girl's hand, knowing what followed. She would not let the girl's hand go, even though re-witnessing this memory shattered her heart.

The girl waited.

The screams fell silent.

The flames no longer burned as high or as hungry.

The roof collapsed.

The smoke became wisps.

Still, the little girl waited.

Dusted in ash and blood from the burns and scratches that told of her escape, the girl didn't move a single inch. Nora remembered why she had held such a strict vigil. She had been so afraid that her family would make their way out and not see her, that they would assume she was dead and leave without her.

What little Nora didn't know was that her family was long gone. The Goddess Jord had already come to collect her mother and brother. She was already alone. Nora wanted to take the little girl she had once been and wrap her in her arms to protect her from what had happened and what was to come.

The little girl's legs trembled and she fell to her knees, her eyes never leaving her home as she released Nora's hand. Nora stood beside her younger self in solidarity, then the sun began to rise and Nora looked on as the girl ignored the people that came to help and inspect the ruin of her home and what was left. Little Nora didn't speak, not when they asked questions and not when they carried her away. Nora watched her younger self go and then the world became fuzzy around her, the field disappearing into darkness.

Suddenly, she was in a garden where small flowers popped out from between green plants. Nora strode towards the sounds of life to find the same little girl, days later, sitting on the steps of a neighbour's house, clean and dressed in fresh clothing that was too big for her small frame. Other children played close by; their laughter was loud as they chased each other beneath the fruit trees.

A tear fell down Nora's cheek as she looked at the girl's face and the way she stared into the distance. She was six years old and already broken.

A man came up the path, his boots crunching on twigs with each step, and Nora felt bile rise in her throat. He knelt before little Nora and pushed back a strand of hair from her face, tucking it behind her ear with a trembling hand.

Nora wanted to protect her younger self, to use her magic against him and slap his fucking hand away. She lunged at him with a growl, only to fall through his body onto the dirt on his other side. Looking up, she watched in horror as the lies spilled from his lips.

"I've found you," he said, shaking his head and closing his brown eyes. "You're safe now. I'm here."

Hatred filled her veins. The man was a well-rehearsed con artist. The way he portrayed a relieved father... she had never stood a chance.

"Who are you?" the girl asked flatly.

"I am your father," he replied. "I've come to take you home."

"No!" Nora shouted at the memory. She shuffled on her knees before her younger self as tears filled her eyes. "Don't go with him, please don't go."

Little Nora looked at the man, her brow creasing. It may have looked like she was going to turn him away, but Nora knew the truth. She'd already lived it.

"Please," Nora begged despite knowing the outcome. "Don't go."

Little Nora couldn't hear the protests or pleas. Instead, she took the man's hand and her life changed forever.

Nora screamed as her eyes snapped open from a sharp pain in her leg. She kicked out, sorrow fuelling her as she scurried up her bed, her room coming into view. With her back against the wall and her heart pounding so rapidly she thought it would escape her rib cage, Nora watched as the contents of her room rushed around her. Clothing, boots and a few books she'd had at Daphne's were caught up in the whirlwind threatening to take Nora along for the ride. Nora was suddenly alert, magic flaring to an almost overwhelming point. Her magic had always been strong, but this power was beyond anything she'd ever felt, fuelled by her emotions like it was revelling in it.

"Florence!" came Will's voice, but Nora couldn't see where he was.

The concern in her friend's voice filled her with panic. What had happened? Her hands shook, and her breathing became quicker. The wind magic shook the room, causing the windows to burst outwards onto the street below.

"Florence!" Will shouted again and Nora gritted her teeth, determined to control her magic. She was its master, not the other way around. She wouldn't let it tear her room apart or hurt her friends.

She closed her eyes and focused on halting the wind. Her body shook as she concentrated, but trying to grasp the magic was like clutching the wind in her bare hands. Another sharp pain ripped up her leg and she cried out, her eyes opening to find a red fox with its jaws clenched on her calf.

Its blue eyes found hers and Nora's determination for control won over her emotional state. The wind stilled instantly and all her belongings hit the walls before falling to the ground. Will rushed into the room looking from the fox to Nora.

"Florence?" Nora asked, breathing heavily.

The fox released her and shifted into a red-haired woman by the bedside. She dropped onto the bed, wiping her mouth before clutching her shoulder. "The one and only."

"Are you all right?" Will asked, coming to her side.

"I'm okay, just a little bruised," Florence groaned, a smile teasing her lips. "I got some good bites in."

"I can't believe you bit me," Nora stated, looking down to her calf and ankle where blood beaded around the red teeth marks. "Twice."

"Serves you right for creating a tornado in your room," Will replied though there was a softness to his chastising.

"Your magic is really strong," Florence said, lying down and turning her head to face Nora. "I knew you were powerful but that was…" She shook her head, blowing out a breath.

"A lot more than expected," Nora finished for her, blocking out the pain of the bites. She deserved it and would take her punishment. Nora wasn't afraid of paying the price for her failures. She'd been conditioned to accept much worse than a couple of bites for her mistakes. "I know I'm pretty amazing, but I was never that strong before. It's probably just my magic coming back in a rush after being dormant for so long."

Florence playfully slapped Nora on the foot and huffed a laugh. "Amazing or not, you'll need to learn to control it."

"I will," Nora replied. "I can. Piece of cake."

She could do it. There was no way she would let anything stand in the way of her new life. Her magic would have to remember whom it answered.

"What were you dreaming about?" Will asked.

"Oh, nothing," Nora said, waving him off.

"Doubtful," Florence said. "It made you go all stormy."

"Maybe I was dreaming about having sex in a hurricane," Nora joked, trying to be playful despite the ache deep inside her.

"Kinky." Florence winked, and Will barked a laugh. "But a lie."

"You can talk to us," Will said. "We're here for you."

Nora chewed her lip. She'd never shared her early childhood with anyone, not even August. He knew her fake father had sold her, but everything before that had been sealed tightly away in her mind. When she did have nightmares, she'd always brushed them off.

"We're your friends," Will added.

"Apparently," Nora teased and let out a breath. "I've never told anyone before."

"About your naked hurricane dreams?" Florence chuckled at her joke.

"No." Nora rolled her eyes. "About what happened before I met the king."

Will tilted his head to one side. "Not even August?"

"I've always had the occasional dream or memory, but ever since…" Nora shook her head.

"Losing the tattoos is making you face more than just what the king made you do."

"Yeah, life's a real bitch huh," Nora sighed.

Florence sat up and edged closer, placing a hand on Nora's. "Maybe it's time you shared it with someone. At least before you blow our house down."

Nora hesitated, unsure of whether she wanted to open the doors to something that she'd kept locked away. Thinking of her mother and brother was beyond painful. She wished she could think of the happy memories, but instead she was faced with wishes that could not be fulfilled. Her life had been stolen from her. Everything she had been and was meant to be had gone up in flames with her home, along with the family who should still be alive today. Nora didn't want to think of what she had lost, of the people that should have been alive. The problem was, the lock was breaking and, even if she didn't want to, it was time to face her past.

Nora took a deep breath.

"When I was six years old, my family died in a fire. Not long after, a man pretended to be my father and sold me to the king."

"An eventful year," Will said.

"No shit," Nora replied. "It's a lot to elaborate on tonight, but I can start with my dream."

Will and Florence waited patiently and Nora decided to no longer keep her secrets. If there was one thing she'd learnt since coming to Forest's Edge, it was that letting in the few friends she had made life better. Steeling her resolve, Nora recounted her dream. They listened as she described what she'd seen, noting the drop in Will's smile and the tears lining Florence's eyes. Nora had never wanted pity, but surprisingly, talking with her friends didn't feel like that.

"That's terrible," Florence said once Nora had finished. "Did you ever find out what caused the fire?"

Nora shook her head. "I was gone soon after, not that anyone would have told me. I was only a little kid, but how suss is it that my house burns down and then a strange man comes along, pretending to be my father?"

"Extremely," Will said. "Had you never seen him before?"

"I don't remember," Nora replied. "I never knew my real father and, to be honest, after my mother and brother died, the idea of a parent whisking me away with the promise of love and safety was kind of hard for a kid to turn down."

"I can imagine." Will frowned. "Do you think you'd ever want to find him?"

"My real father? Or the pretender?"

"Both."

Nora looked at her hands. "Only the man who sold me. The other had years to make contact while my mother and brother were still alive."

"What would you do if you met him again?" Florence asked. "The pretender, that is."

"Find out why he did it and then make him pay for killing my family and selling me to a life of servitude."

She'd never been able to exact revenge for what the man had done. If she ever laid eyes on him again she would make him pay in as many painful ways as she could, and then he would be in Jord's hands.

188

21

Evelyn

Instead of meeting in the drawing room, as usual, Princess Harley had organised for Evelyn and Poppy to meet her in a small hall. When Evelyn entered she was taken aback at the divided room. The first space was filled with fabrics of every colour, design, and texture imaginable, all displayed before two sofas. On the other side, a round table was set with fine dinnerware beside a window with a garden view. Evelyn was amazed at the sheer number of fabrics as she was ushered towards one of the sofas. It was a lot to take in, and now, over an hour later, Evelyn was still overwhelmed by it. So much so, that she'd given up the pretence of being interested in the whole endeavour of choosing fabrics for a wedding gown.

It was hard for her to care about the designs when she didn't want to be married in the first place. She didn't want to play any part in King Dominic's plans.

And then there was Prince Kylan. He had her feeling things she had no right to. His smile and well-timed rescues had butterflies dancing in her stomach. Their argument only added to her confusion when she thought of him, which was more often than she'd like to admit. Her mind was a mess and she didn't like it one bit.

Evelyn watched as Poppy and Harley discussed fashion. Her friend laughed as she held up a particularly ornate design with shiny beads and silver thread, wrapping it around herself. Despite seeing her friend so happy, Evelyn couldn't bring herself to ignore the latest cause of Poppy's changing personality. Zaim had somehow convinced Poppy to forgive him, and the thought made Evelyn feel physically ill. She worried for her friend, but there would be no telling Poppy. Evelyn couldn't convince her that Zaim was an evil monster, and the more Poppy became entrenched in the elite lifestyle of Royal Bay, the harder it was for Evelyn to get her friend to see anything at all. Granted, Poppy still said the king was tyrannical, but her protests were minimal and praises for the rest of the people in Royal Bay were all she could talk about.

Evelyn thought she'd lose her friend by not leaving Forest's Edge with Zaim, but she was losing Poppy anyway. They no longer talked like they used to and Evelyn wasn't sure she could trust Poppy anymore. What was friendship without trust?

"Evelyn," Harley said, coming to sit by her. "Do you have a preference?"

"You two choose," she replied, her smile strained. "You're both much better with fashion than me."

The two women grinned broadly, seemingly happy with her reasoning. From the outside, they would appear to be Evelyn's closest friends. The fact that they weren't only made Evelyn feel more alone.

"The replies have been rolling in for the wedding," Harley said, running her fingers over the sample she held in her hands. It was light pink silk with tiny, crocheted roses sewn to it. "Nearly every lord and lady will be in attendance, Lady Hilde of Ferieton, amongst them."

"Oh, that's exciting, Eve!" Poppy exclaimed, clapping her hands. "Maybe we can go visit her after the wedding, see where you came from."

"I'm from Forest's Edge," Evelyn said, shooting her friend a bewildered look. Just because Ferieton was predominately a Lys Alv city didn't mean she had any heritage there. Lys Alvs, as well as every other race in Valmenessia, had been spread throughout the country for centuries.

"You know what I mean," Poppy said, waving her off. "Semantics."

"Look, the servants have brought some food for tasting," Harley said, and sure enough, maids rushed in to clear the fabrics before trays with roasted meats and vegetables, pies, tarts and other variations were placed on the table by the window.

"I see we are just in time," said Prince Xander as he strode into the room,

Prince Kylan a few steps behind.

The future king had arrived back in Royal Bay that morning and Evelyn was surprised his busy schedule allowed him to be there. "I know it's not customary for us to assist with planning, but I do love a good tasting, especially when a roasted lamb is involved. Don't I, my love?" he said.

"Indeed," Harley replied, rising to meet her husband. She kissed him on the cheek, smiling adoringly at him as they entwined their fingers. "We don't mind your company in the slightest."

Everyone moved to sit at the table and Evelyn found herself beside Prince Kylan. They hadn't spoken since the engagement party and, despite herself, she had missed his kind company.

"This tart is delicious," Poppy said, pointing her fork at the pastry on her plate. "I have never tasted herbs like these before."

"We are fortunate to have access to some fine flavours," Harley replied. "Our chef is extremely talented."

"We have nothing like this in Forest's Edge," Poppy said, taking another bite. "Except for Jasmine, of course—she makes the finest sweets I have ever eaten."

"The traitor?" Prince Xander asked casually, as though inquiring about the weather.

Evelyn gritted her teeth, hating the unwarranted reputation her sister had. Jasmine was far from a traitor. She cared for the people of Forest's Edge and was one of the best people Evelyn had ever known.

"Ahh," Poppy uttered, her gaze darting between Evelyn and Prince Xander.

"Traitor is a strong word. Perhaps she is merely doing what she thinks is right for her people, rather than opposing Father?" Prince Kylan offered.

"She is misguided. A child who thinks she can run a country."

"Better to be a child with open ears than an adult who refuses to listen to those around him." Kylan pushed his plate away. "I don't like this one. Too rich."

"You've never liked anything too extravagant," Harley replied with a hollow laugh before Prince Xander could respond again. She turned to Evelyn, a conspirative look in her eyes. "You should see his study. Only the necessities and a handful of personal items. Nothing more."

"Yes, I've seen it," Evelyn said, looking at the prince curiously. He had not only defended Jasmine, but spoken against the king too. He didn't return her look, instead focusing on filling another plate with food.

"Oh really?" Harley asked, trying to hide her smile. "Then you'd agree. If one didn't know better, you'd think he was a common man."

"Darling, maybe you think he has nothing because you have so *many* things?" Prince Xander said, flicking his brother a glare. "You have enough shoes and gowns to dress the entire kingdom."

"I must be presentable," Harley replied, swatting him playfully. "You have your hobbies. Fashion happens to be mine."

"You have the most exquisite taste," Poppy told the future queen. "You always look so beautiful."

"Thank you, Poppy," Harley said, placing a hand on her chest. "You are too kind and I must say, you fit in so well here. One of the ladies told me you will attend the Royal Bay Women's Association tea tomorrow. I gave my endorsements, of course. I think you have a lot to offer."

"Oh, my goodness! Thank you so much," Poppy exclaimed, then remembered herself. She placed a hand on her lips, taking a few breaths and calming herself. "Sorry, I mean, thank you, Your Highness."

Harley smiled. "A friend of Evelyn's is a friend of mine."

Poppy looked ready to burst from her seat. Evelyn had never seen Poppy this happy before.

"How many dishes are there usually at a royal wedding?" Evelyn asked as more trays were brought to their table.

"As many as you wish," Harley said. "The guest list is extensive and you can never have too much to eat. Besides, it's your wedding. No one will say no to the bride."

"What if I want a small wedding?" Evelyn suggested. "Out of the city."

"Preferably in the woods," Prince Kylan added. "With music."

"And dancing."

"Chocolate cake."

"And it would be at night."

"With small balls of fire like stars floating beneath the canopy," said Prince Kylan.

"And tiny white flowers spiralling around the tree trunks." Evelyn smiled, then froze, realising all eyes were on her and the prince.

"I knew they were a wonderful match," Harley said, tapping her husband on the arm. "Your father has done well."

"I agree." Poppy grinned, resting her chin on her clasped hands. "They are perfect."

Evelyn shot Poppy an incredulous look. She knew Evelyn had feelings for August. Evelyn's guilt rose once more. Since being in the castle, she'd thought less and less of the man. It wasn't that she didn't like August anymore. The thought of him still caused butterflies to dance in her stomach and a smile to grace her lips. But those feelings were fading with each passing day she spent in Royal Bay.

Prince Kylan huffed as he pushed back his seat. "I have somewhere to be."

"Right now?" Prince Xander asked. "I'm sure it can wait."

"It can't," Prince Kylan replied before turning and leaving the room without another word.

"He's in such a mood today," Prince Xander said, stuffing a big piece of meat into his mouth. Gravy dripped from his lips and trailed down his chin. Evelyn grimaced as he spoke his next words, his food visible between his teeth. "He's upset because I told him to remember his place. The kingdom is moving in the right direction; his ideas would only hinder that. Father said I must decide what is best, but Kylan thinks my plans are up for discussion. He needs to remember his role is to negotiate with lords and ladies of other cities and leave running the country to me."

"Love," Harley said, nudging him in the side. "Poppy and Evelyn don't want to hear about your disagreements with Kylan." She stood, dropping her napkin on her plate. "Let's leave these two lovely ladies to enjoy their afternoon."

"Right," he replied, swallowing his food and quickly rising to his feet. He smiled at Evelyn and Poppy with a spot of gravy on his chin. "I'm sure I'll be seeing you both later."

Evelyn and Poppy stood to bow as the future rulers of Valmenessia left the room.

"They are such a sweet couple," Poppy said, sitting back down. Her eyes were on the food as she eagerly helped herself now that the royals were no longer there. "They are going to make such a wonderful king and queen, don't you think?"

Evelyn said nothing. It was hard to think of Harley and Xander when her mind was fixed on what he had said about disagreeing with Prince Kylan. She couldn't help but wonder what the two of them didn't see eye to eye on. And to think Prince Kylan had held such faith in his brother heeding his council.

After the exhaustive day of wedding planning, Evelyn was eager to be alone but not yet ready to return to her room. Being cooped up all the time was suffocating. Luckily, her sentry was happy to extend their walk back to her quarters. He took her the long way and as they walked through the gardens Evelyn tried to find the entrance to the underground area Zaim had brought her up from.

If she could find it she might be able to escape this place.

Her sentry coughed pointedly when she had wandered off too far. She abandoned her search to follow him inside and up a staircase that was lined with busts of past kings in wall nooks. The white marble was crafted so finely, the details utterly realistic, and the display continued along the second floor. Reaching an intersection, Evelyn froze as her eyes caught movement around the corner while the sentry continued straight on, oblivious to her stopping.

Lady Elizabeth climbed from a hole in the wall and closed a large portrait of the Goddess Thyra over it. Evelyn watched curiously, tilting her head around the corner. But when Lady Elizabeth strode in her direction, she quickly backed up and, unmindful of her surroundings, knocked one of the marble busts. Spinning around, she grabbed hold of it and righted it with her heart hammering in her chest.

Smashing a priceless statue and getting caught doing it by Lady Elizabeth of all people would be just her luck.

"What are you doing?" The advisor demanded.

Sweat beaded on Evelyn's forehead as she looked at the woman. She was convinced there was more to her than met the eye.

"I was admiring the work." Evelyn stepped back from the bust slowly, her hands raised as she prayed to the Goddess Nyssa that the marble remained steady. "I must have gotten a little too close."

She looked past the woman to find her sentry had stopped and was now watching the interaction closely. Unfortunately, he didn't come to her rescue, which meant she would have to save herself from the woman's company.

"You need to be more careful," Lady Elizabeth said. "Maybe a few etiquette lessons could teach you a thing or two about poise. It isn't right for a future princess to behave as you do."

"I had an etiquette teacher, but she was murdered. I didn't mean to knock it. It was an accident," Evelyn replied. A glance at her sentry showed that he was still not getting involved.

"Your inaptitude in basic movement is a failure of your upbringing, not an accident. If you had been raised right, you wouldn't have such issues," the woman said, turning up her nose. "I wouldn't want to inform our dear king that you're making trouble around the castle."

Evelyn shook her head, keeping her mouth firmly closed at the woman's threat. She knew not to get involved in political games she had no chance of winning. But she couldn't help but notice that the advisor didn't acknowledge Tina's murder. A sign she truly gave no thought to those she deemed beneath her.

"Good," Lady Elizabeth said, flicking her red hair over one shoulder. "Now get out of my way."

Evelyn quickly stepped aside, letting the woman pass. The woman stormed down the hallway. It wasn't until she was gone that Evelyn walked toward the sentry. She looked at where the painting sat against the wall. It was impossible to tell that a passage lay behind it. The portrait was firmly resting against the wall with no evidence of being moved as though Evelyn had imagined the whole thing.

Instead of going to her rooms, Evelyn hurried to the princess's quarters, eager to tell her what she'd seen and fuel the fire between Harley and Elizabeth. Her sentry had frowned at the course change but didn't complain.

A handmaid let Evelyn in as she knocked on the door, only for Evelyn to find Zaim standing in the centre of the room with his hands clasped behind his back. His curly hair was replaced with the kind of scarred skin that Evelyn knew could only come from severe burns.

"What are you doing here?" Evelyn demanded.

"I invited him," Harley said, stepping into view. "After you hinted at Poppy having a little romance, I just had to meet the person who held her heart."

"And here I am," Zaim smirked at Evelyn, who stood rooted to the spot, stunned by what was happening.

"Evelyn? Is that you?" Poppy called from somewhere nearby.

"Go look at your beautiful friend," Harley said, gesturing towards an archway beside her. "I need to help Zaim prepare."

"Always a pleasure," Zaim whispered venomously under his breath as Evelyn passed.

Harley's quarters were much larger and more luxurious than Evelyn's. Her closet was enormous and filled with gowns of every fabric and colour. Shoes and jewels sat on display as Evelyn moved towards a room at the end where she found Poppy standing before a mirror, pinning the last few loose strands of her blonde hair into place.

"Harley has organised a romantic evening for Zaim and me," she said, twirling her skirt. "What do you think?"

"It's a terrible idea to be alone with him," Evelyn said, shutting the door.

Poppy rolled her eyes. "Not of Zaim. My dress! Do you like it?"

"It's beautiful," Evelyn replied, admiring the flowers sewn around the hem.

"Harley gave it to me," she said, bouncing on her toes. "Can you believe I may call the future queen by her name? I never thought my life would be anything beyond healing, yet here we are. Practically royalty! Well, you will be a true princess soon and I'll be the best friend of another princess!"

"Poppy—"

"I know there are still issues with being here." Poppy sighed. "I'm not delusional, but there are so many positives. It's nice not to feel shitty about all the terrible stuff going on. It's not that I agree with King Dominic, I'm just choosing to stay out of it."

"I'm not sure that's how it works."

"Please don't do anything to risk what we have here," Poppy begged, taking Evelyn's hands in her own and squeezing.

"I don't plan on staying here," Evelyn said with a sigh, tugging her hands back. "We will leave one day Poppy. We are going to escape and go home."

"Why would you want to leave?"

"Because the king is trying to commit genocide of every race that isn't Elementum and these people are letting him do it."

"No, they aren't," Poppy said as though talking to a child. "They don't make the laws and they can't put their own families in jeopardy to help others.

You must think of your own first, Evelyn. That's all they are doing. Many of them are just staying out of his way like I want to. We can be neutral."

"These people live in fancy houses with no shortage of money," Evelyn replied. "That's not taking care of their own. That's greed and a disregard for others."

"They have worked hard to be where they are," Poppy said as she looked at Evelyn and tapped her foot on the tiles. "You are sounding awfully narrow-minded right now, you know that? I'm saying that because I love you."

"What?"

"It's not their fault they are born Elementum and earned an inheritance or worked hard to get good jobs," Poppy said. "Maybe if everyone else wasn't so lazy, they would be living the same lifestyle."

"The king is preventing Anima from bearing titles or possessions—even having jobs!" Evelyn practically shouted. "And that's if he's not arresting them."

"Well, they should follow the laws, shouldn't they?"

"I can't believe you're saying all this," she said. "Can you even hear yourself?"

"I can and, to be honest, I am shocked," Poppy said. "Why can't you just let everyone live their lives? You're being so judgemental. You don't need to change the world to suit yourself. You've been given an opportunity of a lifetime. Don't throw it all away."

"I'm a prisoner!"

"Hardly," Poppy groaned. "You think the king is trying to murder anyone who isn't an Elementum, but that's just not true. You are a Lys Alv, and he is marrying you to his son! You're going to be a princess, Evelyn. Prince Kylan likes you and I know you like him too. I've seen you two together. If you would just let go of August, you could be happy. The guy isn't coming to rescue you, and quite frankly, you don't need rescuing. You have Prince Kylan. Now, I'm going to pretend you didn't say all those things and beg you not to do anything stupid. Please, for your own good."

Stunned, Evelyn gaped at Poppy feeling like she no longer knew the woman before her. It was her greatest fears confirmed.

"All right," Evelyn said. "I'll-I'll let it go."

"Thank you," Poppy replied, pulling Evelyn into a hug. "This is for the best. Trust me."

"Ye—ah, have a great night," Evelyn said as she stepped back. "I'll see you tomorrow."

Evelyn left Harley's room having forgotten the reason she'd gone there in the first place. When she had arrived in Royal Bay with Poppy they'd had the same beliefs and were planning to go against the king. Now, something had broken between them that may never be repaired.

22

The city was quiet
at the library
was feeli
standard she wa
and now that
could se

did and why, and I realised that in setting you up, I hurt Sage, too."

Nora stuffed her hands into her pockets, controlling her magic. As much as it wanted to strike out against the man who'd wronged her, she was not the person she used to be. No king pulling her strings. If she attacked Ashe, it would be on her, and hurting him would ultimately bite her in the ass.

"Maybe you should have thought about that before accusing me of such bullshit. Seems like you have dug yourself into a bit of a hole."

"I know what I did was fucking stupid," he said. "But I mean it, I'm sorry. I thought if you did something terrible, Sage wouldn't be interested anymore and maybe I could get a second chance with her. But all I did was make you look even better than before."

Nora scrunched her nose. "So, basically, you're sorry you got caught and that you've ruined things with Sage."

"That's not what I meant."

"But it's what you're saying," she replied. "You don't give two shits about me and how you've hurt me. You only care about yourself. You're a selfish asshole who's only apologising to make yourself feel better. Probably with some delusional hope that I'd tell Sage about it so she might speak to you again."

"Fuck." He ran a hand over his face. "This is turning out to be the shittest apology I have ever given. Look, the moral of the story? I fucked up."

"Agreed," Nora stated, abruptly turning a corner. "Goodbye Ashe."

"No! Wait!" he called, catching up to her. "Please, I need to make this right."

"So you can get Sage back?"

Ashe shook his head. "Nobody trusts me right now."

"Of course, they don't trust you. You betrayed them by allowing Alta into Forest's Edge. I shouldn't have trusted you either. Trust needs to be earned, and all you've done is work towards the opposite."

"I know, but if forgave me, that would go a long way in building that trust again."

"You're just using me for your own gain, *again*," Nora said, narrowing her eyes. If he kept this bullshit up, she might just let her magic slip after all. "Do you hear yourself when you speak? Or do the words just come out like vomit? Go away Ashe. I don't forgive you. Not when you can't see beyond your own nose. You can't just go around using people and manipulating them, the king has that covered. Your shitty behaviour has consequences."

"And yours doesn't?" Ashe said, stepping in front of her and causing her to bump into him. "That's pretty rich coming from you. You're one of the most manipulative, self-centred people I have ever known. You've hurt more people than I ever have and get off scot-free. But *you're* lecturing *me* on consequences?"

"Not the same Ashe. I didn't have control and now I do. So think of this as the new me with a clean slate," she replied with a smirk, flicking her ponytail with her gloved hand. She didn't need to explain to him how their circumstances were different. "Same smart mouth, more emotional depth."

"As deep as a puddle."

"It's still my choice. Just like you had a choice and chose poorly," she sang, walking around him. "Don't follow me again or I'll end you in the most creative way I can think of." Nora offered him a sweet smile and summoned her wind magic, shoving him back a few steps. "Have a shit day!"

She couldn't believe him. The audacity to think they were the same. True, his actions had pushed her to her emotional limit and been a catalyst to embrace her new life, but he was still wrong. She had trusted him, Forest's Edge had trusted him, and he'd betrayed them.

Traitors didn't deserve forgiveness.

Well, almost all traitors. Nora was coming to realise that there were many different kinds. August had betrayed her to the Faction which led to her tattoos being removed, which was a betrayal to the king. But his actions were born out of love. Now that she was able to see clearly, Nora was grateful for what he'd done. Like true family, he had taken care of her as he'd always promised he would by giving her what she needed, not just what she wanted.

She had thought she was a traitor too, to the king, when in reality he was the one who'd betrayed her all along. He was supposed to care for the people and provide them with a world in which everyone was able to prosper, feel safe and be equal. Instead, King Dominic enforced his twisted beliefs and his own agenda.

Losing her tattoos made Nora see the world wasn't black and white. It wasn't grey either. As cheesy as it sounded, the world was a rainbow of infinite colours and she found she liked it that way. Even though she may have only seen the world in one or two colours for a long time, she now knew each colour was just as important and worth fighting for.

As she walked to the library her mind drifted to August and how she'd told him she wouldn't forgive him. His absence was like missing a limb. She wondered whether she'd ever see him again and if they'd get a chance to make things right between them. She needed him to know she forgave him.

A pigeon landed directly in front of her and she halted to a stop, frowning at it. The bird cooed; the sound was answered as more birds of varying species landed around Nora. She spun in a circle, seeing them perched all over the ground, on snow-dusted rooftops and in the trees.

"What the fuck?" Nora breathed, her wide eyes roaming over the birds as more arrived.

She walked around the pigeon and looked around her. There had to be hundreds of them, all varying in colour and size. They were now eerily still, not a sound or scrape of talons breaking the stillness.

She jogged towards the library, only to come to a halt at the city centre. Nora couldn't help the chill running down her spine as she attempted to count the birds. There were so many. So, so many, all behaving fucking strangely. Nora spotted Gemma standing beside the familiar giant tree with Aeolus by her side, whispering in her ear. Neither took their eyes off the giant pelican standing in front of them.

"What's going on?" Nora asked as she approached. Citizens began filling the streets, watching the scene unfold. The growing crowd deepened her bad feeling.

"I'm not quite sure right now," Gemma replied, her features tightening. She smoothed her long, gloved fingers down her olive-green coat, then adjusted her thick scarf around her neck. "I haven't been told to expect them."

"Lady Royd is on her way," Aeolus said, "but I think you should still address them before she turns up."

"Very well," Gemma replied, taking a step towards the pelican. "You have arrived in Forest's Edge unannounced. I ask that you shift and state your name and business. We are happy to aid those seeking sanctuary from the king, but first, we must know who you are."

The pelican didn't move, nor did it shift. The sight was unnerving as the bird remained like a statue.

"Well, that didn't work," Nora muttered. "Are we sure they are even Anima?"

"Have you ever seen wild birds behave like this?" Aeolus replied, gesturing to the flock.

"Did you send for Florence?" Gemma asked Aeolus over her shoulder. "Maybe she knows why they are here. At the very least, they might talk to her."

"I sent for her. I assume she'll be here soon," he said at the same time as the pelican shifted to reveal a tall man with the broadest shoulders Nora had ever seen. Though his stature was enough to intimidate, the set of his shoulders stated something else entirely which made the situation all that much stranger. Familiar tattoos covered his exposed skin, crawling up his neck and decorating his bald head.

"We are here for your surrender," the man said, his voice carrying throughout the city centre. "King Dominic is offering you the opportunity to give up your leaders and come back to the side of law and reason."

"Are you blind to what he is doing?" Aeolus shouted venomously. "How can you stand there and demand this after all he has done to your people?!"

A dangerous glint danced in the man's eyes. "Where is the traitor who calls herself lady of this city?"

"I am here," Jasmine stated, stepping into view with Omari by her side. "And I ask that you leave. We don't take kindly to threats." She gestured to the avian Anima perched on the rooftops and in the trees. "Take the others with you and return to your king."

"I will give you one last chance to surrender," the man said, reaching up and scratching his tattooed neck.

"Didn't you hear our lady?" Omari shouted notably tense. "Unless you are here for refuge, fuck off back to your pathetic little king!"

"Very well," the man said and Nora could have sworn she heard regret in his voice before he shifted back into pelican form and took off into the sky.

At first, Nora thought he was leaving, but it had only been a signal. The other avian Anima squawked loudly as screams soon joined them. The birds swooped, diving towards citizens with beaks sharp like spears as they attacked.

"Get inside!" Nora shouted. "Lock yourself in and prepare to defend yourselves!"

The people in the street stared, frozen by fear.

"You heard her!" Omari shouted, running by. He lifted a hand, throwing a gust of wind at a murder of crows. "Inside! Now!"

The people snapped to attention, scurrying off to hide. Nora threw out her wind magic, blocking two avian Anima diving towards fleeing citizens. The birds smashed into the invisible barrier, shifting and drawing weapons as they plummeted to the ground.

A door slammed behind her and she heard the bolts sliding home beneath the cries of battle. At least they should be safe inside. Steeling her spine, Nora focused her attention on her attackers. She dove into the fray, using her magic to push back their enemies and give more citizens time to find safety. She summoned her wind magic and threw gusts of it towards four large birds that slammed into buildings and trees further down the street. Instead of waiting for them to attack, she summoned her fire and shot marble-sized balls of fire at their wings. One dodged the attack, but the others' wings went up in flames. They all screeched, thudding onto the ground and shifting into their human forms. The three injured would need to see a Lys Alv healer to be able to fly again, but Nora wasn't giving them that chance. They'd come into her city and she would make them pay.

Three women and a man now stood before Nora, their clothes dishevelled and their skin marred with dirt. Nora summoned her magic at the same time as her four opponents drew weapons. Three pressed forward, two holding swords, the other a dagger, whilst the last of them remained behind, nocking an arrow to her bow.

Water formed into rapidly spinning discs before Nora. The man shouted, running towards her and swinging his blade. She raised one of the water discs, shielding herself from his blow. Water sprayed everywhere as she dropped the discs to summon her wind, throwing him on his ass, along with the two women who had been creeping closer.

"Surrender," the woman with the bow called and Nora saw the arrow rattling against the wood. The woman worried her lip. Nora noted the tattoo around her neck, the ink was dark and fresh. "Please," the woman said.

Nora frowned at the woman and her choice of words. Was the archer afraid? The three Anima got to their feet and Nora decided she'd had enough of this little fight. With one firm gust of wind she threw all four backwards, only this time, they flew past the tree and crashed into the building beyond. Wood cracked and glass smashed as they went through the wall.

She didn't bother checking on them as she ran past the destruction she'd caused and to her next opponent. Nora fought Anima as she moved through the street, defending those cowering in corners or running for their lives. Flaming arrows flew from her fingers, striking birds in the sky and water jets and gusts of wind were thrown at those who had shifted and fought on the ground. As she moved through the city, she noted how each of the avian Anima had the same neck tattoo. They certainly weren't Alta. But the tattoos were undeniably the same.

A woman ran at her from the side with a dagger gripped tightly in her fist. Nora summoned a water shield, but the woman darted around it, coming to Nora's side and slashing. She jumped out of the way before she could be struck and rounded on the woman to throw a punch. Her fist struck the Anima's jaw and the woman cried out. She clutched her face growling in anger as she came for Nora again. Nora blocked her blows and then threw a gust of wind, hurtling the woman down the street and knocking into other Anima as she went.

By some miracle, Nora hadn't been hurt beyond a few shallow scratches and some bruises, despite the overwhelming number of anima. Pausing briefly to catch her breath, she looked to the sky and thanked the Goddess Thyra for watching over her. Shouts sounded around her and Nora took off once more to rejoin the fight to defend the city. She ran down the streets, stopping when a rumble echoed and a giant wave came crashing towards Nora. Water hurtled through the street, capturing those in its path.

Nora ran towards the nearest building and used her wind magic to propel her up the side as she reached for the branches of the nearest tree. She had strong water magic, but she would be no match for the torrent speeding by. Swinging on the branch, she landed on top of the roof and the building groaned beneath her, the water tearing at its sides. Avian Anima took to the skies, but many of Forest's Edge's citizens were not so lucky and were swept up in the water. Some managed to grab hold of buildings, pulling themselves onto rooftops. Nora did her best to help, using whatever power she could muster to drag them onto a roof. The avian Anima swooped, targeting citizens on roofs or in tree branches.

Nora formed three flaming birds at her fingertips that crackled as they speared after the attacking birds. The fire birds tore through the sky, swooping and scratching with their flaming beaks and claws. One sped towards a raven who flapped frantically before the fire bird dived on top of it wrapping its flaming wings around it. The fire bird released it and the raven cried out as it fell into the water with a hiss, its squawks of pain dying with it.

Nora's fire birds continued fighting. Makeshift weapons, as well as Elementum magic, were raised against the attackers. Nora let herself be swept up in the fighting. She never felt more alive than when she put her skills to the test—removing the king's tattoos hadn't squashed that part of her. What that said about her character was something she'd delve into another day. For now, she let the thrill carry her forward.

The endless waves finally dropped and the water spread out like a muscle releasing its tension. Debris and bodies bobbed in the water.

"Let me help you down," Nora said, offering a hand to a man she had saved. "Hold on tight."

The man squeezed Nora's waist, pressing his body to Nora's side as she used her wing magic to lower them carefully to the ground.

"Thank you."

"You're welcome," Nora replied. "You should go find somewhere safe."

The man nodded, not needing any encouragement as he took off. She looked around at the destruction with a heavy weight in her chest. She could no longer hear fighting, only calls for help and those answering the pleas. Nora set her jaw and headed for the nearest voice, joining in the search for survivors while making her way towards the library and Sage.

23

Nora

Flames licked up the shelves and devoured the books within. The library had been ransacked. Furniture lay in pieces, windows were smashed and bodies lay lifeless scattered throughout the rubble. Nora assumed the fire was from wayward Elementum magic, but she couldn't be sure and didn't have time to spare figuring out what had happened. Her mind fixated on one thing: finding Sage.

The fighting had stopped outside with most of the invading Anima either dead or captured. Forest's Edge had won, but the victory had come with a cost and Nora prayed Sage was not part of the collateral.

Nora's heart pounded in her chest as she leapt over a broken chair and ran towards the offices in the back while throwing jets of water to douse the fires still burning. Sage had to be safe. Nora didn't know what she would do if the woman were hurt and she refused to consider anything worse. Slamming wind magic into the door to Sage's office, it opened to Sage tied to one of the wooden legs of a desk. Her purple shirt was torn and there was a gag in her mouth. Her gold-rimmed glasses were cracked. The office was a mess around her with Sage's research strewn all over the place. But she was alive.

"Thank Thyra," Nora breathed in relief.

Falling to her knees, Nora carefully pulled the gag from Sage's mouth and inspected the woman for injuries. She gently untied the rope around Sage's wrists, the rope falling to the floor with a thud as Nora sat back to look at Sage and give her space.

"Who did this to you?" Nora asked, taking Sage's face in her hands. Gently turning Sage's head, Nora inspected the cut about her eyebrow and the dried blood crusted down the side of her face.

"Phillip," Sage said, her plump lower lip quivering.

Nora's brows shot up surprised. He'd always been an asshole, but she'd never imagined he would attack Sage. His name could go right under Ashe's on her shit list.

"He took everything," Sage said through a sob. "All my notes and the pendant."

"Fuck," Nora growled, jerking to her feet and running a hand over her face. "I'm going to kill him."

"I don't want that," Sage said. She stood up and placed her hands on either side of Nora's hips. "I don't want you to kill anyone for me."

"Maybe it's for me," Nora replied, blowing a loose strand of hair from her face. "I hate what he did to you."

Sage's gaze dropped and tears streamed from her eyes, causing Nora's heart to clench. Nora closed the distance between them and wrapped her arms around Sage, pulling her close and holding her as she cried. Her heart broke at Sage's pain. Not only had she been assaulted and betrayed by someone she'd trusted, but years of work had also been stolen. Nora's instinct to protect Sage demanded revenge.

"I'll fix it," Nora said, releasing Sage. The sight of Sage's red-rimmed eyes increased her anger. "He can't have gone far. If I leave now, I'm sure I'll reach the weasel in a couple of hours, max."

"I'll come with you," Sage said, setting her jaw and lifting her glasses to wipe her eyes with the back of her hand. "We can go after him together."

"Is this your way of trying to stop me? Threatening to put yourself in danger?"

Sage placed a hand on her chest. "Phillip did this to me. He stole my research. If you're going after him, I want to be a part of that."

"You'll be a distraction."

"Well, that sounds like a you problem," Sage smirked. "Phillip attacked *me*. Besides, I can handle myself."

"I'd be too concerned about you to focus on finding Phillip and getting your work back. There could be others with him. I can't risk you getting hurt."

"And you think I want you to get hurt? You can't go alone," she replied. "I'm coming with you whether you like it or not."

Nora ran a hand down her face and said, "you're purposely being frustrating."

"No, I'm telling you that I want us to work as a team," Sage replied. "If you are frustrated at not being able to make me do what you want, that's on you. I understand you want to protect me, but I can make my own choices."

"Are you trying to make a point? Is that what this is?"

Sage shook her head. "I'm trying to track down Phillip and get my research back with my girlfriend, who is being difficult."

Nora's heart skipped in her chest. "Did you just call me your girlfriend?"

"Yeah," Sage replied, dropping her gaze and shuffling her feet. "Is that okay?"

"More than okay," Nora smiled. "Though I'd rather *my* girlfriend stay here where it's safe."

"The city was just attacked. I think I'd be safest wherever you are."

"Sage," Nora groaned.

"Nora," Sage said in a teasing tone. "Just give up fighting me already. We're in this together."

Nora sighed, her smile growing. "I like the sound of that."

She leaned in, placing a gentle kiss on Sage's lips, eager for more after thinking she could have lost her. Sage must have felt the same because as soon as they pressed together, their bodies entwined and they kissed with a heated passion. Nora's lips parted and she let desire take over. She moved forward, ushering Sage back until the woman leaned between her and the desk. Sage moaned and that was all the encouragement Nora needed. Her hands slid up Sage's waist, cupping Sage's full breast, awarding her another breathy moan that had Nora squeezing her thighs together. Sage was just as eager, one hand holding the back of Nora's neck whilst the other gripped her ass firmly.

Nora could easily get lost in Sage for the rest of her life, but there was a voice in the back of her head that was slowly getting louder. Sage had just been through something traumatic and the city was under attack. Nora didn't want to take advantage of Sage. She wanted to do things the right way.

Reluctantly, she stepped back slightly. "We should probably not get distracted if we want to find Phillip,"

"Don't talk sense," Sage replied, smiling as she bit her lip. "Why do you have to choose right now to be sensible for the first time in your life?

Nora laughed and said, "if it makes you feel better, I don't want to be."

"One of us needs to. I'm just surprised it's you," Sage teased.

"Me too."

They looked around the ransacked office, gathering anything Sage deemed worth salvaging. Once they'd saved what they could, Nora took Sage's hand and led her from the office. Instead of going into the main floor of the library, they ducked into Phillip's office down the end of the hallway. The door was ajar and smoke billowed from inside. Nora covered her nose with her arm and pushed the door fully open with her wind magic. Inside, everything was blackened and smouldering.

"I'm sorry," Nora said.

"Don't be," Sage replied with a disheartened shrug. "It's not your fault. Should we try his home?"

Nora nodded and they left the smouldering office. They exited the hall and looked around at the destruction with Sage's hand gripped tightly in Nora's as they carefully moved through the dishevelled library. Anything that wasn't destroyed by fire had been doused by Nora's water magic. The damage was done.

"So much is lost," Sage said softly, frowning. "There's so much we will never get back."

They left the library, though outside wasn't much better. Buildings were damaged beyond repair with debris scattered all over the place thanks to the clash. The attack had caught them unprepared and while it looked as though the people of Forest's Edge had won; Nora could see the city was in shambles.

"I don't think the avian Anima weren't here by choice," Nora stated, frowning at the destruction.

"What do you mean?" Sage asked. She quirked a brow, stepping over an abandoned broken cart. "Do you think someone was blackmailing them?"

"Not blackmail, but they didn't attack us willingly. They all had matching tattoos around their necks—the same ink as the ones on my wrists used to be."

Nora was sure the tattoos were a link to the king. It was the only explanation for Anima to attack allies of their people.

Unlike the Alta—who typically joined the king's ranks willingly before receiving the binding tattoos and being brainwashed—the Anima must have been forced. They seemed at war with themselves as well as with the people of Forest's Edge. Nora had seen it in the archer. They had not been on the side they wanted to be in the fight. Nora's stomach churned. For years, all she'd wanted was to please King Dominic. Even before she was tattooed, she'd idolised the man. He had given her a home and purpose. He might as well have been the sixth god because, in her naïve eyes, he had once been everything they represented and more.

She felt so ashamed of whom she used to be, of the thoughts that had filled her mind and her willingness to believe him so easily. Was it the king's fault for making her believe? Or was it her own for being so fucking gullible?

"You think the king was controlling them?"

"I do, and if that's the case, they shouldn't be punished for what they were made to do."

"I agree. If you're right, we will free them," Sage said, squeezing Nora's hand. "We'll free everyone he's ever forced control over. We won't let him win."

Nora offered Sage a grim smile and said, "we'd better find Phillip then."

Phillip's home had given no further clues and could only be described as a blank canvas. The place was bare of possessions, giving no indication someone had lived there. Everything had been tidy and generically bland, not a single personal item in sight other than a sock Nora had discovered under the bed.

"He must have been planning something for a while," Nora said when they were back on the street. The sun was setting as they drew closer to Nora's home and she tugged Sage closer to keep warm... and maybe also because she wanted to be closer to her girlfriend. Nora smiled at the thought. She'd never had a partner before and loved that Sage was hers. "Have you been researching anything else or just the dust stuff in the pendant?"

"Only the dust," Sage replied with a heavy sigh. "He was using me, wasn't he?"

"Yeah, I'm sorry."

"You need to stop apologising. None of this is your fault. Phillip is not your burden. You already have enough to deal with, so don't go adding him to the list."

Nora scowled. "I hate seeing you hurt."

"It's sweet of you," Sage said, smiling. "I like that you care about me."

"I do," Nora said. "I care about you so much. I want to fix this for you, but I don't know how. What do you need from me?"

"To be here." Sage squeezed Nora. "To be by my side. That's all I want."

"I can do that."

Sage's eyes shone, but something captured her attention. Nora followed Sage's line of sight to see a large charcoal-and-caramel-coloured dog bounding towards them, its droopy ears flapping with each step. Nora summoned her wind magic, creating an air shield around her and Sage. It wasn't the best, but her magic was drained, so it would have to do.

The dog halted before them. Its prominent black nose sniffed at the air before the creature shifted to reveal a young woman. "Oh good, you're both together. This will save time. Lady Royd sends for you to her Manor."

"We'll be there," Nora replied, as the woman turned to leave.

"Wait!" Sage called before the woman could shift again. "Can you track someone for us?"

"Depends on who it is."

"My boss," Sage said. "His name is Phillip. He's a researcher at the library."

"Do you have anything with his scent on it?"

Sage frowned, retrieving the sock from her pocket.

Nora huffed a laugh. "Why did you keep that?"

"I don't know," she said, shrugging. "But it's a good thing I did."

The woman shifted back into a bloodhound and sniffed the sock loudly, before shifting back.

"Sorry, I can't help you. There's no scent on that sock other than yours." The woman gave a tight smile, then shifted back into a dog and bounded away.

"Alta can't be tracked by Anima," Nora said, taking Sage's hand. "Phillip could have a way to block himself from being found, too."

Sage's shoulders drooped. "So, what now? He's gotten away?"

"Not if I can help it," Nora said, guiding Sage towards the Manor to meet Jasmine. "We need to make a list of all the people he had contact with.

Friends, family, and places he visited. We'll talk to the other people at the library, uncover every little detail until we find something to go on."

"Is that how you found yourself in Forest's Edge?" Sage asked. "I know you came here looking for Felix."

Nora nodded. "Yes, it was the most infuriatingly tiny lead, too, but it was all we had. Even though it was frustrating at the time, and didn't turn out how I imagined, I'm glad we had it."

"Why?"

"Because it brought me to you… to the best thing to ever happen to me."

"That's a tad romantic," Sage said, her lips quirking at one side as a blush filled her cheeks.

Nora kissed Sage gently. "It's the truth."

24

August

T he temple kitchens were toasty, but the people inside them were warmer. Upbeat chatter and laughter filled the space as they moved about in a sort of dance, preparing and cooking breakfast. August yawned as he stood at a bench, kneading dough for bread. Tyler, his constant companion since August had arrived, stood opposite him. He'd been assigned to share a room with the man and, though he was nearly ten years older, August thought his personality was more akin to that of a late teen.

"Stay up late last night?" Tyler asked with a glimmer of amusement in his black and green eyes.

"I have a talkative roommate," August replied, stifling another yawn. "Wouldn't shut up the last few nights."

"I like a little chat before bed," Tyler said with a shrug of his lean shoulders. "You don't hear me complaining about you being a mouth breather."

"What?"

"You're like this." Tyler stopped what he was doing to emphasise breathing loudly from his mouth. "It's like you forget you have a nose as soon as you fall asleep. I bet you snore when you're exhausted too, so I guess I have that to look forward to."

"I can change rooms," August suggested. He'd be happy to have his own room. That didn't mean he didn't like Tyler. He felt they had become instant friends. There was something about the man that August felt instantly connected to—like he could trust him.

Tyler shook his head, his brown hair flopping around. "Nah, I wouldn't subject anyone else to your torture."

August barked a laugh. He was beginning to think there was a reason the man had no roommate before August's arrival and that Tyler's disposition was also a test of August's control. But if he was honest with himself, he enjoyed the back-and-forth teasing. It reminded August of Nora, whom he missed terribly. He'd never been away from her this long and it felt unnatural not speaking to her for weeks. She was his best friend, his family. He was determined to work hard at his training and return to her and Evelyn. He also missed the Lys Alv, but very differently, particularly when he was alone.

"We have mediation in a few minutes," Tyler continued, reminding August that he was in a crowded kitchen and not a dark room. "You can sleep during that."

"I don't think that's the purpose of the session," August replied dryly.

"Hmm." Tyler tapped his chin with a floury finger, leaving a white dusting on his brown skin. "Maybe that's why it's not working for me."

August quirked a brow, placing his dough aside to rise with the others, then wiped his hands clean. "One of the many reasons, I would think," he teased. "Ready to go?"

"Yep," Tyler replied dropping his over-kneaded dough ball onto the bench and slapping his hands together. "Time for my nap."

August chuckled, removed his apron, and the two men made their way out of the kitchen.

The Temple of the Faithful was bigger than August could ever have imagined, making its invisibility to the outside world all the more impressive. Everyone had a role in maintaining it. Supplies that could not be made here would arrive from an anonymous merchant in Fellbun every week, but otherwise, the place was shut off from the world.

Fellbun's people may not have known about the Mors Alvs' existence, but Lord Havilor certainly did and August was yet to discover whether this mystery merchant and the lord were one and the same. He had his suspicions.

They climbed the stairs from the lower level and walked the expansive hallways, passing the other Mors Alvs awake at this hour. Most would still be in bed as the sun had only just started to rise and filter through the windows. They turned left, ascending a spiral staircase to a circular room at the top of the tower. Fluffy rugs scattered the floor with large pillows and blankets. The air was filled with the scent of lavender.

Tyler winked, patting August on the back, and found a spot near the rear of the room. He lay down, closed his eyes, and appeared asleep within seconds. August rolled his eyes. Unlike Tyler, he wanted to meditate. He was already finding his emotions more manageable after just a few sessions. Between training, meditation, and his assigned tasks, August barely felt the irrational anger and uninhibited need to use his magic anymore.

"Good morning," Jord said as more people entered the room.

He still wasn't convinced that she and Felix were gods, but the more time he spent in Jord's presence, the more challenging it was for him to deny. Felix, or Aren if he were to believe the man, was always so casual. In contrast, Jord had a powerful aura about her. August wasn't sure what to make of all the prayers he'd spoken to the Goddess or the lingering belief that she had been watching over him. It was a lot to process the concept of a Goddess in her physical form on this plane rather than in some ambiguous location in the sky.

August mumbled a reply and found a space to sit down. He immediately closed his eyes, took a deep breath, and waited for Jord to begin. The others settled around him before Jord began guiding the session. He let her words settle over him, allowing his mind to drift to where she commanded and his breathing to match hers.

It was hard for him to marry the now easily snappy August with how he felt during meditation. It provided clarity that made him ashamed of his behaviour. He was mortified that he'd used his magic on Evelyn and Nora and put them both at risk. But, as he listened to Jord speak he let go of the tension inside. He couldn't change the past, but he would do better in the future.

August could see himself staying with the Mors Alvs long term. How easy it would have been for him to wake up each day and follow this routine.

Time moved quickly while meditating and Jord soon encouraged them to open their eyes and leave when they were ready. August sat for a little longer, enjoying the calm within, then slowly opened his eyes to see Jord watching him.

"You thrive on structure," she stated. She wore one of her flowing gowns, though today it was the colour of snow. "You feel lost without the king's

217

direction."

"I don't want to be under his control," he replied stiffly, his calm mood evaporating. "His orders and beliefs are abhorrent."

"I never said you agreed with him," she said, rising from where she sat surrounded by cushions. "He gave a sense of certainty to your life. Without the structure, you appear lost."

"Is that why I am angry all the time?"

Jord quirked a brow. "Are you? You appear calm to me."

"You just said without the king, I have no structure." He shifted where he sat, his shirt and trousers feeling suddenly too tight.

"And aren't you getting that here? Have you felt as angry since your arrival?"

August blinked. She was right. Submerging himself in a routine here had soothed the fire within.

"Your daily tasks and training have fulfilled some of your needs, but it is not enough. Though I wish you would stay, I have a feeling your time here is only temporary. You're looking for purpose."

"I had a purpose," he grumbled, running a hand through his hair. "I was going to rescue a girl from King Dominic, but Felix, or should I say, Aren, convinced me to come here first."

"Because you were no help to her with your magic out of control," Jord said. She folded her arms over her chest. "Aren was right to bring you here."

"I feel like every way I turn is a dead end. I don't know what is expected of me." August sighed.

"Perhaps it's time to work out what you expect from yourself."

When August was growing up, his favourite lesson with Rana was combat training. He loved learning to fight, but mostly he loved seeing his progression. With each lesson, he improved, hitting harder, and moving faster and, as he grew, the feeling never went away. The thing with physical training was that there was always something new to learn, some way to improve. So, when he first arrived at the temple and Jord had said her help would involve three parts—magic, meditation, and combat—he'd understood the first, questioned the second and been excited for the third. The prospect of blowing off steam was exactly what he needed.

"What's going on?" Tyler asked later that day, blocking August's fist and darting back.

"Jord seemed to think I need to sort out my expectations," August said. He'd been filling Tyler in as they sparred, bouncing ideas off his friend.

"I'm guessing of yourself," Tyler replied as he sidestepped. His bare chest gleamed with sweat despite the snow outside.

They were in a large room set up with practice weapons along the walls and circles drawn on the stone floor. There were no real additional safety precautions, other than weapons being made of wood or filed blunt, adding to the intensity of the training.

Around them, others were paired up and practising combat either with a weapon or their body alone. No one used magic. There was no point stealing another Mors Alv's power when it could just as easily be stolen back.

August and Tyler circled each other, walking around the edge of their designated area.

"Am I that obvious?" August asked.

"Yeah, you haven't shut up about Nora and Evelyn and how you're supposed to be riding off on a valiant steed to their rescue since you arrived."

"I don't mention them that often."

Tyler groaned dramatically. "You do. All. The. Time."

"They're important to me."

"You are important to you."

"So, how do I help myself so I can help them?" August grimaced. "I have no idea how to stop the anger alone."

"Seek revenge? Murder the king?"

"It won't change the past."

"No, but it will make you feel better. The king won't be able to hurt anyone else," Tyler said. "Wouldn't that help the situation for your ladies as well? Dead king equals a happy world."

"Are you trying to get me killed?" August said. "Travelling to Royal Bay to murder the king will mean my death too."

Tyler laughed. "You don't think you're capable of a little regicide? I'm disappointed. You're an Alta, not to mention the son of a queen and a general. If anyone can do it, I'd have thought it was you."

"You know about the Alta? And my supposed parents?" August asked.

"Everyone here knows about that stuff," Tyler replied as if it were no big deal. "And if Jord says they are your parents, then that's what they are. She doesn't lie."

"Everyone lies."

"Don't you know anything about the Goddess of balance, *truth*, and passing? Jord doesn't lie. Not to us."

"You believe she is the Goddess?"

"Without a doubt, don't you?"

August paused, letting himself think about it. The thing about Gods and Goddesses was that it was all about belief. They didn't need to prove themselves; it was all about faith. "I guess I do."

Tyler smiled. "Jord told me about you. Well, more specifically, Queen Helen and General Natsky's child. The one that triggered our downfall—not that I'm blaming you."

August groaned. "I'm not that person. I can't be their child."

"Why not? Since you've gotten here, you've spoken only of your need to train. Then about helping your friends. You're so focused on what others want you to be that you haven't thought about what you want or who you are away from them."

"And you think I need to kill a king to work that out?"

Tyler shook his head with a smile on his face. "You're not listening to me. Stop looking for people to give you answers or directions. I can't tell you what to do and neither can Jord. As she said in meditation, you won't be fulfilled unless you work out what you want. Maybe getting to the root of the anger will make that clearer."

"You were supposed to be asleep during that conversation," August grumbled.

"I was, but you two talk so loud."

"How am I supposed to know what makes me angry if I don't even know who I really am?"

Tyler feigned stepping, then turned the opposite way and lunged, punching August in the side. "Sounds like you need to go on a little adventure of self-discovery."

25

Evelyn

The king's outrage was palpable throughout the castle. It didn't matter that he holed up in his quarters. Everyone felt his burning fury as if it were seeping through the very walls. Anima had attacked Forest's Edge and he was using it to make them villains in the eyes of his devotees. It was obvious he had sent them. When Evelyn arrived at dinner, it was no surprise that she was met with an unwelcome reception.

The king made his displeasure with the events in Forest's Edge known, summoning a gust of wind that shoved her out of the dining room before she'd barely stepped inside.

His attack on her home city had failed and Evelyn couldn't be happier. There was something poetic about watching a man who hurt her and the country throw a tantrum.

"I won't tolerate disrespect!" the king growled, using his magic to slam the doors shut in her face. "Not from that damned forest city and not from you!"

Evelyn stared at the closed doors; her body heated from the shock of being thrown out before even properly arriving. But the king's dismissal did nothing to dampen her proud and rebellious mood. Sticking her tongue out at the door like a bratty child, Evelyn was faced with the fortunate fact that she now had the night to herself and wouldn't have to endure any unwanted company.

"I guess I'll go back to my room," she told her sentry, pleased she would not have to endure another dinner.

She grinned to herself as they made their way back upstairs, the expression only faltering when she was dragged into an alcove.

"I'll be quick," Louise said, smiling brightly at the sentry.

Evelyn's sentry grunted, stepping away to give them some privacy but remaining in view.

"What's wrong?"

"Why aren't you at dinner?" Louise asked, clasping Evelyn's hands in hers.

"His attack on my home failed, so he is throwing a tantrum like a child," Evelyn said, unable to hide her smile. She was so proud of her city for not only fighting back but winning too.

"His reckoning will come sooner than you think."

"I hope so. He deserves everything coming to him."

Louise nodded. "Valmenessia will be freed from his tyranny."

Evelyn liked the sound of that—a Valmenessia without King Dominic, where everyone was treated equally and with respect. It sounded like a dream, and one she wanted desperately to come true. She was glad to find Louise shared her joy at the king's small defeat.

"Lady Royd," Louise whispered. "I have found a way for you to escape."

"Leave?" Evelyn asked, her eyebrows raising.

"Yes," Louise said, looking around carefully. "Not now, but soon. We will witness the new age of Valmenessia together."

"Really? You're going to get me out of here? I can go home?"

"Soon. Keep your head down and don't let the royal family bother you. A little longer and we will be rid of this place." She released Evelyn's hands, taking a step back. "I have to go. I'll bring something for you to eat later."

"I don't want you to get into trouble for me," Evelyn said, biting her lip. "I'm not hungry anyway."

Louise nodded; her expression bright. "I'll see you in the morning with an extra-large serving of breakfast then."

Louise smiled again and left Evelyn with her mind in a frenzy. First the victory in Forest's Edge and now a chance to go home. To say she was excited would have been an understatement. The world had looked so bleak and now everything was becoming bright once more. The king was not as strong as he thought he was and soon she would be with her family and friends again. She would see August and she'd be back where she belonged. Her time in Royal Bay was running out, which meant if she wanted to explore the secret passageway Lady Elizabeth had used, then she'd have to go soon.

Inside her room, Evelyn sprawled over the sofa by the fire. Each day had been filled with *pretending* and she was glad for the reprieve. If she could calm herself from the excitement of going home that was. With a sigh, she closed her eyes and imagined being at home by the fire at the Manor instead.

The next thing she knew, Evelyn was waking up to a knock at her door. Her stomach grumbled as she rubbed her eyes and stretched, hoping Louise had brought her something to eat after all. Evelyn waited for her to enter, but another knock sounded on the wooden door. Louise never waited for an answer after knocking, which meant whoever was on the other side wasn't the handmaid. Interest piqued, Evelyn padded to the door and opened it expecting to see Poppy happy that Forest's Edge was safe.

"Oh."

Her golden eyes widened when she found Prince Kylan holding a silver tray. He was dressed in simple attire; a plain maroon shirt and black slacks.

"I assume you were denied dinner in here also," he said, lifting the tray a little higher, his blue eyes sparkling. "Hungry?"

Evelyn eyed him suspiciously. She hadn't seen him after he'd abruptly left the food tasting for their arranged wedding.

"After our last encounter, I'm surprised you're here," she said, reaching for the tray. He stepped out of reach, moving into her room.

Prince Kylan ignored her, placing the tray of food on a table. "You know… you never say my name," he said.

"I do."

He shook his head. "No, you don't. I've never heard you call me anything."

"Is that why you're here?" she asked. "To tell me to start calling you 'Your Highness'?"

"Just Kylan will do," he said simply, turning back to her.

"It's improper for me to call you by your first name."

"You call Harley by her first name."

"That's different."

He laughed softly. "If you say so."

223

"What do you want?" Evelyn asked, folding her arms over her chest. As an afterthought, she added. "Kylan."

He shrugged, though she didn't miss the upward tug of his lips before he moved to stand beside the windows and turned his back to her once more.

Surrendering to the fact that he was staying, Evelyn shut the door and sat on the sofa, ignoring the tray of food even though her stomach grumbled.

"You believe your father was a good person."

"He was better than good," she said, her heart fluttering sadly at the thought of her father. She missed him dearly. The time since his passing hadn't eased the pain she felt when he entered her thoughts. He'd been stolen from her, not by Nora, whom he was trying to help. She never blamed Nora. But by the king who had created the awful situation in the first place. "He was caring and thoughtful. Not just towards his family but to every person he came in contact with. He was a true ruler and a dear friend."

"You're lucky you had a good father."

"I know."

"I'm not," Kylan stated. His shoulders sagged, creasing his pressed shirt. "I wish I could say my father wasn't always this way, that there had once been a kinder, more tolerant side to him, but other than growing crueller, his view of the world has always been this way."

He looked out at the darkened sky instead of facing her. Evelyn didn't speak, waiting for him to continue in his own time. He dropped his gaze from the window, looking at his hands as if they held the answers to his unspoken questions.

"Before my mother died he didn't push such punitive agendas. Whether that was because he was still planning it all, I don't know. He was always talking about how the Elementum were superior, but he never enforced that belief. Then my mother was killed by the General and everything got worse."

"I hope you're not blaming her death for the king's genocide of the Mors Alvs simply for the crime of existing," Evelyn said. Her golden eyes were wide and her tone firm as she spoke. "One terrible act doesn't excuse his behaviour. Your father is a horrible man."

"He is." Kylan frowned, nodding his head. "It was only a matter of time before he chose a race to target. My mother's death was both a tragedy and a convenience for him."

He ran a hand over his face and sighed deeply. They were silent for a moment. The impact of what his father had done fell like a heavy weight over them.

"My brother and I had a disagreement."

"I heard," she said. "He thinks you need to remember your place as a diplomat, not a future king."

"He is not receptive to my ideas just yet," Kylan said confidently. "But I think with time he will come around."

"Please don't tell me you're still pinning all your hopes on your brother being unlike your father?"

"He is a good man."

"You aren't seeing him clearly," she replied. "Can you consider him a good man if what he does only benefits the elite? He wants to continue what your father has started. He said it himself. He might not be the same as your father, but his goals are."

"I will get him to listen to my ideas."

"And what are they? To let Elementum keep the other races as pets?"

"For starters, I want to reform the law, allowing members from every race and city to have input and I want to review our economy so the rich cannot hoard their wealth while others are starving."

"Kylan—"

"I have others too. Unrestricted access to education, assistance in building homes and businesses…"

"Kylan, there is no way he will accept those terms," Evelyn said softly. Kylan's ideas were exactly what the country needed, but there was no way his brother would agree to them.

Kylan shook his head. "You don't know that for sure."

"I won't bet people's lives on a gamble that he might do the right thing when all signs point in the other direction." Evelyn pushed to her feet and moved towards him. "Listen to me. You have great plans, but no one here will see them come to fruition. Not while they all benefit from Elementum holding exclusive power."

"I have to try."

"Then try elsewhere. My sister would listen to you."

"No, I have the resources to solidify my ideas here."

"Seeds won't grow if you don't have someone watering them," Evelyn replied. "If you didn't want my help, why are you here?"

"Because I want you to understand me better."

"Why?"

"I promised I wouldn't pretend with you anymore."

"It isn't with me you are pretending." She sighed defeatedly. He wasn't ready to accept that there were no ears in Royal Bay willing to listen. "You are living in an imaginary world where you think you can change the minds of grown men who show no inclination to do anything other than what they want."

"I'm going to help Xander see," Kylan replied. "Stop thinking the worst of everyone."

Evelyn sighed, realising this conversation was going around in circles. "Kylan, please leave," she demanded, pointing at the door. "I refuse to have this conversation with you. If you cared at all, you would fix what your father and brother are breaking instead of pretending like you can get them to hear you."

"Xander will listen."

Evelyn shook her head. "One day you will wake up and realise you've spent your life begging him to listen rather than having made any change at all." She strode towards the door, opening it wide. "You need to go."

Kylan looked at his hands and said, "it was a mistake to come here anyway." He plucked at the cuffs of his shirt and rolled his shoulders as he moved towards the door. He stopped before her gazing over her features. "I'm sorry to have wasted your time."

She nodded stiffly and he left. His wind magic tugged the door from her grip and closed it behind him. She rubbed her temples, sighing. She couldn't imagine what it was like to be in a family where your ideas were ignored. The feeling only made Evelyn long to be home with her mother and sister more. *Soon.* First, she had a few things to do.

Evelyn waited until after midnight before stepping out onto her balcony. The salty breeze ruffled her skirts and she frowned at the drop below. It was far. Waves violently crashed against the cliffside. Excitement and apprehension warred inside her as she wiped her sweaty palms against her sides. She was dressed in her most practical clothes, which weren't all that sensible. A plain midnight blue dress.

Her door was guarded, leaving this the only way out. Swallowing hard, she tore her gaze from the water and looked to the balcony on her right. Was finding out what Lady Elizabeth was up to worth risking her life? Evelyn shook her head. Of course, it was. The woman was up to something and from what she'd seen and heard since being here, the woman was very close to King Dominic. It was more than likely Lady Elizabeth was aware of the king's plans, or even helping to orchestrate them. Fear would not stop her from doing the right thing. From being part of the change.

Kylan may have been content to do nothing, but she was not.

Evelyn took a few deep breaths and clenched her fists. Her legs wobbled as she climbed onto the railing, avoiding looking down and reminding herself that she was a Lys Alv. Like August had said all those weeks ago when she'd been afraid atop a double-storey building if she fell her magic would heal her. Though the stakes were much greater this time—and much higher.

Evelyn moved from one balcony to another, peering into each room to track her route along the hallway. Her heart raced each time she had to climb between the balconies as the waters churned below waiting for her to fall. She ignored the sea and glanced up, searching for patrolling sentries as they moved around the perimeter. She'd spent enough time in the castle to map out their routines. She hoped their grey uniforms meant they weren't as trained or skilled as the silver sentries she was used to seeing.

Evelyn looked through the window and recognised the empty sitting room. She was sure the next balcony would be the last and the prospect of going inside was more desirable than anything at that moment. Pressing her back to the window, she waited for the sentries to pass her by, but there was still no sound of their nearness. The wind whipped around her and she shivered from the cold as she waited.

When the sentries didn't appear at the point they were supposed to Evelyn began to panic. Had they spotted her and were now waiting to apprehend her from the balcony?

Dread pooled in her stomach. She was not cut out for spying, but she couldn't remain on the balcony forever. She bit her lip and stepped forward, ready to accept her fate. Her heart raced in her chest as she heard the sentries above. She jumped back against the wall. Their conversation didn't falter as they moved on and out of earshot.

Evelyn stepped to the next balcony, eager to move on. Her foot slipped and she cried out, throwing her hands out to grasp the railing before she fell. The crashing waves below drowned out her scream but she prayed to Nyssa the sentries didn't hear or see her.

Evelyn's knuckles whitened as she clutched the wood. The fall would kill her; she knew it for certain. There was no way she'd heal in time if she fell and no one was around to help her. She could feel her hands slipping.

Would she see her father again if she died? Her aunt and cousin?

Tears streamed from her eyes. She wanted so badly to hear his voice and be held in his arms once more. She thought of her mother and sister. They were still part of this world and, as much as she wanted to be with her father, she was not ready to leave yet. She steeled her resolve and pulled herself up with all her strength. Her legs trembled as she dropped to her knees over the railing, placing her hands on the firm ground.

She did it. She was alive and she'd just proven she was capable of saving herself.

After a moment's calm, she stood and wiped her face with her hands. Evelyn straightened, feeling proud of what she had achieved and opened the door from the balcony to the hall. She slipped back into the darkened castle and moved on quiet feet toward the passageway Lady Elizabeth had used.

Evelyn found herself staring at the portrait of the Goddess Thyra. The woman with fiery red hair and bright blue eyes was cast in shadow, making her smile seem villainous as she looked down upon Evelyn.

She took hold of the edge of the wooden frame and pulled it towards her. At first, it didn't move, but she tugged a little firmer and the portrait swung from the stone wall to reveal a dark tunnel within.

Evelyn swallowed hard and stepped into the darkness.

26

Evelyn

Evelyn barely breathed as she made her way through the passage. She was terrified of being caught, especially without any credible excuse for being there. The tunnel was narrow and Evelyn shuffled in almost perfect darkness through tight angles that presumably wrapped around rooms in the castle. Cobwebs hung from the ceiling and Evelyn cringed at the thought of spiders crawling over her, so she did her best to push it from her mind and focus on the task at hand. After she squeezed past a particularly tight corner, the passage widened enough to fit two people abreast and continued more comfortably.

Voices sounded from further down and, with each step Evelyn took, they became clearer until she could hear the conversation from someone's room. Her Lys Alv ears were once again coming in handy as she settled in to listen from the secret place.

"Listen to me, Dominic," came a woman's voice. It was familiar, though Evelyn couldn't quite place it. "You need to command your Alta to deal with the Makers' Murders throughout Valmenessia. It should be a priority."

"Don't you dare tell me what to do," the king replied, instantly recognisable. No one spoke with such condescending authority as he did. "I will command my subjects as I see fit."

"The devotees are not to be taken lightly," the woman urged. "They are more than a misguided religious group. They are out of control. Something needs to be done."

"See, this is why you are no longer in power," he said condescendingly. "You frighten easily over nothing. The Alta are dealing with the murders in Royal Bay."

"But in the other cities—"

"The lords and ladies have it under control."

"You need to see this as a true threat!"

"I do not need to see anything," he growled. "Your time ruling over the Elementum is over. The people may pray to you, Thyra, but that is all. Your eternal life has made you weak. This country needs a strong king who elevates the Elementum. The people need me, not you. *I* am the future."

Evelyn couldn't believe her ears. Did she hear the king right? The Goddess Thyra was alive and on the other side of the wall? It had to be a mistake. Perhaps the woman was named after the Goddess. It wasn't common, yet it was possible. But eternal life...

"I am your advisor, and you should heed my words," the woman replied. "I am far from weak and my long life has granted me experience in such matters that you are a fool to ignore."

The wall shuddered and Evelyn jumped back as the voices became louder.

"Don't you ever speak to me that way," the king bellowed. "I am your king."

"And I am a Goddess," the woman replied. Heat seeped through the walls and forced Evelyn back against the one behind her. "I offer advice and speak to you out of courtesy, but remember this, we are not equals. I will only tolerate your childish tantrums so long as you are useful to me. Have I made myself clear?"

Evelyn heard the king mumble something. How quickly the power had switched on the other side of the wall.

"Now that we have cleared that up, send your Alta to the other cities." There was no reply, but Thyra didn't hesitate before continuing. "We must also deal with a problem closer to home."

The wall shattered with a loud bang, throwing Evelyn to the side, along with rubble that cut her skin and bruised her flesh. She groaned as blood dripped from her head, wetting her hair and the side of her face. Her healing magic instantly went to work sealing the wounds shut as her light sought out injuries.

Hands gripped her by the hair and Evelyn cried out as she was dragged inside the room. Maps of the country and the larger cities covered the walls, lit by a candelabra hanging over a long table covered in paper and wooden figurines. Evelyn was shoved into a chair with Lady Elizabeth standing before her. The woman looked regal in a crimson gown that matched her flowing red hair. She appeared as a living flame, her blue eyes burning with emphasised intensity. King Dominic was behind her speaking gruffly to his silver sentries, though Evelyn couldn't think past the woman before her.

"You're the Goddess Thyra?" Evelyn blurted. Her body trembled beneath that heated gaze.

How had she never noticed the similarities before between Lady Elizabeth and the Elementum Goddess? Not that she would ever have thought that the Gods and Goddesses walked among them. There were plenty of people who could have passed for any of the deities, but finding out this woman was Thyra clicked into place like a bolt sliding home.

Thyra smiled, flashing her teeth. "The one and only."

"How dare you spy on me," King Dominic growled, charging forward and slapping Evelyn hard on the face. Blood pooled in her mouth before it began to heal. "Stupid bitch! I have given you the opportunity of a lifetime and you throw it back in my face."

Evelyn shrank before the king. If she were brave she'd shout or fight back. But if there was one thing Evelyn knew, it was her limits, and she'd been on the wrong end of his wrath before. The king and the Goddess were far stronger than her. She would never stand a chance. Fighting and screaming would only make them angrier with her and that was something she didn't want.

"I've misjudged you," he continued, straightening and smoothing out his shirt. He turned to Thyra and a muscle twitched in his square jaw. "Perhaps you are right. I do underestimate certain threats. I won't be making that mistake again."

"Are you going to kill me?" Evelyn managed. Her voice trembled with each word. She looked between the two people who had more power than they deserved.

The king smiled cruelly, "I still have use for you, but you do need to be taught a lesson. I have given you warnings, but it appears they didn't sink in."

A knock sounded at the door before a silver sentry opened it and bowed even though the king had his back to the man.

"We have her, Your Majesty," he said.

"Bring her to me," King Dominic commanded with a condescending flick of his fingers, not bothering to acknowledge the sentry.

The sentry waved behind him and two guards dragged Poppy through the threshold. She was still in her nightgown. Her loose plait swung limply as she was brought towards the king. Poppy's wide eyes flickered from the king to Evelyn and the blood drained from her face as understanding dawned on her.

Fear churned Evelyn's stomach, her hands becoming clammy as she looked at Poppy. They'd speculated as to why the king had wanted Poppy in Royal Bay and now it was clear. Poppy was Evelyn's weakness.

"The thing is," the king began, pacing back and forth with his hands behind his back. "Whilst I may underestimate a threat, I always have leverage."

Evelyn's heart sank, and she shook her head as she said, "please."

"Please, what?" King Dominic sneered like a feral beast. "Regretting your choices now that your little friend is involved?" He laughed, Thyra joining in with sparkling eyes. "What did you think she was here for?"

Poppy whimpered as the sentry shoved her to her knees.

Evelyn made to move from her seat but was instantly held down by an invisible force. Someone was using their wind magic on her. She was outnumbered by the Elementum.

"I begged you not to do anything," Poppy cried. "Why couldn't you just listen?"

"I'm sorry," Evelyn said as tears fell from her eyes. "Please don't hurt her, I'll do anything you want."

"It is a shame really," the king said, ignoring Evelyn's pleas. He gripped Poppy's chin in his large hand and turned her head from side to side. "Not only is she an Elementum, but she is quite pretty too." He sighed, his hazel eyes meeting Evelyn's as he shook his head. "If only you had behaved."

With a swift movement, he drew a shiny dagger from his belt and plunged it into Poppy's chest.

"No! Please! No!" Evelyn screamed. "Poppy!"

Over and over, the king thrust a new hole into her friend, all the while grinning. Blood splattered on the king and sentry holding Poppy. Evelyn struggled against the magic holding her, but it was no use. The king laughed, wiping the dagger on his shirt, and released Poppy. Her body fell to the floor and her blood began pooling around her.

"Next time," Thyra said, leaning down towards Evelyn, their faces inches apart, "you will think twice about disrespecting those above your station."

She stepped back and Evelyn's eyes shifted to where a woman appeared, dressed in a black uniform with her long blonde hair tied up in a ponytail.

"Rana," the king barked. "Have the Alta fetch another from Forest's Edge to keep this one in line."

Rana nodded, taking in Evelyn and Poppy's still form on the floor, though she didn't appear shocked by what she was seeing.

"Oh, and make it an Anima," he added. "It'd be a shame to kill another Elementum."

Evelyn stood in a black gown beside Kylan and whispered prayers of passing. Bitter rage still simmered inside her. King Dominic had spun a lie that declared Poppy's death a Makers' Murder. The nobles took to the story like bees to pollen, their voices joining Evelyn's in prayer as they filled the small temple.

She hated the idea of Poppy being buried so far away from their home, but what was she to do? Evelyn wasn't sure she would ever escape now. She was afraid of risking Louise's life. The handmaid was Evelyn's only ally now and the thought of her being hurt for helping Evelyn kept her up at night. Not that it was the only reason Evelyn lacked sleep. Her mind was busy enough grieving for all she'd lost. All she wanted was to shut her brain off.

Warmth touched her hand, and she looked down to see Kylan's fingers wrapped around hers. She didn't want or need his sympathy. Tugging away from his grip, she clasped her hands before her and continued praying. A small voice inside her wondered if there was any point. If Thyra was alive, maybe the other Gods and Goddesses were too and, if that were the case, Evelyn doubted any of them were answering prayers. If they were all here walking the land then none of them cared enough to stop what King Dominic and Thyra were doing to the people.

The prayers ended and Evelyn was led from the temple, leaving Poppy's body lying on the cold stone altar in an elegant black gown. She spotted Zaim. His face was expressionless, but when their eyes met he dared to smirk at her. She hated him more than words could describe. Poppy would *never* have been in Royal Bay if it weren't for him.

Kylan appeared, blocking Zaim from her view and gently taking her hand before she could attack the Alta. He led her towards a carriage, helping her in and shutting the door.

"I'm sorry for your loss," he said as the carriage moved up the street.

"Won't your father be mad that we left before him?" Evelyn asked, ignoring his sympathies.

"Probably." Kylan shrugged, leaning forward and reaching for her hand. "Evelyn—"

"What?"

"You don't need to be strong in front of me. You just lost your friend."

"I didn't lose her. I know exactly where she has gone and how she got there," Evelyn snapped. "How I deal with that is none of your business."

"*You* are my business," he said, maintaining his closeness, his hand still outstretched towards her. "You're suppressing your emotions."

Evelyn glared at him. "Again, what I do with my emotions is my choice."

"It's not healthy to bottle it all up."

"I'm not."

"Your father died a few weeks before you arrived in Royal Bay. The Anima attack on Forest's Edge must have you worried about who and how many casualties there were. Now your best friend has passed too," he said.

"I'm well aware of the losses I have had to endure because of your family," she replied coldly. "I am allowed to deal with all this how I see fit."

"You are, but you are blocking it out. You're so invested in what is happening in the country instead of dealing with your grief. I can see it in your eyes. The fight within to feel your grief fully."

"You want me to curl into a ball and cry?" she asked, narrowing her eyes at him.

"I want you to feel it," he said. "Whatever that looks like."

"I do."

He shook his head. "No, you don't. You let it fuel your anger towards my father, but there is more to grief than that. You have been held here against your will and other than yelling at me, you act almost as if it's a typical situation."

"Maybe that's what I choose to show you."

"Really? Because Harley thinks you are fitting in perfectly. That you're so compliant," he replied, his bright blue eyes holding hers. "Are you really happy for her to control your life? For my father to do so and kill the people you love?"

"Stop assuming you know what I feel. That you know what's best for me."

"Stop hiding."

"Fuck you," Evelyn shouted, surprising herself at the anger she directed at him.

She lashed out, making to slap him across the face only to have him catch her wrist. They stared at each other, neither moving. Her breaths came quick and she felt tears in her eyes.

"It's not fair," she said, her voice barely audible.

"I know," he replied, releasing her wrist and running his fingers gently over her cheek. She leaned into his touch.

Closing her eyes, Evelyn let herself feel. She hadn't properly grieved for her father and now with Poppy gone, she found it hard to breathe. A sob escaped her and she let herself cry for the two people she loved so very much. Instead of shoving it all down like she'd grown accustomed to doing, she let her grief tear through her. Her heart hurt and she worried that now she'd opened the door she'd never be able to close it again.

Strong arms wound around her, and she was pulled against a hard chest as she cried for her loved ones.

27

Nora

Phillip's disappearance had
flimsy scrap of evidence
without a fucking tr
eyes, but her girlfriend w
working on replacing wh
her work. Not only di
cells with their ta
who needed th
the Anim
attacki
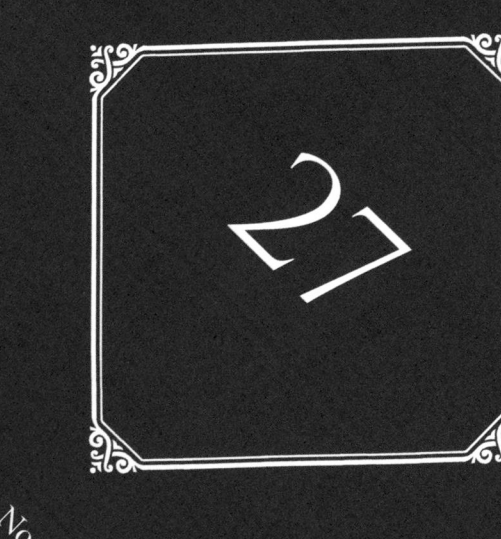

Nora couldn't help but feel that even though they had won, they had lost too. The death toll was high and the survivors were scared. Morale was low as people prepared for the worst. The king's manipulation of the Anima had opened a whole new set of terrifying possibilities.

How were they supposed to fight against their own people?

After the attack, the Faction meetings consisted of war strategies and no longer took place at the Faction headquarters. Instead, guards, Faction members and anyone else eager to fight against the king were invited to the Manor.

Nora stood in the ballroom, the faction banner hanging high above all their heads, unsurprised by how many people had arrived for the meeting. Forest's Edge was angry and sought revenge, despite their fear.

"Good turnout," Florence said beside Nora as she looked over the gathered crowd.

"I heard someone say there's a line out the door," Sage said on Nora's other side. "Looks like the whole city has turned up."

"The king got the opposite of what he was hoping for," Nora replied with a smug smile. "Most look ready to march to Royal Bay and kill him themselves."

"They'll have to get in line," Gemma said as she passed on her way to the makeshift stage where Jasmine stood dressed in a gown of forest green. Her hair was pinned at the sides with the length falling down her back. The lady of Forest's Edge held her chin high as her brown eyes moved over her people. Jasmine was the image of a true ruler. Her appearance put those she cared for at ease, but it was her fortitude and kindness that earned the respect of all in the room. Omari stood beside her in black trousers and a coat the same colour as his lady with his hands clasped behind his back. Like the woman by his side, he looked refined but, more importantly, approachable. Someone for the people to look up to.

Gemma approached Jasmine and they clasped hands. The tension Nora had witnessed the last time she'd seen the two women together was gone. Omari raised his hands and the room quietened.

"Thank you all for coming," Jasmine began, stepping forward and smiling at those gathered. "I am filled with hope and determination at seeing so many faces here. The king tried to knock us down, but he underestimated the people of Forest's Edge. We are a formidable force not to be dismissed so easily!"

The crowd cheered and Nora found herself joining in, swept up in the victory with everyone else. She was part of this city now.

"I am repulsed by his forceable control of the avian Anima that attacked our home," she continued, as she fisted a hand. "His laws are bigoted towards the Anima, but still he uses them to enforce his will. It is proof of what a despicable and hypocritical man he is. I have sent word for other city leaders to come and witness themselves what the king has done to the Anima here. They will see that the king holds them captive and forces their hands to further his agenda. I'm certain once they see the tattoos we will gain more allies."

"As it stands, Fellbun, Kaldom, and the Northern Wolf pack are allied with Forest's Edge and more refugees flock from the southern cities. However, we can no longer wait idly to fall into the king's hands."

"He will come for us again. I have decided to merge the city guard and this division of the Faction. Gemma has been appointed General of the Forest's Edge Army and together we will lead this city and the rest of the north to victory over the king. We will not let him take Valmenessia."

Everyone erupted in applause as Jasmine stepped back, giving Gemma the centre of the stage. The Lys Alv strode forward with her head held high and confidence in her stride.

"I do not take this position lightly," she said, looking out at the crowd. "Lady Royd has declared we press an attack and I support her with my whole heart. Volunteers from Forest's Edge and Northern Alliance will move to take back Midskopas. We will hold the central city and use it to prevent the king from gaining any ground in the north. Guards will visit each home to ask for expressions of interest. We will not force any of you to fight if you are not able."

"What about the avian Anima?" someone called from the crowd. "They didn't need to travel through Midskopas to reach us."

"You're right," she said. "We have weaponry being made to defend ourselves from another attack. However, we cannot let that keep us from our plans. We cannot remain on the defensive."

Gemma continued her speech. Then after a time, Jasmine took the floor once more and provided updates on what was happening around the country. But Nora had stopped paying attention. The prospect of going to Midskopas was far too distracting. If she helped free the city, it would be a big step in making amends for all she'd done as an Alta. Helping protect Forest's Edge had been a step in the right direction, but taking away some of the power she had helped to create would be a leap. Nora wouldn't be able to bring back the lives she'd taken, but she could stop King Dominic from ruining any more.

"What do you think?" Florence asked, bouncing on the balls of her feet once the announcements were over and the ballroom began to clear. "Reckon either of you will come to Midskopas with us?"

"Us?" Sage quirked a brow. "You're going?"

Florence nodded.

"I'm going to volunteer," Nora said with a nod. "I want to help."

"I'll come with you," Sage replied.

"You know you can't," Nora said with a shake of her head. "You need to continue working on another pendant filled with that dust stuff. The Anima are relying on you to free them from the king's hold."

Sage sagged slightly and said, "I hate that you're right. But I hate Phillip more. I can't believe that old bastard ran off with everything. I hope the king kills him for his troubles."

"Still think he went to the king?" Florence asked.

"Most likely. I can't imagine where else he'd go," Nora replied. "The king will want that kind of power. Think about it. It's the surest way for him to rid the world of all the Anima and anyone else who grows too powerful."

"That and he wants to prevent us from possessing the pendant and the knowledge to make more."

"Luckily we have you, so he can go stick that little victory up his ass," Nora said, kissing Sage lightly on the cheek. "I know you'll piece it all back together soon."

"I hope so," Sage sighed.

Florence smiled. "We have faith in you. This is the rise of the Northern Alliance. Nothing's going to stand in our way now. Not the king, not his sentries and not the King's Guild."

Nora grinned. "I'll drink to that. Speaking of which, we should go and do just that. Right now."

"Smooth change in topic," Sage laughed. "Barely noticeable."

"Did I hear something about a drink?" Will asked, striding towards them. "Sounds like a fantastic idea."

"Of course, *you* overheard that part," Florence teased, taking Will's hand. "Did you plan that?"

Nora watched as her friends walked away, letting herself enjoy the small happiness before they were to face a world of horrors.

Nora walked down the steps to the prison cells. She hated being back there. She wasn't afraid of being behind bars. It was more that she didn't like the reminder of who she had been. The last time Nora had walked the dark corridors, she had been a slave to King Dominic. A spy and, worst of all, a murderer. She never wanted to be that person again.

Sage must have sensed her unease as she slipped her palm into Nora's. The touch was instantly calming and Nora was glad Sage had agreed to accompany her. It had been hard to ask—each time she was vulnerable with Sage, she worried it would make the woman walk away. That it'd be too much. Sage never left though and Nora was learning that the more she let Sage in, the tighter Sage held on to her.

"Thanks," Nora said in a low voice.

With a warm smile from Sage, they continued. Nora's orb of flame bobbed above them as they followed Gemma through the foul-smelling place to the end of the row. Two figures dressed in black sat behind the bars in side-by-side cells. If Nora was a normal person, she might have felt a twinge of sorrow for Jolene and Owen… after all, she'd known them most of her life. But because of that fact, she felt nothing but Satisfaction. The two Alta had been cruel to her and August and seeing them filthy and trapped was like a gift.

"See if you can get them to talk while you're at it," Gemma said before leaving Sage and Nora alone with the prisoners.

Nora stepped forward, placing her hands on the cool bars and looking down at Jolene where she rested against the bars separating the two cells.

"Come to gloat?" Jolene asked, lifting her gaze to Nora. "Because we both know you won't be getting any information from us."

"We could always cut your arms off," Nora replied casually. "See if that works in removing the tattoos."

Jolene didn't flinch. She was a Lys Alv and losing a limb was more an inconvenience than a threat when one could be regrown.

"You can try," Jolene said with a wicked grin. "It would spice up the monotony of this place, though the ink would reappear with the limb and we'd be back at the beginning."

"Why are you here?" Owen asked. He sat deeper in the cell than Jolene, his back pressed against the stone wall.

"You may not be free from King Dominic yet, but I've been told your tattoos have faded," Nora stated. "I know when August's were disappearing, he started to feel more like himself. I noticed the change in him and I just wanted to see if I could glimpse the real you."

"You know us," Jolene replied with a roll of her eyes. "With or without the tattoos, nothing will change. We became Alta because of who we are."

Owen shifted, lifting his head to look Nora in the eyes. "We aren't like you and August. The king always had to command you two to do every little thing. I remember the first time you came back from a mission. You'd killed the target but left witnesses. We had to go and clean up your mess."

"Shut up Owen," Jolene snapped. "Don't you dare tell her anything."

"I'll tell her whatever I fucking please. You're not in control of me and soon the king won't be either. Without the tattoos I have allegiances to no one," he said.

"I remember our first mission. Rana said we did a good job," Nora said before Jolene could continue arguing with Owen. "She would have punished us if we stuffed up like that."

"You two are the closest thing that woman ever had to children," Owen scoffed, tilting his head back and looking at the light trickling in through the narrow window above his head. "It's pathetic really."

"Her tattoos wouldn't let her favour us like you're saying," Nora insisted. What he was saying couldn't have been true. There was no way Rana could get away with something like that. "If we did wrong by the king she would have done something."

"You were punished plenty," he replied. "But when commands weren't black and white she always protected you and made one of us do the dirty work. After your first mission, King Dominic had to give you specific commands to be more violent, and more murderous. Seems his child experiments had too much heart, unlike the rest of us."

"That's enough!" Jolene shouted, rising to her feet. She gripped the bars between the two cells and shook them as she looked down at Owen. "Do you think by telling her this shit that she will save you? That these people will be lenient on you?"

Owen shook his head. "I'm telling her because I fucking feel like it."

"They won't take you here," Jolene said with a sneer. "And when we escape, King Dominic won't have you either. You're a dead man living on borrowed time." She looked over her shoulder at Nora. "So are you. No one leaves the Alta."

"Jolene, you really need to pay attention," Nora smirked. "I'm the third person to leave. You and Owen will be the fourth and fifth."

"I will never leave the service of the king," Jolene snapped, spit flying with her words.

"Then you will die with him," Sage said, and Nora turned to see her girlfriend had stepped closer and was narrowing her gaze at Jolene.

"Thanks for the chat, Owen," Nora said without turning around. She took Sage's hand and they walked out of the darkness together.

28

August

Jord paced around August as he tried to focus on his magic rather than being blindfolded in a room with someone he barely knew. That Jord had shown him a table of weapons before restricting his sight wasn't helping. The sound of the fire burning in the hearth was all he could hear.

"Focus," Jord commanded from his left.

"Kind of hard when you could stab me at any moment," he replied, earning a chuckle from the Goddess. He'd been trained to endure torture as an Alta, but the training never took away the pain or apprehension.

"That's the whole point of this exercise," she replied, sounding further away. "Pull your magic back in."

He did as she said, drawing it back to himself, only to have his fingers burn painfully.

"Fuck!" August hissed, darting to the side and bringing his hand to his chest.

"I told you to rein it in," Jord said simply. "I can still feel it."

August let his magic flow back into himself, determined not to let it simmer beneath the surface.

"Good."

Jord's soft steps disappeared from him once again and he thought about the table and her next weapon of choice. They continued the process. Each time, August was instructed to let his magic reach out a little further and she would do something to cause him pain whilst he was trying to bring it back to himself. He could feel his anger rising but stamped it down. August was determined not to be controlled by it. He recalled his breathing techniques.

"Summon it again. Only this time let it go out even farther," Jord said. "If you are losing control of it, let yourself."

Again, August did as she asked, summoning his magic and letting it move out of him. In his mind, he imagined dark smoke curling through the air as it pushed out. He could feel it searching for others' magic, igniting the thrill of the hunt in him.

"Nicely done," Jord said. "Extinguish it."

Like pulling an invisible rope, he tugged it back and, like every time before, it did his bidding. He continued forcing it to bend to his will, only to have a sharp pain burst from the side of his thigh. August cried out and crumpled to the ground. Then, resting his weight on his healthy knee, he tore the blindfold from his eyes. Rage burned through him.

"Fuck!" August snarled, looking down at his thigh where blood seeped around the handle of a blade. He knew instantly that it wasn't fatal, but that didn't lessen the pain. "This is fucking bullshit!"

His magic grew with his rage and he didn't fight it. Instead, he felt it moving beyond the walls, searching for health to mend his wound.

Jord came to stand before him with lips moving, but he couldn't hear a word. He was too angry to give a shit about what she was saying to justify this sort of training. He'd left the Alta and its fucked-up way of doing things to be here.

"Rein it in," Jord commanded, her voice breaking through his thoughts. She looked very much like a Goddess as she stood before him in her flowing black gown with the emerald rings in her dark eyes glowing. "You will not use your magic on anyone here."

August gritted his teeth and narrowed his gaze at her.

"Now."

With a snarl, he focused on pulling his magic back, though this time, it put up a fight. Like a wild beast fighting against a leash around its neck. He tried to think of things that didn't make him angry, like kissing Evelyn or hanging out with Nora. With every memory that flashed through his mind the beast calmed and soon, he could rein his magic in entirely.

"We'll work on it," Jord said as August panted. She reached out a hand. "Take my health."

August shook his head. "Just give me a tonic and some stitches."

"I am immortal," she replied. "Don't be stubborn and heal yourself."

He held her gaze and their dark eyes took each other in. He weighed the possibility of this being another test, but the pain in his thigh was persuasive. He sighed and took her hand, letting his magic seep from his fingers into hers.

Whilst he could feel that her magic had limits, Jord was like an endless ocean of vitality. If he hadn't believed she was a Goddess before, he certainly did now. He remembered how Felix—Aren—had felt similar when they'd fought back in Forest's Edge—like there was no limit to the life inside of him.

"You felt it," Jord stated, taking her hand back from him once his leg was healed.

August nodded. "Your life doesn't have an end."

"Not a natural one," she frowned and her shoulders sagged.

"The Makers gifted you with immortality."

"No," she replied with a shake of her head. "What they gifted me is a curse."

After an afternoon practising his magic with Jord, August was beyond starving. Unlike the Goddess, he didn't have an endless supply of life to sustain him and his magic. So, he lined up for stew and bread in the dining hall. The scent within the big pots made his mouth water with each step he took towards the front of the line.

The hall was one of the biggest rooms in the temple. There were multiple communal areas, but only one dining hall. Which meant all the Mors Alvs ate together. Long wooden tables ran the length of the room, though August noted how seats were not free to just anyone. Like everywhere else in Valmenessia, the place had a hierarchy. The closer the seat to the head of the table, the more influential the person was.

Mors Alvs gathered over dinner or moved about their business around

August. As much as they were like him, he still felt like an outsider and wasn't sure he'd ever fit in. These people all had a shared experience and he didn't feel like he could relate.

Accepting his serving from one of the kitchen staff on duty, August quickly found Tyler on the far table and headed towards him. Tyler didn't mingle with more prominent groups, mostly hanging out with August or anyone else who appeared to be on their own. It was as though he was drawn to people who didn't quite fit in.

"It's not the best," Tyler said as August sat down. He angled his head towards the stew with a grimace and his brown hair fell over his eyes.

"I don't care," August replied simply, picking up his spoon. "It smells good and I'll still eat it if it tastes like shit. I'm starving."

Tyler laughed. "I'm sure the cooks would love to hear that compliment."

"Don't go making any trouble, Tyler," a man with silver hair opposite them grumbled. "Or next time, you won't get fed at all."

"Okay, okay," Tyler replied, raising his hands in defence. "I won't tell them August's excellent compliment."

"August?" said an older man, who shuffled closer along the bench. His grey hair was tied into a bun at the base of his neck, and a scar was slashed through one dark eye, the coloured ring no longer visible amongst the black.

Tyler waved a hand in August's direction. "This handsome gentleman."

The older man looked at August and frowned, his wrinkled skin creasing around his lips. "You're the new one."

"Yeah," August said with a shrug. "I arrived a few weeks ago."

"Been hiding from the rest of us?" the man asked, quirking a brow.

"Not intentionally. I've been busy with getting used to the place and with Jord's lessons."

"I hear she has taken a liking to you," he said, dipping a chunk of bread into his bowl of stew. "You must be important for her to spend so much time with you."

"She likes me so much that she stabbed me in the thigh," August replied with a chuckle, dropping his gaze to his meal.

"You don't look like someone who has been stabbed," Tyler said, sitting up straighter in his seat so he could give August a proper look over. He leaned over the table, his grey shirt unintentionally falling into his stew.

"She let me take some of her health."

Tyler whistled. He sat back and wiped the dinner from his shirt with his sleeve. "Yeah, she must really hate you."

"Don't be an idiot," the man grumbled at Tyler. Then he turned to August and asked, "how did you survive out there all this time? Luck?"

"I wouldn't call it that."

"Must be lucky," he said. He pointed to his scarred eye. "Last time I was out in the world, people were trying to murder me."

"Not much has changed," August replied, dropping his gaze to his meal. "It's worse."

"I heard about the Anima. We may be isolated in these freezing mountains, but we still get some gossip. The king is trying to get rid of them as he did us."

"He's taking his time with the Anima," August said. "Making their lives difficult with politics—dogmatic laws and fear-mongering."

"No queen to kill and blame on the Anima to get the people riled up this time around," Tyler added with a shrug of a shoulder.

August frowned and Tyler quickly shot him an apologetic look. He wasn't sure that Queen Helen was his mother, but either way, the story held more weight for him. She was no longer just someone in the history books.

"How did he make everyone turn on Mors Alvs so quickly?" August asked the man. "The death of the queen couldn't have been the only reason."

The man shook his head. "There were rumours about us for a while. Every race has gossips talking about them in a negative light, but for some reason, we always had the worst reputation. Our magic frightens them. People forget everyone is capable of murder. An Elementum could light you on fire and burn you alive, but because their flames also provide heat for warmth and to cook food their magic is viewed as a good thing."

"When the queen died it was just an excuse to let the fear spread," Tyler added, tapping his spoon on the wooden table. "So many people already wanted to hate us."

"But why go slow with the Anima? There are reasons to be afraid of them, too."

"Yes." The man nodded. "However, they pass as humans when they aren't in their shifts. Elementum don't fear those without magic so it's more difficult to convince the people of the Anima being a threat."

"Not to mention, some can shift into adorable little puppies," Tyler said with a pout. "Who could hate that?"

"The king needs to shift the mindset of the population to keep them on his side," the man said, rising from his seat. "It takes time."

August dropped his spoon, no longer hungry. "I'm worried we are running out of it."

The man simply sighed deeply before leaving August and Tyler alone. August looked at his new friend, eyeing him suspiciously.

"You said everyone here knows about my parents and the Alta," August stated.

Tyler nodded. "I did."

"But that man didn't know me."

"It's not common knowledge that the new guy is the same person as the son of the queen," Tyler said, shrugging his lean shoulders. "I don't think Jord has told anyone that particular little detail."

"But she told you?" August leaned on his elbows, his shirt tightening around his muscular arms and eyed Tyler.

Tyler seemed to consider his next words before saying, "we may be friendlier than I have let on. We keep each other… informed about certain things."

August frowned. "You mean I was put in your room so you could spy on me."

"More like to guide and make you feel welcome," Tyler replied, then sighed. "It sounds worse than it is, but I think it's all worked out for the best. We're friends now."

August felt his trust betrayed. Which only made him feel more shit about lying to Nora back in Forest's Edge. Tyler had become a friend and even this small lie stung. August could only imagine how Nora felt about what he'd done to her. Fuck. He needed to see her and make things right.

"August?"

"Yeah, we're friends," August replied, waving Tyler off.

Tyler grinned and jokingly said, "So should we get matching tattoos?"

"Nope," August laughed. "Had one with my last friend and that turned out terribly."

He didn't have many friends and despite how their friendship had come about, August trusted Tyler to have his best interests at heart. In a world where his life was constantly under threat, he wasn't about to go throwing away true friendships. Valmenessia was too dangerous to be alone.

29

Nora

In a couple of hours, Nora would leave Forest's edge. A fact she was regretting committing to. Her bed was too warm and cosy and the idea of lifting the sheets and bracing herself against the Frost Season chill was far from ideal. She stuck the tips of her fingers out of the top of the blanket and summoned a ball of fire to heat the room. Shutting her eyes once more, she curled up and settled in to wait for the temperature to rise. The bed dipped and something gentle touched her head.

Nora blinked her eyes open, finding Sage lying beside her with her fingers running through Nora's hair. The morning sunlight streamed in through her bedroom window and Nora took a moment to appreciate the beautiful woman beside her. Sage's dark, tight curls were tied back with a bright yellow ribbon, giving Nora the perfect view of her face. Nora's gaze roamed slowly over Sage's features. Taking in her small nose, long lashes and bright brown eyes. She wore a new pair of golden glasses. Except this pair was a little too big for her round face.

"You're here early," Nora yawned, resting a hand on Sage's waist. "Not that I'm complaining."

"You leave today and I wanted to say goodbye," Sage said, then grinned wickedly. "So, goodbye!" Snatching back her hand, Sage sat up abruptly and shuffled to the end of the bed.

"No way!" Nora laughed, scrambling out from under the blanket and reached for Sage's arm. She tugged her girlfriend back, determined not to let her leave so easily.

Sage's laughter joined Nora's as she fell back onto the bed. Nora quickly took advantage of the movement, straddling Sage.

"Thank you."

"For what?" Sage asked, tilting her head in confusion.

"For forgiving me," Nora said. "And for helping me to see whom I want to be."

"Nora—"

"I mean it. I was so messed up after losing the tattoos and August leaving. Then having you, Florence, and Will not give up on me and continue to accept me…" Nora shook her head. "I didn't deserve it. I still don't."

"You do," Sage said, reaching out to cup Nora's face. "Being an Alta is not who you are and, after what Owen said, it never was. You deserve to have friends that care for you."

"A girlfriend too?"

"Yeah, one of those. I wonder where you can find yourself one?" Sage teased, a mischievous glimmer in her brown eyes.

"I'm claiming the beautiful woman currently beneath me," Nora replied, tickling Sage's sides.

Nora leaned down and planted a kiss on Sage's plump lips. Despite her giggling, Sage kissed Nora back and her hands moved to stroke Nora's bare thighs.

"If you keep doing that I'm not going to be able to leave."

"Maybe that's the plan," Sage replied, her fingers moving higher until they were squeezing Nora's ass.

"I doubt it," Nora replied, running a hand along the collar of Sage's dress. "You are wearing way too much clothing if it had been."

Nora leaned forward and captured Sage's lips with her own.

Their kiss was gentle. Their lips moved slowly, taking their time to savour each moment. Nora took her girlfriend's face in her hands as she deepened their kiss. There was something about Sage that set Nora on fire in the most amazing way and she couldn't believe how lucky she was to have Sage in her life. Nora broke their kiss and grinned down at Sage; she was the most beautiful person in the whole world.

"Stop staring and kiss me," Sage said, and Nora did as she was told, pressing her lips to Sage's.

This time, their kiss was almost bruising. Sage placed her hands on Nora's hips, but Nora had other ideas. She grabbed the woman's wrists and tugged them above Sage's head. Sage gasped as Nora used her wind magic to hold Sage firm against the bed, completely at her mercy. Nora smiled mischievously as she pressed her lips along Sage's jaw, venturing lower. Sage let out a moan of pleasure when Nora kissed the spot just behind her ear.

Nora sat back up and ran her fingers down the front of Sage's dress, tapping each silver button as she went. Nora bit her lip, looking up at Sage between her lashes. "Can I?"

"Yes," Sage breathed, and Nora pushed the first button from the loop.

She took her time, slowly sliding down Sage's body with each button she undid, her eyes never leaving Sage's.

"Tease," Sage chuckled.

Nora grinned and pushed aside Sage's dress to reveal her naked body beneath. Fuck, this woman was going to be the death of her. Leaning down, Nora placed gentle kisses on each of Sage's breasts before continuing down her stomach. When she reached Sage's tights, Nora gripped the waistband and tugged them down in one fluid motion.

"I want you so bad," Nora said, her eyes taking in every inch of Sage's exposed body. "I've never wanted anything in my life as much as I want you."

"You have me," Sage replied, her breath hitching when Nora crawled back onto the bed, parting Sage's thighs as she did so.

Nora held her girlfriend's eyes as she stopped at Sage's hips and lowered her face before the woman of her dreams. Sage bit her lip as she watched. Nora ran her tongue up Sage's centre, drawing a moan from the woman, her legs opening further, giving Nora greater access. Nora didn't need more of an invitation and moved between Sage's legs, licking and tasting.

"Fuck," Sage breathed as Nora pushed her fingers inside and picked up the pace.

It wasn't long before Sage cried out, her body quivering with pleasure. Nora dropped to the bed beside Sage, released her wind magic on the woman's wrists, and smiled.

"I've been wanting to do that for a while," Nora said as Sage rolled onto her side to face her.

"You're more than welcome to do it whenever you like," Sage replied, and Nora laughed before leaning in to kiss her tenderly.

"I wish, but I need to get ready to leave," Nora said leaning back. She traced her fingers over the soft skin of Sage's cheek. Nora wasn't sure she'd ever get enough of Sage, but she had to maintain some sense of control or she'd be lost to the woman forever. "I'm thinking signing up to go to Midskopas was a bad idea."

"I'll be here when you get back," Sage replied, then wiggled her brows. "And then we can make up for lost time."

Nora laughed. "Well, when you put it like that…"

"You're doing the right thing," Sage said. "And I have so much work to do here anyway without you distracting me. Those tattoos aren't going to remove themselves."

"Unfortunately."

"Time to go back to reality," Sage said reluctantly.

"Yep," Nora said, popping the 'p', though made no move to get up.

"We should really get up," Sage said, though she wasn't moving either.

"Uh-huh," Nora replied and kissed Sage once more.

Nora walked to the fortified entrance of Forest's Edge with a pack on her back and Florence by her side. Will had said his goodbyes at their home. He was not one for public farewells because other people would be too emotional—his words. Nora and Florence had exchanged a knowing look and laughed before leaving.

Nora felt a little apprehensive about departing the city. There was safety behind the new defensive walls and beyond them were factors Nora wasn't sure she was ready to be tested by. Inside Forest's Edge, she was certain of her desire to do the right thing and fix what she had helped to break, but what if there was something out there that made her question everything she had come to believe about herself all over again? Nora steeled her spine. Sage had confidence in her and that was enough.

As they walked closer to the open gates, she saw Faction members,

Forest's Edge guards and volunteers gathered in groups. There were the odd family members too, wishing their loved ones goodbye. Nora spotted her trainees huddled by the wall, inclining their heads to her in acknowledgment. They had taken her teachings more seriously recently but she still wasn't their favourite person. They respected what she had taught them and that they all had the same goal, but Nora was under no delusion that she had to be liked by everyone. So their lack of interest in anything beyond those two things didn't bother her.

Movement sounded beyond the wall and Gemma called out. Florence leapt forward, shifting mid-air and ran ahead towards the open gates. Another fox appeared from the other side of the gate—its fur almost identical to Florence's—and collided with her. The two tumbled to the ground wrestling. Nora summoned her magic to her fingertips, ready to defend her friend from the unknown threat.

"It's okay," Omari said, coming to her side and placing a firm hand on her arm. He laughed and his brown eyes were alight as he watched the two foxes. "It's only her brother."

"Florence has a brother?"

"Yeah." Omari nodded. "Looks like the Northern Wolf Pack has arrived."

Anima prowled through the entrance to Forest's Edge. There were so many of them and, despite the name of the group, the ranks were a mixture of species. Some shifted into their human forms to greet those from Forest's Edge, but most remained in their animal shift and kept back.

Omari nudged Nora's arm playfully, then stepped forwards to greet a tall man with chestnut hair. His skin was as pale as a spirit which was only worsened by his dark grey coat and slacks. He looked like he haunted a village in his spare time.

"Carl," Omari said, shaking the man's hand. "Good to see you again."

"And you," the man named Carl replied, then glanced down at the foxes still tumbling around on the ground. "So immature."

The foxes stopped, their ears perking before their bodies shifted. Nora faced a man with the same red hair and freckled cheeks as Florence. The siblings dusted themselves down with wide grins on their faces.

"All right, old man," Florence's brother said, looping an arm around Carl's waist whilst Florence came to stand beside Nora once again.

"Is Lady Royd here too?" Carl asked glancing around those from Forest's

Edge.

"Yes," Jasmine replied as she appeared from the crowd, her guards parting the throng to give her room. She looked regal in her green gown beneath a luxurious black coat.

Carl smiled broadly at her approach, then his features turned sombre as he embraced the woman. "I'm sorry for the loss of your father. How is your mother?"

"She doesn't leave her rooms," Jasmine replied with a heavy sigh. "With Evelyn captive in Royal Bay, it's all too much for her."

He frowned. "Understandable."

"What news do you bring?" Jasmine asked. "How is your pack?"

"It has grown to the size of a small city. We cannot stay hidden for much longer with numbers like that, even deep in the forest."

"We can take more into the city," Jasmine said. "Do you need more supplies?"

Carl nodded. "Whatever you can spare. We have the population, but not the means to provide for it."

"I will send resources today."

"Thank you. It will boost the people's morale," Carl said. "Things have been uneasy of late. The Makers' Murders have finally reached us. I'd thought we were protected from them, but they killed five people before we caught the culprit. A young woman." He shook his head. "She was caught in the act, otherwise I never would have suspected her."

"It doesn't matter how the killer was found," Jasmine said. "Only that they were. We haven't been able to find anything that links them beyond the terrible crimes they are committing. Even the victims appear to be chosen at random."

"We will figure it out," Carl replied. "Until then, we have a king to keep us busy."

"We do indeed," she said. "Gemma will lead my people within the Alliance. As for Lord Kaldom, he has chosen not to send help right now, but will send forces to hold the city once we have taken it."

"Doesn't want to fight but will share in the winnings."

Jasmine breathed a small laugh. "Something like that."

"And Lord Havilor?"

"His people will meet with you and Gemma before you reach Midskopas."

Carl nodded, looking around at those gathered. "How many are going with us?"

"One hundred and fifty from Forest's Edge," Jasmine replied. "Give or take."

"So, we are trying to take a city with less than five hundred," Carl said, scratching his stubbled chin. "I like a good challenge."

"Me too, but those odds aren't great," Florence's brother said.

"We will make it work. We have some powerful people here," Gemma said as she came to stand with Jasmine and Carl. She looked back at those from Forest's Edge, her golden eyes falling on Nora. Nora held the woman's gaze, inclining her head in acknowledgment. She would not let them down.

"I expect little resistance for your journey," Jasmine said. "There have been fewer attacks on our walls from King's Guild members and our scouts have reported a decrease in sightings."

"Good," Carl replied. "Hopefully that means they are a dying breed. We will keep a lookout but I think it's time we leave."

Carl raised his hand and the people started moving towards the gates to begin the journey to Midskopas. Nora made to follow, only to be stopped by Jasmine.

"I thought you'd might like this," Jasmine said. The lady of the city stepped closer to Nora and slipped a piece of fabric beneath Nora's arm, tying it around her bicep.

Nora looked down to see the faction's symbol proudly sitting over her clothing. She couldn't help the smile that tugged at her lips. "Ah, thanks."

"Take care of yourselves," Jasmine said, looking between Florence and Nora, then she did something Nora had not been expecting; Jasmine drew them both into an embrace.

Nora stood there awkwardly as the Lady of Forest's Edge held her in a three-way hug. She glanced over the woman's shoulder and spotted Omari chuckling at the sight.

"I expect you both back," Jasmine said, releasing them. "That's an order."

"I'll do my best," Florence said. She slapped Nora on the back, grinning. "Nora, on the other hand, is a stickler for commands, so you know she'll return to Forest's Edge now."

Nora glared up at Florence. "You're an ass."

"You always say the nicest things," Florence teased, backing up and waving at Jasmine and Omari. "Bye!"

"Ah, bye," Nora said to the leaders of Forest's Edge before joining Florence and the flow of people leaving.

They may not have the numbers, but the newly formed Northern Alliance had something the king did not. Each other. Where he divided the races, they united them. As they set off to take Midskopas and rise against a tyrant king, Nora thought about how much the king had to lose. Which was everything they had to gain.

30

Evelyn

E velyn was no longer allowed to leave her quarters unless the king commanded her presence—not that she had any desire to step foot out of them now. Ever since Poppy's funeral and the carriage ride with Kylan Evelyn hadn't been able to stop the flow of tears whenever she thought of Poppy or her father. And she thought of them a lot. There were so many things that reminded her of them and, at night, the darkness welcomed her with open arms.

Sitting on a chair by the window, she watched the clouds slowly drift through the sky. The cool sea breeze caressed her cheeks, blowing her hair around her shoulders. Evelyn breathed in deeply, memorising the scent and feel. Despite disliking the people in Royal Bay, the place itself was beautiful and she wished to visit a seaside city in the future. First, however, she needed to return home and help dethrone a king.

It was the one thing that kept her from crumbling completely. Louise had said they would leave soon and Evelyn was determined to do just that. She had information to bring home. Lady Elizabeth was the Goddess Thyra and if she was alive then chances were the other Gods and Goddesses would be too. If the Faction could find them, maybe they had a chance to stand against the king and Thyra and win.

And then there was August. There was something about him that had the king concerned. Maybe even afraid.

"How are you feeling?"

Evelyn jumped, turning her head to see Kylan dressed in an immaculate red coat, black trousers, shiny boots and a sword belt, though there was no weapon hanging in it. She hadn't heard him come in, not even with her Lys Alv hearing and it unnerved her. Not his presence, but that her instincts were off. She needed to snap out of her grief. It was leaving her more vulnerable than she already was.

"What are you doing here?" she asked, looking up at him.

"I came to check on you," Kylan said, halting before her and leaning on the window frame. He folded his arms over his broad chest and light glistened off his dark hair.

"Your father employs guards to ensure I am alive and held captive," she replied, pursing her lips. "Has he started giving you coin, too?"

Kylan sighed deeply. "I'm here because I care about you."

"No," she snapped. "You can't care for prisoners when you're the one holding the key."

"Please don't push me away," he said, his blue eyes softening.

"It's better this way. I'm leaving soon," she blurted before she could stop herself. She bit down on her tongue and mentally berated herself for the slip, his gaze boring into the side of her face.

"What?" he asked. "I assume you're only threatening me with your departure. How do you actually plan on going... Do you really plan on leaving?"

A breeze brushed her face like a gentle caress. She held her hand to her cheek and realised it hadn't come from outside, but rather from Kylan's magic. Evelyn stood, storming away towards her dressing room. She would not ruin her opportunity of getting out of this place. It had been a slip of the tongue and she wished she could take the words back.

She would not fall for his charms.

"Wait," Kylan said, catching hold of her wrist. "Don't go."

"I'm supposed to be dressing for dinner," she lied. Louise wouldn't be there for at least another hour to help her dress.

"I don't mean now," Kylan replied, dropping his gaze though his hand was still firmly holding onto her. "Don't leave Royal Bay. Stay here... with me."

"Why would you want me to stay?" *Shit. Why did she ask that?*

He looked up, his eyes searching her own and said, "Maybe I like the idea of marrying you."

"You've got to be kidding me," Evelyn replied, throwing her other hand in the air.

"Why? We get along, we want similar things—just different ways of trying to achieve the same outcome," he countered with a wry grin. "And you're incredibly beautiful."

Evelyn raised a brow. "You've hit your head."

"Why is it so hard to believe?" he asked, tugging her from the seat to draw her closer to him. "Tell me you don't feel something between us."

She opened her mouth but couldn't speak the words. They would have been a lie because she *had* felt it. Every time she'd been in his presence her heart beat faster in her chest and all her senses felt heightened. She'd told herself it was because he wanted something from her, but what if all he had wanted was her?

Kylan quirked a smile. "I knew you felt the same."

He closed the distance between them, his mouth capturing hers and her lips moved of their own accord. Kylan wrapped an arm around her, pressing her tightly to him as she grasped the back of his neck. Their kiss deepened, the need to be close to him consuming her. She'd never felt like this before and the thought scared her.

"I can't," she gasped, stepping back and pressing a hand to her lips. "You have to go."

"Evelyn," Kylan said, reaching for her.

She shook her head and ran from him into her dressing room, slamming the door behind her. The kiss shouldn't have happened. Nothing could come from her feelings for Kylan. Evelyn pressed her back to the wood, sliding down until she was sitting on the floor, and pulled her knees to her chest.

With the grief still so raw, Evelyn didn't need this confusion in her heart on top of it. She let out a whimper and tears streamed from her eyes. She made no move to wipe them away. She let them fall, let herself feel it.

How had she made such a mess of her heart?

31

August

August's eyes were closed as he focused on those in the temple, counting each magical presence he felt. His magic moved through the hallways and rooms, searching and he let his magic delve into each corner. He would not miss a single person.

"Six," August said with certainty. He opened his eyes to Jord's study. He sat in the chair before her desk with his broad shoulders and neck stiff from concentration. He released his grip on the wooden arms of the chair.

Snow fell beyond the stained-glass window. It was a beautiful sight, though somewhat obscured by the frost spreading across the multicoloured window. Without an Elementum in the temple to regulate and guarantee warmth they had to rely solely on natural fires. Some days the fires kept the chill away and some days the ice won out.

Jord clasped her hands on the desk and nodded. "You're getting better."

There were far more than six Mors Alvs at the temple, though Jord had instructed only those six to act as beacons for him to find. He'd only ever been able to identify magic close by and only of those he knew well. But now with Jord's teaching, he could recognise it in an entire building. He wondered whether he could track Nora down in one of the larger cities—it was something he would test when he left the mountains. He missed his friend and had so much to tell her. They'd never been separated this long before and he hated not having her close. Especially as he had so much to tell her.

"You are strong," Jord said with a small smile. "But I'd expect no less from the son of Queen Helen and General Natsky. As I'm sure you know, King Dominic would allow no one without exceptional magic to hold such high positions and your parents were some of the strongest magic wielders I have ever seen. You have their power running through your veins."

"We don't know if that's even true," August replied. He rubbed the ache in his neck. "Queen Helen was murdered by General Natsky. Why would he kill her if they were going to have a child?"

"Exactly," she said, tapping her temple. "Why would he kill the woman he loved?"

August leaned back in his seat. "*Did* he love her?"

"Aren seems to think so."

August shook his head. "It doesn't add up. Not with the facts I have been taught."

"Tell me," Jord drummed her fingers on the desk. "Who told you those so-called facts?"

Everything he knew about the country's history had been taught to him by Rana— leader of the Alta and a general to King Dominic—who wasn't exactly a reliable source.

When August didn't reply, Jord continued walking around the desk to stand before him and said, "Queen Helen was due to have a third child, but they never survived the birth, or so the story was told. A few months later she was killed—along with her staff—and the General was blamed and quickly executed before an angry crowd hours later. Interesting that those killed were the ones privy to not only the Queen's death but the birth of the third child."

"You think the king killed them," August replied flatly as he looked into her dark eyes.

It was tempting to believe Jord, but everything she said went against all he'd ever known. He realised much of what he knew was wrong, but he also didn't want to believe her word blindly. The Alta and King's Guild didn't question the king's word and look at how they behaved.

"Is it so farfetched that he would do something like that?" she asked, raising a brow. "Look at what he did to our people. The tide had been turning on the Mors Alvs for years before he came into power. But not until a ruler enforced laws that benefitted one race over another or called for the extermination of an entire race. Thyra had spent years spreading rumours of the Mors Alvs being dangerous creatures and once the king lied about the Queen's murder, the truth was eclipsed. Mors Alvs were protectors of the people—mostly humans— keeping them safe from those who used magic to harm them. We were carers and healers too, like the Lys Alvs. We have the power to cure magical illnesses caused by conjuring magic and can help those who are terminally ill pass peacefully. Mors Alvs are not the monsters you have been raised to believe."

August frowned. There had to be truth to her words, at least in part. His short time at the temple was proof enough that every Mors Alv was unique. It was an obvious thing, but for so long, August just hadn't been able to see what was right in front of him.

"Your anger and unwillingness to use your magic to its full potential proves you still believe those lies."

"I use my magic," he huffed, looking up to the ceiling. "I was using it just then."

"To sense people," she replied. "But you do not use it on anyone, at least not intentionally. You are afraid of your own power."

August stilled. He had been hesitating to use his magic that way, even before coming here. Ever since the tattoos on his wrists started to fade back in Royal Bay he'd avoided using it, finding excuses or relying on Nora to use hers. Felix must have noticed back then, and probably Ashe too. Ashe had followed Nora and August from Royal Bay to Forest's Edge on Felix's orders, but August was still unsure of the reasoning behind it all. August thought Felix wanted to keep tabs on him because of his heritage, but perhaps it was because he suspected the tattoos had been fading.

August turned his attention back to Jord. "Felix told you a lot about me."

"Aren has a keen interest in you," she agreed with a nod of her head. "You didn't think he brought you here just out of the kindness of his heart, did you?"

"He brought me here to train."

"For someone who has been exposed to a lot of awful things in this world, you are rather naïve. Aren thought to use you to come here so he could persuade me to help prevent the Anima from ending up like us. He knew I would let only another of my people into the temple and he knew you—the lost Mors Alv prince—were the perfect candidate."

"You don't want to help?" August asked, dark eyes wide.

Jord shook her head. Her long black hair swayed with the movement. "Why would I put the last of us at risk?"

"Because there are lives in danger."

"They aren't Mors Alvs lives. Why should I care?" she replied, pursing her lips. "They didn't lift a finger to help when my people were being slaughtered."

August stood and looked down at her. "A lot of them weren't alive or old enough to do anything at the time."

Jord shrugged.

"What if there are Mors Alvs out there?" August asked, thinking of the Mors Alv he'd seen in Forest's edge. The one who had been killing people in the name of the Makers' Murders. Evelyn had examined the bodies of the Mors Alv's victims and had accused August of being the culprit. He'd been so angry, but he understood how she reached her conclusions. Until the bodies were found August had been the only Mors Alv she'd ever known. "I saw one in Forest's Edge. What if there are others?"

"There is a slim chance of that," she said, coming around the desk to stand before him. "But I can't doom the people here on that gamble."

"Are you so afraid of Thyra that you are going to spend the rest of your life, which I am assuming, by the way, is the rest of eternity, hiding up here?"

"I am not hiding!" she snapped, fury burning in her gaze.

August scoffed. "Sure looks like it."

"Don't pretend to understand the affairs of Gods." She pressed forward so that their chests brushed and her tone dropped to a heated whisper. "You are but a flicker of time in my long existence."

"At least my flicker is going to be worth something," he replied through gritted teeth.

Jord's hand moved quickly, slapping August hard enough to make him turn his head.

"You have no idea what I have given up, what I have done, in order to live a worthy life," she said. Jord shook her head. " I cannot go relive it again."

"When she trapped you?"

She swallowed hard. " My place is here."

He watched as she stormed from the office. If Felix thought he'd convince her to help, then he was delusional. The woman was determined to stay up in the frozen mountains. She held too much hurt for what had been done to the Mors Alvs. As much as August wanted her to act, to do something about the lives that would be lost, he couldn't blame her for not wanting to get involved.

The eastern communal hall was one of August's favourite places in the temple to unwind. Most people hung out in the main hall, so there was always a free spot to sit and it was much quieter too. August wasn't used to being around so many people wanting to speak with him. He'd been in crowds before but, beyond the mountains, most people had kept their distance or didn't engage him in chit-chat because he actively had to hide his identity and keep to himself. It wasn't only because he was an Alta and had needed to stay hidden on the king's orders. If people had seen his race there was no question that he would have been attacked and killed purely out of fear of what he was.

When August worked in the kitchens, everyone but Tyler left him alone, but in the main hall… he had no such luck. Social interactions with multiple people, especially in large groups, were fucking exhausting.

August contemplated his training session with Jord as he sat by the fire. He'd had other sessions since then to continue working on his magic, but that one kept running through his mind. They hadn't broached the subject again of helping the Anima and everyone else who wanted freedom from the king's rule. He understood her hesitations, but that didn't stop him from wanting her to act. To help the Anima and the other races. The division was the first step to making them weaker. They were all playing into King Dominic's plan.

After the altercation with Jord, his rage had all but disappeared. It was as though wanting her to act had opened his eyes and given him a more solid target for the pent-up anger he felt. He'd been mad at the king for all the man had done, but now he had direction. Jord may not have wanted to involve herself or the other Mors Alvs, but that didn't mean August was going to hide up in the mountains with them. He now had a plan. All he needed was an ally to help him. Luckily, August already had one in mind, and the man was walking towards him.

"How's your day been, Dark Prince?" Tyler asked, coming to sit beside August. He leant back into his corner of the sofa and propped a boot onto one knee.

August groaned. "I wish you wouldn't call me that."

He wasn't a prince, only an illegitimate child of a queen who, without her husband, would have had no title at all. He was a bastard in both senses of the word.

"I think it has a nice ring to it," Tyler replied, quirking his lips into a smile. "A title people can rally behind."

"It's not accurate, not to mention extremely cliché," August said, running a hand through his dirty blond hair. He'd let Tyler cut it, the side now shaved, whilst leaving a bit of length at the top. The man had done a surprisingly good job considering he joked and flailed his arms around during the whole process, setting August's nerves on edge. "I don't need a title anyway."

"Everyone needs a title."

"Oh yeah?" August raised a brow. "What's yours?"

"I'm still working on it."

"How about Giant Pain in the Ass," he teased, laughing at his joke.

"It's all right." Tyler jutted out his bottom lip and looked at the ceiling. "Wordy, but we can work on it."

"August grinned at his friend. Then made a decision. It was now or never. Taking a deep breath, he broached the subject on his mind. "I think it's time I leave."

Tyler sat up, leaning his elbows on his thighs, and clapped his hands together. "Where to?"

"Back to Fellbun, then onto Royal Bay," August replied, scratching at the worn leather of the sofa arm. "Some crazy Mors Alv convinced me to think about what I wanted."

"Sounds like a smart guy," Tyler said, wiggling his brows and smirking. "So, what have you decided you want? Will you return to your ladies?"

August shook his head. "If I have learned anything from this place, it's that I need to deal with myself before I can help anyone else. Plus, Nora is more than capable of taking care of herself. And Evelyn…"

"She's still your girl, right?"

"I hope so. I plan on going to Royal Bay to find her, but also to speak to the only parental figure I have ever known," August said, thinking of the woman who'd raised him. "I'm going to visit Rana."

"Who?"

"She's the leader of the Alta and has known me my whole life or at least more of it than anyone else. If anyone were to know about who I am, it would be her."

"And once you get the answers?"

"Then I'm going to rescue Evelyn and kill the king."

"Big job," Tyler said, blowing out a long breath. "Want some company?"

August smiled. "As a matter of fact, I do."

32

Nora

Travelling to Midskopas had given Nora a lot of time to think and only reaffirmed that her past and the old relationships in her life were something she hated dwelling on. Whilst she had Florence and the anima's brother, Chester, to fill her days with stories of the siblings' childhoods and general banter between the two they made Nora miss August. They had been separated for months and as far as Nora was concerned it was far too long.

She wondered whether he'd made it to the Periculum Mountains with Felix to train with the Mors Alvs hiding there. As much as she hoped he was learning not only about his magic but the people there too, Nora couldn't help the pang of jealousy that they might give him something she could not. She and August had always considered each other family, but she knew there were things about his life she couldn't possibly understand. It didn't help that she never had the courage to tell him how much he meant to her. To be fair, she had never been an emotionally intelligent person—always hiding behind her pride and snappy remarks. Thankfully, Sage, her new friends and the removal of her tattoos had changed that to a degree.

Nora hoped she had the chance to see August again soon and tell him she didn't mean all the horrible things she'd said to him. That she loved him. He was her brother and she prayed to the Goddess Thyra that he still thought of her as his family, too.

Nearing Midskopas, the Northern Alliance halted their travel and set up camp. The journey had been uneventful with only a few run-ins with the occasional King's Guild member, but nothing that warranted any sort of panic or fight. The Guild in the north had lost numbers thanks to their unsuccessful skirmishes against the major cities and was no longer much of a threat as Jasmine had predicted.

Instead of leading the Alliance closer, Gemma and Carl were discussing their next moves. Nora was surprised that she'd been asked to stay during the meeting and now watched as the leaders crouched over a map of Valmenessia on the tent floor. They were both dressed in thick, brown leathers with swords at their hips, almost like a matching pair, though Gemma had the Forest's Edge emblem sewn onto her upper arm.

"Chester will lead my people to the northeast border where the river runs out from," Carl said, placing a stone on the spot at the edge of Midskopas. He picked up another one, putting it down on the northernmost point. "Your people will check out the gate here."

Nora eyed the city pass between the north and south of the country. It sat between the Grenblad Woods on the west and a mountain range to the east and, though the city had been run down the last time Nora had ventured there, it held value when fighting over a country. If the north could take Midskopas it would provide a barrier to the king's forces, making it harder for them to attack the northern cities.

"Lord Havilor's scouts said their main camp will wait in the Grenblad Woods for our signal to attack the western border," Gemma added, and Carl marked the spot. "The only way to go is south if they choose to flee."

"If they get the chance," Aeolus chuckled, looking over the map. His tan hand sat on his sword hilt at his hip, as though ready to draw it at a moment's notice. "I don't plan on letting any escape. They wouldn't give us the luxury."

"Very true." Carl sighed as he rose to his feet. "My scouts are ready to leave."

"So are mine," Gemma replied, waving a hand towards Aeolus, Florence, and Nora.

Nora's eyes shot up in surprise. "Me?"

"Yes," Gemma said as Aeolus marched out of the tent. "You and Florence will go with Aeolus. Make sure you are well-equipped."

Nora didn't need telling twice, rushing out of the tent with Florence after Aeolus. She didn't need any weapons other than the dagger strapped to her belt. Her magic would be more than enough.

"Did you bring your gun?" Nora asked Florence as they walked through the camp.

Florence shook her head. "I left it with Will. I know he is safer in Forest's Edge, but I felt better knowing he had something stronger than a blade to protect himself. Not that he wanted me to leave it with him. He can be so stubborn sometimes."

"Can't argue with that." Nora chuckled.

The rest of the Alliance had settled into preparations for their impending attack. As they strode through the camp, Nora glimpsed people sharpening their blades or practising drills, whilst others prepared by filling their hungry stomachs and talking with friends.

"See you soon," Chester called out before shifting into his fox form and bounding into the darkness.

Florence waved at his departing form and the three of them took off, heading west towards the northern gate. Nora stayed close to the others who headed for the city, keeping hidden as best as possible. It wasn't easy as there was little natural coverage, but they made do. Florence took the lead, shifting into her fox form to travel in stealth. With only the three of them, it didn't take long to reach their destination.

Hiding behind a crumbling stone wall, Nora saw that like the last time she'd been to Midskopas with August all those months ago, the walls were guarded by Royal Sentries, though this time it appeared the new lady had been establishing more of her own. The mixture of grey and blue sentries were visible in the moonlight as they monitored not only the top of the wall but the front too.

At first, Nora thought the city had been notified of the impending attack and fortified themselves with extra men on the walls, but as they crept closer, she saw how relaxed they were, slouching, talking, and playing card games by firelight. Turned out, rushing to bolster sentry numbers left little room for adequate vetting of applicants and Nora hoped that meant poor training too.

She smirked, feeling cocky for the first time in a while. Fighting was what she'd been trained for and, despite the reasoning behind her training, her confidence grew at knowing she was about to help and that she was capable of doing so. Her trainees had come from Forest's Edge to free Midskopas and she couldn't wait to see how they fared. Looking at the people on the wall, she felt her trainees were worth at least twice that of the city's sentries before her.

"Thoughts?" Aeolus asked, crouching beside her.

"They're lazy," Nora replied. "If we can maintain the element of surprise, we should be able to cut down their numbers fairly easily. What if I go over the wall?"

"That could work," he agreed with a nod of his head. "Send a few to assassinate as many sentries as possible and open the gate for our forces. If we don't need to use Elementum magic to knock the walls or the gates down, it would be a lot cleaner. Problem is, we don't know what's beyond that wall. For all we know, the first few over would be sent to their deaths."

"I'll go," Nora said. "I have the magic and experience."

Aeolus looked at her, deciding whether he could trust her. He probably would never do so completely. "You could betray us. Tell them of our arrival."

"I won't," Nora said, shaking her head. "You've got to learn to trust me at some point."

"Send me with Nora," Florence said, appearing at her side. Nora had no idea when she'd appeared—or shifted from her fox form for that matter. The woman was deathly silent when she wanted to be. "We can be the first over." She turned to Nora. "You can lift me too, right?"

Nora nodded. "Easy."

"I'll have to run it by Gemma and Carl," Aeolus said, looking between them. "If they agree, you will follow all orders given. Understood?"

"Yes," Nora replied, unable to contain her grin as she nodded.

Turning from the city, Aeolus led them back, and Nora readied herself for what was to come. Training Faction members and busy work were never her strengths, but having a mission to complete? This was something she could do. Her mind focused on what she needed to achieve. She would not let these people down again.

After the sun had set the following day, ten Alliance members snuck towards the city walls. They spread out in pairs, and Nora stayed close to Florence as they moved to their appointed position. The air was still with no cool breeze or sound coming from any wildlife. It was as though even nature was watching the events unfold. Nora hoped it was a good sign and that the Goddess Thyra was watching over them.

Nearing the wall, Nora summoned her wind magic and lifted Florence and herself up before quietly lowering them both on top of the stone beside a tower.

Keeping hidden in the shadows, they waited only the briefest moment to get their bearings, then Nora lifted Florence once more and watched as she moved swiftly towards those stationed on the tower above. Without a sound, Florence crept between the sentries, moving like a spirit, and sliced the throats of those nearest. When she was done, she looked down at Nora with a furrowed brow. Nora had made no move to kill those nearest her.

Nora grinned at Florence, then focused on the three sentries near her, summoning the air from their lungs simultaneously. The sentries grasped at their throats, but it was no use. Nora would not let a single drop of air in. They fell to their knees, dying soundlessly. It had always taken so much magic to do that particular trick, but now that her magic wasn't restricted by the tattoos, it wasn't as taxing as it used to be.

"Okay, that was both awesome and terrifying," Florence whispered after climbing down from the tower. "Once again, I'm happy we are friends."

Florence and Nora's attack had been flawless. Unfortunately, they were not so lucky. Shouts rang through the air and the sentries drew weapons to defend themselves against the Alliance attackers. With a glance at each other, Florence and Nora raced to take down as many sentries as they could on their way to the ground. They needed to open the gate.

The sentries were alert, the silent attack no longer viable, so Nora decided it was time for brute strength over stealth. Summoning her water magic, Nora threw waves at the sentries, knocking them from the wall as she ran. Florence shifted into her fox, lunging at sentries with her sharp teeth bared and biting down hard.

Beyond the wall, the Northern Alliance rushed forward. Elementum launched their attack, fire orbs and water jets shooting towards sentries atop the wall whilst Anima, Humans, and Lys Alvs used blades, teeth and claws to tear down their opponents. Nora angled her head to see where the sentries she'd thrown had fallen. Their fellows stationed on the outside of the wall weren't prepared for the Alliance's attack, though they mounted some defence. The way they fumbled to do so only proved Nora's observation of their lack of training true, especially in the case of the Lady Ignisto. The Royal Sentries on the wall were the more dominant of the force, but they would fall to Nora's magic and blade soon enough. She would make sure of it.

Shouts echoed as the fighting continued, but she ignored it, not letting herself become distracted from the task at hand. Archers nocked their bows and Elementum shot fireballs in every direction, only for their attacks to be knocked off course or extinguished in a hiss thanks to jets of water from the Elementum in the Alliance.

She summoned her water magic into whips and lashed out at sentries, the water curling around them and throwing them in every direction. She spotted Florence descending the steps and raced after her friend, fighting off as many sentries as she could as she followed her friend.

"We need help!" one sentry shouted over the ruckus. "Sound the alarm!"

Two sentries scurried away, Nora's attack missing them by seconds as her fireballs hit a wall, leaving scorch marks.

"Fuck," Nora growled, reaching the ground. She hated that they'd got away, but she could not go after them.

A stocky man ran at her, bellowing unintelligibly with an axe raised above his head. Nora dodged out of his way, spinning, then threw a ball of water at his back. The man flew forward onto the ground, his axe flying from his grip and wedging itself into the chest of another sentry.

"Convenient," Nora smirked, turning her attention back to the gate as the bell chimed loudly for all to hear. It needed opening *now.*

Nora raced to the gate lever, pulling up short as two sentries blocked her path. She dodged their blows as they ran at her, their swings slow and wide. Darting closer to the sentry on the right, she drew her dagger and stabbed it deep into the man's chest. Blood seeped through his coat as she pulled the weapon out.

Not waiting to watch his death, she spun toward the other sentry. The man came at her. His face was red as he bellowed a war cry and she ducked under his blade. She threw a punch at his face, splitting his brow, and he growled, summoning his wind magic and throwing her back against the wall. Stalking towards her, she let herself hang against the stone, readying her fire magic to come as soon as he was right where she wanted him.

When he was one step away, the gates exploded inwards with a loud boom that shook the ground and threw the sentry away from her. His magic released her as debris flew in the air and groans echoed around her. Ears ringing, Nora rose to her feet and cursed the Alliance.

"Could have given warning that the plans were fucking changing!" she shouted at no one in particular and turned to see a giant hole. She was a few feet away from the opening—any closer and she would have exploded into a million pieces too.

When the smoke cleared, the Alliance came storming in at the same time as more sentries appeared from further inside the city. Magic clashed with magic. Weapons were drawn and sharp teeth and claws were bared.

The place erupted in battle and Nora joined in eagerly, determined to make her mark and right the wrongs she had committed in her life. With each summons of her magic, she let go of the guilt within her. This battle wasn't about killing, it was about taking a stand against a worldview that was doing harm. It was rising against an evil king.

33

Evelyn

Evelyn's eyes snapped open. Louise stood over her, hands gripping her shoulders. "Lady Royd," the maid whispered, "it's time."

Evelyn looked up at the woman with her brows furrowed and then realised what Louise meant. "We're leaving?" Evelyn asked.

"Yes, I've collected some clothing for you," she said, disappearing into the dark. She returned quickly, dropping a bundle onto the bed. "We need to hurry."

Not needing to be told twice, Evelyn rushed out of the bed, changed into trousers, a loose shirt and a jacket and then stuffed her feet into boots. Once dressed, Evelyn followed Louise through her quarters to the door.

"Won't the sentry catch us?" Evelyn asked, keeping her voice low.

Louise shook her head, pushing the door open. "He won't be following you around anymore."

Before Evelyn could ask Louise to elaborate, the woman took off quickly through the dim hallway. As Louise had said, the sentry who had been guarding her day and night was nowhere in sight, though she didn't ask her handmaid to explain his whereabouts unsure she wanted the answer. It was the middle of the night. Sconces were lit to provide a small amount of light while outside was pitch black. Evelyn hurried to keep up, doing her best to tread as silently as possible on the tiled floor in her boots.

They made their way downstairs, pausing on the bottom step to drop to a crouch as two sentries walked by. Evelyn held her breath, shuffling silently towards the more shadowed end of the step and waited for them to pass. By some miracle, they didn't notice Evelyn and Louise and she breathed a sigh of relief, giving thanks to the Goddess Nyssa. Louise tapped Evelyn's arm and the pair took off once more, only for the two sentries who had passed to turn and spot them as they moved. The women didn't hesitate to run.

Shouts rang behind them as Louise and Evelyn raced to the ground floor and through the expansive hallways. Louise took sharp turns around corners and Evelyn found herself skidding along the tiled floors more than once in an attempt to keep up. Evelyn pushed on, determined to not get caught. Finally, they made their way along a passageway to the gardens. Louise turned, disappearing ahead, but Evelyn kept going, determined to not get caught. She would not suffer another one of King Dominic's punishments.

Evelyn reached the spot she'd last seen Louise. She entered through the door and stifled a scream as she was suddenly pulled back by her hand and spun around, coming face to face with Kylan.

Louise silently shut the door behind them and Evelyn realised where they were. They had been running past his study, though why he'd been in here at this hour was beyond her.

"What are you doing?" she whispered, her words coming out harshly as her heart thumped.

"I'm coming with you," he replied in a hushed tone.

"What?"

"I thought we'd been through this," he said, drawing her closer. "I want you."

"Kylan," Evelyn said, tugging her hand from his.

"Why do you think Louise brought you here?" His gaze was fixed firmly on Evelyn. "I'm going with you."

"I'm not coming back," she stated, eyeing him. "This isn't a night-time outing. I'm going home."

"Why are you so adamant about ignoring me? I'm going with you," he replied, stepping closer.

"Why would you want to do that?"

"I've been thinking on what you said about my brother and you're right," he said, reaching for her hand. "He won't listen to me, but if I go, maybe I can make a difference another way. I want to try."

"Is this some kind of trap?" she asked, looking up into his eyes and searching for any sign that he was lying.

Kylan shook his head. "No. I want to help and… I want to be wherever you are."

Evelyn did not know what to say. Why did Kylan have to be romantic at a time like this? And why did the thought of him escaping with her make her heart skip? When it came to Kylan she was in over her head.

"We need to go now," Louise said, saving Evelyn from saying anything, and waved for Evelyn to join her at the door. She pressed her ear to the wood, then gestured for Evelyn once more. "We don't have much time. They will be back this way soon."

Evelyn looked up at Kylan.

"Fine," she said, earning a grin from the prince that had her smiling too, though she tried to hide it by following Louise out the door.

As they made their way through the passageway, she could feel Kylan close to her back and couldn't help but admit to herself how comforted she was to have him there with them.

"Where to?" Kylan asked as they reached an archway that opened onto the gardens beyond.

"There," Louise replied, then took off into a sprint.

Evelyn and Kylan exchanged a look before following the woman as she ran towards the edge of the castle island. Waves crashed loudly outside, but nothing hid the shouts sounding behind them. Kylan reached for Evelyn's hand, gripping it tightly as they ran.

"Hurry!" Louise shouted as they reached her at the cliffside.

"What now?" Kylan puffed.

"This way!" she replied, using her wind magic to lower herself over the side. Evelyn glanced down in horror, only to see the woman dropping to an edge. "Come Lady Royd, I won't let you fall!"

"What happens when we enter the water?" Evelyn asked Kylan. Magic didn't exist outside of Valmenessia, and she had no idea how far into the water they would need to be for her magic to leave her. "Will we lose our magic?"

Kylan shook his head. "We won't be far enough from land for it to affect us. I'm told you need to be further out to sea for your magic to disappear."

Nodding, Evelyn hesitated only for a second before the shouts had her putting her life in Louise's hands. She stepped off, heart racing, and almost cried when she felt the catching wind beneath her feet. She kept still as Louise lowered her down.

"I know what you're thinking. Why are there ledges here?" Louise said as Kylan landed beside Evelyn. Evelyn reached for him, gripping his shirt tightly in her hand. "It's an old escape route for those who couldn't use magic to escape an emergency. Pretty handy considering if we tried to get down any other way we would have jumped to our death."

"That makes me feel a lot better," Evelyn replied sarcastically, earning a chuckle from Kylan.

"You know you can heal rapidly," he said into her ear, putting a hand around her waist and lowering them together to the next ledge. "You would probably survive the fall."

"It would still hurt," she groaned as he took off again, moving them quicker to each ledge on the side of the castle cliff.

They'd made it almost halfway down when they heard shouts echo above, followed by fireballs soaring towards them.

"Now what?" Evelyn shouted as Kylan pressed her against the rock, shielding her from an orb of flame.

"We swim!" Louise replied and with a gust of wind magic, she shoved Evelyn and Kylan off the ledge.

Evelyn shrieked as she fell. The water was rising far too quickly to meet her. She slammed into it. Her body screamed as she was shoved under the surface. Her magic rose, healing and keeping her alive as she struggled to reach the surface. Water tumbled her around and she lost all sense of direction. She had no idea which way was up—not that she had any idea how to swim in the first place. Strong arms encircled her waist and they tugged her to the surface. She gasped for air as she leant back on whoever had saved her.

"You're okay," Kylan puffed. "I've got you."

"Louise just tried to kill us."

"No, I didn't," Louise said from somewhere close by. "We need to keep moving."

The water moved them, guiding them away from the island thanks to either Louise or Kylan's Elementum magic. Once Evelyn had her breath back, she slipped from Kylan's grip, not wanting to encourage his feelings—or hers for that matter. As soon as she was out of his arms though she dropped back beneath the water.

His arms pulled her back up and she gasped clinging to Kylan's body.

"Can't swim?" he asked, holding her above the water.

"I live in a forest," she sputtered.

"Let me help you, then."

He kept hold of her and guided her to his back, helping to loop her arms around his neck. The closeness sent shivers that had nothing to do with the water over her skin and her heart beating rapidly in her chest. She could have lied to herself and said it was the cold, but in the darkness, with no one to see her face, she let herself smile as he carried her to wherever Louise was leading them.

Thanks to Louise and Kylan's Elementum magic, it didn't take long for them to near the shore. Evelyn detached herself from Kylan so that she could walk the rest of the way. Louise had taken them past the city limits and, now that the sun was rising, Evelyn could better see the rocky area they were walking towards.

"Just behind those jagged rocks is where we need to be," Louise declared, waving her hand to dry herself with her Elementum magic, then did the same for Evelyn.

"Thanks," Evelyn said, chuckling as Kylan grimaced at his drenched clothes. With a quick flick of his wrist, he was dry too.

They walked in silence over the sandy terrain and passed the jagged rocks Louise had pointed out, finding a small cabin nestled in the middle of them. It was set lower into the ground and had roof tiles a similar shade to the surrounding rock, hiding it from view.

Louise produced a key and, without knocking, the trio stepped inside the cabin to find a woman with violet hair waiting within. Louise instantly went to greet the woman and they threw their arms around each other like old friends.

"Where are the others?" the woman asked, looking at the open door expectantly.

"They'll be here on time," Louise replied with a dismissive wave of her hand. "Don't worry Sloane."

"When do I ever?" Sloane said, her eyes landing on Evelyn and Kylan. She yelped, stepping back and slapping Louise on the arm playfully. "Forget what I said. That's the prince and his bride. Now I'm going to worry."

"They want to help our cause."

Sloane nodded, though didn't look at all convinced as she strode over to the centre of the room and knelt. Beside her, pots containing various coloured concoctions were filled to the brim. She dipped her fingers into the closest one and began drawing on the wood with her stained fingers, creating intricate patterns and chanting under her breath.

"What is this place?" Kylan asked, stepping closer to Evelyn. His shoulder brushed hers and she leaned into his touch for comfort.

"This is Sloane's home," Louise replied. "She's a conjurer and a very good one too."

"And what did she mean about the others?"

"We aren't the only ones leaving Royal Bay this evening," she said. "Tonight is the beginning of the rebirth of the country."

"Rebirth?" Evelyn asked.

Louise smiled and said, "you'll see."

Evelyn glanced around the room, taking in the space, instead of pushing the subject. She had tried to question Louise more about her plans to escape, but the woman had been very secretive. She figured Louise would be much the same about this as well.

Sloane's home was eclectic. It was filled with strange statues and shelves and a dusty collection of jars. Evelyn stepped closer to some of the jars and peered at the various preserved fruits and vegetables inside, each labelled in a script she didn't recognise. She raised her hand to one of the glass containers stacked upon the ledge and carefully rotated it, eyeing what she thought were pickled onions within. She gasped in horror and reared back, chills running up her spine as she backed into Kylan's firm chest.

'They're only animal eyes,' came Sloane's voice. Evelyn looked at the woman who was still tracing some lavish swirl in purple. 'They were already dead when I found them.'

Evelyn shuddered and turned away from the shelves to see four people stride through the front door. Three men and a woman were all dressed in plain clothing.

"Everyone's here," Louise said, making no move to greet them the way she had Sloane.

"Yeah, yeah," the man in front grunted. He moved to stand over Sloane, his tall frame casting a shadow in the dimly lit room. "Please tell me you're almost finished."

"Portal magic cannot be rushed," Sloane replied simply, drawing a swirling pattern onto the floor with her silver-ringed and tattooed fingers.

"What's portal magic?" Evelyn asked, looking at the woman's work. The swirls and loops created a circle in the centre of the room.

"None of your business," one of the new arrivals snarled, shooting Evelyn a glare. He was not as tall as the first man, though he was equally lean. "I can't believe you actually brought them."

"They are here to assist," Louise replied, sticking her chin out. "They want the same future as us."

"Doesn't mean they need to know all our secrets," the first man huffed.

Sloane tsked, sounding far older than she appeared. She couldn't have been much older than Evelyn, judging by her smooth complexion and youthful features. "They aren't your secrets to keep. Portal magic moves objects or people from one place to another within seconds."

Evelyn shuffled on her feet. "How far? Like from here to Forest's Edge?"

"Precisely," Sloane nodded, finishing her drawing with an elegant swish before moving on to another design. "You can go as far as you like."

"How come I've never heard of it before?" Kylan asked, scrunching his brow.

"You royals don't know everything," she said, earning a chuckle from the others. "Your father may use old magic to enslave people, but not all conjurers know every trick."

"Why don't more conjurers know this one? It would be extremely useful," Kylan said, ignoring the snickers around the room. Evelyn glanced up at him to see that he was genuinely interested in the topic.

"It is complicated conjuring," the woman said. "If done incorrectly, those travelling in the portal could disappear."

Evelyn's jaw dropped. She turned to look at Sloane with wide eyes, forgetting about Kylan. "As in *die*?"

Sloane shook her head, her violet hair dancing around her shoulders. "Not die, simply cease to exist. No afterlife with the Goddess Jord. No peace. Nothing."

Evelyn swallowed hard. "Maybe—"

"Shut up and stop distracting her," the first man scolded. He moved to lean against the wall, remaining close enough to have his presence known to the violet-haired woman. "I want to be gone within the hour."

"Don't speak to her like that," Kylan barked, placing a hand on the small of Evelyn's back.

"She's not my ruler," the man replied, narrowing his gaze. "And neither are you."

"Doesn't change the fact that she is a person," Kylan rebuked. "Learn some manners."

"He's got a point," the female newcomer said, stepping further into the light. Her curly red hair was bright, even in the low light. "You're awfully rude, especially to Sloane."

"Both Evelyn and Sloane *are* on our side," Louise insisted.

"Ha! The Alv maybe, but don't let the conjurer lull you into her trap," the man replied, his lip turning up at Sloane in disgust. "She is a crafty woman who'd happily carve you up and put you in jars on those shelves with the rest of her victims."

Evelyn felt the blood rush from her cheeks and said, "they're animals."

"Yeah," he scoffed, rolling his eyes. "And *she's* only twenty years old."

Her eyes snapped to Sloane, searching for evidence of what he was implying. The woman couldn't have been older... could she? And the animals in the jars, were they really... No, he was only trying to frighten her and as much as she hated to admit it, he had succeeded.

"It is done," Sloane said, connecting the swirl she'd been painting to another. She rose to her feet and rubbed her lower back.

"Finally," the man huffed, stepping into the circle. He narrowed his eyes at the rest of them. "Hurry and stand beside me."

Evelyn hesitated as fear stopped her from moving. What if Sloane had made a mistake? The idea of no longer existing was beyond terrifying.

"If you'd rather stay by my side, you are more than welcome," Sloane offered, placing an inky hand on Evelyn's arm and looking into Evelyn's eyes.

"A-ahh," Evelyn stammered, feeling herself being drawn in by Sloane. It would have been lovely to remain with Sloane, but would the woman let her be by her side forever? The idea of an eternity with Sloane sounded perfect.

"She's staying with me," Kylan said firmly, his hand slipping from Evelyn's back to her waist as he pulled her into his side and led her into the circle.

Evelyn reached out for the other woman, but Louise moved quickly over to her. The handmaid wiped a hand over Evelyn's arm and smudged ink that hadn't been there a moment before.

"Pity," Sloane said with a wave of her hand. "The Lys Alvs have always had such a pull on me. No other race helps me maintain my youth like her kind."

Red smoke twisted through the air around them as Sloane's conjuring magic took hold. It swirled around the edges of the circle, gathering speed and whipping Evelyn's hair against her face. She leaned into Kylan as he held her more tightly.

Soon the little cabin was no longer in sight as Evelyn and the others were portaled across the country. It was the strangest sensation, like being inside the centre of a storm, and she prayed to the Goddess Nyssa that she would not be lost to the swirling oblivion. The smoke dissipated and Evelyn found herself in a darkened room. Her heart hammered in her chest. Had they made it or was this what it was like not to exist any longer?

A creak sounded and a thin sliver of light slipped into the room.

Louise turned to Evelyn, half her face illuminated by the small bit of light, giving her smile a sinister look as she said, "We have arrived."

34

Nora

The Royal Sentries in Midskopas were putting up quite the fight, but the Alliance wanted the victory more. They had gained the advantage and pushed forward with triumph in their sights. Nora remained by Florence's side, using her magic to take down opponents while Florence fought with tooth and claw in fox form. They'd fallen into a sort of rhythm, one that had Nora thinking of August. It was strange that such a violent thing had her longing for her best friend, but she and August had never been conventional, and she kind of liked it that way.

The fighting had moved deeper into the city where most civilians hid behind locked doors. Some were not so smart and were either stuck outdoors or had attempted to join the fight but they quickly paid for that lack of critical thinking. Nora avoided anyone who wasn't a sentry at all costs, not wanting to harm someone who may have only been in the wrong place at the wrong time. Most people were purely running for their lives and she would not harm an innocent anymore.

They followed in the sky obscuring the rising sun as Nora and Florence neared the lady of Midskopas' home. They followed Marco's command and kept moving, but their hope of finding Lady Ignisto within looked grim. Smoke engulfed the dark stone building and many of the others surrounding it.

"Over there! That woman fits the description!" Marco shouted, and Nora looked to see people in fancy coats running across wooden bridges away from the fire. Marco went after them saying, "quick! Don't let them get away!"

Two foxes took off along the ground and chased after the people fleeing above on the bridges. Nora did her best to keep up with Florence and Chester as they wove through the streets but they were quick and it was difficult keeping them in her sights, let alone keeping up. Marco ran to Nora's side, directing her through the streets as she scanned the bridges overhead. She spotted the targets and Nora threw out balls of smouldering blue flame in quick succession, lighting the bridge on the far end. A Midskopas woman threw water to douse the fire but the damage was done. The blackened bridge would no longer hold the people's weight and they would have to turn back or risk falling to where Nora and the others were on the ground.

Nora continued throwing flames as magical attacks started flying their way. Beside her, Marco had shifted into his wolf form and was growling as he dodged water and fire. A gust of wind came hurtling their way and they ducked behind a wall to prevent being knocked off their feet. Nora pressed her back against the dark stone and glanced around the corner, then suddenly jumped back as a fireball flew at her face. Marco shifted back to his human form beside her and pointed to the sky.

"Aren himself aids our cause!" Marco shouted for all to hear as a giant eagle in the sky called loudly.

Howls from the Northern Wolf pack filled the air and the eagle descended, spinning as it propelled itself to the ground. Nora and Marco moved out of their hiding spot and watched as the eagle swooped down at those on the bridge, catching them in its giant claws and carrying them high into the sky. Their screams filled the air as they plummeted down. The bodies splattered with a thud on the ground a few feet from Nora and Marco. She stepped forward to see if any survived, but was faced with limbs in impossible directions and crimson spilling in pools around the crumbled forms.

The eagle flew low to the city once more, earning an eruption of cheers from the Alliance. Nora raced towards the sound to find the Northern Alliance attacks growing stronger with the prospect of having a God on their side. They fought with renewed vigour; a new sense of determination helping their attacks land true. Nora spotted her trainees among them and felt a surge of pride at the skill they were displaying. They were doing better than most, taking on more than one attacker at a time and with no injuries to boot. They may have disliked her, but her lessons were keeping them alive.

Nora re-joined the fight and summoned wasps made of flame, urging them towards her attackers. They sizzled and hissed as they swarmed around the sentries, causing them to stop their attacks and focus on the flaming bugs. It was a simple but effective move as the sentries could not concentrate on anything else.

"You don't have to fight," she shouted at them. "You don't have to follow the king!"

"Never!" one growled as a fire wasp burnt her long nose.

"The rest of you?"

Each called out various forms of devotion to the king in between hisses at her magical attack. Well, she had given them a chance.

With a heavy sigh, Nora used her wind magic to lift the debris from the destroyed buildings. The objects levitated all around her as she raised her arms and launched them towards the enemy. Jagged planks of wood, broken glass and other sharp items flew at a rapid speed. They hit their mark, and the sentries dropped to their knees with cries of pain. Wood and glass protruded from multiple wounds on their bodies with blood staining their uniforms and their faces and hands covered in burns from the fire wasps.

They were on the wrong side of this fight.

Nora had carried guilt for the people she'd killed and hurt in the king's name, but for the sentries fighting for the king, she held no such emotion. Now that she knew what she was fighting for—what she *chose* to fight for—she could stomach shedding more blood for its cause. Freedom.

These sentries were enabling the king's tyranny and at some point simply doing a job was no longer a good enough excuse. She'd given them a chance to choose differently and they had stuck by the king.

Nora didn't linger once they'd fallen and ran to help others in the Alliance. The thrill of battle sent her heart pounding in her chest and kept her going despite her waning magic. She'd used so much of it already, but she would let it run dry completely before she stopped. The buildings in the street were in bad shape. Their stone walls were beginning to crumble from the magical attacks flying around.

She sprint around the corner and rapidly ducked, avoiding a blow to the head. Nora picked up a large stone from the ground before whirling on her attacker and smashing it into his temple. The man stumbled, dropping the makeshift wooden bat and attempting a meagre retreat. Though Nora wouldn't let him get away so easily. She followed, kicking him in the gut. He fell over a half-crumbled wall, landing on his ass and hitting his head with a sickening crack.

Nora saw there was no point in checking if he was dead and sprinted through the streets, noticing fewer and fewer sentries alive to attack her. She searched for Florence as she went, keeping an eye out for the red fox. The fighting was almost over. The last of the king's followers were dealt with by other Alliance members.

The Northern Alliance had won.

"Nora!" came a familiar voice, and she turned to see Florence shouting as she ran towards her. The rising sun's glow shone brightly behind her, illuminating her red hair.

Nora was part of something good for a change and it felt amazing. They were going to change the world and this was only the first step. They would free Valmenessia one city at a time if they had to.

As they closed the distance, Nora couldn't help but grin at Florence's dirty smiling face. Before long they would be sitting around a fire telling Will all about this fight.

A man stepped from an alley and shouted, "long live the king!" His clothing was charred and torn; a Guild tattoo was visible on his arm. His bloodied blond hair clung to his dirty face as he looked between Florence and Nora. His voice was hoarse as he said, "the Guild will fight for our king against those who wish to tear down all he has built!"

"He has built nothing! Only caused division!" Florence yelled back.

"Bullshit!" The man stumbled, blood staining his pale grey pants. "You are the ones invading cities!"

A flicker of movement from the man caught Nora's eye and then everything seemed to move slowly. Suddenly, there was a flash of light gleaning from a polished blade followed by a gasp from Florence's lips. The anima woman stumbled, falling to the ground as Nora let out a piercing scream and threw a fireball towards the Guild member. The man burst into flames.

Nora ran towards her friend and begged the Goddess Thyra and every other fucking God and Goddess to come to Florence's aid. She skidded to a halt and dropped to her knees to turn Florence over. A dagger protruded from her chest. There was so much blood.

"Stay with me," Nora commanded, panic filling her. "I'll find a Lys Alv."

Florence gurgled a reply, her eyes unfocused as she looked up to the morning sky. Nora tapped her friend's cheek.

"Look at me. Florence, look at me," Nora said, gripping Florence's chin. Florence's blue eyes landed on Nora and the woman tried to smile. "Will."

"Yeah, he'll be so pissed with you if you die," Nora replied. She summoned the last of her wind magic, raising Florence gently off the ground, ready to float her to the nearest healer. "We've got to tell him all about our victory. And how badass you were… Stay with me. No. No. No. This can't be happening. We won. Stay with me…"

"Tell him I love him," Florence rasped.

"You tell him," Nora said through her tears. "Do you hear me? That's your job."

Florence let out a final breath and fell still.

35

Evelyn

Evelyn looked around the dimly lit room for clues to suggest where they had arrived. Dread pooled in her stomach as she saw nothing familiar. She'd thought Louise was taking her home to Forest's Edge—that her handmaid was part of the Faction—but now she had a feeling that wasn't the case. Evelyn's desperation to leave had clouded her judgement and she only had herself to blame.

"Where are we?" she asked Louise as Kylan pressed closer to her.

The room was plain with dusty shelves lining the walls and empty wooden crates stacked haphazardly in the corner. Light trickled in through dirty windows that obscured the view outside. One of the group members opened the door. Dust caught in the rays of light that now illuminated the room.

One by one, the others started filing out and Evelyn's nerves increased with each departure. She would be expected to leave momentarily and face whatever was outside, but she couldn't help her hesitation.

"You'll see," Louise replied, her eyes bright with an excited smile plastered on her face. The woman practically skipped through the door behind the others, clearly eager for what lay ahead.

Evelyn looked at Kylan and swallowed deeply before following Louise. To her surprise, they strode into a lush garden. The grass was a vibrant shade of green, and the flower beds were filled with hedges trimmed to geometric shapes and rich-coloured petals. They walked along a brick path and under flowering arches until they reached a brick pavilion. Vines crawled up the pillars, and the sound of cascading water filled the air. Yet, despite the surrounding prettiness, a sense of dread still filled Evelyn. There was something *wrong* about this place.

The garden was surrounded by mountain peaks and, judging by the thinness of the air, Evelyn could only guess that they were high above the ground. There were many mountainous regions in Valmenessia, but there would have been snow at this time of year if they had travelled to the north. Judging by the lack of ice, she deduced they were still south, but she was unfamiliar with the south and did not know where they could be.

"I bet this is where we'll witness the beginning of the end," Louise told them excitedly as they entered the pavilion. "Valmenessia shall be made anew."

Kylan lowered his brows. "What's that supposed to mean?"

"Any moment now the last sacrifice will take place and—"

"Sacrifice?" Evelyn gasped, her eyes snagging on the pit in the pavilion's centre. Splotches of dark red stained the cream bricks. Above it sat a hole where the sun shone brightly through, though it did nothing to hide the grimness of it. Evelyn's stomach dropped. What had she gotten herself into?

Louise nodded. "A sacrifice to the Makers."

"You're involved in the *Makers' Murders*?" Evelyn rasped, terror running through her as memories of the night she'd almost become one of those so-called sacrifices tore through her mind. "*You* killed Tina?"

"I had to," Louise snapped, placing her hands on her hips. "Her sacrifice and the many others are for the true gods—the creators of the five deities—and they will gift us a new world. Her sacrifice was a gift to this world."

"Not quite," came a deep male voice, and Evelyn turned to find two men striding towards them.

They stopped on either side of Sloane with the one on the left giving her a wide smile. He was lean with cropped black hair and a knowing glint in his brown eyes. The man on the right was tall with broad shoulders and tousled blond hair that match the stubble on his jaw. Both exuded confidence and power.

"What do you mean by that?" asked the rude man they'd travelled with through the portal. "That is what we were promised. What was foretold."

The blond shook his head. "It is what you were led to believe. For centuries, Thyra, Jord, Nyssa, and Aren have clashed over this country and I won't stand for it any longer. I'm sick of their power-hungry ways."

Evelyn examined the man more closely and noted how his features were somewhat familiar. As though she'd seen a caricature of him somewhere before. She got a similar feeling as Lady Elizabeth—Thyra—from him.

"You're Frode," Evelyn said, and Kylan tensed at her side. She hadn't told the prince what she knew about Lady Elizabeth being Thyra and wondered whether he was already privy to the information. Did he know as much as his father or was he kept as much in the dark as the rest of the country?

To see the Human God standing before her was still a shock, despite having seen Thyra in the flesh herself. Unlike the other Gods and Goddesses, he had no magic, but that didn't make him any less impressive. Frode was an intimidating figure.

"I am," he replied. "And it is time to end my siblings' rivalry."

He nodded to Sloane, who stepped to the pit and began chanting as she tilted her head back to the bright sky above. Frode moved with purpose towards those who had travelled from Royal Bay and Kylan tugged Evelyn against his chest. The God smirked at the movement. Then, without warning, he reached for Louise and drove a blade straight into her chest.

Evelyn gasped and shoved out of Kylan's grip. A desperation to heal Louise overcame her even though the handmaid had tricked them. She couldn't let someone else die when she could heal them.

She barely made it a step before being drawn back. Kylan again held her tightly against him. His arm was immovable around her waist as she struggled to get free.

"Stop," Frode commanded without looking her way, his attention on the pit before him. He dropped Louise into it and turned, pointing the bloodied blade at each of them. "If any of you try to sabotage this I will kill *all* of you as punishment. At the moment that won't be necessary. It would be a waste to bleed you all so soon."

Evelyn stilled as the ground beneath them shook with Sloane's chanting growing louder.

Darkness crept up the walls and tears streamed down Evelyn's face as she watched the conjurer's magic work.

"If you try to heal her I will kill them all," he continued, singling out

Evelyn this time as he gestured to the others with his blade. "You can't heal them all."

Louise smiled at the sky as she took her final breath and the ground rumbled beneath her. Evelyn held back her sob for the woman. Tears continued streaming down her cheeks as darkness spread from Louise's body like the roots of a tree.

"What are you doing to her?" Evelyn demanded weakly.

"The same thing that is occurring all over this country with the other sacrifices," Frode replied. "Her body will fester and spread darkness. You wanted a new world?" Frode nodded towards the pit. "You're going to get one."

A shiny gold perimeter appeared around the pit, halting the spread, and Sloane's chanting fell silent.

"It's done," she declared, stepping back. She reached for the black-haired man who had remained silent and took her hand. "We will finally finish this," Sloane said.

Evelyn didn't understand. Who were these people and why would they help Frode do such a thing? The world wasn't perfect, it was unfair and cruel, but this? This was too far.

Kylan spoke before Evelyn had the chance to question them. "Who are you both?" the prince asked, his eyes intent on the dark-haired man and the conjurer. He must have had the same thought as Evelyn.

The man looked lovingly at the conjurer as he said, "Sloane is my great-grandmother, and I'm Elliot." His gaze turned to Evelyn and Kylan, its coldness sending a shiver down her spine. "Elliot Maker."

36

Nora

T he victory was short-lived, at least in Nora's eyes. It was hard to rejoice in the glory when Florence's body lay lifeless before her. Nora sat alone in the dining room of an abandoned tavern, grateful that Marco had organised for everyone else to clear out so she could see Florence with no other eyes around. The tavern was where they had brought their dead. Each of the long tables had one or two people laying upon them, bodies motionless. Some were covered with blankets whilst others were left uncovered appearing as though they were in a deep sleep.

Tears streamed down her face as Nora stared at her friend. The last time she'd grieved on this level was when her mother and brother had died in the fire, though she couldn't recall feeling as though the ground had disappeared from underneath her at the same time as her heart was simultaneously being pulled from her chest. Maybe it was because she'd lost them so young before she understood the meaning of death. It is hard for a six-year-old to process something so huge.

All that was minuscule from what she felt now as she looked at her friend. Florence had been the friend Nora had never thought she truly deserved. Florence had been faithful, honest, and beyond supportive. She'd been able to see something in Nora that she, herself, could not. The world would be a darker place without Florence's smile, laughter, and warmth.

The Northern Alliance had taken Midskopas and Florence should have been celebrating together with Nora and everyone else right now.

It wasn't supposed to be like this.

Nora wanted to go back to Forest's Edge to be with Sage, to hold her and be held by her. Florence was supposed to return home back to Will.

Fuck.

Will.

Nora's heart ached for him. He was oblivious to the pain he would soon meet. Life was so fucking cruel. He didn't deserve this. Florence didn't deserve this. How was Nora supposed to tell Will of Florence's last words?

It was all King Dominic's fault.

His greed and fucked-up beliefs had brought nothing but pain to Valmenessia. He was a curse upon the country, on the entire world.

She would make him pay.

The bench groaned and Nora looked to find Felix sitting beside her. He'd come to their aid in eagle form and solidified the Alliance's win.

"I'm sorry for your loss," he said, frowning at Florence. "I wish there was something I could do."

"Bring her back," Nora replied, wiping the tears from her eyes. "I know you have access to magic stronger than just your eagle form—I saw your shift and how you killed the leader of this city. Everyone did. You scooped Lady Ignisto up in your claws and let her fall to her death. You're more powerful than you let on."

"I don't have the power to raise the dead," he replied solemnly. "And I have no magic beyond my Anima shift."

"Bullshit," Nora scoffed. "How did you do it, hmm? How did you leave if you're only a dumb giant bird?"

Felix huffed. "I assume you are talking about leaving the Alta?"

"Evelyn's father died freeing me," Nora said, her words coming out strained. "Who did you kill to break free?"

"No one," he replied, looking down at the wrists covered by his shirt. "A conjurer helped me. The tattoos faded soon after the ceremony and then I had fake ones put on. I was only ever under the king's control for a couple of hours."

"As simple as that."

"I wouldn't call that kind of magic simple."

"Did your conjurer also make your shift larger to match your ego?"

Felix shook his head and smiled. "The eagle is all me."

"Why did you leave?"

"Things got complicated," he said. "An old friend was too close for comfort. I didn't want her identifying me."

"Who are you?" she asked, looking at him carefully, as though the answers were written on his face. "Really?"

"August didn't believe me when I told him. I have a feeling you won't either."

Nora lifted her chin. "Try me."

"Who do you think I am?"

Nora pursed her lips and thought for a moment. There had been hints all along that pointed to who he truly was. "If I didn't know better, I'd say you were the Anima god, but that's impossible."

"Is it?" Felix smiled coyly. "Trust your instincts."

Nora blew out a breath, remembering when she and August had first set off to look for Felix all those months ago. She'd told August about Felix quoting Aren and he had teased her about Felix being a god. Looking back, she'd been piecing it together the whole time. Maybe subconsciously she'd always known there was something more to Felix.

"Aren."

"The same," he replied, his lips quirking to the side. "Walk with me."

Nora took a last look at Florence and nodded. She rose from her seat and wiped her nose on her sleeve then followed him from the tavern.

"The other Gods and Goddesses?" Nora asked as they strolled through the streets. Now that the smoke had cleared and the fighting was over citizens and Faction members were cleaning up the destruction. Homes and businesses were being prepped for repairs and the community was coming to terms with their new reality.

"They are alive, too," Aren said. "I took August to meet with Jord."

"Is that why you were so interested in him? You planned to offer him as a gift to the Mors Alv Goddess?"

Aren shook his head. "August is important."

"Care to elaborate?" she asked pointedly.

Aren halted his steps and caught her gaze. "The rest is his story to tell you."

Nora looked around at the rubble and ruins stained with blood and thought of the people lost on both sides. "I might never see him again," she said softly. "Just tell me."

"No." Aren sighed. "You will see him again soon; I am certain of it. You two can't be separated for too long. You're like salt and chocolate."

"That's a weird combination."

"It's not," he grinned, taking off again. "Try it and you'll see. You're the salt, by the way."

"I assumed as much."

They walked through the streets of Midskopas watching civilians take in their new situation. Some wandered looking lost, others were searching for friends and loved ones, and a few simply sat on the ground and cried. Not all were unhappy tears though.

"You believe me then? About who I really am?" Aren asked.

Nora shrugged. "It makes sense. You've always had a chip on your shoulder."

Aren laughed.

"Plus, my problem has never been belief. August has always been the more sceptical one about bigger things, like royalty or religion. He's not overly trusting of authority." Nora chuckled tiredly. She was so drained, both magically and emotionally. "I, on the other hand, used to trust authority and question everyone else's motives."

"Used to?"

"I'm trying to do better with the latter," she admitted. "The other Gods and Goddesses are roaming about too then? Sitting in taverns and tending to crops?"

"Jord won't come down from the mountains. She is too afraid," Aren explained. "Nyssa lives like a queen without the title and I haven't seen Frode in a few hundred years."

"And Thyra?" Nora asked.

"She's the reason I left the Alta. She's an advisor to King Dominic. There was only so long until she figured out I was there. I was lucky to get the time I did."

"Of course." Nora sighed. With the Elementum being put on a pedestal, it made sense that the Elementum Goddess had a hand in everything occurring.

To think Nora had offered up prayers to the Elementum goddess only hours before. She thought of her friend. If Nora's Goddess was to blame for Florence's death, then she would make Thyra pay. "Do I know her? Thyra's secret identity I mean."

"Lady Elizabeth."

"Ugh, did it have to be her?" Nora groaned. "Why couldn't I get a cool deity?"

"Like the Anima God?"

Nora rolled her eyes and they walked a time in silence.

"It will get easier, you know," Aren said, placing a hand on her shoulder. "The pain of losing someone you care about will never disappear, but you will learn to live with it."

"Have you lost someone?"

"More than I can count," he said, tapping two fingers over his heart. "They all live here and are the reason I wake up each day and keep fighting against King Dominic and Thyra. I owe it to them."

There was something comforting in thinking that Florence would be in her heart, always kept close. Nora smiled sadly at the thought.

Shouts came from around the corner and Nora and Aren picked up their pace, turning to see what the commotion was about. Panicked faces were huddled around Marco and Aeolus waiting for direction.

"What happened?" Aren asked, moving through the crowd to stand beside Marco. Nora stuck by his side, eager to know what was going on.

"A darkness has broken from the ground, like black tentacles," Aeolus said. "It's spreading rapidly."

"Take me to it," Aren commanded.

Nora remained with Aren as they followed Aeolus through the streets of Midskopas.

As they moved, Marco updated them on their plans now that Midskopas was theirs. "Chester and I will remain until someone is appointed the new lord or lady of the city," he said. "The rest of my pack in the north has everything under control for now, so I can stay a little longer."

Nora hadn't seen Florence's brother since the fighting. "How is Chester doing?" she asked.

"Much like you," Marco said grimly. "My husband's heart is broken."

Nora nodded, biting her lip to hold back the fresh wave of tears threatening to fall.

"He is lucky to have you by his side," Aren said, smiling at Marco. He placed an arm around Nora's shoulders and tugged her close to offer comfort.

Nora was conflicted. Her old self would have stubbornly swatted him away and told him to fuck off like she used to back when they both were Alta, but now she wanted his comfort. Maybe it was because he was now a God in her eyes, or perhaps she purely enjoyed his familiar presence. Most likely it was because *she* had changed since seeing him last. Either way, it didn't matter. She was learning to trust her instincts and they were currently telling her to soak up as much solace from Aren as possible.

"There," Aeolus declared, pointing towards the distance.

Nora looked out and saw what had the soldiers so on edge. It was unlike anything she had ever seen or heard of.

"Aren… what is it?" Nora angled her head to him with wide eyes.

Aren looked grimly at the blackness in the distance and shook his head. "I don't know. I've never seen anything like it before."

EPILOGUE

August

Jord had accepted August's departure, though he could tell by the set of her shoulders and the crease between her brow that she hadn't been entirely happy about it. Nevertheless, with the support of Tyler and the others who had joined him, August had felt invigorated by the departure. He only hoped that she and the rest of the Mors Alvs would join them one day soon.

August's boots crunched along the gravel as they strode up the path and he tugged his cloak tightly around himself. He still wasn't used to the chill, despite all his travelling via the frosty mountains first to the temple then back to Fellbun. The city may have had better weather than the peaks surrounding it, but it was still fucking cold. Lord Havilor's mansion sat perched on a cliff in the distance, overlooking the city. Beside it, Thyra's Firefall rushed towards the ground. Today the colour of the fall was a bright blue, unlike the fiery red it had been the last time August had seen it.

"How many powerful people do you know?" Tyler asked, walking by August's side. His brown hair was hidden beneath a knitted hat, flecks of snow speckling the green wool. Behind them, a group of ten had joined them from the temple. "You're friendly with Jord, Aren, Lord Havilor…."

"Lady Royd," August added with a quirk of his lips. "Not that many people."

"Four more than most of the population, I would gather. Not to mention you share a mother with the two princes in Royal Bay." Tyler grinned mischievously. "You're pretty well connected, Dark Prince."

August halted his steps. Tyler's words repeated in his mind with an effect he hadn't expected. He had brothers. Relatives that were *alive*. To think the princes had lived in the castle above the Alta quarters—had walked the same grounds as August and been in the same rooms. August might have remained hidden, but his brothers had been so close... and yet so far.

"August?" Tyler asked, turning to face him. The rest of the group slowed, now paying attention to them both.

"Lord Havilor might not let us stay, let alone welcome us through the front door," August said instead of what he had been thinking. Tyler and the others didn't need to know everything in August's head. "There's just as much chance he'll turn us away."

"Doubt it." Tyler rolled his eyes. "Powerful people love you, remember."

August huffed a laugh. "I wouldn't go that far."

August and Tyler had planned to make a stop in Fellbun after they left the Temple of the Faithful, preferably lodging with Lord Havilor. August knew no one else in the city and there was still distrust amongst the people in Valmenessia regarding his kind. Lord Havilor hadn't seemed fazed by August's nature. Rather than cause a scene, he thought they'd try their luck with the lord.

A cool breeze drifted past, bringing with it the scent of decay. August held his arm to his nose.

"What's that smell?" one of the men exclaimed, gagging.

"Death," August said, glancing around. "Something's wrong."

They continued as open land turned into homes. They drew their hoods to cover their Mors Alv eyes as the scenery only became eerier. There were no sounds of life, no people coming or going. Instead, homes stood with doors wide open, clothes hung on lines long forgotten.

"This is starting to freak me out," Tyler said, sticking his head into an open window. "Where are all the people?"

August walked around the house and froze, his eyes fixed on the ground. Black veins spread out like roots, weaving over the land. "Have a look at this!"

"What the fuck?" Tyler hissed, coming to stand at August's side.

"What in Goddess Thyra's name?" one woman whispered.

August hesitantly placed a foot forward, his boot squishing the vein and releasing darkness that oozed into the gravel path. The scent of rot intensified and the men's gagging worsened. August looked out into the distance to where the veins grew more prominent. He could have sworn the damn things were pulsing.

"Don't go any further!" came a shout, followed by the sound of galloping.

The group of Mors Alvs turned to find men riding towards them. Their purple coats identified them as Lord Havilor's sentries. Their horses' hooves ground to a halt and the men looked down at the group.

"If you value your lives, you will step back," one of the sentries said in a deep voice.

August glanced down at his boot and obediently stepped away. "What the fuck happened here?" he said.

The sentry frowned and gazed at the darkness that spread far into the distance. "Something we thought was only a legend. A bedtime story to frighten children and miscreants into behaving. Something that put the fear into those who dared disrespect the Gods and the Makers." August saw deep-rooted fear in the man's eyes, though he did well not to let it sound in his voice. A chill ran through August's body as the man continued, "But the tales of the Morken are nothing like this. This is something entirely different... It sprouted from the bodies of those who have been murdered."

Tyler swore. "You mean that came out of people?"

The sentry nodded solemnly. "It's the beginning of the end. The end of all things, friends... It's the Makers' Curse."

Acknowledgements

Unlike my last book, these acknowledgements are going to be short and sweet!

A huge thank you to my wonderful husband Mitch and my two children, Liam and Zoe. Thank you for all your support and love. You are my world, and I love you so much.
Thank you to Jess and Zia Rita for reading the unedited versions. Your support and insistence on getting spoilers are the best and make me love writing.

Thank you to my editors, Chloe and Emily. Your advice and feedback are always so valuable. Also big thank you for never turning me away no matter the hour or obscure the question :P

And last but certainly not least, thank you to everyone who has made this book possible, including K.D Ritchie at Story Wrappers for the stunning cover art, my lovely beta readers and of course all of you for reading!

I am so appreciative of everyone who has wanted to read all about these characters that are constantly causing chaos in my head. I love being able to share them with you, and I can't wait to introduce you to more in the future.

If you enjoyed Rise and Reverence, please consider leaving a review on Amazon and Goodreads. It would mean the world to me!

THE VALMENESSIAN CHRONICLES

THE WORLD

THE GODS AND GODDESSES

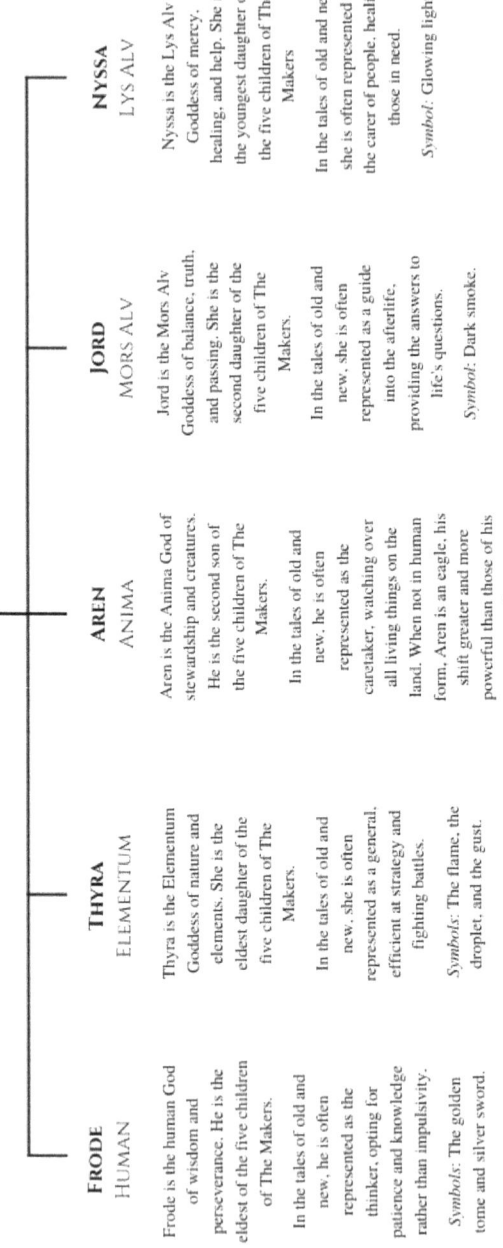

FATHER SUN
SOLARI

MOTHER MOON
LUNIA

The Makers, also referred to as Solari and Lunia, are the parents of the five Gods and Goddesses of Valmenessia. Though they are said to have created the five races, there are no accounts nor stories about the Makers other than The Dawn, in which the tale of the children's births is told.

Today, The Makers are not widely worshipped. However, they are not overlooked either. The Maker's Temple in Royal Bay is one of the only known locations dedicated to the disappearance of their worshippers centuries prior.

Symbol: A sun and moon surrounded by a circle

FRODE
HUMAN

Frode is the human God of wisdom and perseverance. He is the eldest of the five children of The Makers.

In the tales of old and new, he is often represented as the thinker, opting for patience and knowledge rather than impulsivity.

Symbols: The golden tome and silver sword.

THYRA
ELEMENTUM

Thyra is the Elementum Goddess of nature and elements. She is the eldest daughter of the five children of The Makers.

In the tales of old and new, she is often represented as a general, efficient at strategy and fighting battles.

Symbols: The flame, the droplet, and the gust.

AREN
ANIMA

Aren is the Anima God of stewardship and creatures. He is the second son of the five children of The Makers.

In the tales of old and new, he is often represented as the caretaker, watching over all living things on the land. When not in human form, Aren is an eagle, his shift greater and more powerful than those of his people.

Symbol: The eagle.

JORD
MORS ALV

Jord is the Mors Alv Goddess of balance, truth, and passing. She is the second daughter of the five children of The Makers.

In the tales of old and new, she is often represented as a guide into the afterlife, providing the answers to life's questions.

Symbol: Dark smoke.

NYSSA
LYS ALV

Nyssa is the Lys Alv Goddess of mercy, healing, and help. She is the youngest daughter of the five children of The Makers

In the tales of old and new, she is often represented as the curer of people, healing those in need.

Symbol: Glowing light

R A C E S

There are five races that live in the world of the Valmenessian Chronicles.

Humans

- People born without natural magic or special abilities.
- Humans can become conjurers who learn how to use magic through spells and rituals.

Anima

- Look like humans but can shift into an animal.
- Familial animals are common but not a rule, especially for those with mixed heritage.

Elementum

- Look like humans,
- Can wield fire, water, and air,
- The strength of magic and the use of various elements differ between people.
- Most can only wield one element.

Lys Alvs

- Speed healing that requires taking on others' injuries,
- Can sense the degree of injuries,
- Their healing magic is more potent during the day,
- Pointed ears,
- Golden irises,
- Some have sharper senses and movements.

Mors Alvs

- Can absorb health and magic from people and objects,
- Can sense others' power/race/degree of magic.
- Pointed ears,
- Black eyes with coloured irises.
- Their magic is more potent at night.
- Some have sharper senses and movements.

LOCATIONS

MAJOR CITIES AND TOWNS

Royal Bay
- City on the mainland and a castle on an island in the centre of the bay
- Guarded by Ferieton and Ocean's Harbour navies
- Castle on water and connected by bridge
- Sandstone with red tiles
- Cobbled/paved streets

Midskopas
- City in the centre of Valmenessia
- Tall stone buildings with wooden bridges over muddy streets
- Grey dark stone

Forest's Edge
- Wooden city in the trees
- Arts
- High anima population

Kaldom
- Small town in the north near the sea
- Frozen and snowy
- Cold, harsh and quiet
- Separated from other populated areas by the northern forest and mountains

Giland
- Farming/agriculture
- High Elementum population

Fellbun
- Base of Periculum Mountains
- Thyra's Firefall
- Clusters of small stone buildings/houses leading to larger clusters
- Buildings carved into mountains
- Over the river are the wealthier houses/estates

LOCATIONS

Sorby
- Human only town
- Isolated and mostly independent
- Magic free

Ferieton
- Located in the west
- Predominately Alv city
- Half of Valmenessia's navy military stationed there

Ocean's Harbour
- Half of Valmenessia's navy military stationed there
- Trading city, ships from other countries trade here before entering Valmenessia
- One of the only safe places to enter the country and so is the gateway

Dostvet Harbour
- Trading harbour
- Loose rules and lots of contraband

Crestoy
- South of Valmenessia
- Beside a large coral reef known as the Blessed Reef
- No ships are able to travel through it so the people are protected from threats from the sea

Rovton
- Very small city
- Known for fishing and beaches

LOCATIONS

OTHER LOCATIONS OF NOTE

The Temple of the Faithful
- Located in the Periculum Mountains
- Harsh terrain

Northern Wolf Pack Hideout
- Hidden deep in the Great Northern Forest
- Ruins and underground buildings covered by nature
- Surrounded by thick forest wall

The Great Northern Forest
- Located in the north east
- Separates Forest's Edge and Kaldom

Misfortune's Wood
- Located in the south east
- Dark forest
- Many are superstitious of the wood as most who venture in do not return

The Mines
- Located in the east of Valmenessia
- Where prisoners are taken

The Periculum Mountains
- Located in the north west
- Mostly unknown lands

Grenblad Woods
- Located in the west and borders Midskopas

Sailor's Peril
- The eastern coast of Valmenessia
- Unsafe for naval travel due to the rocky coastline

Blessed Reef
- Located on the southern coastline

THE RULING FAMILIES

ROYAL BAY

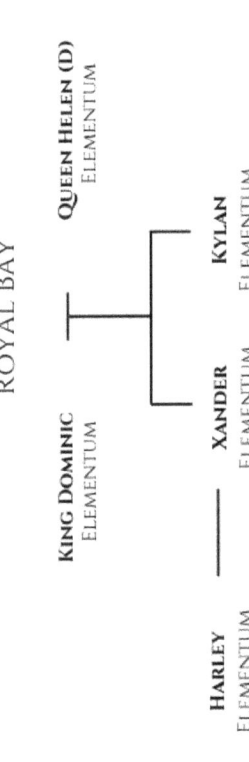

KING DOMINIC
ELEMENTUM

QUEEN HELEN (D)
ELEMENTUM

HARLEY
ELEMENTUM

XANDER
ELEMENTUM

KYLAN
ELEMENTUM

NOTABLE FIGURES

LADY ELIZABETH (THYRA)
ELEMENTUM
ADVISOR TO THE
KING
GODDESS

TINA
ELEMENTUM
ETIQUETTE TUTOR

ZAIM
HUMAN
ALTA

BLAINE
ELEMENTUM
LORD IN WAITING
OF OCEAN'S
HARBOUR

LOUISE
ELEMENTUM
HANDMAID

THE RULING FAMILIES

FOREST'S EDGE

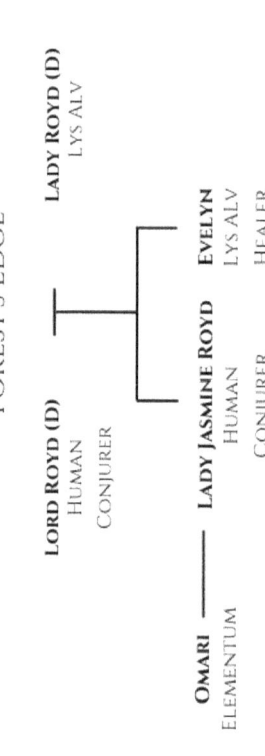

LORD ROYD (D)
HUMAN
CONJURER

LADY ROYD (D)
LYS ALV

OMARI ——
ELEMENTUM

LADY JASMINE ROYD
HUMAN
CONJURER

EVELYN
LYS ALV
HEALER

POPPY
ELEMENTUM
HEALER

NOTABLE FIGURES

FLORENCE
ANIMA (FOX)
FACTION MEMBER

WILL
HUMAN
FACTION MEMBER

SAGE
HUMAN
FACTION MEMBER
RESEARCHER

GEMMA
LYS ALV
FACTION MEMBER
LEADER

AEOLUS
ELEMENTUM
FACTION MEMBER
SECOND IN
COMMAND

PHILLIP
HUMAN
FACTION MEMBER
RESEARCHER

NORA
ELEMENTUM
EX ALTA

ASHE
ANIMA (LEOPARD)
FACTION MEMBER

THE RULING FAMILIES

FELLBUN AND THE TEMPLE OF THE FAITHFUL

LORD HAVILOR
LYS ALV
LORD OF
FELLBUN

JORD
MORS ALV
GODDESS

NOTABLE FIGURES

AUGUST
MORS ALV
EX ALTA

FELIX (AREN)
ANIMA (EAGLE)
FACTION MEMBER
GOD

TYLER
MORS ALV

THE RULING FAMILIES

The Northern Wolf Pack

Carl
Anima (Wolf)
Leader

—

Chester
Anima (Fox)
Florence's
Brother

NOTABLE FIGURES

Mya
Anima (Wolf)
Scout &
Messenger

Lou
Anima (Mouse)
Scout &
Messenger

OTHER NOTABLE FIGURES

Sloane
HUMAN
CONJURER

Frode
HUMAN
GOD

Elliot Maker
HUMAN

Nyssa
LYS ALV
GODDESS

ABOUT THE AUTHOR

Rebecca Camm was raised in Melbourne by a single mother who encouraged her passion for reading and all things magical. She has been writing stories since she was a child to help manage her anxiety and make sense of the world.

Rebecca strongly believes in the power stories have in changing lives. Just like her, Rebecca's characters are flawed, yet they are continually learning. Unlike her, they are confident, witty, and just generally more exciting.

Rebecca lives with her husband and two children. When her children allow her free time, she is either writing or attempting to conquer her ever-growing tbr pile.

Stay in touch!

Website rebeccacamm.com

Newsletter rebeccacamm.com/contact

Instagram @readingwritingdaydreaming

TikTok @readingwritingdaydream

Facebook @readingwritingdaydreaming

Facebook Group facebook.com/groups/rebeccacammsreadergroup

Lightning Source UK Ltd.
Milton Keynes UK
UKHW012018250123
415976UK00016B/209/J